The last thing Lady Katherine wants is to take the matchmaking job for Mrs. Burwick, whose daughter, Prudence, clearly does not want to be matched... until she realizes it provides her the perfect cover to investigate the string of robberies that have been taking place in the holiday town of Bath.

Katherine, her loyal maid, Harriet, and her tenacious Pug, Emma, soon find themselves knee-deep in troubled waters as they try to piece together the baffling clues to reveal the truth. To further complicate matters, Katherine's investigation is impeded by the incompetent detective hired by the Marquess of Bath to flush out the burglar.

Now Katherine must juggle advising Prudence on how "not" to land a duke while she dives into the investigation in the hopes of narrowing down the suspects without making waves amongst the aristocracy, some of whom are her primary suspects.

When the burglary attempts turn violent, Katherine must take drastic measures to ensure her detective career isn't all washed up before it even gets started.

THE BAFFLING BURGLARIES OF BATH

LADY KATHERINE REGENCY MYSTERIES - BOOK 2

LEIGHANN DOBBS
HARMONY WILLIAMS

LEIGHANN DOBBS PUBLISHING

CHAPTER ONE

—————

S aturday, September 7, 1816
 Bath, England

IF KATHERINE'S CLOSEST FRIEND, Lyle Murphy,
turned any stiffer, the patrons of the Sydney Hotel
would mistake him for a decoration. The lanky Bow
Street Runner sat as straight as the neoclassical pillars
outside the terrace doors. His pallor matched the walls,
his shock of reddish hair the only sign that he was
living and not carved of marble. That, and the words
spilling out of his mouth.

"I don't see why you asked me to come."

Lady Katherine Irvine exchanged a look with the
third person at their table, Prudence Burwick. Every

bit as tall as Katherine, though with her weight distributed more solidly along her frame, Pru wore a pinched expression that emphasized the sharp cast to her chin. She forgot to smile yet again. Had Katherine's true aim been to match Pru with Lord Annandale as she'd been hired to do, Pru's less-than-welcoming air would have boded ill for the endeavor.

Fortunately, Katherine was here to solve a crime instead.

"The robberies," she reminded him.

Lyle pulled a face. "I'm from London. Bath has its own city watchmen."

"It does, but are they as skilled in catching criminals as Sir John's Men?"

From the moment he had been accepted into the ranks of the detectives, Lyle had preened over his profession. As well he should. Although the name Bow Street Runner had a derogatory association, ever since Sir John Fielding had organized them, London's first overt detective ring had thrived and made the streets safer than ever. This was particularly necessary now that the war with Napoleon was through and those previously employed by the military supplemented their income with thievery. The Royal Society of Investigative Techniques, of which Katherine was a member, regularly invited Sir John's Men to share their expertise.

Lyle's stance altered as he puffed his chest. "Of course not. We pride ourselves in being the leading detectives in England."

Katherine opted not to take offense to that statement. After all, although she had been solving crime ever since she was in pinafores, she had done so at her father's heels. The earl had taught her everything he knew, but only recently, shortly before her twenty-fifth birthday, had she solved a crime on her own. The Pink-Ribbon Murders had vexed even her father, but she had had help to solve them — from Lyle in particular. This time, she had to prove to herself that she was capable of solving a crime on her own.

Nevertheless, she valued her friend's insight, and his many tools.

He added, "That isn't to say the Bath city watchmen aren't perfectly capable of solving this particular case on their own. I'll only get in their way."

Pru tapped her fork against the round wooden table, one of many in the ground floor of the hotel. The ping of sound only added to the hum of conversation around them. Everyone seemed far too engrossed in their own conversations to eavesdrop.

With a disapproving twist of her mouth, Pru

pointed out, "They've had ample time to solve the robberies. This is what, the fifth? Sixth? By Jove, they've been going on since June!"

The conversation at the table next to them stilled, where an older gentleman, new money, given the way certain others in the room avoided their table, plied his young wife with praises about her beauty. She wore a ring, earrings, and a necklace laden with citrines the size of robins' eggs. A lewd display of wealth at the least — with the recent string of jewel thefts in the area, it was downright foolish.

Katherine tapped her fingernail on the table and lowered her voice to a hiss. "Tarnation, Pru. Keep your voice down."

"Perhaps you ought not to swear," she countered in a quieter tone.

Katherine couldn't argue with that. She turned instead to her longtime friend, who looked as wary as if he feared he might spontaneously burst into flame. He didn't often accompany her into polite society, a world away from the criminal underbelly of London with which he was far more familiar.

"If I don't have need of your expertise, perhaps you can use the time away from London to finish your latest invention. I know you lament you're too often on patrol to give it your due diligence."

His shoulders relaxed from their position around his ears, and a slim smile curved one corner of his mouth. "I do have a sketch for an apparatus that uses steam to render the recent oils left by a person's touch visible on certain surfaces. I've heard that the healing waters of Bath contain a rich array of minerals. It's possible, when vaporized, these minerals will adhere—"

Katherine had only a rudimentary knowledge of science and sensed that if she allowed him to continue to muse aloud, she would soon be out of her depth. With a fond smile, she tapped him on the back of the hand to draw his attention away from the theoretical. "There are springs galore near the baths in the center of town."

Leaving his half-eaten bun and empty teacup, Lyle started to stand. "If you don't object, perhaps I'll visit and discover for myself if the water will do for my invention."

A woman's gnarled hand, her fingernails buffed to a shine, clasped his elbow in a vise that made him jump. "An invention, you say?" The woman, wearing an outdated dress with a high neckline, and an enormous feather hat better suited to twenty years prior, looked to be ninety if she was a day. Age bowed her spine, reducing a form that might once have been over five feet tall when standing straight. Spectacles perched on her long nose, threatening to fall off the tip. Judging from the way she squinted, Katherine thought they did little to improve her vision. Her hearing wasn't much improved, given her piercing voice. "Do you mean to create an invention in our lovely little town?"

As the woman beamed up at him, Lyle turned several different shades of pink in succession. He stumbled over his tongue. "Why, yes I— If it is permitted, I mean to say. I would be ever so grateful for the opportunity to—"

"Permitted! Of course it is permitted. I encourage all bright young men to draw inspiration from our great town." She latched onto his arm with a hawklike grip and patted the snowy coiffure peeking from beneath the brim of her hat as she steered him toward the exit. "In fact, I can introduce you to a few good men nearby who are skilled in construction or who might sell you any materials you need to build your invention."

As he was led away by the enthusiastic old woman, Lyle shot a bewildered look over his shoulder. His lanky form, well over six feet tall, loomed over the slight woman on his arm, yet he looked as helpless as a stray puppy. Katherine waved at him and giggled into her hand then tore off another piece of the Sally Lunn and popped it into her mouth. She savored the taste of the rich, sweet bun.

Pru frowned. "Was that the Marquess of Bath's grandmother?"

"I can't say. I've never met her."

Fiddling with a lock of her brown hair, Pru turned back. "Yes, I'm certain it was. He came in with her, and he's impossible to miss. Those unfashionably wide cuffs make him look as if he's a bird about to take flight."

Katherine bit her lower lip to contain a smile, her eyes wandering to the gentleman in question. Him, she recognized, for he ventured to London every year to sit in Parliament. Her father also had a seat. The trim, jovial man was nearing forty, a fact evident from his receding hairline. However, his ready smile put anyone, young or old, at ease. As Pru had mentioned, he did wear wider than usual cuffs, having an aversion to restrictive clothing around his wrists. Papa had never mentioned why, though the two were friendly and Lord Bath had dined with him on occasion.

The marquess frowned and paused in his conversation with a pair of gentlemen in fashionable buckskin breeches and dark jackets. "Grandmama?" He stared in the direction of the exit to the street, where Lyle and Grandma Bath were now headed.

As the marquess took a step to follow, a lady's voice cut through the chatter. "Emma, no!"

Katherine's mouthful of Sally Lunn suddenly tasted like ash. *Tarnation!* She swallowed hard and stood, but she wasn't quick enough to match the black-and-tan blur racing in from the terrace. Emma, her pug, arrowed for the marquess and jumped up on his leg as she begged for attention. She reached no higher than his knee, yipping and snapping playfully at his wide cuffs, her back end wiggling back and forth as she attempted to wag her short, coiled tail.

Sard it all. Lord Bath was more congenial than most, but those who mingled with polite society were a strict and stuffy bunch. If he took offense to Emma or, worse, hurt her...

The marquess bent to pat Emma's head. He spoke to her in a low tone, too soft for Katherine to hear the words as she rounded the table to join them. Emma seemed pleased enough with the response, for she stuffed her head into his wide cuffs and snorted.

Katherine's maid and close friend, Harriet, bolted in from the terrace. Her dark hair escaped its plait, forming a riotous halo around her head. Emma's leash and collar, from which she must have managed to slip free, dangled from Harriet's fist. Her harried expression turned to one of horror as she caught sight of the escaped dog.

Katherine neared the group as Harriet curtsied deeply. "Forgive her, my lord. She didn't mean any offense. I'll take care that it doesn't happen again."

The marquess straightened, looming over Harriet. "She's a friendly sort. No harm done. However, do take care to keep her restrained. There are a good number of older women and gentlemen in residence who might trip. Speaking of which, if you'll excuse me—"

He had already turned away, dismissing the situation, much to Harriet's visible relief.

"Grandmama?" As Lord Bath hastened across the room, Katherine had never seen a man move so quickly in pursuit of a woman. He headed the pair off moments before they were about to slip onto the street.

Katherine hoisted Emma into her arms when the enthusiastic pug waddled past in pursuit of the marquess. The dog whined then shifted to lick Katherine's chin. Still chewing the last of her bun, Pru stood from the nearby table and dusted off her hands as she stepped close to Katherine. She swallowed before speaking.

"I can't say as I blame the marquess. In his position, I'd be just as alarmed to watch a relative saunter off with a fellow like Mr. Murphy."

Katherine raised an eyebrow, at the same time tilting her chin out of Emma's reach. "What do you mean by that? Lyle's far from a reprobate. In fact, I'd be wary of half the men in this establishment, including the two with whom Lord Bath was just speaking. They have that look to them."

"As does Mr. Murphy," Pru countered. "The way he took charge at Lord Northbrook's house party was frightening."

There *had* been a murderer on the loose, so Katherine couldn't fault him for acting with authority at the time. In fact, she'd been rather relieved.

As she opened her mouth to counter, her maid approached to wrestle Emma back into her collar. Upon catching the tail end of the conversation, Harriet snorted. "Lyle? He wouldn't hurt a fly."

"At the house party—"

"He wouldn't hurt a fly that hadn't proven a danger to society," Harriet amended. As she expertly secured the collar, she raised her eyebrows at Pru, undaunted by the differences in their statuses. "Besides, weren't you the one to wallop the murderer over the head with a lantern?"

Pru colored up. Looking contrite, she mumbled under her breath. "He might have killed Katherine..."

Harriet smirked. "You see? You both acted in pursuit of a just cause. Come to think of it, you two have quite a bit in common. I'd think you'd be much more apt to... get on." Her suggestive tone as she scooped Emma from out of Katherine's arms was mirrored by her smirk.

Pru and Lyle? Not precisely the pairing Katherine had in mind. Besides, she'd been hired by Mrs. Burwick to pair her daughter with the Marquess of Annandale. Not that she planned to make much effort to accomplish that goal, certainly not with Pru's aversion.

However, Prudence was no dolt. She understood Harriet well enough, given the way she wrinkled her nose in distaste. "Mr. Murphy and I do not *get on*, as you so succinctly put it. We have very little in common."

"He's tall," Harriet pointed out, her smile widening.

Pru crossed her arms before she recalled their public location and relaxed her hostile stance. "Height isn't everything," she bit off.

"He's also a decorated detective. Since you also have an interest in the investigative arts, I'd think it would behoove you to find a husband who shares that interest."

Pru scowled. "I have no need or desire for a husband at all. Katherine doesn't intend to marry. I don't see why I should have to."

Thank Zeus Katherine had been able to persuade Mrs. Burwick to stay behind in London. She would have a far more difficult time on her hands trying to investigate if her client were dogging her steps and asking inconvenient questions such as, "Why haven't you made any effort to match Pru with Lord Annandale?"

Then again, she hadn't made much effort to match Miss Annie Pickering with Lord Northbrook, yet they had managed to find their way into one another's arms while she'd been catching the Pink-Ribbon Murderer. Although Pru's scowl spoke volumes in this case. Annie had, at the very least, wanted to make the match.

In a high-pitched voice, Harriet answered, "Perhaps Lady Katherine can answer that question for you in detail after you've spoken with Lord Bath. Is the weather clearing up? I should resume my duties. Excuse me, my lady, my lord." Harriet dipped in a deep curtsey before turning on her heel and scurrying through the open terrace door.

The weather did, indeed, seem to be clearing up from the dismal cold rain that had battered the gardens all morning. But who had she called "my lord?"

"Lady Katherine."

The marquess!

Katherine turned, forcing a smile as she met Lord Bath's twinkling gaze. She dipped in a polite curtsey as he inclined his head. "Lord Bath, so good to see you."

"And you, my dear. I must admit to some surprise, however. Your father didn't write to let me know that you would be arriving, or else I would have offered you a room on my estate."

No, that would never do. Katherine was here to investigate a string of thefts! In order to be most effective, she had to be alongside the would-be victims. Perhaps she should have brought some gaudy jewelry of her own to tempt the thief. All Harriet had packed were a few modest pieces, as Katherine didn't tend to bother with that sort of frippery when on a case.

She forced a smile. "Thank you for the offer, but I've let rooms here for the week. I thought it better to give back to the town."

Grandma Bath, hanging from the marquess's arm, harrumphed. "Quite right. A sensible girl you've found for once, Ernest." She squinted and adjusted her spectacles as she leaned forward to stare at Pru. "Two sensible girls. For once I don't feel blinded by the amount of jewelry worn."

"Hush, Grandmama," Lord Bath said with a fond smile and a pat on her hand. "The entire room doesn't need to hear your condemnation. Are you thirsty? You're looking a bit flushed."

"I'm not at all out of sorts—"

He guided the old lady toward the chair Katherine had recently vacated. "Here, why don't you sit down a moment, and I'll fetch you a flute of lemonade. Ladies, would you care for one as well?"

"No," Katherine began, but he didn't wait long enough to listen.

With a jaunty "I'll bring three," he turned on his heel and expertly navigated through the crush of round tables and patrons with jewels sparkling brighter than their gowns. His cuffs flapped as he walked toward the footman standing at attention at the side of the room. Come to think of it, they *were* rather ridiculous.

Grandma Bath beamed as she beckoned Katherine and Pru closer. "Come now, I can't hear you from over there." Neither of them had said a word.

Katherine smiled as she stepped closer. "It's nice of Lord Bath to be so attentive to your needs. I don't see many grandsons so doting."

"Doting?" The old woman's smile slipped. "Smothering, is more like. I was Marchioness for thirty years before his grandfather passed. I raised four children and a dozen grandchildren. I am perfectly capable of standing on my own for a few moments." She harrumphed and patted her hair.

"I should say so," Pru said, raising her chin. "We women are perfectly capable of getting on without male interference."

Oh dear. Neither woman cared to keep her voice down. Across the tearoom, the score of men and women whispered as they eyed their group. Including one particularly tall man in the corner, with auburn hair and an unfashionable beard.

Katherine had never had the privilege of meeting Lord Annandale, since his estate resided in Scotland and he famously eschewed the *ton*, but the description matched that of the man Mrs. Burwick had described. He looked more amused than appalled, like the shorter blond dandy at his side, but Katherine was willing to wager that Pru had destroyed all chance of drawing his amorous eye.

A fortunate thing, then, that she didn't seem to want it.

When Katherine returned her attention to the women, both stared at her with open curiosity. Had she missed a question? "Forgive me, I was woolgathering. Did you say something?"

Grandma Bath's mouth tipped up in a sly smile. "I see what's caught your attention."

She did? Katherine glanced over her shoulder and bit her tongue to keep from swearing. Beyond Lord Annandale and his friend, the Marquess of Bath collected three flutes from a footman.

"He needs to marry soon, you know. He isn't getting any younger, and he hasn't got an heir. Perhaps with another woman to dote on, he'll have less time to chase after me." She winked.

"Ah." For once in her life, Katherine was rendered speechless. How should she reply? The old woman couldn't possibly be suggesting Katherine marry her grandson. Grasping for words, she said the first thing that entered her blank mind. "I'm in Bath to find Pru a husband."

Pru's amused smirk fell away, replaced by a glower. She didn't bother to hide it even as Grandma Bath turned toward her. The old lady turned back to Katherine with alacrity.

"It's so good of you to think of others before yourself. But you know, my dear, you aren't getting younger either."

Katherine felt older the longer this conversation

was prolonged. Fortunately, Lord Bath returned with the promised refreshments. He set the flutes on the table, his cuff catching the lip of one and nearly spilling it before he righted it. He handed that one to his grandmother.

"What poison are you dripping into Lady Katherine's ear, Grandmama? She's in the pink of health."

The old woman harrumphed but took a healthy gulp of the lemonade despite her earlier protests. She half finished it, occupying her long enough for her grandson to distribute the other flutes. As he handed one to Katherine, he said, "I hear from your father that you mean to seek an independent residence. That is brave of you."

No, what was brave of Katherine was staying in the same house as her father and stepmother as they made no secret of their efforts to conceive an heir. She smiled thinly and sipped the tart beverage.

Lord Bath added, "If you go through with it, I'd advise you to hire a chaperone. A woman of your stature cannot be too careful with her reputation."

Some days, Katherine wanted to throw dirt on her reputation herself, simply to have others stop discussing it. "I've managed with my maid this long, and I'm serving as chaperone now, besides. I'm no longer an eligible young debutante."

The marquess laughed heartily, drawing the attention of those closest. "My dear, a woman as comely as you is far from on the shelf."

And rich — don't forget my dowry, now. No one else does. However, now that Katherine had signed the papers to secure the funds for her own personal use — rather than the funds being released to her husband upon her marriage — she hoped to dissuade fortune hunters from sniffing at her skirts. For all intents and purposes, she was no longer available. If she ever had been.

"No, no, your maid simply isn't enough protection to your reputation. You must hire a professional companion. I'll ask around discreetly for you and see if I might find a recommendation."

Katherine finished her drink to keep from swearing. This was precisely the reason she went out of her way to avoid drawing a man's eye. Most of them had strong opinions about what she should and shouldn't do — opinions that she would never follow.

Before she angered a friend of Papa's, she set the flute on the table. As she leaned past Grandma Bath, the old lady whispered, "You see? Smothering. Though he means well."

Katherine didn't answer. She turned to Lord Bath with a strained smile. "Thank you. Now that the weather has improved, I fear it's time for me and Miss Burwick to take a tour of the gardens. For my health."

The old woman suggested loudly, "Ernest, why don't you escort her? We can't have Lady Katherine out there on her own."

I wouldn't be alone.

Lord Bath looked worried as he glanced between them. "Grandmama, I know you aren't up to such exertion. I wouldn't dream of leaving you on your own."

"Miss Burwick here can keep me company. She seems a sensible sort, at the very least not parading her jewels like every other ninny in here." The feather on her hat wobbled as she shook her head. "Not that you need worry, of course. We keep a vigilant patrol on the area. Our watchmen are most capable of apprehending this thief."

The marquess looked pained. "Grandmama, please don't draw attention to the matter, let alone in such a tone."

"Nonsense. They have nothing to fear. It's true, I was afraid this scoundrel would scare off our patrons, but that hasn't proven to be the case. If anything, we've only attracted a more daft set of visitors."

"Grandmama!" Lord Bath hovered near her elbow. "Perhaps you aren't feeling quite the thing and we should return home."

"But Lady Katherine..."

"Is perfectly capable of walking in the Vauxhall with Miss Burwick. Come." He shot an apologetic look at everyone within earshot. "Please do forgive her. Lady Katherine, Miss Burwick, I hope to see you later at the Assembly Rooms? I've opened it on Saturdays for a second dress ball, given the prominence of the visitors to Bath of late."

Katherine nodded. "Of course." She'd planned on attending tonight in any case, to discover what she could about the previous thefts and unearth suspects. However, when the old woman beamed, she wished she hadn't agreed so readily.

"Perhaps I'll come tonight as well."

Tarnation! The very last thing Katherine needed was for the old woman to throw her at Lord Bath. She had important work to do! However was she to find the Jewel Burglar of Bath if she was destined to be distracted? She had to solve this one on her own this time, to prove to everyone she was capable.

Especially little old ladies who thought her better suited for marriage than investigations.

CHAPTER TWO

K atherine and Pru strolled all the way to the nearest hedge before Pru burst into raucous laughter. Katherine scowled. "A fine lot of help you were."

The other woman wiped her eyes. "I didn't want to get in your way. It's terribly selfless of you, to be looking after *my* future before your own."

"If I were you, I'd mind how you treat me. I might try to arrange the match with Lord Annandale, after all."

Pru's mirth disappeared like the sun in a down-pour. She straightened. "You wouldn't dare. I thought we had an agreement."

As a woman's loud conversation hailed that they were soon to be interrupted, Katherine paused. She and Pru waited to one side of the path as a trio of older women passed. Lady Dalhousie, in the center, was the only person Katherine could name, having crossed paths with her once or twice in London.

The fifty-year-old gossipmonger cared for nothing as much as she did a winding tale, true or not. As she passed, excitement flushed her round cheeks, turning them nearly as dark as the rouge she wore on her lips. Her eyes twinkled, and her manicured hands flapped as she drew attention to her neck, where a necklace of diamonds and aquamarines fell in waves reminiscent of a waterfall.

"That scoundrel Napoleon had it commissioned for Joséphine, I'll have you know. He wanted something to adorn her that shone as bright as his love for her."

To her left, the graying woman with a robust figure made little effort to hide her scorn. "If that's so, then why doesn't Joséphine have it?"

Lady Dalhousie's mouth pursed. She scoffed as she turned down the nearest path, but her voice carried. "Why would she want to keep something that reminded her of the heinous man who cast her off like a common doxy? Fortunately, we happen to have a friend in common. She gave the jewels to him, and he to me. Oh, it was the most delightful thing to receive!

You see, I hadn't expected him at all, but a storm had blown up and..."

Katherine didn't need her years of investigating to have honed her instincts in order to recognize Lady Dalhousie's story for rubbish. More foolish than her blithering tale was the fact that she openly wore such expensive jewelry in the middle of the day when there was a known burglar about! What did she hope to accomplish?

The moment she was out of earshot, Pru leaned forward and said in a hiss, "You cannot match me with Lord Annandale! What if he is the thief?"

Linking her arm through Pru's, Katherine turned her down the path opposite the one the trio of women had chosen. Here, the tall shrubberies rose over even their heads, the thick growth of the labyrinth walls shielding them from prying eyes. "He most likely is not the thief."

"You cannot possibly know that."

Pru had a point, but Katherine didn't want to encourage it. Truthfully, everyone she met was a suspect until she learned more about the previous thefts and how long certain parties had been present in Bath. At the moment, all she knew had been gleaned from the news rag. Secondhand knowledge, at best.

"Lord Annandale might be the culprit, or it might be his friend — I think I heard him called Sir Hugh."

Katherine bit the inside of her cheek. She hadn't heard of Sir Hugh, but clearly Pru seemed bent on disparaging the man her mother wished her to marry. "Lord Annandale is a marquess. What possible need could he have for jewels like these? He has fortune enough to buy his own."

"He's Scottish. I hear they're all a bit wild up there."

Katherine pinched the bridge of her nose. "Thank Zeus your mother isn't here to hear this."

"Indeed. She'd likely be defending his honor when he's likely no better than a hulking barbarian in a fashionable jacket. Bravo on convincing her to stay behind in London, though. I don't know if I could have done it. There aren't many she trusts to pursue this sort of thing. She must have great confidence in you."

Although Pru likely meant her words to be encouraging, Katherine's spirits flagged. This was precisely why she needed to solve this crime by her own merit without help from anyone, including Pru. Not that the young woman hadn't been instrumental in the last case, but because Katherine's reputation would be ruined if she claimed credit publicly. No one knew she'd been the one to capture the Pink-Ribbon Killer. Everyone simply thought she was a matchmaker.

It was a great cover that allowed her access to house parties and balls without anyone asking questions, but she didn't want to get a reputation for being *too* good at it. The very last thing she wanted to do was orchestrate love matches for the rest of her life. She was destined for far more convoluted puzzles, and she needed to prove to herself that she could solve a case on her own, even if she could never let the general public know.

Tightly, she answered, "Yes, fortunately, your mother does seem to put great store in my ability to chaperone and make a match for you. I'd never be able to investigate properly if your mother were butting her head into my every endeavor."

Pru radiated smugness as if it were warmth. "Her presence would make it difficult for *us* to investigate."

Katherine raised her voice by a hair. "I'll have to ask you to keep out of it as well. If Lord Annandale is involved, I'll investigate the matter myself."

Pru's mouth flattened, and a furrow formed between her eyebrows. "Why? I thought—"

"It's nothing personal, Pru. I need to do this myself."

"Then why bring Mr. Murphy all this way to aid you?"

After a glance down the nearest junction to ensure they still had relative privacy, Katherine continued along the damp stone path. "His inventions are invaluable, and speaking my thoughts aloud regarding the case often helps to refine my theories."

Next to her, Prudence stiffened. Her footsteps fell heavy in the strained silence between them. "Very well," she said after a moment. "If you want me to steer clear of potentially the most exciting investigation to cross my path, then you'll have to promise me something in exchange."

Wary, Katherine asked, "And what might that be?"

Her companion's smug air returned. When her lips tilted up, they softened the sharp cast of her nose and chin. *If she'd only smile more...*

"Vow not to match me with Annandale or anyone else. In fact, I want him to think of me as the very last woman he will ever marry. If you can do that, I promise to leave you be."

Perhaps she ought to smile less, in that case.

"I won't match you with Annandale against your will." That would be a match doomed from the start, in any case.

"Good." Pru's smile faded. "You will use me to help refine your theories, though, won't you?"

Katherine laughed and squeezed the other woman's arm. "That, I can do. You know, Pru, you're a lot like me."

"I know. That's why we'd make a good team," the other woman said pointedly.

"This time, I won't need a team. With all these ladies parading their jewels about, they're all but begging to be robbed. All I'll have to do is keep an eye on the proceedings and catch the thief in the act."

It would be the easiest investigation she'd ever conducted.

———

KATHERINE CATALOGUED each item as she put it in her reticule: string, since that had proven useful in place of plaster to take the size of a shoe print, a small pair of scissors, some powder and a brush for illuminating clues, a small empty vial in case she needed to sample something, a few handkerchiefs to wrap larger items, a small notebook, and — confound it, where was the pencil?

Crack. Katherine bolted to her feet at the sounds of chewing. "Emma!"

The pencil was rendered unusable, but the graphite could make the dog sick. Katherine bolted after the furry thief and caught her by the behind a second before she slipped beneath the narrow bed. She wagged her tail, pleased with herself, as Katherine hoisted her.

"That isn't for eating," she admonished. She wedged her fingers into Emma's mouth, checking for remnants of graphite, before she groped along the floor, one handed. She deposited every pencil shard she found on the cramped writing desk. Aside from the desk and bed, there was precious little furniture in the quaint hotel room. In fact, she had scarcely enough room to maneuver, with her trunk taking up most of the space. Once the floor no longer posed a hazard for Emma, she dropped her pug to the ground once more. The dog happily sniffed the area in search of other ill-gotten goods.

Katherine checked her appearance in the hand-held mirror Harriet had packed to make certain she looked presentable — presentable, not comely. After the attention Grandma Bath had bestowed upon her that afternoon, Katherine wanted to appear ordinary and unremarkable in every way. Her height and wide hips drew enough attention as it was; she did not need to compound that by battling off Grandma Bath's unsubtle suggestions. How was she to investigate if the dowager and her grandson were following at her heels? With her brown hair tucked into a simple chignon, and wearing only the most modest of jewelry, Katherine looked utterly forgettable. Satisfied, she crossed to the door to seek the company of Harriet, who she had sent across the hall to help with Pru's attire.

The moment she opened the door, Emma squeezed between her legs and scurried out of sight. Maids and valets entered and exited various rooms, the pug disappearing amongst the polite chaos. As the last whisked out of sight, shutting the door behind her with a firm click of the latch, she left the corridor quiet and deserted.

Darn! Emma might have gone anywhere. In the hope that the dog had learned how to reach the gardens, Katherine hitched her skirt above her ankles and hurried toward the staircase to the first floor. Along the way, she cocked her ears at each doorway, hoping for sounds to indicate that her pet was within. Nothing. "Where are you, Emma?"

Whoever she terrorized, they had yet to find her. Her heart in her throat, Katherine slipped down the stairs to the silent first level, then the ground floor.

When she asked a passing maid whether she'd seen a dog, she had not. As Katherine mounted the stairs again to the cramped floor containing the hotel rooms, she bit the inside of her cheek.

At the top, Emma waited in the corridor, tail wagging. She cocked her head as if to ask, *Where have you been?* Katherine sank to her knees to pat her.

"Don't do that to me, you rascal."

Emma spat out something sparkly onto the runner. With a sinking feeling, Katherine reached for the moist item and lifted a diamond earring. The intricate spray of metal and precious stone dangled two inches long. Katherine groaned.

"I could have gotten a parrot. Philomena Gray-locke has one, and the worst he has ever done is insult someone."

The pug grinned, her pink tongue hanging out one side of her mouth.

"This is not something to be proud of," Katherine admonished.

Emma didn't appear to notice her chiding tone. She rolled on her back, asking for a rub. Instead, Katherine scooped her up and deposited her in her room. With the door shut and the thieving dog safely on the other side, she stared down the daunting line of doors. From whom had Emma stolen the earring?

Katherine prayed it hadn't been taken directly from some poor woman's ear, though she suspected she'd have heard a great deal more screaming if that were the case.

Across the hall, Pru's muffled voice pierced the wooden door between them. "This is a disaster! I need Katherine's help. Where is she?"

Katherine didn't have time to walk down the line of doors and knock on each in search of the earring's owner. Instead, she slipped it into her reticule and opened the door to tend to her charge.

Pru looked close to tears. Clad in her undergarments, she held a shawl in front of her like a shield and faced off against Harriet and her hairbrush. The moment Katherine shut the door, Pru met her gaze and blurted, "Harriet keeps trying to make me beautiful."

The maid scowled. "What woman deliberately wants to look unappealing?"

"I do," Pru snapped. "I don't want Lord Annandale to think of me as a desirable woman in any way." She raised her gaze, beseeching. "Katherine, please, won't you help me dress unattractively, like you do?"

"*Like me?*" Katherine didn't look that unappealing, did she?

Harriet snorted. "I advised you to wear something in a brighter color."

She had. Her first choice had been a dove-gray dress with a spray of lace around the collar. However, when Harriet had mentioned that she looked as if she were in mourning, Katherine had chosen a faint sea green instead. Her earrings were gold studs; she wore no other ornament.

Pru made a face as she looked at the bed, atop which draped a dress. "Harriet wants me to wear the puce, but it's the finest dress I own. What do you do to make yourself look so... dowdy?"

When Katherine glanced at Harriet, she had her face downcast as she stepped to the side, out of the way. In any other woman, Katherine might mistake that expression for meekness. However as she stepped closer, she caught the smirk curving Harriet's lips. Her maid was enjoying this!

Scowling, Katherine turned her attention to the other woman. Despite her disparaging words, Pru didn't look as though she meant to insult. She genuinely looked as though she hoped for Katherine's guidance. Katherine sighed. "Show me your dresses. We'll pick the least offensive."

"The most offensive," Pru countered. "I want him to think me the ugliest woman alive."

"Better he not think of you at all." Upon crossing to the open trunk, Katherine rifled through the contents, looking for a plain gown. "You haven't yet been introduced, so he'll have no reason to notice you exist if you don't draw attention to yourself."

"Plenty of gentlemen seek out inoffensive brides, the sort that fade into the background and they don't believe they'll have to bother with after the wedding." She tugged a beige dress out of Katherine's hand and dropped it back into the trunk. "I want something that makes me such an eyesore they can't stand to look at me. Something that makes me look — oh! Like a pumpkin!" With a triumphant grin, she fished out an orange dress.

Truthfully, the dress might be better described as peach than orange, but if it was an eyesore Pru hoped to present, this gown seemed her best bet. Katherine pointed at the bodice. "What are those?"

"The flowers?" Pru shook her head with a sigh. "You see, I gained a bit of weight since last Season. My mother had to replace the buttons. She bought a lot of these, thinks it's the latest fashion. Wears them herself. Honestly, I had to wrestle her to the ground to keep her from sewing them on everything I owned."

Buttons seemed like such an innocuous term. The size of Katherine's fist, the flowers were made of a gleaming marbled ivory material. They shimmered in the candlelight, catching it along their polished surfaces and making them as much a noticeable fixture as the gaudy jewelry of the other patrons. Pru would fit in splendidly.

"Very well. That dress will do."

As to the weight, it couldn't have been terribly much. Certainly, Pru was no shrinking violet. She was big-boned, with her weight distributed solidly along her frame, and couldn't be called petite in any sense of the word. To any man who preferred a woman to have a bit of meat on their bones — admittedly, most of them — she had an ideal figure.

If she recalled to smile instead of scowl.

Harriet laid down the hairbrush on the writing desk and navigated the crush near the bed to help Pru don the dress. As she did so, she seemed a bit wilting. The buttons on the back were the same hideous ones as the ornamental three on the front.

With a wan smile, Harriet quipped, "Well, you certainly don't need a man to send you a posy. You are one all on your own."

Pru glowered. "Of course I don't need a man. I don't need one for anything. What use is a posy, in any case?"

Harriet cast Katherine a despairing look. Tucking away a smile, Katherine continued to rummage through the chest in search of some earrings that wouldn't draw too much attention. Fortunately, Pru seemed to own no other kind.

The moment Harriet finished with the dress, she cajoled, "What do you say to a bit of cosmetics?"

Pru frowned as she turned to Katherine, assessing. Katherine had declined cosmetics, on account of coming to Bath to investigate rather than socialize. She didn't care how she looked, so long as she didn't manage to draw the Marquess of Bath's admiring eye in the process, as his grandmother seemed adamant to promote.

With a nod, Pru answered, "Perhaps a little. Can you make me look as sallow as Katherine does in that dress?"

Perhaps she ought to change into the dove gray, after all.

The opening and shutting of a door along the corridor alerted her to the fact that the other women were readying to leave. She had no time to change dresses, even if Harriet could be spared from her task. "Hurry, if you can," she instructed her maid. "We don't want to be late."

However, Pru didn't make the task easy. She twisted, trying to meet Katherine's gaze. "How else should I act unappealing tonight? You must know."

She means well, Katherine reminded herself. At the

steely look in Pru's eye, she recalled the ultimatum the young woman had given. Very well, if it was the cost to keep Pru from stepping on Katherine's toes, she would make her the least marriageable woman in the room.

Forgive me, Mrs. Burwick. With luck, she would be able to enact this trick without tarnishing Pru's reputation overmuch.

"Lords want ladylike wives." The conventional ones did, at least. "If you act contrary to everything that you've been taught, you ought to be able to repulse them."

Pru pursed her lips. "What does that mean?"

"In essence, act like they do when not in mixed company."

The young woman seemed a bit out of her depth at that very notion. "My father used to smoke and drink in his study."

"That will do." Though how Pru thought to find a cheroot, Katherine didn't know. She only hoped the young woman wouldn't ask her for help on that measure. Katherine didn't smoke, nor did she wish to take up the habit.

"What of loo?"

"I beg your pardon?"

"Five-card loo, the game. Is that unladylike?"

Considering that it was usually played in gaming hells and not at polite events... "Yes. Do you play?"

"I do. I'm quite good at it, in fact."

Katherine laughed and shook her head as Harriet finished and stepped away. "If you have the opportunity tonight, flaunt your prowess." It couldn't hinder her goal.

The first to exit into the corridor, Katherine nearly collided with Lord Annandale's blond friend, Sir Hugh. She took a step to the right, offering him the ability to pass, but he did the same. She stepped to the left instead, as did he. It was like dancing with a much paler mirror. Katherine stopped and smiled. "Sir, if you want to dance, perhaps you ought to put your name on my dance card."

The thin curve of his lips he gave in return couldn't be called a smile, for it fell far short of his eyes. If Pru thought Katherine looked sallow, she clearly hadn't compared her to Sir Hugh. The dandy's skin looked waxen, which made his blue eyes seem all the brighter and the curl of blond hair draping over his forehead seem like straw. His pinched expression was nothing like the easy manner he had adopted while in Lord Annandale's company.

Katherine frowned as her investigator's instincts

buzzed. Something was amiss. "Are you quite all right, sir?"

He laughed, but the sound rang hollow. "Of course, I'm in the pink of health."

"You seem agitated."

"I'm set to meet a friend before venturing to the Assembly Rooms this evening. I don't want to be late. If you'll excuse me, ladies."

He tipped his head, his forelock dripping to obscure his eyes as he stepped past. As he did, Katherine noticed the wear on the silver fastenings of his emerald jacket. Although once covered in gilt, the oblong buttons had chipped in places to show dark metal beneath. It wasn't the only sign of ill fortune. The coat was faded along the shoulders and back, where the sun might have shone, and darker beneath the arms. Her gaze caught on a darned hole near the elbow as he passed.

Sir Hugh wasn't as flush in the pockets as he appeared to be. However, if so, why hadn't he begged residence with his friend Lord Annandale? In her cursory inquiry into the Scottish marquess, Katherine had learned that he'd let a townhouse in Sydney Place for the duration of his stay in Bath. Certainly, if the pair was as close as they seemed, Sir Hugh would have been welcome in that townhouse. Was pride stopping

Sir Hugh from begging assistance? Or had he rented a room at the Sydney Hotel because he didn't want his friend to look too deeply at his dealings?

"That was odd," Pru muttered as she shut the door behind her.

"I couldn't agree more."

"Should we follow him?"

If he truly meant to visit the Assembly Rooms, he would be traveling in the same direction where they meant to go. Katherine nodded. "Yes. Discreetly." She took the lead, following in the dandy's wake as he descended the stairs to the ground floor. At the mouth of the staircase, an older lady and gentleman stepped in front of them.

Sard it, move faster! The old couple blocked the staircase. Katherine and Pru couldn't slip past until the first floor. As she excused herself, hurrying down, Pru followed in her wake. However, they were too late. The moment they exited into the brisk pre-autumn air, their breaths fogging in front of their faces, Katherine caught sight of Sir Hugh through the door to a closed carriage as a footman shut it. The driver flicked the reins, and the matched pair of horses lurched into motion.

"Tarnation," Pru cursed, not as softly as she might have. She drew the eye of another couple stepping into a second black carriage. They sniffed and begged the footman to shut the door at once.

"Mind your language."

Pru scowled. "If ever there was a time to use that word, it is now. He's gotten away."

"We don't know that he has anything to do with—" She paused to scan her surroundings. Aside from the third and last carriage waiting on the cobblestones in front of the towering hotel, the old couple they had passed on the way out exited the building. Lowering her voice, Katherine finished, "Recent events. At any rate, he'll be at the Assembly Rooms, and you promised not to interfere."

Although she heaved a long sigh, Pru didn't speak a word in contradiction.

The old woman's face fell as she beheld the scene. "Oh, dear. Did Lady Dalhousie leave without us?"

Hers must have been the carriage Pru had scared off with her foul language. Using a word Katherine had inadvertently taught her, no less. Masking a pang of guilt, Katherine beckoned to the couple. "Do you mean to attend the event at the Assembly Rooms tonight?"

The woman, in her fifties and graying, though her figure was much more limber than that of her husband, who seemed a bit older and who leaned on her arm, answered, "Yes, indeed." She, like the rest of the bacon-brained ladies who had come to Bath, had swathed herself in jewels. Sapphires winked at her ears and on her finger. Several strings of shining gray pearls drew attention to her long neck. "It's much too far to walk, especially in my condition."

Her condition? She didn't seem unable to walk, but perhaps her husband's difficulty masked hers.

Katherine gestured to the carriage. "Would you care to come in my carriage?"

"Oh, what a sweet girl. Thank you. Is that the Earl of Dorchester's seal I espy on the door?"

As prompted, Katherine used the inquiry to expedite the introductions. "It is. I am his daughter, Lady Katherine, and this is Miss Burwick. Do you know my father?"

A carriage was one more thing into which she would have to delve once she lived on her own. How much did it cost to keep a team of horses and a carriage? She didn't want to overreach her dowry, but the ease of having one's own carriage was worth considering. She didn't want to rely on her father for anything other than occasional companionship and advice.

The older man shook his head, his white whiskers trembling with the motion. "We don't quite move in those circles, I'm afraid. Mr. Oliver, at your service, and this is my wife."

Mrs. Oliver added, "We have heard tremendous things about your family. Is it true you are a successful matchmaker?"

Pru looked as sour at the suggestion as Katherine felt. "Indeed, I am." The words tasted bitter on her tongue. "I am here to arrange a match for Miss Burwick, in fact."

If Pru pressed her lips together any harder, her entire face would turn as white as the rim around them. Hoping to defuse the situation, Katherine motioned for the Olivers to precede her into the carriage. After handing his wife into the conveyance, Mr. Oliver insisted the ladies go next.

Mrs. Oliver had chosen the seat facing forward, so Katherine and Pru had no choice but to face the rear of the carriage. They pressed hip to hip as Mr. Oliver huffed getting into the carriage. Once he was seated across from her, a hotel footman shut the door, and the driver directed the coach onto the road.

Determined to make the most of the situation, Katherine steered the conversation in a different direction. "Have you been in Bath long?"

"Not terribly long, I don't say."

"I'm surprised the thefts haven't frightened you

off. The first must have been quite the cause for alarm."

Mrs. Oliver fluttered her hand over her chest. "Oh, dear me, I think it might have, if we'd been in town for that misfortune. What a shock! No, no, we've only been in Bath since the end of the Season."

"You aren't afraid of the risk?"

"Aren't you?" Mrs. Oliver countered, but from her tone, she didn't seem terribly concerned.

Not wanting to reveal her true purpose, Katherine grasped at an excuse. "I left my most expensive jewelry at home."

The older woman glanced at Katherine's bare neck. "Well, I shall say you'll never find yourself robbed then."

She sounded almost as if that would be a disappointment.

Pru found her voice before Katherine. "What sort of imbecile would want to find themselves robbed?"

With a sniff, Mrs. Oliver turned her face toward the small window. "Only the best jewels are robbed. The burglar has impeccable taste, which reflects upon the person he robs, wouldn't you say?"

The women of the *ton* were more vapid than Katherine thought. No wonder she usually avoided them.

Katherine narrowed her eyes. "Forgive my boldness, but have you been one of the victims?"

The silence soured like curdled milk. After a moment, the older woman snapped, "No. But neither has Lady Dalhousie, and she's practically throwing that atrocious necklace into his hands. He doesn't want it." She sounded smug.

Clearly, there was some sort of rivalry between the two women. Perhaps Katherine ought to delve into the matter further another night.

Instead, she asked, "Who has lost their jewels, then?"

"Well..." Mrs. Oliver drew out the word. "I cannot speak for those who ventured here before I arrived, of course."

"Of course," Katherine muttered, trying to encourage her.

Seemingly content to be the bearer of such news, the woman informed them, "Mrs. Tatton was robbed of her prized sapphire-and-diamond earrings last month. And only a few weeks ago, Lady Carleton lost that atrocious ring her husband gave her upon the tenth anniversary of their wedding. You know the one, the emerald encircled by diamonds?"

Although she wasn't familiar with either victim, Katherine nodded.

Pru muttered, "That seems more a travesty than a blessing. Imagine the cost of replacing such items!"

"Cost," Mrs. Oliver scoffed. "Dear me, anyone with any sense has those sorts of valuables insured these days, with all the threats of highway robbery."

Katherine bristled. "The streets of London are perfectly safe, both in and around the city." Lyle and his compatriots saw to that, relentlessly hunting down all reports of highway robbery and seeing the culprits to justice.

Mrs. Oliver harrumphed.

The carriage turned a corner and started to slow. As it did, Katherine recalled the earring in her reticule. She straightened and fished it out. "Oh, while I have your attention, I found something, and I think it might be yours." She lifted the earring near to the window, to allow for the meager light streaming in to catch upon the jewels. "Do you recognize this?"

All occupants in the carriage looked confused at the question. Pru narrowed her eyes as she looked at Katherine askance. The other woman perused the earring closely.

"It isn't mine," Mrs. Oliver said with a sniff, turning her face away. "Perhaps ask Lady Dalhousie. It looks the sort of monstrosity she might favor. It matches well with her precious necklace."

With a small sigh, Katherine returned the item to her reticule. "I'll ask her. Thank you for your help."

Mrs. Oliver leaned forward as the carriage stopped, her eyes gleaming. "Do tell, how did you come by it? Did you catch someone in the act of stealing it?"

Katherine raised her eyebrows. "If I had, I'd know who the rightful owner was. Unfortunately, my dog, Emma, has a singular talent of finding things that ought not to be hers. She's rather like a magpie that way."

Pru smirked as she leaned back against the squabs.

Nudging her husband, Mrs. Oliver joked, "Did you hear that? A dog. Perhaps Emma is the thief of Bath!"

Everyone in the carriage laughed except for Katherine.

CHAPTER THREE

On the outside, the Assembly Rooms looked no different from any other building on the street. Rather plain, actually. Faint music wafted from within, so the clock must have struck six of the evening while they had driven through town. Katherine disembarked last from the carriage and instructed the driver to come for her at eleven o'clock that evening. She didn't want to leave a moment earlier than anyone else, or risk missing a vital clue.

She and Pru entered by the northwest door. If the façade was plain, the interior, by comparison held enough decoration to render the viewer breathless. Corinthian columns dotted the walls, with ornate swags carved between them and scrollwork decorating the perimeter. Niches held elegant painted vases. Light shone from the intricate chandelier overhead.

Everyone in Bath seemed to be in attendance. As Katherine stepped inside so she wasn't an obstacle to others, a footman dressed in a turquoise coat with gleaming buttons stepped into her path and held out a hand. "May I have your ticket, madam?"

Perhaps she should have seen to it earlier in the evening. "I'm afraid I don't have a subscription. How much will it be to attend the evening's entertainment?"

"Five shillings. Each."

Katherine had expected to have to pay some small amount in order to cover the cost of tea, but that number taxed the amount she carried in her reticule. Would she have enough? As she reached for the strings to root around inside the bag hanging from her wrist, the Marquess of Bath appeared with a smile as wide as his cuffs.

"Lady Katherine, do forgive me, I meant to meet you outside the door but was detained a moment. You haven't paid, have you?"

"I was about to do so now."

Lord Bath waved off the notion. "Please, put that away. I've obtained tickets for both you and your guest." He handed them over to the footman and offered an arm to both ladies. Katherine accepted and allowed herself to be led in. After the marquess's cuff nearly caught on Pru's front button, she gingerly accepted his arm, keeping a healthy distance between them.

He deposited them both in the mouth of the left-hand arch. "Here is the ballroom. We'll have minuets here until eight, and I hope to claim one." He caught Katherine's eye with a pointed look.

How was she to investigate while dancing? Katherine forced a smile. "Thank you, but you know I don't care to dance."

"Just this once. I won't take no for an answer. You must tell me how your father is getting on." He glanced anxiously around the entranceway. "If you'll forgive me, I must find Grandmama and convince her to sit a moment. She'll overexert herself. Ladies." He inclined his head.

Katherine curtsied in answer. "My lord." By the time she straightened, he'd turned away and disappeared into the growing crush. Tarnation, Katherine hadn't even known there were so many members of polite society in Bath!

Pru looked every bit as dismayed. "How are we to find Sir Hugh in this?"

"We aren't," Katherine said. "I am. I'm sure I can trust you alone for a few hours?"

The other woman scoffed. "I'm two years older than you. I don't need to be chaperoned."

"Good."

When Katherine turned away, Pru caught her arm with a sly expression. She pulled her out of the doorway and into the ballroom. This long, magnificent hall was lit with more chandeliers, the principle decoration in the room save for the walls themselves. Square, intricate sections of Vitruvian scroll framed the mooring of each chandelier down the middle of the high ceiling. More scrollwork above the wainscoting and Corinthian pillars decorated the walls, culminating in a second-floor alcove with a delicate white railing situated in the center where the musicians had taken up their instruments. Several marble hearths were lit, shedding light and warmth on what looked to be five hundred guests or more. Men and women danced in elegant pairs down the middle of the room, adding little to the conversation humming along the perimeter and tiered rows of benches near the windows.

Katherine was rendered speechless. A private ball couldn't compare to the splendor; even Almack's had competition. Fortunately, she had Pru to ground her in the present.

"If you'll be too busy dancing, I'd be happy to conduct an investigation in your place."

Katherine glared at her charge. "You will do no such thing. You promised."

"And *you* promised to make me undesirable. Why then are so many of the men staring at us?"

Perhaps because we are blocking the door. Katherine bit the inside of her cheek and guided Pru a few steps further into the ballroom. As they side-stepped a group of mixed men and women, a man's lowered voice reached her ear.

"I don't believe I've seen those two ladies before. Can anyone provide an introduction?"

Sard it all! There was only one reason a gentleman would seek an acquaintance at such an event, and Katherine didn't have the time to be dancing all night. Fortunately, she doubted anyone in that cluster of debutantes and suitors knew either of them.

"I know the lady on the left. She's the Earl of Dorchester's daughter. I met her once in London."

Tarnation!

"Lady Katherine," called the woman.

Pretending not to hear, Katherine quickened her step. She and Pru passed the second-floor alcove, drawing more attention along the way. The men looked them over but apparently didn't find their attire as unappealing as Katherine had hoped, for she caught the scattered questions as she stepped past. Were they married? Chaperones? Did anyone know them? Katherine, at least, had the illusion of her duties as chaperone behind which to hide. Should anyone make introductions, however, Pru would be most unhappy — and would make Katherine equally so.

As they neared the set of open doors leading to another room on the far end of the ballroom, her companion proved as much by hissing in Katherine's ear. "This is unseemly. I have never been so ogled. Are you certain this dress makes me look unappealing?"

Katherine's vanity made her mutter, "Perhaps they're looking at me."

Pru raised her eyebrows as if to say, *In that dress?* She pursed her lips and thankfully didn't spout the words aloud.

Nevertheless, Katherine needed three deep breaths before she could answer in a tone that wasn't biting. "More likely, we're oddities, being new to Bath. That must be the root of our apparent popularity." The local gentry must lead a dull existence if the mere presence of two women caused such a stir, but Pru was right. They had both dressed plainly, in such a fashion as to avoid admiring looks.

"How, then, do I convince them that I'm not worth courting?"

"Act unladylike," Katherine advised.

"Yes, but how?"

The door on this end of the ballroom opened into an octagonal chamber with a high roof and a single lustrous chandelier. The light glinted off the carved marble fireplaces at intervals, each still lit to provide warmth for the early arrivals, but burning low and likely to soon be extinguished. Above each of these fixtures was a curious, ornate mirror in a shape reminiscent of a pumpkin. The wide expanse in between held round card tables, with another room to the left containing more.

Katherine gestured to the Octagon. "Start with five-card loo, and if any other opportunity arises, seize it."

Pru smirked. "Now that, I should be able to do."

The moment she departed for the other room, Katherine squeezed in behind a row of matrons to seat herself on one of the chairs. Here, she was hidden enough to take a moment to get her bearings.

She had two aims tonight. First, she had to find the owner of the earring Emma had filched so she might return it. However, with the way Mrs. Oliver had joked that Emma — or worse, perhaps Katherine —

was responsible for the string of thefts, Katherine hesitated to ask those staying at the hotel outright.
Although she would be able to convince the authorities
that she wasn't responsible, being that she had recently
attended the Earl of Northbrook's house party, so she
wasn't even in Bath when the last theft happened. But
if she were even suspected because of the earring, her
investigation might become infinitely more difficult.
The very reason she masqueraded as a matchmaker
was so that her suspects would find her unassuming
enough to speak in her presence. Therefore, she had
no choice but to seek out the owner of the earring
without seeming to do so.

That promised to be a Herculean task in itself.
How was she to find the handful of people staying at
the hotel amidst these hundreds of guests? She had to
try. Perhaps, if she was lucky, she might be able to use
the overwhelming amount of people to coax out gossip
about the Burglar of Bath. Beginning her investigation
was a far more important task.

Her decision made, Katherine waited for the music
of the song to fade. Hoping to use the influx of people
from the dance floor as camouflage to avoid anyone
who wished to flirt with her, she slipped off the bench
at precisely the wrong moment. Her heart skipped a

beat as Lord Bath entered from the Octagon with his grandmother hanging on his arm.

The old woman's face lit up as she spotted Katherine. "Oh, Lady Katherine, there you are!"

Bally! Of all the people... Katherine couldn't possibly be so rude as to turn away, especially not when Lord Bath had arranged for her entrance into the event. Biting back a sigh, she fixed a smile in place.

"So nice to see you, my lord." She curtsied. "My lady."

Grandma Bath narrowed her eyes with a sly smile. "No need to stand on such formality. Ernest is so fond of your family, I think of you as an extension of ours. Please, call me Grandmama, as he does."

She would never do that.

Her smile wavered, but she tried not to show her sudden trepidation. "Thank you. I fear I don't have time to chat. I seem to have misplaced my charge. I make for a frightful chaperone, don't I?"

Lord Bath answered her smile with a warm one of his own. *Stop it!* Didn't he see that he would only encourage this sudden delusion his grandmother had cooked up?

"Don't discredit yourself. We saw her but moments ago at the card tables. She seems well off, deep in luck, it seems. Why, I even saw her correct

Annandale's hand. They're in plain view, no harm to come of it."

It seemed that Pru had found a way to make herself undesirable to Lord Annandale, after all. Katherine had yet to meet a man who enjoyed being corrected.

"Nevertheless, I should collect her before the gossips start a hum over this."

As Katherine tried to sidestep the pair into the Octagon — silently apologizing to Pru for having to interrupt the game — Grandma Bath stopped her with a hand on her elbow. For such a frail old woman, she had a frightfully strong grip. Katherine swore she heard her bones creak.

"Miss Burwick can tend to herself. She is a sensible woman. Why don't you enjoy yourself? This is the first time I've seen you in our lovely town. Enjoy what it has to offer!"

"It is the first time I've been in Bath," Katherine admitted. Her family spent the bulk of their time in London or among their estates. "However, I'll have to enjoy it with Miss Burwick. I've been hired to find her a husband, I'll have you know."

"Ernest knows every eligible gentleman in town. Why doesn't he tell you while you dance a minuet?

I'm afraid I'm feeling faint and need to sit down for a spell, in any case."

Concern overtook Lord Bath's friendly expression. "I was afraid this would be too taxing an excursion for you. Let me fetch you some lemonade." He helped her to the nearest bench, immediately vacated by its occupant, who moved with her companions farther back in the row.

Grandma Bath waved her hand. "No, I won't hear of it. You're too often caring for me and forgetting to enjoy yourself. I don't wish to be a burden. Why don't you dance with Katherine, and if I'm still feeling poorly in ten minutes, I'll have you fetch me that drink."

With a shrug, the lord turned to Katherine. "You did promise me a minuet, my dear."

Actually, she'd never promised, but Katherine didn't want to insult one of her father's friends. She capitulated with a graceful incline of her head. "Only one, then I must reunite with Miss Burwick."

The marquess offered his arm as music wafted into the air again. As he led her onto the dance floor, she spotted several faces that she recognized from the hotel. Perhaps this dance was the very thing needed in order to find the earring's owner! Since she had already garnered a reputation for clumsiness while at Lord Northbrook's house party, she didn't see the harm in stumbling once or twice to get a better look at the ladies' jewelry and find a similar style. Rarely did a lady purchase the earrings on their own. She had to have the matching accoutrements as well.

They took their places in the line of dancers. Lord Bath adjusted his wide cuff before holding his arm aloft. Katherine rested her hand atop his as they began the elegant minuet. With her free hand, she dug into her reticule for the earring. As she palmed it, she realized that the marquess had said something to her.

"Forgive me, I was woolgathering. What did you say?"

"I asked after your father. I haven't heard from him since the close of the Season. How is he?"

"He was in good spirits when I left him. He keeps busy, what with visiting my sisters and their children." Not to mention attempting to have another of his own.

As she completed the next step of the dance, Katherine flung her free arm a little harder than necessary, whapping a woman in the collarbone. As she apologized with a simper, she compared the earring with the necklace the woman wore. It didn't match.

Lord Bath added his apology to the innocent dancer and returned his attention to Katherine with a frown. "Are you quite all right?"

"I'm a trifle out of practice, I'm afraid. I don't often dance."

He circled Katherine, and upon returning offered her a crooked smile. "You ought to amend that more during the Season next year. I'll see it as my solemn duty."

Oh dear. Surely he was only being polite to a friend's daughter. He couldn't possibly share his grandmother's aspirations. Katherine was *not* on the marriage market.

Lord Bath added, "I'm certain your father would rest easier if he knew you were taken care of."

Katherine bit the inside of her cheek, grateful that the dance afforded her a moment to breathe. She compared the earring to a gaudy ring, having to stumble in order to come close enough to the woman to do so. They didn't match.

Lord Bath dropped her hand in order to steady her by the shoulders. "Forgive me, my dear. It seems I'm not the best dance partner."

In terms of conversation, not at all. The clumsiness was deliberate on Katherine's part, but she couldn't confess that much. Perhaps he would be so discouraged by the dance's end that he would give up the notion of asking her to stand up with him again.

"Not at all. The fault is all mine. Shall we continue?"

"Certainly. I'll try not to arrange us quite so close to the other dancers."

Tarnation! She needed to be close in order to continue with her ruse. Although she had eliminated two potential owners, she still had several down the line, including... was that Lady Dalhousie? Most matrons opted to gossip rather than dance, but the woman's profile was uncannily similar... Mrs. Oliver had fingered her as being the rightful owner. Katherine had to get closer.

She and the marquess danced for a moment in silence before his previous statement festered too long. When she couldn't hold her tongue any longer, she blurted, "Papa supports and encourages my independence. He gifted my dowry to me this past birthday, so I might have complete control over my finances and my future. I take care of myself."

Lord Bath pursed his lips. He circled her again before he said, "It appears I've offended. Please accept my apology, Lady Katherine. It was not my intention."

She inclined her head.

Unfortunately, he did not let the subject rest. "Forgive me, but I cannot see your father being satisfied in his daughter taking up a profession such as matchmaking. Aiding a family member is one thing, but accepting money for the service... it's rather bourgeois for a woman of your heritage."

"It's good business sense," Katherine answered in a clipped tone. "In fact, my father insisted on it."

Granted, he knew Katherine's true purpose, whereas the marquess did not. Her matchmaking business was less a means to support herself and more a ruse to conceal her investigations. If Lord Bath didn't approve of her matchmaking, he certainly wouldn't approve of her detective work.

Frowning, the marquess stepped forward to do another circuit. His cuff flung wide, catching on the necklace of a woman who had stepped closer with her partner. It was Lady Dalhousie! She shrieked as her necklace pulled tight against her throat.

"Thief!"

The dancers grew still, turning to the growing spectacle.

Panic crossed the marquess's face, and he froze in place. "I'm not trying to rob you, madam. My cuff is caught!"

Katherine took advantage of the moment to leap into the fray. "Allow me to help." She took her time unhooking Lord Bath's sleeve. The shadows cast by Lady Dalhousie's hair made it difficult to tell if the diamonds on the earrings were at all similar to the ones on her necklace. Finally, reluctantly, Katherine ruled that they were not.

Nevertheless, as Lady Dalhousie huffed over the indignity and the marquess ushered her and her partner off of the dance floor so the gathering might resume the festivities, Katherine took the opportunity to tap the woman on the arm. "I found this in the hotel earlier this evening," she whispered, angling her hand to display the earring. "Mrs. Oliver thought it might be yours."

Lady Dalhousie scoffed. "As if my tastes run so ugly. No wonder you found it tossed away. Even the thief wouldn't want it!"

It seemed Mrs. Oliver had been wrong. Katherine bit the inside of her cheek. How was she supposed to find the rightful owner and return it?

The matron added, "Perhaps you'd do better to keep it for yourself. You could do with a little adornment. Has your family fallen on hard times?"

"No," Katherine bit off. "I left my jewels at home."

"Whyever would you do that?"

Perhaps because there is a thief about town!

Katherine didn't have the chance to answer, for the moment they were safely out of the way of the dancers, Lord Bath took Lady Dalhousie in hand. "My lady, I assure you that you are perfectly safe while in my town. You will not be robbed, certainly not in plain view of five hundred people! I have the best investigators looking into the matter of the recent misfortunes, and patrols around town are stringent. Come, perhaps if you have a sip of our fine healing waters, you'll feel better."

Lord Bath cast an apologetic look over his shoulder as he led Lady Dalhousie, who pretended a fit of vapors over the "sudden fright," and her escort toward the entrance. The matron's penchant for exaggeration was perhaps the best stroke of luck Katherine had yet had this evening. At last, she had time to investigate, and she'd eliminated half the women at the hotel as the owner of the earring.

All she had to do now was find the other half. With that aim in mind, she toured the perimeter of the room. Grandma Bath had disappeared from her pedestal, which gave Katherine a frisson of trepidation. Had she spotted her grandson leading Lady Dalhousie out of the room? If so, Katherine suspected the old woman had pursued the pair with the aim of throwing Lord Bath into Katherine's path once more.

Spotting no one familiar from the hotel, Katherine ducked into the Octagon. To her astonishment, she didn't spot Pru at any of the cloth-covered tables.

Where had she run off to? Katherine wove between the tables, smiling to the men and women playing whist and quadrille as she passed. On the far wall, the door to the tearoom was shut, indicating that no one was permitted inside. A glance toward the card room to her left rewarded her with a glimpse of peach-colored fabric.

Katherine stepped closer. As she lingered in the doorway, Pru didn't appear to notice her. The young woman took a swig from a flask. Tarnation, was that spirits? They were forbidden in the Assembly Hall, but it seemed that hadn't hindered some opportunistic young fop. Katherine thanked her luck that Mrs. Burwick hadn't accompanied them to Bath. She would not approve in the least.

Pru, on the other hand, seemed to be having the best night of her life. She was seated in front of the biggest pile of fish tokens, and her cheeks were rosy as she passed on the flask with a triumphant glint in her eye and a wide smile. At ease with herself and the cards in her hand, she looked radiant. Not that Katherine would dare utter such sentiment aloud. Pru might box her ears at such a pronouncement.

Lord Annandale sat to her left, squinting at his cards. On his far side was Sir Hugh. Among the others gathered around the table, one gentleman in particular caught her eye. Unlike the others at the table, he wore nearly as much jewelry as the women in the ballroom. His coat was a brilliant scarlet, but not in the military style. His golden hair flopped in a devil-may-care fashion over his forehead and onto his high cheekbones, some strands kissing the top of his square jaw. Whereas Sir Hugh and some of the others assessed their cards with all seriousness, this particular gambler tossed his fish onto the table as if he had hundreds more of the metal tokens in his pockets.

Katherine stopped a passing debutante. "Excuse me, but do you happen to know who that is?"

The young woman smirked. "Reaching a bit above yourself, aren't you, miss? That's Prince Karl of Prussia, and if you're hoping for a ring, the only ones I hear he's inclined to give out are at the card table."

With his lackadaisical approach to gambling, Katherine could only imagine he was a rake of the highest caliber. In fact, it wouldn't surprise her to learn that he'd been the man to smuggle in the flask of spirits. She frowned. "A prince, in Bath?"

The debutante shrugged. "I think he arrived at Bristol during the Season. Who am I to dictate the whims of royalty? Perhaps he has need of the healing waters."

"It's a wonder he's stayed in town with a thief on the loose."

She laughed. "It's a wonder he hasn't been one of the victims, with the way he flaunts it. One more reason for these haughty Londoners to brag. The thief chooses *their* jewels over those of a prince."

She must live locally, to have so much disdain for those choosing to vacation in the city. Not that Katherine blamed her — in fact, she shared the sentiment. Blind fools, the lot of them. What sane person *hoped* to be robbed?

"I think it likely has more to do with the accessibility of the jewels."

The debutante shrugged. "That would require an ounce of forethought on their part. Ever since the second theft, there have been wagers over whose jewelry is likely to be snatched next. They got so up in arms over the notion that when a few weeks passed after the second theft, some took it as a personal affront and returned home! The rest might have as well, if the robberies hadn't resumed."

"Senseless. Have they all been robbed from the same place?"

"Hardly. Each one seems to be in a different location, and the Londoners are always the victim. Yet still, they continue to come in droves."

Katherine leaned closer. "I overheard the Marquess of Bath tell a lady that he's hired the best investigators to find the burglar."

"The best?" The woman hid a delicate snort behind her hand. "It's not my place to judge the decisions of His Lordship, but if you ask me, he's daft as well." The girl made a face as she peered across the room. "Forgive me, that's my mother. I have to go."

She left Katherine with much to think about.

CHAPTER FOUR

As the debutante hurried across the room, Katherine continued to walk, mulling over that information. She spotted one of the women from the hotel playing whist and made a show of leaning over that woman's shoulder while she checked the diamond earring. No match. She continued on into the entrance room, hoping that Lord Bath and his grandmother had continued on to a different room to search for her. There, she stumbled into another group. They were snickering behind her back by the time she detached herself, and she thought she distinctly heard a scathing comment regarding her dancing.

If nothing else, that minuet must have frightened off any gentlemen wishing to further their acquaintance.

Katherine frowned at the profile of a matron on

the arm of a portly older gentleman. She was tall and regal, with steely gray hair, and there was something about her that niggled at the back of Katherine's mind. Had they met? As the woman glanced over her shoulder before beginning the painstaking task of helping the gentleman into the ballroom, recognition surged. Katherine had crossed paths with Mrs. Julien frequently almost a decade ago, near her father's country estate. Shortly thereafter, her sisters had taken their bows in society, and the family had spent a great deal more time in London.

Eager to renew the acquaintance and curious at finding them in Bath, Katherine followed the pair into the ballroom. Mrs. Julien helped the man, presumably her husband, onto a chair at the edge of the nearest row. Katherine stepped closer.

"Mrs. Julien?"

The old woman's face lit up. "Lady Katherine, darling." She reached forward to clasp both of Katherine's hands. "It's so good to see you. What brings you to Bath?"

"I might ask you the same question. I've been tasked with finding a young woman a husband."

"Ah, yes." Mrs. Julien's eyes crinkled in the corners. "I'd heard you'd acquired a bit of a romantic eye. You matched your sisters with their husbands, did you not?"

"I did." That had been before she had taken up the ruse of matchmaking to facilitate her investigations. At that time, she had only sought to further her sisters' happiness, and they, unlike Katherine, had viewed marriage as an essential part.

"But no one for yourself?"

Katherine took a deep breath to ward away the mounting frustration that accompanied that particular question. When she had herself under control, she answered, "No. I'm far too busy to think of marrying and giving up my independence." Proud of herself for maintaining an even tone, she changed the subject. "You haven't answered why I find you so far from home."

Mrs. Julien glanced at her husband. The weight of the day seemed especially heavy at that moment, deepening the lines in their faces and making them appear a decade older than Katherine's estimate of late sixties or seventies. Mr. Julien looked solemn.

"It's Scottie, I'm afraid."

"Oh yes. Your grandson is about my age, isn't he? Is he here?" Katherine frowned. She resisted the urge to look. Not only would it be a futile effort in such a crush, but after so long, she doubted that she would recognize him.

Mrs. Julien's face fell. Mournfully, she shook her head, lowering her gaze and worrying her lower lip. "He went into the army, you know. After the Battle of Toulouse... Well, I reckon we're lucky to have him alive." She blinked rapidly, the light glinting off of moisture gathering along her eyelashes.

After clearing his throat, Mr. Julien took up the tale. He reached out to squeeze his wife's hand. "He took a bullet to the thigh. Can't walk anymore, let alone dance. Spends most of his days inside the house."

Mrs. Julien plucked at a stray thread in her brown gown. As Katherine's gaze was drawn to her weathered fingers, she noticed the worn state of her dress. A hole was darned near the cuff of the sleeve. It looked a bit thinner in places than in others, showing more of her plain under gown. The state of Mr. Julien's clothes was no less shabby. How could they afford to visit Bath?

In a soft voice, Mrs. Julien confessed, "We hope that the curative powers of the water here are more than myth. Perhaps if they can bring some relief to the pain we know he endures..."

Katherine touched her arm. "I'm terribly sorry. If

there's anything I can do..." Unfortunately, there wasn't. She couldn't eliminate another person's pain.

As she thought of the earring in her reticule, she fished it out again. "Are you staying at the Sydney Hotel? I found this..." If it belonged to the Juliens, perhaps they could sell it. They seemed to have done everything else possible to see that their grandson got the care he needed.

Unfortunately, Mrs. Julien pursed her lips and shook her head. "No, dear. We're letting a house not terribly far, but the earring doesn't belong to us."

Tarnation! It had to belong to someone. Emma couldn't have left the hotel in order to find it. She hadn't had time to leave the floor! If not anyone Katherine had encountered this evening, then who...?

Katherine's gaze lit upon a woman she had hoped not to see for the rest of the year. Perhaps the rest of her life. Inwardly groaning, she excused herself from Mr. and Mrs. Julien and hoped to make her escape before the wicked woman in question noticed her.

Mrs. Fairchild was a short woman about ten years Katherine's senior with a generous figure, a reddish tint to her brown hair, and an air of superiority. Tonight, she wore a garish white gown, the color of which seemed to imprint itself on Katherine's vision even when her eyes were shut.

She could not be missed, nor the biddable young debutante at her side. Although Mrs. Fairchild had lost her matchmaking client a few weeks before when the young woman had fled home in fear of being attacked by the Pink-Ribbon Murderer, this defeat didn't appear to have hindered her matchmaking business at all. Already, she seemed to have found a new client.

Which, when she learned of Katherine's ruse to conceal her investigation, would only instigate a rivalry Katherine didn't want or need. Pru didn't care to be matched with Lord Annandale, so if he was the husband Mrs. Fairchild's client hoped to marry, then Katherine wished them well of it. Preferably from afar, where the bitter woman couldn't drag her into a nasty battle of wills.

As the debutante tilted her head to speak to another matron, presumably her mother, Katherine glanced skyward. She recognized them from the hotel, which could mean only one thing: They were the last people who might own the stray earring Emma had pilfered. Katherine couldn't simply offer it to them. Last month, Mrs. Fairchild had accused her of murder — Katherine wouldn't put it above her rival to accuse her of theft next. That was the very last thing she needed. In fact, she would rather find a way to sneak into their chambers and leave the bauble as if they'd lost it.

When she opened her eyes again, she found Mrs. Fairchild glaring at her.

I've done nothing, you wicked woman.

She glanced around the room, searching for any excuse not to speak with her. She frowned as she spotted a familiar figure standing stiffly next to the hearth as if he, too, were made of marble.

"Lyle?"

He was too far away to hear her. He stood, in a fresh jacket and cravat that couldn't hope to match the expensive high fashion of the others gathered, perfectly still but for his eyes. They darted every which way as if he were trying to catalogue each and every person. The oddity of finding him at such a genteel event was matched only by his obvious distaste for attending. Why was he there?

Katherine glanced at Mrs. Fairchild, hoping she hadn't seen the Bow Street Runner. So different was his demeanor tonight than it had been when he'd taken charge at Lord Northbrook's house party that he might as well have been two different people. Katherine knew him to be in a delicate enough state at such times without the added acerbity of the gentry toward him.

Fortunately, Mrs. Fairchild seemed engrossed in

instructing her charge. She whispered madly in the young woman's ear. A moment later, the brunette turned her head to look where the matchmaker pointed. A stir started in the ballroom from that direction, the door to the Octagon, and Katherine squinted to make out the reason behind it.

Prince Karl. *Excellent.* If he was the man Mrs. Fairchild hoped to match with her mousy, forgettable client, then all the better. Katherine wasn't setting her cap for him in any way. They would be unlikely to cross paths at all, with any luck.

Before the matchmaker noticed her in the crowd again, Katherine hastened to the side of her dearest friend. Up close, Lyle looked to have no more color than the white marble hearth. His hair looked unnaturally dark in contrast.

"What are you doing here?" When Lyle jumped and whirled on her, his eyes wide, Katherine raised her hands. "It's only me. My, you're easily startled tonight."

"This isn't my sort of event. I prefer a gathering of minds, not" — he waved his hand to indicate the dancers gliding past — "this."

Katherine pressed her lips together to contain a smile. "Precisely why my surprise at seeing you is justified. What possessed you to attend if it's so torturous an event?"

Lyle's shoulders slumped as he sighed, defeated. "The Dowager Marchioness of Bath."

As a giggle bubbled to the surface at the thought of the little old lady sinking her hooks so far into Lyle as to entice him to a soiree, Katherine recalled the dance through which she'd recently suffered with Lord Bath. Her mirth faded. Grandma Bath was a force to be reckoned with.

Lyle added, "She was very taken with my invention and insisted that I attend. I didn't want to insult the resident Marquess or his family by refusing."

Katherine patted his shoulder in comfort. "It's only one evening. You'll survive."

With a grimace, her friend added, "I hope that it will only be one." His expression smoothed as he turned to his left. He bowed. "My lady."

Grandma Bath nodded her head brusquely. "There you are, Mr. Murphy. I'd begun to think you'd run off. Lend me your arm a moment. I've been walking for a while."

Concerned, Katherine offered, "Why don't we find a place to sit for a moment?"

The old woman waved away the suggestion as she

leaned heavily on Lyle's arm. "No, no. I'll be happy to stand just as soon as I catch my breath."

Katherine frowned. "Where is your grandson?"

As she scanned the knot of people nearby, she spotted Lord Bath with his wide cuffs flapping as he spoke to a taller gentleman. For a moment, Katherine couldn't breathe. *It can't be.*

She hadn't seen Captain Dorian Wayland since he had departed Lord Northbrook's house party with Lyle and the Pink-Ribbon Murderer in their custody. That silhouette was unmistakably him — broad shoulders thrown back in a straight, military posture, head and shoulders taller than everyone else in the room, Katherine included. His short-clipped brown hair was a bit longer in the front, curling across his forehead. Why was he now *here* of all places?

A sly expression crossed Grandma Bath's face. "Are you missing him already?"

Wayland? *Not sarding likely.* Ever since he'd returned from war, he was her father's foremost rival in detective matters. Papa didn't approve of Wayland's methods of closing cases, and neither did she. She'd managed to outwit him during her pursuit of the Pink-Ribbon Murderer and solve that crime first. Would she be able to do it again this time?

Lord Bath had mentioned hiring the best investigators. Could he have meant Wayland? If Wayland had access to the marquess's resources, she didn't have a hope of succeeding. Though if he was her opponent, she refused to quietly step aside. She had beaten him once, after all.

Grandma Bath leaned forward, claiming Katherine's attention once more. In a voice that wasn't nearly as hushed as the old woman likely thought, she confessed, "You needn't worry about him keeping company with that old widow. He was only seeing to her well-being."

Lyle frowned as he turned to Katherine. "What are you worried about?"

"Nothing," she answered in a clipped tone. She had only asked after the marquess because he doted so upon his grandmother.

Fortunately, Grandma Bath seemed to recognize that Katherine didn't intend to warm to the subject. She changed it, patting Lyle's arm. "Have you heard about the wonderful invention Mr. Murphy is creating here? He wants to use the steam from our special water to identify criminals from the traces they leave at the scene of a crime! What a brilliant fellow."

Lyle's cheeks turned pink at the praise. "I haven't yet begun to build the apparatus—"

Smiling, Katherine spoke over him firmly. "He is brilliant. Among the sharpest minds I know."

The color in his cheeks deepened.

Grandma Bath craned her neck to look up at him. "Have you had a chance to speak with those craftsmen I recommended here in town?" She asked Katherine, "I'm rather proud of all the capable men hereabouts. It is true, with this year's crops faring no better than anywhere else in England, I was a bit worried for our town, but they've come together to prove that they are very skilled in a variety of areas and willing to put in the work needed to get through this hard time. Luckily, men like Mr. Murphy here" — she patted his arm — "come to town every day, in need of all the things my good people can provide for them. Why, have you met Sir David Brewster? He's here from Scotland, working with light and glass to create... Oh dear. It's not a telescope..." She frowned then shook away the thought. "You know, you can ask him yourself. I saw him just a moment ago. Why don't I introduce you?"

Lyle stumbled over his tongue at the abrupt change in the conversation.

Beaming, the old woman extracted her arm. "Wait here a moment, and I'll fetch him. I'm certain you'll get on smashingly, given that you're both bright inventors!" With that pronouncement, she started an arduous journey around the perimeter of the ballroom.

Katherine glanced at Wayland once more, still deep in conversation with Lord Bath and smiling.

Lyle followed her gaze. "He isn't as bad as you think he is."

Lifting her eyebrows, Katherine feigned innocence. "The marquess?"

"Captain Wayland."

She twisted her mouth with distaste at hearing his name aloud and turned away before he noticed her watching him. Picking invisible dust from her bodice, she mumbled, "He'd best not get in my way if he knows what's good for him. I must solve this crime myself."

"You solved the last one. I have every confidence that you'll be able to solve this one as well."

"Yes, but in the last, I had your help."

Lyle frowned. "And I publicly took all the credit. Forgive me. I thought, erroneously, it seems, that you didn't want to announce your involvement."

She laid her hand on his arm. "No, that's not it at all. I can't announce my involvement, or I'd be shunned from the very events I need to gain access to in order to solve these crimes. I'm happy you got to take the credit, rather than *him*." She'd half expected to open the news rag and find Wayland's name on the first story.

For a moment, Lyle glanced at Wayland, deep in thought. "The clerk at Bow Street wanted him to take credit, since he is the heir to a viscount. He refused. He said he had no part in the discovery or capture of the murderer save for escorting the knave to London and insisted I take credit."

The man had never shied away from public praise before, so Katherine couldn't account for his change of heart. She pressed her lips together.

Her friend added, "We spent a great deal of time talking on the way to London. I think you misjudged him."

I think not. Katherine didn't want to argue with her dearest friend, however. Fortunately, the arrival of Lord Bath — *without* the accompaniment of the man they had been discussing — put the conversation to rest. Although Lyle stiffened again and bowed for the new arrival, Katherine merely smiled as the marquess drew close. "My lord, nice to see you again."

She followed his former companion with her eyes, ensuring that Wayland didn't intend to insinuate himself in their conversation. Fortunately, he stepped away. He paused to speak with Mr. and Mrs. Julien, of all people. Did he know them as well?

Katherine fought back a frown and returned her attention to the marquess. "If you're searching for your grandmother, I believe she meandered toward the Octagon in search of a man named Sir David so she might introduce us."

"Ah, yes. She's been quite enamored with him since he arrived a week ago. It's lucky he has a wife," Lord Bath said with a wink.

Katherine couldn't help but laugh at the image of Grandma Bath setting her cap for a man at ninety.

The marquess added, "I hope you don't mind my deserting you earlier this evening, Katherine. I didn't want Lady Dalhousie panicking the other dancers."

With his hands clasped behind his back, Lyle looked resolute not to comment and thereby draw attention to himself. However, when the conversation paused, he glanced from one to the other, curiosity worming its way into his expression.

"Forgive the intrusion, but did you say you thought she might panic the others? Has there been another robbery?"

"Keep your voice down!" Lord Bath glanced around, but no one seemed to be paying their conversation any mind. "There has not been anything of the sort. My cuff caught on Lady Dalhousie's necklace, and she jumped to unreasonable conclusions. No one was trying to rob her."

"I should hope not," Grandma Bath said loudly as she returned on the arm of a modestly dressed gentleman with wide brown side whiskers. "Oh, I was so afraid at first that this business of the jewel thefts would scare off our visitors, wasn't I, Ernest?"

With a pained look, Lord Bath answered her between gritted teeth. "Fortunately, that didn't happen, Grandmama. Brewster, it's nice to see you again."

"Oh yes!" Grandma Bath beamed and patted her escort's arm. "Sir David, this is Mr. Murphy. He is an inventor, like yourself."

"Oh? What field of science do you study?"

"Forensic," Lyle answered. He paused a moment, looking uncomfortable, before he added, "I serve as one of Sir John's Men in London."

The newcomer frowned. "Forgive me, but I'm not familiar with that organization. Where is it located?"

"Bow Street."

"Ah, you're a—"

Katherine shook her head, hoping he would take the hint.

Fortunately, the man seemed astute. He frowned at her and ended with, "Ah."

Silence fell over the group. No doubt it dug beneath Lyle's skin, for he was the first to break it. He turned to the marquess. "As one of Sir John's esteemed Men, I would be at your service to investigate this unfortunate string of thefts you've been having."

Lord Bath looked dubious. Even Grandma Bath didn't warm to the idea as Katherine would have expected, not until Lyle added, "I recently apprehended the Pink-Ribbon Murderer. I know what I'm doing."

He shot Katherine a sheepish sort of smirk. Luckily, she knew him well enough to know that even if he was awarded the task of pursuing the Burglar of Bath, he wouldn't do so in earnest unless Katherine asked. This was her case, even if she needed a proxy to claim it for her. Come to think of it, she needed someone to arrest the thief once she found them. Perhaps having Lyle on the case would be best.

Lord Bath, on the other hand, didn't seem to agree. "Catching a thief is a far different matter than arresting a murderer."

Was it? Katherine raised her eyebrows, exchanging a look with Lyle, but the marquess pressed on.

"In any case, I've already hired someone."

Please don't say Wayland. Katherine braced herself to hear his name.

Instead, Lord Bath said, "Mr. Salmon is handling the matter."

Katherine gaped. What lunacy was this? "Mr. *Harvey* Salmon?"

The marquess preened. "Why, yes. Do you know him?"

When Katherine glanced at Lyle, she imagined she mirrored his look of horror. In unison, they answered, "Yes." Mr. Salmon was the most inept, bumbling fool in the Royal Society for Investigative Techniques. Frankly, it was a wonder he hadn't been asked not to return. To date, Katherine couldn't name a single case that he hadn't bungled. It had gone on to such an extent that she had begun to suspect him of taking bribes from the thieves he pursued and polluting the good name of detective, as his forbearers had.

Weakly, she added, "Perhaps you ought to give further thought to hiring Lyle in his place. Lyle has a much better record of solved cases."

The marquess puffed up and adjusted his cuffs. "Of course you would say that, being as familiar with him, as you are."

Grandma Bath frowned. She adjusted her spectacles and peered up at Katherine. "Just how familiar with Mr. Murphy are you?"

What in Zeus's name? Was she trying to insinuate

that she and Lyle had a carnal relationship? "We are close friends," Katherine answered, biting off her words. She turned back to the marquess to add, "And even one solved case would be more than Mr. Salmon has to boast. I'm fairly certain that he'd be more apt to hand the thief some jewels than to apprehend him. He is the least recommended detective in all of London!"

"Come now, don't get yourself in a snit. I assure you, I asked for letters of reference before I hired him."

She balled her fists. "They must have been forged. I have never spoken to anyone who had anything good to say of Mr. Salmon." At times, her compatriots lamented that he botched a case so badly as to scare off the criminal and make them impossible to find.

"And who would you have spoken to who might shed light on the situation?"

Lyle bristled. He answered, "Me."

At the same time, Katherine spat, "My father, for one." She bristled with indignation. Why did every man assume that she sat by the parlor window all day and did needlepoint? Even the well-meaning ones — or, in Lord Bath's case currently, the patronizing ones. She had a brain, and she used it often. More often than he had when hiring a complete dolt to find a clever thief!

With a fond smile, the marquess said, "Don't

worry your head over it, my dear. It's well handled. You see? He's doing a splendid job of searching for clues as we speak."

Katherine followed the gesture of his arm to spot a man in a dusky-brown coat looming over a lady, jotting down notes in a handheld notebook. His forehead was creased with concentration beneath a lock of his silver-threaded hair as he examined her bosom — no, wait, her necklace. Good grief! No wonder Lady Dalhousie had shrieked of a thief so readily, with a cretin like Mr. Salmon lurking about. Watching his foolish efforts and knowing that others thought worse of her profession because of it made her blood boil.

She turned away. "So it seems," she said, her voice laced with venom. Lord Bath, it seemed, didn't want to be swayed, so she didn't see the point of trying. "If you'll excuse me, I must check on Miss Burwick to see if she requires my presence. My lord, my lady." She dipped her knees briefly to each of the esteemed hosts before striding away. She didn't wait for a response.

By the time she reached the far corner of the ball-room, across from the Octagon, she felt more in control of herself. She started to make her way across the line of occupied chairs toward where Pru likely awaited her in the card room, but caught movement in the corner of her eye. The door in the far left corner of the ballroom... hadn't that been shut earlier? Now it was ajar.

When she took a step toward it, she caught a glimpse of movement in the darkened room beyond. A tall figure, the hood of their cloak drawn to cover their face. Her heartbeat quickened. Could it be that the Burglar of Bath was here, after all?

Picking up her skirts, she rushed toward the room.

But she only made it a few steps before a figure stepped in her path. Mrs. Fairchild.

No! The figure is getting away!

Katherine craned her neck, looking over the woman's shoulder to keep her eye on the door.

Mrs. Fairchild cocked up her nose. "Fancy seeing *you* here, Lady Katherine. Did you follow me from London just to spite me?"

"I beg your pardon?" Katherine snatched her gaze away from the door to examine the woman. Had she had a nip from the flask passed around the card tables as well? "Of course I haven't."

Arms akimbo, Mrs. Fairchild glowered. "You expect me to believe that your presence at the event where I mean to match my next client is a coincidence?"

"Yes." She didn't have time for this. She made to move to the left, but Mrs. Fairchild moved to block her.

"You won't fool me. What bit of deviousness are you up to, without your client at your side?"

Katherine drew herself up, towering over her rival. "I could ask you the same question."

With a wave of her hand, the matchmaker indicated the dancing couples. There, with a perfectly plain gentleman, Mrs. Fairchild's young client danced gracefully. Somehow, even in doing all the steps of the minuet perfectly, she seemed to fade into the background.

Katherine's attention wavered between Fairchild, the dancers, and the dark doorway. Was the figure still lurking there in the shadows, or had it disappeared?

"Miss Newcomb is dancing."

"Not with the prince, I see." Katherine turned her attention back to Mrs. Fairchild and raised her eyebrows pointedly. "That is who your client has set her cap for, is it not?"

The grooves around Mrs. Fairchild's mouth deepened as she scowled.

"You needn't worry," Katherine informed her. "I've been hired to match Miss Burwick with somebody else. We shan't get in your way. Now if you'll excuse me—"

Katherine made to push past Mrs. Fairchild, but again the woman stopped her.

Sard it all! She'd never catch the thief if Mrs. Fairchild didn't leave her alone!

"So you say, but I know you don't play by the rules."

Katherine pressed her lips together and glanced toward the ceiling. She didn't have time for this argument! "And what rules might those be? I'm afraid I never received my copy of *A Matchmaker's Etiquette.* Lord Northbrook chose Annie to be his bride because he fell in love with her. For no other reason!"

"Miss Young wasn't even in attendance when he announced his engagement! You scared her off."

Katherine would have thought the murderer to have done so, but she was tired of arguing.

Mrs. Fairchild crossed her arms. "Pray tell, why are you asking after women's jewels? The only reason I can see is so that you can trick Miss Newcomb into thinking she's been robbed."

Zooks! That got Katherine's full attention. She wasn't about to stand here and let Mrs. Fairchild accuse her. Two could play at that game. She retrieved the diamond earring from her reticule and presented it to Mrs. Fairchild.

"I intended no such thing. I found this in the corridor. *You* can have it back."

Her rival dropped her arms and stepped back,

appalled. "Have it *back?* I never took it in the first place! Of all the conniving accusations—"

"This doesn't belong to you or the Newcombs?"

"No!"

For a moment, Katherine was struck dumb. Mrs. Fairchild had to be lying. She had already determined that the earring didn't belong to any other woman in the hotel.

The matchmaker took advantage of Katherine's silence to lean forward and hiss in a venomous tone. "If you think for a moment that I'll sit idly by and allow you to frame me for theft—"

Katherine couldn't possibly do that. Not only would it go against her integrity, but Mrs. Fairchild had been with Katherine at Lord Northbrook's house party at the time of one of the robberies. She couldn't be the thief.

"That isn't what I meant. I'm trying to find the rightful owner."

"Of course you'd say that. How am I to know you didn't pilfer that yourself?"

"I was at Lord Northbrook's house party with you," Katherine snapped. "I only just arrived in Bath. I wasn't even here when most of the thefts took place."

The woman sniffed and arranged a lock of her auburn hair. "Perhaps there is more than one thief, each capitalizing on the last. You might be the latest in a long string."

"Don't be ridiculous. I am not a thief. My dog stole—"

"*Stole?*" The woman's voice rose sharply.

Katherine wished Mrs. Fairchild would be quiet. As it was, her annoying conversation and accusations had cost her the chase after the cloaked lurker who could be the *real* Burglar of Bath. The culprit was probably long gone by now, and she didn't need the whole of the Assembly Rooms overhearing Mrs. Fairchild's words and watching to see if she was the Burglar.

A man's steely voice rang in the hollow of silence that followed Mrs. Fairchild's exclamation. "Is there a problem here?"

The breath gushed from Katherine's lungs as Wayland stepped alongside her, as if lending his support. She didn't so much as look at him. Great, now she'd never be able to give chase to the lurker.

Mrs. Fairchild, on the other hand, couldn't avoid looking at Wayland, not with his shadow cast across her. Her expression smoothed to one of polite disinterest. "A minor misunderstanding, Captain. Nothing that requires a second opinion."

"I see."

"Isn't that your charge?" Wayland asked as the music ended. He didn't turn his head.

Mrs. Fairchild nodded vigorously. "It is. If you'll excuse me, I have work to do." She raised her eyebrows at Katherine, as if reminding her yet again that she was without her charge.

The moment she walked away, the gossips in the vicinity lost interest and returned to their conversations. Katherine turned to Wayland. As he gazed down at her, his icy demeanor thawed. His hazel eyes warmed, and the dimple in his chin winked at her as he opened his mouth to say something.

Confound it, she didn't have time for polite conversation! She grabbed him by the hand and towed him through the door and into the room where the cloaked figure had escaped. The room, of course, was empty.

The moment he entered fully, she whirled on him and shut the door before someone followed.

"If you wanted to thank me, a dance would have sufficed."

"Have you been at the card table?"

He frowned. "No, why?"

She turned to examine the room. The long, narrow length was packed with sedan chairs pressed up against the wall. A thin path along the glazed windows, punctuated with columns, led down the corridor to a door situated at its end. Was that movement she espied? She started to move down the path then paused and turned back when Wayland followed on her heels.

She jostled her hip on the hard corner post of a sedan chair. Wincing, she stumbled a step. Wayland steadied her with his hands on her waist. She pulled away quickly.

"Thank you."

Despite the glass windows, she couldn't make out his expression. The sun had dipped nearly below the horizon, shrouding the city in deep twilight. The meager light peeking into the corridor wafted from the street lamps on Bennett Street. It provided little more than the silhouette of the sedan chairs and a few solitary details from closer artifacts... or people. Was the cloaked lurker in here?

Wayland seemed to be staring at her intently. Perhaps he couldn't see any better than she could.

"You look lovely tonight."

Perhaps he had gone blind.

"I beg your pardon? You can't possibly see me any better than I can you."

"I saw you perfectly well in the ballroom."

"Perhaps you need to have your eyes examined,"

Katherine mumbled under her breath. Not only had she dressed plainly on purpose, but Pru had been relentless tonight in her criticism. Katherine couldn't possibly look lovely to anyone. Was he teasing her? If he genuinely thought she looked comely, she needed to find another means of making herself plain.

"Pardon me? I didn't catch that."

"Pay no mind to me. We don't have time to tarry."

As she started to turn away, he laughed. With a frown, she turned back to him.

"What amuses you?"

"You weren't precisely subtle, my dear. If you're worried that the ballroom will notice our absence, I assure you, they already have."

Dang! He was right. She had less time to investigate than she thought.

"I'm a chaperone. I'm practically on the shelf. They'll think nothing of it as long as you don't make a fuss." At least, so she hoped. Granted, she'd never been so bold before. She should have left him in the middle of the ballroom, no matter how rude it would have been. Even if he would have been dogging at her heels in any case.

"You are nowhere you don't seek to put yourself. You could be a diamond of the first water, if you chose.

In fact, you could have any man in here with you. Why this sudden change of heart?"

Katherine frowned. "I don't know what you're talking about."

"You were outright antagonistic to me at Northbrook's party. Now you're pulling me into secluded rooms to steal a kiss? That qualifies as a change of heart, if you ask me."

"I am not!" Steal a kiss? He was the last person with whom she would seek to do so. He might have charmed Lyle, but he hadn't fooled her. Stepping back, she turned and scanned the corridor. Not that she had much hope of finding the cloaked figure now. Wait, was that a trick of the light, or did she catch movement in the shadow near the last sedan in the line?

Wayland caught her arm, turning her back toward him. "If not for a... private moment, why did you bring me here?"

"I spotted a cloaked figure, and I didn't want you to draw attention to us when I left. Though it seems I overestimated your investigation abilities."

He mumbled something under his breath that sounded vaguely like, "So did I?" The warmth faded from his stance, replaced by something urgent. His voice deepened with disapproval. "Were you planning to slip away from the ballroom on your own?"

"Of course. I don't know why you're in Bath, but I'm here to find the thief and bring them to justice."

"Alone."

"Yes," she spat, pulling her arm away. "I'm perfectly capable of solving a case on my own."

He drew himself up, separating the distance between them. "Perhaps I overestimated your sensibilities. Think, Katherine. There is a felon on the loose. What do you think he would do if he found himself alone in here with you, and you were moments away from arresting him?"

"There is a *thief* on the loose, not a murderer. And that's Lady Katherine to you. We are not at all familiar, *Captain* Wayland."

"We're more familiar than you care to admit. I could be an ally to you, not an enemy."

She narrowed her eyes. "You sound as though you intend to find the Burglar of Bath yourself. Is that why you're here, to claim the reward and the glory this time?"

"You can't possibly be angry that I gave your friend the credit for arresting the Pink-Ribbon Murderer. Or did you want me to expose you for a detective?"

Katherine didn't have any answer to that. She still couldn't fathom why he'd done it. If word got out that she made a habit of trying to solve crimes, she'd be shunned by every member of the aristocracy. That would certainly put a damper on any future investigating.

When she didn't answer, he added, "As I suspected. And what nonsense is this about a reward? Lord Bath hasn't posted one."

"Not to my knowledge," she answered, her voice weak. In fact, why hadn't the marquess posted a reward for the capture of the thief? It would keep his town safer.

Perhaps he hoped to minimize the cost by hiring the most bumbling fool in existence.

Silence charged the air between them once more. After a moment, Wayland murmured, "There's no one here but us. Will you return to the ballroom now, or do you mean to go haring through the streets in pursuit of anyone keeping warm on this frigid night? You probably saw a servant checking on his master."

Katherine hadn't considered that. She'd caught no more than a glimpse of the figure, enough to tell that they were of a height comparable to hers and wore a hood. Berating herself, she followed Wayland to the door once more.

By the time he reached for the latch, she shook off her momentary doubts. If the figure had been a servant, why had they run and hid when Katherine had entered the corridor? No, something more suspicious must be afoot. Her instincts wouldn't lead her so astray.

She stopped Wayland with a hand on his arm before he opened the door. "I'll go first. It wouldn't do for us to be seen emerging together, as you've pointed out."

He blew out a gusty breath. "I don't see why not. It's probably already circulated the building that we entered together. You know how the gossips like to wag their tongues."

"Be that as it may," Katherine said through gritted teeth, "I must go check on Miss Burwick. Promise me you'll stay here until I cross the room, at the very least."

He nodded, opening the door. "As the lady wishes." The light from the ballroom spilled onto his expression, but it didn't illuminate what she'd hoped to find. Wayland's expression was impassive, the same bored mask any man wore for entertainment in polite society.

She turned away and stepped into the much warmer room. Although the fires had been extinguished, the heat of so many bodies filled the air, wafting up into the high ceiling. Katherine kept her head down as she strode across the room.

Her gaze caught on Mr. Salmon, who started to

guzzle a glass of lemonade and spilled on his precious notebook. With a look of panic, he waved the sheets in the air as if trying to dry them. That buffoon hadn't even noticed the cloaked figure to begin with. If he was her only opponent in hunting the Burglar of Bath, then she would win handily.

As she reached the threshold of the Octagon, she glanced over her shoulder in time to notice Wayland slip into the room. For all his rakish confidence tonight, he was a clever investigator. He might prove more difficult to outwit. However, she had some hope that, if he did have his eye on the Burglar of Bath, he would soon leave. With no reward and no compensation from the Marquess of Bath, why would a man like Wayland possibly stay in town?

CHAPTER FIVE

T he clock struck eleven of the evening without a
further glimpse of the cloaked figure, the
person Katherine suspected to be the Burglar of Bath.
With a sigh, she collected Pru from the card table,
waiting as the triumphant woman collected her enormous pile of fish-shaped metal tokens. One of them, at
least, seemed to have done well for themselves.

Together, they joined the stream of people leading
down the length of the Assembly Rooms to the
entrance, where the carriages awaited on schedule.
She craned her neck, searching the crowd.

"What are you looking for?" Pru asked.

"Lyle. I told him to ride with us back to the hotel in
the carriage."

Pru smirked. "If you say so."

"What are you smiling about?"

Her grin widened. "I happened to see Captain Wayland here earlier. Did you offer him a ride, as well?"

Katherine gritted her teeth. That confounded rumor must have reached the card table! Through clenched teeth, she said, "I did not drag Wayland into the corridor to... become familiar with him. I thought I spotted the thief."

At this pronouncement, Pru straightened, growing serious. "Did you catch him?"

"No," she informed her. The word tasted sour. She hadn't so much as gotten a better look at the figure's face or form.

"A pity. If you had, we might have escaped this drudgery and spent a week or two in one of the small towns we passed along the way before we crawled back to Mother in disgrace."

Katherine raised her eyebrows as they squeezed out of the doorway and into the cool open air. "You just schooled every man in Bath in the game of loo. Tell me you didn't enjoy yourself."

The other woman colored up. "Perhaps I did, a little. It was nice to win. I didn't know all men were such poor hands at loo."

Perhaps Pru underestimated her abilities.

Her heels clicked on the stone steps as they

descended to the row of carriages. Katherine paused in front of hers, searching again for Lyle. She smiled as he appeared.

That smile dissolved instantly when her gaze lingered on the abnormally tall figure by his side. With an easy lope, Wayland kept pace with the Bow Street Runner as they approached the carriage.

Once they were within earshot, Wayland offered a debonair smile and an explanation. "I hope you don't mind the intrusion, but Murphy indicated there might be room in your carriage. The friend with whom I'm staying seems to have departed without me."

Katherine had half a mind to turn him away, but she didn't want to put Lyle on the spot for having offered. No doubt, after hearing of the rumor that had spread through the Assembly Rooms like wildfire, he had assumed that Katherine and Wayland were now on friendlier terms.

"Where are you staying?" she asked in a clipped voice. "We're going to the Sydney Hotel."

"What luck, my friend is letting a townhouse on Sydney Place not far from there. There's no need to go out of your way." He caught her gaze, his eyes dark in the light of the streetlamp. "Besides, it might be providential to have me along in case of unforeseen interruptions."

Katherine understood his pointed words altogether too well. She released an exasperated breath. "Come along if you will, but we are not going to be waylaid by a band of cloaked highwaymen. Even if we were, we have Lyle for protection."

Wayland smiled. "I'd rest better knowing that you have added protection. Besides, Lyle and I make a smashing team."

Since her friend made no move to protest that announcement, nor the prudence of having him along for protection, Katherine had no choice but to admit defeat. Biting her cheek, she turned and climbed the steps into the closed carriage. After a moment's pause, Pru followed next. Much to Katherine's consternation, she chose the spot directly across from Katherine. Lyle wedged himself beside her, leaving the last open position at Katherine's side for Wayland.

Katherine laid her head back on the squabs and pretended to ignore Wayland's presence. After a moment's delay, the driver lurched into motion. She counted the seconds until they reached the hotel and she could be rid of her unwanted companion. Meanwhile, Lyle filled the silence.

"What is that bag filled with, stones?"

"Fish, actually," Pru answered with a sniff. "I didn't have time to change them for coin, but I'll do that on Monday during the next dress ball. I won them at loo."

"Loo?" Lyle made a musing noise. "You know, I've never understood the mechanics of that game."

"It's different if you play with three cards or five, but essentially…" Pru launched into an enthusiastic explanation of the mechanics and merit of the game. To Katherine's surprise, Lyle seemed interested in the topic.

Katherine was not. She never gambled.

Wayland leaned closer to murmur in her ear. "How is Emma?"

Katherine laughed. "Your more enthusiastic female admirer, you mean? She's in perfect spirits."

"Is she getting up to the same mischief?"

The diamond earring in her reticule suddenly weighed twice as much. Should she confess the matter to Wayland? He had interrupted her and Mrs. Fairchild during that unpleasant exchange. If he'd eavesdropped before approaching, he might already know the severity of the matter. Could he help?

What was she *thinking*, asking help from her father's greatest rival? No. One way or another, she would find the owner of the earring herself.

"If you mean to ask whether she is shamelessly begging for attention from any man who walks past,

I'm sorry to say that you're only one in a long line. She's likely forgotten you."

He chuckled. "I should hope not." A passing streetlamp illuminated his expression as his gaze wandered across the carriage to the pair on the opposite bench. "You're in Bath to match Miss Burwick with her future husband?"

"Yes." That was her cover, after all. "Though it isn't my primary aim." Wayland ought to know her well enough after their previous encounters to be able to extrapolate that much.

"I did think the thefts more likely to hold your interest. You managed to make your last matchmaking job a success despite catching a murderer in the process."

"I did..."

"Precisely why I have every confidence that you'll be able to do anything you put your mind to do while in Bath, as well."

Katherine narrowed her eyes at him. Was that a compliment? Coming from him, it was as baffling as when he'd called her comely. They were not friends. At best, they were rivals — at worst, enemies. If he meant to use his silver tongue to convince her to share the details of the thefts as she learned them, he was destined to be disappointed. That approach hadn't worked at Lord Northbrook's house party, and it would earn him no more victories here.

Had he known that she intended to make the thief in Bath her next case so soon after the last had been solved? If so, who had informed him of that secret? Her gaze drifted to Lyle, still deep in conversation with Pru. Despite his apparent good opinion of Wayland, she didn't think he was likely to have spilled her secrets to the man. Lyle was a stalwart friend.

Perhaps Wayland's appearance here was mere coincidence.

Unaware of her thoughts, the blackguard asked, "With whom has Mrs. Burwick asked you to pair her daughter?"

Absently, Katherine answered, "The Marquess of Annandale."

"Oh?"

The interest and enthusiasm in Wayland's voice caught her full attention once more. What had she said?

"As it so happens, Annandale is the friend in whose rented townhouse I am staying. Why don't I put a good word in his ear regarding Miss Burwick? Perhaps I'll be able to speed the matter along."

"No—" Katherine choked on the word. Tarnation, that was precisely what she and Pru *didn't* want.

The carriage stopped. Wayland moved to get the door before Katherine could protest further. She pressed her lips closed, not wanting to alert Pru of the blunder. Perhaps she would have a few more hours of investigation time to herself before the other woman turned the matter into a test of their abilities. If the thief was so desperate for more jewels as to linger in the shadows of the Assembly Rooms, then perhaps they had already made a grievous error that she might exploit. All she needed to do was dig a little deeper.

Cold night air penetrated the carriage as Wayland disembarked to help the driver lay the steps for the rest of them. As he handed Katherine out of the carriage, she leaned closer, hoping to dissuade him from mentioning anything to Annandale. Unfortunately, Pru hunched behind Katherine, close enough to hear and no longer distracted with a conversation of her own. *Sard it!* If Wayland managed to somehow spark Annandale's interest in Pru despite her unladylike behavior that evening...

Then Katherine and Pru would work doubly hard to turn him away from the match. Surely the marquess was discerning enough in the woman he wanted for a wife for that to be an easy matter. If Katherine could arrange matches, she could certainly undo them as well.

The moment Wayland handed them both down the stairs and onto the cobblestone street, he tipped his hat to them. "Thank you for the ride, Lady Katherine. Now that I've seen you to your destination unmolested, I will continue on my way."

Katherine glared. She propped one hand on her hip and wagged her finger at him. "We were in no danger to begin with—"

He claimed her hand and bowed over it, brushing his lips against her knuckles. Katherine snatched her hand away fast.

Wayland looked amused. "Goodnight, ladies. Murphy."

Lyle nodded to Wayland as the taller man turned and strode along the well-lit street.

Straightening, Pru stepped up next to Katherine and stared off after him. "What a curious man. He does seem rather eager to be in your presence tonight. What were you talking about in the carriage?"

Katherine blew out a breath and turned her back. "Nothing significant. Did you learn anything of use while you were at the card tables tonight?"

Pru frowned as they strode toward the hotel door, opened for them by a footman. Lyle trailed behind them.

"Anything of use? What do you mean?"

"You don't think I situated you there simply to make a spectacle of yourself. There is always gossip at the card table. Did you learn anything that might be prudent to the investigation into the robberies?"

Pru faltered for a moment before a broad smile capped her face. "I thought you didn't want my interference. I knew you wouldn't shut me out of the investigation like that." She threw her arm around Katherine's shoulder and squeezed. "You had me fooled!"

Guilt niggled at Katherine's belly because she'd meant every word earlier. Yet if she could use any of the gossip Pru had gleaned at the card tables to further the investigation, all the better.

"I played most of the night at the same table with Sir Hugh, Lord Annandale, Prince Karl of Prussia, and a few other gentlemen who came and went. Most didn't care to stay after they lost their fish to me."

"Did anyone talk of the robberies?"

Pru frowned. "Aside from Mr. Oliver, no. He whined about his wife insisting on wearing her best jewels around town, though they haven't been the target of the thief yet. The prince, though..."

"The prince?" Katherine mounted the stairs alongside Pru. "I heard he hasn't been a target of the thefts. Do you think he is the thief?" She couldn't think of a single reason why a prince would need to resort to thievery.

He *was* a prince, wasn't he? Perhaps she should ask around and verify his heritage. If he was only pretending to be visiting royalty...

Pru made a face. "I can't be certain. He certainly wears enough jewelry for him to be sporting the efforts of the thief's labors. Though if that were the case, I imagine the victims would remark upon him wearing their jewelry..." Shaking her head, she opened the bag containing her winnings and pulled out a large amethyst ring. "He goes through money as fast as he does spirits. When he was out for the evening, he tossed this down on the pile. A horrible player, but a good sport, I suppose. He never accused me of cheating."

Katherine gave Pru a pointed look and paused on the landing of the first floor to examine the ring. Only a single tallow candle provided light on this floor for the moment. "I hope you weren't cheating."

The other woman scoffed. "As if I needed to. I had more skill than everyone else at the table combined, even if the cards weren't always to my advantage." She shrugged. "The ring is rather pretty, even if it is too big for me."

Katherine memorized the shape and flourishes in

case she later found a report of a stolen ring matching this description. What had Lady Carleton's anniversary ring looked like, again? She would have to ask or consult the newspaper clippings she'd brought with her.

Footsteps on the stairs alerted her to someone following them up. She passed the ring back to Pru, who quickly hid it from sight just as Sir Hugh slipped past Lyle onto the landing. He frowned as he beheld them.

"Lady Katherine, Miss Burwick." His gaze strayed to Lyle, but they must not have been introduced because Sir Hugh didn't greet him by name. In fact, he didn't greet him at all. "Why are you congregating on the first floor? Is something amiss?"

Pru opened her mouth. Although Katherine had no clue what the other woman meant to answer, she jumped in to do so first. "We were trying to think of who might be the owner of this earring, actually." She fished it from her reticule. Since he had been in Bath longer than she, perhaps he would better know to whom the jewel belonged. "I found it in the corridor earlier this evening."

The moment Sir Hugh peered closer at the earring, he stiffened. His friendly expression turned to ice. "The corridor? No, it couldn't possibly have been there."

Her chest constricted as if an unseen hand squeezed her. Should she confess to Emma's part in this? Her voice as brittle as her smile, she asked, "Have you seen it before?"

"It is mine."

His? Katherine exchanged a dubious look with Pru. Men didn't wear such elaborate earrings. They resembled small chandeliers in the intricacy of the interlaced diamonds.

"I beg your pardon."

"I have the other." He dipped his hand into his pocket and emerged with an identical earring. "I have to thank you for finding it, even if I was certain they never left my room aside from being in my pocket."

Hesitantly, Katherine held out the jewel for him to take. Weakly, she asked, "Are you certain they weren't in your pocket and didn't fall out?"

The stony look in his eye chilled her. "Quite."

When he snatched the earring from her hand, she couldn't think of a single reason to stop him. At the same time, she couldn't think of a reasonable explanation as to why an unmarried man might be in possession of women's jewelry, either.

Unless that man happened to be a thief. Had she

just given the Burglar of Bath precisely what he wanted?

"Thank you for returning it," he said sharply. He tucked the matching pair into his pocket once more. "They belonged to my mother. Now that she's passed, I like to keep them with me... for sentimental reasons."

An heirloom.

Katherine ducked her head in a polite nod. "You're quite welcome." She wrestled with doubt and suspicion as he mounted the steps to the next floor, where their rooms resided.

Judging by the speculative look on her face, Pru shared Katherine's misgivings. No one said a word as they followed in Sir Hugh's wake. At the top of the steps, Pru beckoned them toward Katherine's room, silently. Her lips were pressed together.

Emma gave a happy yip upon spotting so many visitors entering her domain. Wagging her tail, she set upon them, twining between their legs and threatening to send them down in a heap.

Harriet jumped off the bed. Her cheeks darkening, she hastily shoved something that resembled a notebook beneath the pillow and stood, clad in her nightdress. Because the room was so small, Katherine had invited her maid to share the bed during their stay in Bath, rather than sleeping on the floor. The hotel didn't have accommodations for servants or enough rooms at hand for Katherine to rent another. She had hinted for Harriet to share with Lyle, but that had only earned her a look of befuddlement on both their parts. Despite how she'd sung Lyle's praises to Pru, Harriet, it seemed, did not think of him in a romantic light regardless of her penchant for teasing him.

Pru ushered Lyle inside and bade him to close the door. Although he obeyed, he turned as red as a rose and examined the ceiling rather than look directly at Harriet. Normally, that would have been the sort of thing that would have earned him a cheeky word from the maid, but tonight she was much too busy rearranging the pillow over the book she'd hidden.

Frowning, Katherine followed Harriet's movements. "What were you reading? Was that my journal?"

"As if I would bother," Harriet answered with a high little laugh that told Katherine she was lying. "Your journal is as dull as ditchwater." A sly look overtook the guilt in her expression. "Unless, of course, you've had something to add of late. Perhaps featuring a tall, handsome captain and a secluded ballroom corridor?"

Katherine gaped. "How do you know about that? We've only just left the ball!"

Harriet laughed and stepped closer to scoop Emma off the ground and provide the attention for which the dog begged. "Gossip travels fast. Does he kiss well?"

Lyle cleared his throat, blatantly uncomfortable as he shifted from foot to foot. "Am I needed here?"

"Yes," Pru snapped.

At the same time, Katherine protested, "I did not kiss Wayland. I was searching for clues!"

Harriet's grin grew. "And did you find any in the poor captain's clothing?"

"No. I didn't look in his clothing. He was with us at the house party and cannot be the thief. The person lurking in the corridor, on the other hand—"

Pru interjected, "If we could discuss Katherine's indiscretions at another time..."

Katherine threw her hands in the air. "There was no indiscretion! I pursued the cloaked figure into the corridor. Wayland followed. The End."

Continuing to pat the dog, Harriet quipped, "That isn't how I heard it. My sources tell me you dragged him into the other room with the promise of a kiss."

Katherine held up her hands in surrender. With the scrutiny of her friends, her cheeks flushed with heat. She grasped for dignity as she said firmly, "There is no conversation. In fact, there is no foundation to justify having this conversation, as there is no romantic inclination on either part."

Lyle frowned, removing his gaze from the ceiling to study her. "Actually..."

Harriet spoke over him. Relieved, Katherine gratefully turned her full attention to her maid, even if she endured further teasing. She didn't want to know what he had to say on the matter.

With a false look of exasperation, Harriet said, "Pity. I have nothing about which to gossip with the other servants. You spend all your time working, plying your intellect to solve one puzzle or another, and the balderdash you wrote in your journal at the house party is all drivel about clues and murders."

A laugh slipped from between Katherine's lips. "I know. I wrote it."

"I was hoping for something more exciting! A titillating tale of you and the captain in the garden, for instance."

Katherine let out an exasperated breath. "That never happened, just as—"

She cringed as a piercing whistle split the air. All eyes turned to Pru, who looked cross. She braced her hands on her hips and glared at them.

"I did not bring you in here to discuss Captain Wayland or any other hanger-on in Katherine's life."

She wrinkled her nose at Katherine, giving her a studious look. "In fact, I have to wonder at the fact that she *would* have a man at her heels in that outfit."

Katherine balled her fists. She had had enough of Pru disparaging her choice of clothing for one night, even if she had hoped to look plain. "I'll have you know he said I looked comely tonight."

"He wants something from you," Pru stated, her voice frank.

"I know." What she hadn't yet deduced was what he hoped to gain.

"I know what he wants," Harriet said with a lascivious smile.

Katherine glared her into silence. "He likely wants to seduce me into telling him the details of my investigation."

"Oh, yes," the maid grinned. "*Seduce.* That's what I was thinking, as well."

Loudly, Pru interrupted, "I herded you in here for good reason. Unless, of course, your primary aim while in Bath has changed from finding the thief to seducing Captain Wayland?"

"I think not," Katherine bit out, her jaw clenched with irritation.

"Would you like to hear what I learned about Sir Hugh or not?"

Her interest piqued, Katherine immediately turned her full attention on the other woman. Her suspicions about the baronet rekindled, she leaned closer and urged Pru to continue with a wave of her hand. "Of course. I'm listening."

Smug, Pru stood taller. She drew out the silence, seeming to revel in the attention directed to her by the three other people in the room. She would have made an admirable opera singer.

"Sir Hugh has recently come into a large sum of money."

Katherine frowned. "How large?"

"No one knows, nor from whence it came, but he's been freer with his money at the card tables these past few weeks, I've been told."

If he had such an influx of quid, then why were his clothes in such a shabby state? Katherine frowned, mulling over that information.

Pru added, "He seemed most attentive whenever Mr. Oliver was complaining of his wife's insistence on bringing her jewels everywhere, including the King's Bath, where they mean to go tomorrow after church."

"Do you think he means to rob them?"

She widened her eyes in a look of innocence. "I would never presume to form such a theory when knowing so little. *I* am not the investigator in this matter. What do *you* mean to do?"

Clearly, she had yet to forgive Katherine for telling her she could have no part in the investigation. As long as Katherine could limit the other woman's role to that of information gathering, she ought to have a reasonable chance of solving the thefts on her own. After all, she had to learn her gossip from *someone*. Why not Pru?

"The thief has yet to rob anyone at the public baths. I suspect there are far too many people nearby for them to try."

As Pru scowled, Katherine held up her hands.

"Nevertheless, I think it is prudent that we also attend the baths tomorrow, just in case Sir Hugh — or someone else — intends to help himself to somebody's jewelry. Perhaps we might be able to catch them in the act. Lyle?"

At her question, he shrugged. "The Pump Room, where the Dowager of Bath has graciously allowed me to access the water for my invention, is next door. I'll be nearby."

"Excellent!" Pru opened the door and slipped out to the corridor. With a wave of her hand, she said, "Feel free to resume taunting Katherine." In a lower tone, she mulled, "I wonder what I'll wear to look horrid..."

Katherine didn't want to know. She turned to her companions. "It's too late in the night for taunting."

"In the morning, then," Harriet said with a twinkle in her eye. "I'll be sure to let you know if you whisper the captain's name in the middle of the night."

Katherine heaved a sigh. Why did she have to be such close friends with her maid? Others of her station didn't have to put up with such insolence.

Beleaguered, she shooed Harriet toward the bed. "I will not be whispering his name in my sleep. In fact, unless we cross paths again, I shan't even think of him."

Cradling Emma, the maid sat at the foot of the bed. The dog wiggled in her arms but settled the moment Harriet started rubbing her belly. "Well then, if you're right in thinking he's interested in the investigation, you're bound to think of him often."

Katherine sighed. She herded Lyle into the corridor. "My apologies for all... this. I know you'd rather not hear it." Truthfully, neither would Katherine.

Instead of accepting her apology with aplomb, he paused on the threshold of her room and caught her gaze. "I think you're wrong."

Katherine frowned. "I beg your pardon?"

"Wayland is not interested in the investigation. Goodnight." He nodded to her and Harriet before striding down the corridor to his room.

A stroke of luck, on Katherine's part, for she hadn't the faintest idea of how to answer him. If anything, *he* had to be wrong. Wayland couldn't possibly have any other reason to be in Bath except to solve the very investigation upon which she had turned her attention.

And she was determined to solve it first.

CHAPTER SIX

The respectful hush shrouding the congregation lifted the moment the gentlemen and women strode through the carved arched doors of Bath Abbey and into the square. Katherine's gaze skated past the epitaphs artfully carved into blocks in the wall and floor as she exited. She paused, craning her neck to view the cloudy gray sky. The trees, angels, and bishops carved into the façade of the abbey loomed over her between the elaborate arched stained-glass windows.

Pru approached and steered her to the left, out of the stream of people. "Should we return to the hotel and change clothes?" The woman had been in a sour mood all morning, upon finding that she didn't have a day dress ugly enough to suit her needs. She had been forced to accept Katherine's advice of choosing a plain one instead, in the hope of fading into the background.

Katherine's dress was beige, she hoped neutral enough to match the stone walls of the King's Bath and render her presence unremarkable. Pru had chosen gray for the occasion.

In answer to the question, Katherine shook her head. "We have no time. I want to install myself at the baths in time to see everyone lingering nearby. We cannot risk the thief striking while we are away."

The other woman pulled a face. "Surely you're being too stringent. Won't everyone want lunch before they use the pool?"

Katherine smirked. "Haven't you heard not to swim after eating? They'll bathe first in the healing waters then adjourn for lunch. If we're lucky, they'll take lunch in the Pump Room and we won't need to stray far to keep everyone in our sights."

Her gaze meandered across the square to the brown stone building by that name. A covered walkway, the roof held aloft by carved Ionic columns, separated the square from the street beyond and adjoined the building. Latticed windows, Corinthian pillars, and elaborate scrollwork decorated the Pump Room, noticeable even from a distance. Although Katherine had yet to set foot in the building, she had been told that they served refreshments in the afternoon and housed the spring of healing water accessible to the public. Lyle must already be ensconced within those walls, for he hadn't attended the sermon with Katherine and Pru.

Katherine slipped her arm through Pru's and steered her into motion. "Come, let's go to the King's Bath."

Although Pru didn't protest, she glanced over her shoulder every few feet. Whatever she saw had her agitated. She leaned closer. "Are you certain that acting unladylike is the proper way to dissuade a man from thinking of you romantically?"

"Why do you ask?"

Even as the words left her mouth, Katherine turned to discover what agitated her companion. Lord Annandale strolled no more than six feet behind them. Although he spoke with his companion, Sir Hugh, he didn't lift his gaze from the pair of them for a moment.

Pru lowered her voice and hissed, "He stared at me all through the sermon."

Perhaps, if she had noticed, whereas Katherine had not, she had spent a good deal of time staring back.

"I don't think winning at loo was enough to

convince him I'm undesirable. I even sat out one hand and advised on his, but he didn't seem the least bit offended at the advice. He isn't the most skilled of card players."

This is Wayland's fault. As Katherine glanced behind her to note that Sir Hugh had parted ways with Annandale, leaving the marquess to dog their steps alone, she could only assume that Wayland was at fault. He had promised to put a good word in Annandale's ear, much as Katherine *didn't* wish him to do that. It seemed the rival investigator held as much sway over his friends as he claimed. If he, for a second, believed this would ingratiate him enough with Katherine for her to spill the secrets of the thefts she uncovered, he was wrong. If anything, this was going to make things more complicated.

As they stepped past a short row of carriages awaiting the arrival of their owners from the church, Katherine had an idea. If her prowess at cards wouldn't work, perhaps she could have Pru act unladylike in other ways. Wayland's promises of Pru's well-mannered traits wouldn't stretch far. A twinge of guilt had her wondering if it was fair to Pru to foist her off while Katherine's attention was otherwise occupied.

"Your plan isn't working," Pru hissed. "I've never had a man pay so close attention to me before. I have *much* better things to do than hold a lord at bay. Why, I could be solving the string of thefts here in Bath. If I only gave it my full attention, I'm willing to wager that I'd be able to solve it faster than you."

"We solved the last case at the same pace," Katherine snapped. She needed a way to keep Pru occupied for a few hours while she investigated at the King's Bath. If not, the other woman would certainly make good on her threat and seek to investigate herself. Any lingering guilt over what she intended to do dissipated.

Pausing in front of the entrance to the King's Bath, Katherine turned to Pru. "Do you want to help investigate that badly?"

"Of course." Pru looked shocked that Katherine would ask. "It's the most interesting thing happening here in Bath!"

Katherine motioned for the other woman to keep her voice down. "Very well, then I'll need you to do something specific for me."

"Anything."

"How well do you know horses?"

Pru frowned, as though trying to connect horses to the investigation. In actuality, there was no connection. Katherine merely needed something with which to occupy Pru to prevent her from following Katherine into the baths.

"I can ride, if that's what you're asking."

"Sidesaddle or astride?"

Pru hesitated a moment before she admitted, "Both. I went hunting with my father a time or two before he passed."

"Excellent." It might be easier than Katherine thought to convince Lord Annandale that Pru wasn't the match for him. She had never met a man who welcomed a woman's input on hunting, not that she tried unless it involved hunting a criminal.

She shot a quick glance at the man who had prompted this conversation. He had halted next to a marked carriage emblazoned with a thistle in the seal, where he softly exchanged words with the driver.

"Go speak with Lord Annandale. Keep him by the horses and prove you know more than him about those, as well."

Pru shot a glance over her shoulder to the marquess. She looked dubious. "How will that help with the investigation?"

"He seems friendly with Sir Hugh. Try to discover how long they've been in Bath and whether he knows anything about the jewel thefts. Most importantly, if

Wayland arrives, keep him out with Lord Annandale. I don't want him interrupting my investigation again."

Pru sighed. "Very well. For what it's worth, I still think I'd be more help inside with you." Squaring her shoulders, she marched upon Lord Annandale as if confronting the French army.

The moment he noted her approach, he greeted her with a smile.

I hope this cools his interest, Katherine thought. If, by some bizarre coincidence, he was even more interested in Pru as a potential wife, Katherine would have one very disgruntled woman on her hands.

For now, she resolved not to think about it and stepped inside.

The King's Bath was the only bathing pool in Bath that catered to both men and women. The Queen's Bath, a short ways away, was open to women only. Katherine chose to attend the mixed baths, figuring that if the thief meant to strike, it would be there. To date, none of the robberies had happened at one of the public baths. However, with the way the visitors to town flaunted their jewels in the hopes of drawing the burglar's eye, in Katherine's opinion, it was only a matter of time. These women made no secret of coming to the baths, nor did they bother leaving their jewels in their rooms while attending church. It was a veritable feast to a thief.

The door to the baths led to a wide, vaulted antechamber. The ceiling was intricately carved with Vitruvian scrollwork and flourishes. Several red divans, a dark contrast to the pale walls and floor, were situated around the perimeter of the room. On the back wall, a window showed glimpses of the large bath below, even now populated with people — men, in their shirts and drawers, women wearing shifts that covered them to their ankles. A footman, in matching red-piped livery, smiled at Katherine as she entered.

"The women's dressing chambers are this way, madam. Bess will have everything you need inside."

He indicated one of two doors, situated on opposite walls. The other must be for the men. Thanking him, Katherine slipped through the door to the other side. It led to a long, sparsely lit corridor. The sounds from the bathers seemed amplified and distorted to her ears. At the end, a neat little cubbyhole was guarded by a single female servant of middle age. The moment she spotted Katherine, she helped herself to a pile of towels on a bench by the entrance.

"Here you are, my lady. Will you need help undressing?"

Undressing? Katherine smiled tightly. "No, thank you. I don't mean to go in the water."

The woman looked confused. "I beg your pardon, my lady, but everyone who comes here bathes in the King's Bath, unless of course they are an attendant of one of the bathers. Forgive the assumption, but you look far too deep in the pockets to be in such a position."

That, Katherine was. She peered around the small room, plain in comparison to the grand antechamber through which she had journeyed to get here. The walls were plain, unadorned stone. Shelves lined them, each with neatly folded clothing and jewels sitting atop them, sparkling in the daylight spilling through the arch into the pool.

"I am not an attendant," Katherine informed her. However, when it seemed as though the woman would protest her venturing to the bathing area if she had no intention of immersing herself in the water, Katherine added, "I'm afraid of water. Terrible affliction. I can't swim, but I'd hoped to dip my feet in the water. Perhaps the healing powers will have the same effect."

Mollified, the woman allowed Katherine to pass to see the bathers, but not before first confiscating her slippers and stockings. Frankly, Katherine was lucky she'd been allowed to keep her dress rather than stripping down to her shift as everyone else had been. Despite the warmth seeping into the air from the hot spring filling the baths, the day was far too chilly for that.

By the time she entered the area with the pool — dressed in Neoclassical pillars holding the roof of the covered walkway aloft on all sides, with the large, rectangular water in the center, open to the sky above — she felt as though she'd survived a battlefield. Adjusting the sleeves of her dress, she lingered in the shadow of a pillar as she surveyed those gathered.

She found Mr. and Mrs. Oliver at once, both swimming in the water at the near end of the pool. The older woman conversed loudly with Lady Dalhousie, who... tarnation, was she wearing that diamond necklace even in the pool? Her hair wasn't wet, nor was the top of her shift, attesting to the fact that she intended to remain in shallow waters to preserve the gems, but it seemed a foolhardy choice, if you asked Katherine. Every few minutes, Lady Dalhousie lifted her hand to touch the necklace, wetting it as she assured herself that it remained around her neck. They spoke with another couple of affluence, the woman younger than the man by at least three decades as they boasted of the jewelry they'd left at home, of course, so as not to chance it becoming damaged by the minerals in the water. Lady Dalhousie didn't at all look pleased to hear such a proclamation, even if it was the truth. Katherine heard her refer to the woman as Mrs. Quicke.

Annoyed at such insipid conversation, Katherine walked along the warm tile of the outer floor and circled the perimeter. Across the pool, a young man was being helped out of his bath chair by an attendant in the livery of the King's Bath. Recognition toyed with Katherine at the sweep of his brown hair and the set of his chin. Had they met? As her gaze traveled lower, to his bare leg where his clothes ended, revealing his puckered scar, she deduced that he must be Scott Julien. She barely recognized him.

Where were his grandparents? She didn't see them nearby, but perhaps they required assistance them-selves in order to use the baths. Mr. Julien, in particu-lar, moved with difficulty and could likely benefit from the purported powers of the baths. They were certainly too old to help their grandson safely out of the chair and into the water. Out of respect, Katherine averted her gaze and wished others would do the same to grant Scott a moment or two of dignity while the footman lowered him into the water. Even from across the pool, the pain on his face was prominent.

The moment she averted her gaze, Katherine

spotted Mrs. Fairchild in a particularly high-necked, frilly shift, and grimaced. She took a step back, deeper into the shadows cast by the covered walkway, in the hopes that she wouldn't be seen. Fortunately, the rival matchmaker seemed much too occupied in attending to her charge, who was presently swimming after Prince Karl. Oh dear. That wasn't the way to woo a man at all. Katherine almost felt sorry for the poor girl.

Her gaze paused on the broad shoulders of a man as he resurfaced midway along the pool. The water dripped from his dark hair, flattened to his head, along the translucent white shirt that now clung to his muscular shoulders, back, and arms. As Wayland turned, Katherine's breath caught, and she clasped the cold column by her hip. Their gazes locked. She tried not to notice the way his wet shirt clung to his chest, but it was impossible. Although it had been over a year since the Battle of Waterloo had marked the end of the war, Wayland clearly continued to keep himself fit for battle. Why was she even noticing? She certainly had no interest in taking up with a man, and if she ever did, it wouldn't be Wayland.

He had noticed her momentary interest. As he turned fully toward her, Katherine tried to make a subtle gesture to tell him to remain in the pool. Thus far, no one had remarked upon her presence along the perimeter, but if he approached to speak with her, that would certainly change. Not to mention the rumor circulating about them. She had to negate that somehow, before a tarnished reputation prevented her entry into the very events she needed to attend in order to solve crimes.

First and foremost, she had a thief to catch. Movement at the corner of her eye drew her attention to another shadow, one across the pool from her. The sun peeked out from between the clouds, glaring down at her and inducing sunspots that made it difficult to make out the figure. Tall, the figure wore far more clothing than Katherine expected anyone to be let in with. Was there another entrance? At this distance, with the shadows and the sun in her eyes, the figure looked to Katherine to be wearing a long cloak and... was that a bicorn that had lost its shape or a shepherdess hat? The wide brim obscured the wearer's face. Katherine's heartbeat quickened as she realized that she must be looking at the same lurker whom she had seen the night before at the Assembly Rooms. The thief!

Blinking away sunspots, she started around the perimeter of the pool, shortening the distance between her and her primary suspect. Although she tried to appear casual, the figure bolted. *No!* Katherine wouldn't let them escape again.

She rounded the far end of the pool, the tile slick with moisture. Her foot slipped, and she nearly toppled into the water. Someone shouted her name, but she paid them no mind. The moment she had her footing, she raced toward the suspect. Cloak billowing, the figure followed the shadows behind the pillars toward the open doorways leading into the dressing rooms.

Katherine skidded to a stop halfway along the pool edge as she nearly collided with Mr. Oliver, groaning with effort as he climbed out of the pool. He startled, losing his balance. If Katherine hadn't reached out to clasp his arm, he might have fallen in and injured himself. The others nearby climbed out and gathered around them.

"Mr. Oliver, are you hurt?"

"Shame on you, Lady Katherine! You should watch where you walk."

"Walk? I saw her running as if her life depended upon it."

"Youth these days..."

With empty placations, Katherine managed to extricate herself from the wall of people. Her heart thundered as she glanced around. Where was the thief? Nowhere did she spot where the figure must have run. They had escaped.

Sard it all! Why must everyone have gotten in her way? Frustration gripping her, Katherine fought the urge to smack her fist into the nearest pillar. That was twice now that the figure had eluded her, for no reason other than that other people seemed determined to delay her progress.

"Katherine?"

She stiffened and nearly turned at Wayland's voice. The water sloshed as he exited the pool. She didn't look. *Think.* The women's attendant, Bess, would never have let the figure pass with so many clothes on. Katherine doubted that the men's attendant would, either. That left only one explanation; there was another means by which the thief had entered the pool. How?

Wayland touched her arm from behind. Water soaked through the thin material of her dress, making her shiver despite the warm humidity rising from the bath.

"Are you all right?"

About to answer in the affirmative, Katherine lost her voice as a woman screamed. Where? It sounded as if it came from the direction of the women's dressing rooms.

"My necklace! It's been stolen!"

Katherine bolted for the dressing room, weaving between startled men and women who gawped at the open door and sluggishly followed in her wake. She paused in the threshold to catch her breath. Mrs. Oliver clutched a towel to her ample bosom as she pointed to a pile of clothes on the shelving unit. Bess, the attendant, looked so pale that she might swoon.

Although her expertise as an investigator wasn't known, Katherine took charge nevertheless. She turned to address the women hovering behind her like a gaggle of geese. "Stay back. The investigator who Lord Bath has hired will want to look for clues."

Not that she intended to wait for Mr. Salmon to arrive and examine the scene before her.

Violating her own advice, Katherine turned and approached the two women. "This is a very great shock for you both, I'm certain."

"Of course it is," Mrs. Oliver exclaimed. "My pearl necklace has been stolen!" She shot a look of triumph to the door.

Katherine gritted her teeth and shooed both women toward the bench where the towels were stacked. Once the women were seated, Mrs. Oliver close enough to tell the women gathered by the door exactly what had transpired while Bess shut her eyes and leaned back against the wall in a fit of vapors, Katherine turned to look at the shelf containing the clothes. What had changed since she had last been in here?

When she was small, her father had played a game with her called Magic Music. While she was out of a room, he would rearrange certain items and then have her return to seek them out again. As a clue, he would hum loudly if she was nowhere near the correct area, and grow quieter the closer she came to discovering what had been misplaced. The older she became, the less he hummed. The last time they had played the game, he had simply sat back and read the latest news-paper while she catalogued precisely what had changed in the room. Over time, it had honed her mind to notice small details.

Taking a breath, she pictured the room as she had seen it when she had passed through. Judging by the neatly stacked clothing and jewelry, three women had arrived after her. Curiously, of those who had already been in the pool, only Mrs. Oliver's jewelry had been snatched. The others, often in plain view and sparkling atop the pile of clothing, hadn't so much as been moved to be examined. Either the thief hadn't had time — which was the case if that cloaked figure had passed through and robbed Mrs. Oliver on the way

— and had snatched the first item to meet their fingers, or else they had known precisely what they intended to steal.

Why the pearls? Could there be merit to that ridiculous rumor of the thief having good taste?

As she stepped closer, Katherine noticed the wink of metal from the floor. She stepped closer and knelt in front of Mrs. Oliver's discarded slippers. A curl of silver leaf resided in the heel of the shoe, newly deposited since it hadn't been flattened by someone stepping on it. Positioning her body to shield her actions from the view of the other women, Katherine opened the reticule on her wrist and removed her tweezers and a small vial. Gently, she plucked the delicate piece of silver and examined it. At her guess, it hadn't fallen off any piece of jewelry, but had chipped off something larger. A large button, perhaps? The top of a snuffbox, a buckle... the possibilities were endless. It might even have fallen off Mrs. Oliver's clothing. Not her shoes, for they had not the slightest hint of silver, but her clothes. After depositing the sample into the vial and slipping it out of view once more, Katherine stood to examine the folded clothing. It didn't look to have been touched. The dress had no embroidery in silver thread, no silver embellishments, buttons, or buckles. That curl

of silver could not have come from Mrs. Oliver's
clothing.

Which meant only one thing: It had to have been
left there by the thief!

A man's voice echoed along the narrow corridor
leading to the dressing room, distorted by the walls.
"No need to panic. I have everything well in hand."

Mr. Salmon entered the modest chamber with his
jacket buttoned to his throat and his shoulders thrown
back. He passed a hand over his clean-shaven chin as
he surveyed the interior. His eyes narrowed as he
spotted Katherine.

"You are contaminating my crime scene!"

I am a better detective than you, and you know it.
However, Katherine couldn't admit as much aloud.
Glaring, she skirted the room to make way for him.

"There's nothing to see here," he said loudly.
"Carry on."

He rummaged through the nearest stack of clothing, topped with jewels.

"I beg your pardon," a woman gasped in indignation. "Those are *my* things. I haven't been robbed!"

"Oh, yes."

Katherine pinched the bridge of her nose. "It's
Mrs. Oliver's dress, the bottle green. Her pearl necklace is missing." She suspected that, without her telling

him, Mr. Salmon would have continued to create chaos in the dressing room as he examined everyone's clothing.

He approached the green dress instead. As he grabbed it by the sleeve and shook it out, Katherine cringed. If there had been any delicate pieces of evidence lodged in the fabric, they were now destroyed. A fact that the bumbling fool assured when he thoughtlessly trampled the floor in front of the shelf as he leaned closer to inspect it.

"*Mister* Salmon," Mrs. Oliver exclaimed. "I will thank you not to step on my shoes! It is bad enough that I have lost my prized necklace, but I cannot fathom the cost of replacing my shoes as well!"

In the doorway, Lady Dalhousie sniffed. "Do you mean to say that you *didn't* take out an insurance policy for your necklace? I have all of my jewels insured by Featherstone's Goods Assurance. *I* would not be in dire financial straits were this blackguard to turn his eye toward *me*."

Katherine gritted her teeth and fought not to call them both dolts. It wouldn't help the matter, even if it might give her a moment's satisfaction and soothe the sting of Mr. Salmon systematically managing to destroy all possible evidence in the room. Thank Zeus Katherine had managed to arrive first. If she hadn't, he would certainly have destroyed the sliver of silver as he ineptly stomped around and heavy-handedly examined the items left untouched by the thief.

Mrs. Oliver quipped, "Even if you were reimbursed, it couldn't possibly compare with a necklace once owned by an empress. It's a wonder the thief didn't take your jewels, Lady Dalhousie." Her voice dripped with scorn.

"Yes, well... it must be because I was wearing them at the time! A lucky thing. I do feel for the poor thief, though, having to settle for something as dull as a pearl necklace. Perhaps everyone is wrong about his taste in jewelry."

Before she snapped at these old gossips, Katherine stood and meandered closer to Mr. Salmon, still in the process of spoiling any hope of finding clues inside the room. She paused by his elbow, but he was such a dullard that he didn't notice her presence a mere foot away. She dodged as he carelessly flung his hand through the air, narrowly missing her.

She cleared her throat. "Mr. Salmon."

He frowned as he turned. "Lady Katherine, please wait by the door. This is a matter for professionals."

Katherine seethed with indignation. She leaned closer, fisting her hands to keep from doing something she might regret, such as boxing his ears. In a low, lethal voice, she spat, "I *am* a professional, as well you know. We've crossed paths in the Royal Society for Investigative Techniques before."

The wrinkle in his forehead deepened. "I was merely trying to preserve your reputation. Since your pastime isn't widely known, I thought I'd do you the courtesy."

Pastime! You sarding halfwit. Katherine was more a professional detective than he was! Even if the world at large didn't recognize her as such. She had her father's support, and his reputation was sterling.

"Why don't you do us all the courtesy of investigating this thief? Check for footprints, or—"

"Footprints!" Mr. Salmon scoffed. "We're indoors, my lady. What footprints might there be to be had?"

She would have at least attempted to search before dismissing such a thing.

"They might have left something behind—"

Once again, he cut her off. "So I am attempting to discern, but I've found nothing thus far."

"Perhaps that's because you're using your fingers instead of your eyes!"

Katherine regretted snapping at him almost immediately as he drew himself up. He still didn't match her for height, but she could tell from his demeanor that he was seconds away from shutting her out of the investigation altogether. Given how insistent Lord Bath had been that Mr. Salmon handle the matter, the only way Katherine was going to have access to any official clues that were found would be if she remained on Mr. Salmon's good side.

Quickly, she added, "Perhaps it might be wise to interview those gathered here in case one of them might have seen the thief."

Katherine had — at least, so she assumed — but she kept that thought to herself. Until it was corroborated by someone else, she couldn't be certain.

"You need keep us from our clothes no longer," a woman said, indignant. Katherine turned to see that Mrs. Fairchild had wedged her way to the front of the group by the door. She clutched a towel to her chest, but it must not have staved off the relative chill of the air, for she had gooseflesh on her bare arms. "I know precisely who the thief is."

If you tell him I did it just because you think I might interfere with your matchmaking... Katherine pressed her lips together and attempted to warn her rival with her eyes.

Mr. Salmon turned toward the matchmaker. "Oh? And who might that be?"

Lifting her chin and cultivating an air of superiority, Mrs. Fairchild announced, "I saw her skulking about the front of the bathhouse, the ne'er-do-well. Here she is now, come back to admire the scene of her crime!"

"Who?" several asked.

Mrs. Fairchild lifted an accusing finger and pointed to the corridor leading toward the antechamber. Everyone's gaze turned in that direction.

There was no mistaking whom Fairchild was accusing. Only one person stood in the corridor. Pru.

CHAPTER SEVEN

P ru looked as though she wanted to spontaneously combust. Her cheeks lost their color, nearly matching the gray of her dress. She flapped her mouth, attempting to speak, but no words came out.

"Miss Burwick cannae be the thief."

Katherine should, perhaps, have been the person to state that herself, rather than the looming shadow behind Pru, who turned out to be Lord Annandale when he squeezed out of the corridor, planting himself firmly between Pru and her accuser. Never having spoken with him before, Katherine hadn't realized how thick his Scottish burr was.

His eyebrows low over his eyes and his frown disappearing into his neatly groomed beard, he loomed over the much smaller Mrs. Fairchild. Not that she appeared the least bit intimidated. Hands on her hips, she glared back at him and answered, "Wishful thinking will not make it so, sir."

"*My lord*," he corrected her, accentuating the words. "Mayhap ye didn't see me out by the carriages, shawin' her the horses. Miss Burwick did nae leave my side."

Pru's eyes widened as she closed her mouth. His back to her, he couldn't possibly see the look of gratitude and adoration she gave him, but Katherine did. Was Pru as opposed to this match as she pretended?

If Katherine continued to encourage unladylike behavior and other devious methods of assuring that his attention wandered to someone else, she might be dashing Pru's hopes of future happiness rather than building them. Simply because Katherine had no inclination to marry didn't mean that other women felt the same, even those in her profession. Her sisters were proof enough of that, each happily settled and content with the paths they had chosen. With the way Pru looked at Annandale just then, whether she did so consciously or not, Katherine suspected she might be more amenable to the thought of marrying the marquess than she let on, even if she did not yet realize it herself.

Mrs. Fairchild didn't seem the least bit pleased to

hear of Pru's alibi in the thefts, even though she must only have been attempting to make trouble for Katherine by suggesting it. She must have known Pru couldn't be the thief. They had been at Lord Northbrook's party until recently! Katherine's head throbbed.

In an obvious ploy to distract those gathered from her blunder, the matchmaker clutched the towel to her chest and looked scandalized. "My lord, what are you doing in the women's dressing room? We aren't clothed!"

"Ye were in the bluidy pool dressed as ye are."

Lord Annandale's presence — and his profanity — stirred the gaggle of gossips into a frenzy. The old women followed Mrs. Fairchild's lead, squawking in indignation over a man seeing them in such a state and the indecency of being forced to stand and become spectacles there rather than don their clothing once more. Mr. Salmon bowed to the pressure exerted by the ladies and relinquished the room to them, allowing them to dress. Meanwhile, Lord Annandale escaped down the corridor, where he wouldn't be harassed.

Katherine struggled to make sense of the resulting cacophony. Scooping up her shoes and stockings, she followed on Mr. Salmon's heels as he vacated the room. "Wait!"

He pretended not to hear. Fortunately, she had long legs and caught up to his brisk pace as he reached the antechamber.

"Mr. Salmon!" She dashed in front of the would-be investigator and barred his exit.

He peered down his nose at her, quite the feat when he happened to be the shorter of them. "Why are you harassing me now, Lady Katherine?"

Because you're investigating poorly! She pinned a smile on her face. "Mr. Salmon, don't you think it would be prudent to question those gathered at the pool today? Stop them from leaving before it will be impossible to tell who was here?"

She would do it herself if she could. However, her role in Bath was that of matchmaker, not investigator. The Marquess of Bath had declined Lyle's assistance in the investigation — and unfortunately, she hadn't seen him or his grandmother since the sermon. Who hadn't she seen in the baths at the time of the theft? Sir Hugh must be about somewhere, though admittedly she hadn't seen him. And where were Scott Julien's grandparents? They'd never entered the bath, as she'd expected them to.

Chafing, she ground her teeth at the inconvenience of having to work alongside someone as inept as

Mr. Salmon. She prayed he would see the sense in questioning those present.

Unfortunately, he looked dubious. "Lady Katherine, I know you are new at this—"

No, I'm not! I've been at every Society meeting you have since I could walk!

"But I have been hired by the Marquess of Bath, whose primary concern is that we don't frighten the guests away from his city. If we insist on questioning them, they might take it as license to leave."

Tightly, Katherine countered, "If they continue to be robbed, they definitely will leave."

Even that bit of logic didn't seem to sway Mr. Salmon's mind.

She released an exasperated breath. "Surely you've seen the cloaked figure lurking about."

Mr. Salmon stared at her blankly. The groove in his forehead deepened. "A cloaked figure?"

She frowned. "You *have* seen him, haven't you?" If not, Salmon was a bigger bumbling fool than she'd expected! In a place like the King's Bath, such an over-dressed figure could not be missed. Katherine could only imagine where else the figure must have lurked in the past few months.

Puffing out his chest, Mr. Salmon huffed, "Of course I have! He is my primary suspect. Always lingering in the shadows, wearing a dark suit of clothes."

When had Katherine mentioned a dark suit of clothes? She hadn't even described the cloak. She frowned. The thought of Mr. Salmon having noticed this figure before her rankled, never mind that she had only arrived in town yesterday!

Unless... Yes, it seemed much more likely that he hadn't encountered the cloaked figure at all. He was fabricating details that didn't exist to make him look more competent.

Nonetheless, on the off chance that he spotted the culprit in the future, Katherine informed him, "No, the figure to which I'm referring wore a dark cloak coupled with a broad-brimmed hat."

He nodded vigorously, the loose skin by his chin wobbling with his enthusiasm. "Yes, that's the one. He... wears something different each time."

You sarding liar. She bit her tongue, hoping to use his willingness to agree with her to her advantage. "We're in agreement, then. Since this figure has proven elusive thus far, we must ask the bath patrons what they've seen."

Mr. Salmon hesitated.

Gritting her teeth, Katherine added, "Unless, of course, you aren't trying to catch the thief after all."

The inept investigator drew himself up. "How dare you accuse me of such! Of course I'm trying to apprehend the thief. The good Marquess of Bath has hired me to do that very thing."

Katherine's eyes narrowed. She wondered about the terms of Salmon's employ. Would he be paid only when he caught the thief, or was the Marquess paying him to investigate? If the latter, perhaps it would be in Salmon's best financial interest to drag the investigation out as long as possible.

With a wave of her hand and a winsome smile, Katherine indicated the two doors. "Then perhaps we ought to station someone to alert the patrons to remain for questioning."

Mr. Salmon hemmed and hawed but ultimately capitulated. With a weary sigh, he dragged his feet as he crossed toward the nearest divan and sat. "Let's give them a few minutes to dress. We can interrogate them here, when they've set themselves to rights."

Katherine smiled and settled next to him to wait.

Mr. Salmon proved every bit the fool that Katherine thought him. Tenfold, in fact, with the sort of questions he asked. Had they seen Mrs. Oliver wear the pearls today? Perhaps she was mistaken about their theft. Had any of their belongings been disturbed? Did they know anyone with ill will toward Mrs. Oliver? The last question might have had merit had the theft been an isolated incident, but at this point Katherine believed the victims chosen on the basis of opportunity more so than enmity.

Since Mr. Salmon seemed more likely to ask the witnesses for old family recipes than for anything useful, Katherine took it upon herself to butt in. However, she soon found herself baffled in that no one seemed to have noticed the cloaked figure. Mrs. Fairchild went so far as to say that it was Katherine's imagination, though with a gleam in her eye that told Katherine she was lying. Mrs. Fairchild, if no one else, had also noticed the cloaked figure. For all her rancor, she was an astute woman. Would she withhold vital information in order to spite Katherine? It seemed so.

Unfortunately, when quizzed as to their whereabouts at the time of the robbery, all persons at the King's Bath at the time claimed to have been in the pool. Bathing, it seemed, now numbered among the social events of the *ton*, and they had been far too preoccupied with gossip and grasping to make social connections to notice who had entered or exited the women's dressing room.

Bess, the attendant, was little better than wreckage. She had only stepped away for a moment, to find someone to better assist Mr. Julien, who appeared to be having difficulty moving in the bath. When she'd returned, nothing had seemed amiss, but the necklace must already have been stolen.

Katherine wanted to scream. Her frustrations over the entire event centered in a throbbing knot of pain near her temple. As Mr. Salmon dismissed the servant, Katherine massaged her skin.

He turned to her, an air of superiority curling around his shoulders like a mantle. "There. You see, Lady Katherine? There was nothing to be found. We were wasting everyone's time."

She balled her fists in her lap to keep from strangling him.

"How did you know that we would discover nothing?" Her tone was biting, but she didn't have the patience for niceties. "Were you nearby?"

"Not terribly close," he hedged, shifting on the divan and looking toward the ornate ceiling. "I was next door, in the Pump Room. With the Marquess of Bath, I'll have you know!" He preened, his confidence returned as he informed her of that fact. "The moment he heard the scream, Lord Bath was most distraught. He dispatched me, his trusted investigator in this matter, straight away."

It was clear to Katherine that Lord Bath didn't know the first thing about investigations. He seemed like a trusting soul, and Katherine worried that he was being taken advantage of by Salmon.

Nevertheless, he had been assigned the case far longer than she. If she had to suffer his presence anyway, she might as well learn all she could about the investigation thus far.

"Who do you suspect the thief to be?"

"Me?" Mr. Salmon huffed. "I cannot point a finger at anyone without first finding proof. That is the investigative way. I would have expected you to know that, Lady Katherine."

She fought the urge to smack the smug look off his face. As much as he might deserve it if she boxed his ears, she required information from him. In fact, if she was barred access to any future thefts, she wouldn't be able to complete the task she'd set herself. Therefore, she had to remain on his good side... as much as was possible.

"Do you think the culprit might be one of the gentlemen or women visiting Bath?"

The middle-aged man expanded his chest with such a large breath that Katherine braced herself for a blistering admonishment.

She hurried to spill out her theory, to prevent him from aggravating her further. "Sir Hugh, for instance, seems in a desperate way, and he wasn't in the pool today. Neither were Mr. and Mrs. Julien." She didn't want to consider them, being as they were such congenial folk. However, they obviously loved their grandson and would do anything to see to his comfort. They appeared to have fallen on hard times in so doing. She wanted to discount them immediately... but they had motive enough to steal the jewels.

Mr. Salmon harrumphed. "I highly doubt it was either of those people. As you said, they weren't at the baths."

"I said they weren't *in* the baths. The thief must not have been, in order to have stolen the necklace."

The wrinkle in his forehead deepened as he shook his head. "No, indeed. If you ask me, it is much more likely that someone *at* the baths would have stolen the necklace. Any woman has reason to enter the dressing room."

"And where would they have hidden the jewels?" Katherine snapped. "We questioned them all."

"We didn't look in their bags or their bosoms."

Her mouth gaped like a fish as she imagined the indignity of asking the women to strip once more in order for them to check them for jewels. Reticules were small drawstring bags hanging from the wrist. They could barely hold a few handkerchiefs without creating a noticeable bulge, let alone such a long string of pearls, made to wrap several times around the wearer's neck. Katherine had looked and seen no such bulge in anyone's reticule.

Unable to formulate a response to the image of Mr. Salmon using a magnifying glass to peer down the bodices of all the old ladies, Katherine stood.

"I imagine we're done here," he said cheerfully before he strode out the door and into the street.

This time, Katherine didn't stop him. Her head throbbed as she tried to recall everyone she had seen in the King's Bath. Had she spoken with them all?

Movement across the antechamber, from the door leading to the men's dressing room, drew her eye. Wayland separated from the shadows, where he'd been leaning against the wall. He carried his jacket, thrown across one forearm. His wet hair curled around his ears and dripped onto his collar. His damp shirt clung to his torso, much the way the one he'd worn to bathe had.

"How long have you been waiting there?"

Katherine asked, her voice sharp.

Wayland shrugged. "A few minutes. You seemed deep in conversation, and I didn't want to disturb you."

She pulled a face. "You mean you didn't want to subject yourself to that dolt's company."

He smiled, a wide and welcoming expression that made the dimple in his chin deepen. "That, too."

"Coward," she said, but an answering smile curved her lips.

He fell into step with her as they strode toward the exit, donning his jacket on the way. "How goes the investigation?"

She narrowed her eyes. "Why should I share my leads?"

His smile shrank as he cocked an eyebrow. "You still don't trust me, I see."

"You'll get no reward out of this. I don't see why you're still here."

On the threshold to the street, Wayland paused. He rubbed a hand across his mouth. "Not everything is about money, Katherine."

"Notoriety, then? I thought you weren't interested in that, either."

"I'm not."

She released a long breath as she studied his face. He seemed earnest, but he must have another angle, something he would gain from solving this investigation. No matter the cost, she refused to let him steal her glory this time. This case was hers to solve, and hers alone.

However, unlike Mr. Salmon, Wayland was a keen investigator. If he hadn't been, her father would never have taken enough interest in his doings to label him a rival. Wayland might have insight into this investigation — or perhaps even clues that she hadn't yet found.

"What do you make of the investigation? Salmon doesn't seem to have made any headway, for all that he seems thick as three in a bed with Lord Bath."

Wayland chuckled. "The marquess does seem quite enamored with him."

"But why?" Katherine pulled a face. "I've never met someone so inept! You should have heard the questions he asked the witnesses." She shook her head as she added, "Not to mention, he refuses to consider the possibility that the culprit might not have been in attendance in the King's Bath. They might have snuck in."

The captain mulled over the information before nodding shortly. He held the door for Katherine to exit into the late-afternoon air. A chill gathered around her, necessitating the need to wrap her arms around herself. Where had her pelisse disappeared to?

Perhaps she'd left it in the dressing room. Or perhaps she'd handed it off to Pru when her charge had seemed overly flustered even once Mrs. Fairchild's erroneous accusations had been straightened away. When Katherine had begun interviewing the witnesses, she'd sent Pru back to the hotel with Lyle for an escort.

Stepping out onto the street on her heels, Wayland shut the door and offered his arm. "To the hotel, I presume?"

When she shivered at the unseasonable nip in the air, he shucked his jacket and laid it around her shoulders. She held him off with a raised hand. "Don't be ridiculous. Your shirt is damp. You'll catch a chill."

"I'll chance it."

His jacket, when he wrapped her in it, proved to be a bit damp as well, but warm from his body heat. He didn't offer his arm again, which was just as well, for Katherine's arms were crossed beneath the fabric, huddled for warmth. They strode briskly out of the square, toward the Sydney Hotel. With luck, they would reach it in less than ten minutes.

Wayland asked, "Are you hungry? We could stop nearby for a Sally Lunn."

Katherine's stomach had been grumbling throughout the interrogations, when the scent of food had drifted in now and again from the Pump Room. By now, the refreshments and social niceties would be over, and the people would have disbanded to return to their beds for an afternoon nap, or else engage in some other planned activity. Admittedly, Katherine usually preferred to spend Sunday afternoon with a good book, a game of chess, or an unsolved mystery.

"Thank you, but I'll eat at the hotel."

"I'll join you. I didn't want to miss the interviews, so I forwent attending the luncheon at the Pump Room. I'm feeling rather peckish."

He wasn't a friend. In fact, given that Lord Bath was a friend of her father's, she should be avoiding Wayland at all costs, lest reports of her association with him reach Papa's ears. Why did he want to take tea with her, if not to gain the upper hand in some way?

Frowning, she asked, "You were listening in the entire time?"

"Far from it. Since you were situated closer to the women's dressing room than the men's, I barely heard a thing. If it will help, I'll happily volunteer my services to provide a sounding board for what you've learned."

"You've yet to answer my last question."

"Of whether or not the thief could have snuck into

the baths to steal the necklace? Are you referring to the cloaked figure or someone else?"

Katherine's knees weakened with relief. She hadn't known how much she'd needed to hear someone else acknowledge the figure's existence until that moment. Perhaps, subconsciously, she *had* worried that her mind had played tricks on her.

"You saw them as well?"

"This time, yes, but only out of the corner of my eye. I'm rather cross with myself for being so obtuse. By the time I turned to look, you were chasing them. You nearly fell into the pool and..." He looked away, examining the people traversing a cross street. "Suffice it to say that I was more concerned with your safety than with the lurking figure."

Katherine frowned. "Why? I can swim, even in a dress." It wasn't so different from swimming in a shift, to be honest.

"Can you?" He glanced at her, curious. "I heard from Mrs. Fairchild that you were too terrified to get in because of a lack of ability."

Of course the spiteful woman would say such a thing. She must have entered the baths directly on Katherine's heels and lingered in the corridor as Katherine argued with the attendant.

"That was a convenient lie to give me an excuse to

observe from outside the pool. I can swim quite well."

"Oh."

They fell silent, walking on a short ways.

She asked, "Did you see where the figure went? I collided with Mr. Oliver, and when I looked up, the lurker had disappeared."

"I'm afraid I was paying more attention to you. The cloaked figure escaped my mind for a moment."

Katherine sighed. "At least you saw them this time."

"Yes," he agreed with a grin. "Unlike at the Assembly Rooms. That, I'm certain, was no more than an excuse."

Was he flirting with her? He must be extraordinarily bored with Bath if he sought her out for diversion. She'd never thought him much of a rake, being as he pursued a mystery with as much single-minded focus as did she, but given that his first assumption when she'd pulled him into the corridor was an amorous one, perhaps she'd misjudged him.

In any case, she had yet to find a way to defuse that rumor, and walking with his jacket around her shoulders wouldn't help one bit. She shrugged out of the warm fabric and held it out to him, bracing herself against the chill air.

"Thank you. I've warmed up sufficiently now."

He hesitated but took the jacket from her and donned it.

"Do you think the cloaked figure might have managed to enter the women's dressing room while everyone's attention was upon us?"

"It's possible..." Wayland said, drawing out his words.

She completed his thought aloud. "But you don't think it likely."

"Unless they then removed the cloak and hat, no. It is far too conspicuous an outfit for no one to have remarked upon it."

Katherine sighed. She hugged herself for warmth, though their brisk pace kept all but her fingers cozy. "And yet no one seems to have seen the figure."

"No one?" He sounded incredulous.

"Not that anyone cares to admit."

He grumbled several insults about the self-centered leanings of polite society but voiced none clearly, so Katherine didn't deign to comment. Technically, she and her father were a part of said *polite society*, as was Captain Wayland. However, she often shared his sentiments. There was much more to life than what color dress was all the rage or whose jewels would go missing next.

"These peahens have been flaunting their jewelry

enough that it's a miracle nothing has disappeared from the King or Queen's Bath before now. Someone as conspicuous as the lurker feels more like an amateur to me than someone who has preyed on these unsuspecting fools for months, but perhaps I'm wrong."

"I might be inclined to agree, were we not the only two people" — and potentially Mrs. Fairchild — "to have seen the cloaked figure. Even Salmon hasn't, though he claims otherwise. And he spent little time on the subject, so there might have been a few men or women who slipped past without being asked. You'd think he would want to unmask the lurker, given that they might very well be the thief."

"His avoidance of the subject might have been by design," Wayland mused.

She frowned. "You think he is being deliberately obtuse?"

The fellow investigator shrugged. "It's hard to say. If I didn't think Salmon was too stupid to fashion such an elaborate scheme, I might be inclined to believe him the thief all along. It would be ingenious, to ingratiate himself to the marquess enough to install himself as the sole investigator in this matter. Were you discouraged to pursue your line of inquiry?"

Reluctantly, Katherine answered, "Yes." Though

in her case, Lord Bath had seemed to think it impossible that she had a sharp enough mind to contribute.

"I was, as well," Wayland added.

He had been? She worried her lower lip as she walked. Perhaps there was some merit to the idea of Mr. Salmon being the thief. He had been in town for long enough, hadn't he? Several months for certain, though she'd have to verify the time when the Marquess of Bath had hired him. Granted, the thefts would have to have already begun at that point, creating a problem that Mr. Salmon alone could solve. He'd been accused of taking bribes from the thieves who slipped through his fingers in the past; perhaps it was a small leap to thievery.

However, Katherine had already asked Mr. Salmon about his whereabouts. She shook her head. "He can't have been the thief. He was in the Pump Room with Lord Bath at the time of the theft." Or at the very least, at the time Mrs. Oliver had screamed. Katherine would confirm who had been present in the Pump Room with Lyle, who had been there working on his invention. He'd been reluctant to leave with Pru earlier, stating that he was making good progress on the apparatus; however, given that the Pump Room was soon to be flooded by the bacon-brained members of polite society, he had masked his disappointment and capitulated.

"No, he wasn't."

Lost in thought, Katherine started. "I beg your pardon?"

"Salmon. He couldn't have been with Lord Bath at the time of the theft. Or at the very least, not at the time Mrs. Oliver had screamed. I imagine there isn't a very large window between the theft and when it was discovered."

"I imagine not," Katherine agreed, though her mind was on how he could possibly know that Salmon wasn't in the Pump Room when he said. Wayland had been in the pool. What wasn't he telling her? "Bess, the attendant, gave an approximate time of when she left the women's dressing room unattended, and it was no more than five minutes before Mrs. Oliver found her jewels stolen."

Wayland nodded, his expression resolute. "Then he couldn't have been in the Pump Room with the marquess."

"Whyever not?"

"I spotted Lord Bath driving past in his barouche mere seconds before you took chase of the cloaked figure and diverted me."

"You were certain it was the marquess inside?"

Wayland gave her a contemptuous look. "It's a barouche. Open to the air, ridiculous when we haven't had a proper summer this year to begin with. Lord Bath was the sole occupant other than the driver. He's impossible to miss with his cuffs flapping as he waves to his tenants, and I know it was his carriage because of the silver-embossed seal on the door."

"You were in the pool. How could you possibly have seen him?"

"The rear of the King's Bath is more window than wall, none of it glassed in. It faces an alley, but if you're on the north side of the pool, you can see onto the street just south of the baths. Those windows are likely how your lurker gained entrance unnoticed."

Katherine wondered if all those patrons realized how easily they might be spied upon.

However, if Wayland was telling the truth, then the Marquess of Bath couldn't have been in the Pump Room at the time of Mrs. Oliver's scream. He couldn't have been rendered distraught enough to dispatch Mr. Salmon to apprehend the thief. Someone here was lying. Was it Mr. Salmon?

Could he be the thief all along?

CHAPTER EIGHT

F or what felt like the first time all summer, the sun deigned to peek through the clouds. Sydney Gardens Vauxhall teemed with gossiping women, most swarmed around Mrs. Oliver as she recounted, yet again, the tale of her missing necklace from yesterday. Katherine had gathered what information she could in the afternoon and evening, but none of it brought her any closer to finding the thief. She needed her friends' input.

If only it weren't quite so crowded in the garden! Emma pulled at the leash, her tongue lolling as she tried to peek between the legs of the old ladies. Katherine kept a firm hand on the lead, lest the wily dog slip out of her collar and wreak havoc again. As she wrangled the animal past the knot of women, the old gossips' laments peppered the air.

"Why would the thief take pearls? My diamond bracelet is worth ten times as much!"

"Your bracelet? The ruby in my ring is the biggest in all of England!"

"My earrings have been passed down ten generations!"

Lady Dalhousie was the loudest of all. "That can't possibly compare to the heritage of *my* necklace." She draped her hand across the fall of jewels.

Katherine wondered if she ever took it off.

"Did you know, after it left Empress Joséphine's possession, a notorious band of highwaymen nearly took possession of it? It was en route to Britain, to me, at the time. I'm sure you've heard of Alexandre Montereau and his band of thieves? They're infamous in France..."

Katherine doubted very much that such a band of thieves had ever come within sniffing distance of Lady Dalhousie's jewels. She steered Emma away from the gossiping group and around a bend in the gravel walkway. The hedges soared above even her head, soon shutting out the sound. Katherine let out a relieved breath, mirrored by her three companions.

Harriet held her hand out for the leash. "Will you let me walk her, my lady? It is my job."

Shaking her head, Katherine informed her, "I'd like your full attention on the matter at hand."

She sighed. "You're the detective. And Miss Burwick and Lyle. What can you hope to gain from my insight?"

"A fresh perspective."

Striding on Katherine's far side with his hands clasped behind his back, Lyle interjected. "I'm happy to give my opinion, you know, but I fear I must be quick. I have an appointment with Sir David this morning. We're comparing notes regarding our inventions."

"That's wonderful." Katherine covered a momentary sting of envy that Lyle had someone new with whom to spend his time. After all, that had been her design, to have him occupied in completing one of the inventions he lamented often that he had no time to puzzle out. That he was doing so alongside a like-minded friend should have been for the better. "How is your invention coming along?" she asked, genuinely invested in its success. Lyle's inventions had helped many a detective apprehend a criminal.

"Excellently! My hypothesis has proven correct so far. The minerals in the healing waters here will do very well for the purpose I have in mind. All I need to do is build an apparatus to boil the water into steam in a timely fashion and point it toward a contained object. With a few additions, the minerals in the steam should adhere to the recent residue left by a person's touch. I should be ready to test the device soon."

"Fantastic! Brilliant as ever."

Lyle turned pink with the praise. Katherine meant every word. She was proud to have him as her friend. If only she were more adept at discussing scientific principles with him. Alas, their commonality began and ended with investigative techniques.

Pru coughed into her fist. "Not that this isn't fascinating, but aren't you going to tell us the clue you discovered?"

"Oh, yes. I've told you all about the cloaked figure."

Harriet nodded. "We'll be on the lookout for such a scoundrel. Hardly anyone notices a servant; should I see them, I'll follow and see where they lead."

Katherine nibbled on her lower lip. Although she would dearly like Harriet's help, she didn't want to put her maid in danger. "Only do so if you're certain not to be seen. We don't know what this thief is capable of when cornered."

"Of course."

"The clue?" Pru danced behind Katherine, clearly impatient.

After a surreptitious glance to make certain they were shielded from prying eyes, Katherine opened her reticule and removed the vial containing the sliver of silver.

"This was on Mrs. Oliver's clothes?"

"In her shoe," Katherine confirmed. When Pru reached for the vial, she relinquished it reluctantly.

Lyle peered at it closely as well. "It appears to be from some sort of filigree."

"It's a small sample," Katherine answered. "It might be scraped from something larger."

Harriet nodded. "Like a buckle or a button. Should I keep my eyes open for anyone who wears something that might be scratched or tarnished?"

Katherine began to nod, but Pru interjected.

"No need. We already know more than one person who fits that description. Sir Hugh, for example."

"And Mrs. Julien," Harriet added in a small voice. When Katherine glanced at her, she wrinkled her nose in shame. "Forgive me, Lady Katherine. I know you think fondly of the Juliens, but you must consider it."

Katherine knew as much, but hearing it spoken aloud felt like a kick to her kidney. She nodded, her lips pressed together.

Pru held the silver higher to catch the light. "It might even be from something larger. A snuffbox, perhaps the frame of a painting... tarnation, even some of the carriages out front had silver inlay like this! I spotted it while Lord Annandale was showing me his horses."

Lyle took the bit of silver from her to examine it himself. "If it came from the thief, it must have come from his person. Who opens a snuffbox in the middle of pulling a heist?"

Raising her chin, Pru countered, "Perhaps it was a box larger than a snuffbox and the thief carried it to hide the necklace in." She glared daggers at him, daring him to refute her.

Lyle shrugged and handed the vial back to Katherine, who quickly stuffed it out of sight again. "Did any of us see anyone carrying a box? The most likely explanation is that it came from the clothing of one of the two people you mentioned or someone else whose clothing is in disrepair. In fact, the shelf of the dressing room might have been the sharp edge that scraped this bit of silver away."

With a harrumph, Pru crossed her arms over her breasts.

Harriet asked, "Did you see Sir Hugh or Mrs. Julien yesterday?"

"At church, yes. In the King's Bath..." Katherine hesitated. Where had Sir Hugh gone when he had parted ways with Lord Annandale? Could he have rounded the building and entered as the cloaked figure by means of the windows along the back wall?

Lyle clapped Katherine on the shoulder, jolting her back into the present. "It sounds as though they weren't there. Perhaps your next move ought to be discovering where they were at the time of the theft? I don't mean to press you, but I have to hurry along."

Katherine waved her hand, shooing him as they turned the corner of the path, coming full circle. "Run along, then. Thank you for your insight."

He tipped his hat to her. "Always happy to help." Lengthening his stride, he loped toward the nearest exit to the Vauxhall, through the hotel.

Pru immediately insinuated herself next to Katherine. "*Did* you see the suspects near the baths?"

"I did not," Katherine admitted. "Unless Sir Hugh entered after I did..."

She shook her head. "I was out front with Lord Annandale. He never approached."

"Then he wasn't there." Katherine pressed her lips together to keep herself from confirming the same about the Juliens. She'd remarked on their absence earlier, when she'd spotted their grandson in the healing waters. Neither had they shown their faces after Mrs. Oliver had screamed. Where had they been at that time?

She didn't want to suspect such dear, sweet people, but there seemed to be no other explanation. If they didn't have a plausible explanation for their whereabouts at the time...

No. It had to be someone, anyone else. Perhaps they and Sir Hugh weren't the only people to have tattered silver ornaments on their clothing. Somehow, Katherine had to fashion an excuse to look more closely at the long-term visitors.

As they approached the gaggle of gossips once again, Emma yapped happily. She lurched forward with such vigor that she tore the leash from Katherine's hand. Katherine lunged to catch her. She slipped on the loose gravel as she plunged toward the waving leather ribbon of lead, grasping it at the last moment. As she wrapped it firmly around her hand, catching her balance, Emma bolted across her path. The leash pulled taut against Katherine's legs, and she catapulted headfirst toward the nearest gossipmonger, Lady Dalhousie.

They collided in a pile of flailing limbs. Emma cheerfully jumped into the fray, barking. The old ladies shrieked as Lady Dalhousie toppled backward. Several jumped out of the way. Another two tried to save the old woman from a nasty meeting with the walkway. No one tried to save Katherine, and she landed in an ungraceful, stinging heap at their feet.

The moment they righted Lady Dalhousie, everyone set in to scold Katherine.

"You should pay better mind to where you're walking!"

"That mongrel needs to be kept indoors!"

"I've never been so insulted." That, said by Lady Dalhousie as she dusted herself off, was accompanied by a sniff as she gathered up the women following and proposed they all take tea inside the hotel, where it would be safer.

As they walked away, Katherine heard the biddies as they resumed wagging their tongues. This time, Katherine was the subject of their juicy bit of on-dit.

"She's made quite a reputation for herself, you know."

"Aside from dragging good men into hall closets?"

Katherine winced. At all costs, *that* particular rumor needed to find its end. She examined her hands for scrapes as Emma bounded into her lap, planting her paws on Katherine's chest in order to lick her face.

"No, for clumsiness. She was falling over everyone at the Earl of Northbrook's house party, I hear."

The women scurried out of earshot. Katherine

narrowed her eyes as she watched their backs. Her mind was awhirl. Perhaps she had found just the excuse she needed in order to examine people's clothing for traces of broken silver. All she needed was to play on her clumsy reputation while at the Theatre Royal tonight.

CHAPTER NINE

"What is it you wish me to do tonight?"

"Nothing," Katherine answered, her voice a hiss as she escorted Pru down the stairs. The other occupants of the Sydney Hotel followed in their wake or a few mere steps ahead. She didn't dare raise her voice, lest she draw undue attraction.

Unfortunately, Pru had no such qualms. "Nothing?" she repeated, her voice laced with dismay.

Katherine shushed her.

Scowling, Pru leaned her head closer to Katherine's and persisted in protesting. "You can't mean to have me watch the performance." She sounded as though Katherine had suggested she bathe her feet in boiling water.

"That is what one does when one is at a theatre."

"But there's work to be done. An investigation! I cannot sit by and do nothing."

On the first-floor landing, Katherine ensnared her companion's elbow and led her to the threshold of the long hall. It was dark and cold, not open to the public with the Assembly Rooms hosting another dress ball tonight. "You promised if I helped you steer Lord Annandale's attentions away from you that you wouldn't butt in to this investigation."

Pru held herself stiffly. "You can't ask me to twirl my thumbs when there's something I might be doing! Not to mention, whether or not we succeeded in rebuffing Annandale's interest remains to be seen."

"He didn't call upon you yesterday afternoon, nor today," Katherine pointed out.

"Perhaps... but neither did Captain Wayland call upon you."

She rubbed her throbbing pulse in her forehead. "Wayland is not courting me. He has no reason to seek out my company." Perhaps she'd succeeded in driving him away from Bath. After their awkward tea together during which he'd probed for more information regarding the Burglar of Bath and she'd met him with just as much inquiry, without revealing too much of what little she did know, she hadn't so much as seen his shadow. She only hoped that didn't mean he had taken it upon himself to solve the thefts himself.

Katherine fell silent as the last of the hotel patrons filed past. She herded Pru toward the staircase after them. "If you don't hurry, we'll be late to the theater."

"Why are we attending the theatre tonight instead of the dress ball? Won't there be more people at the ball?"

Katherine fought to keep her expression neutral. Her pulse pounded in her throat, an uncomfortable reminder that the true reason she had chosen to attend the theater tonight was because she was afraid. She was hiding from the place where she'd committed her social blunder last time. And perhaps a small part of her was hiding from Wayland as well, until she sorted out these hideous rumors.

"More people, yes. However, the bulk of those who become the victims of the Burglar of Bath are older ladies visiting the town to seek out the healing waters for their aching joints. Older ladies tend not to dance, meaning they'll be more likely to attend the theater instead of the ball."

"I suppose..." Pru didn't sound as believing of Katherine's hasty explanation as she'd hoped.

Katherine added, "Whoever has been stealing from them must keep a close eye on their victims.

They would need to know certain things such as when the jewels would be left unattended and where. The thief took only Mrs. Oliver's necklace yesterday. Clearly, they had come to the King's Bath solely in pursuit of it."

Pru shook her head, befuddled. "But why?"

"That... I haven't quite puzzled out. However, how they must have learned of Mrs. Oliver's intention to go to the King's Bath, as well as her penchant for bringing the necklace with her wherever she went... that, I believe we can lay squarely at Mr. Oliver's feet."

"How so?"

Katherine smirked as they reached the ground floor. "Why, you yourself complained of him whining over his wife's habit of always wearing the necklace. He was also the person who, at the card table, informed everyone of his intention to go with his wife to the King's Bath after church."

Pru loped across the wooden floorboards toward the exit, seeming irritated when she had to wait for the older patrons ahead of them to step through and vacate it. She leaned closer to Katherine and whispered, "You think the thief must have been there, with me?"

"Certainly within earshot."

Why Mrs. Oliver's jewels, that Katherine still couldn't fathom. As the biddies didn't fail to remind everyone, Mrs. Oliver's pearls were worth far less than some of the other items left unattended in that room. Had the necklace simply been the closest thing to the thief's questing fingers? Or might this be more personal? Perhaps they chose their victims based not on fashion — a ridiculous theory — but because Mrs. Oliver had angered them in some way. Katherine mulled over the notion as she followed Pru into the open.

There, she stopped short as she nearly collided with the other woman.

"Did you arrange for an escort?"

"No..." Katherine stepped around her and nearly groaned. Instead of finding her carriage waiting to take them, she found a coach with Lord Annandale's crest on the door — and two men flanking it.

With a smile, the Marquess of Annandale stepped forward. "I heard a whisper ye meant to be takin' in the show tonight. Cap'n Wayland and I foind ourselves without escort. How about we offer our services to you foin ladies?"

Did his brogue get thicker when he looked at Pru? That couldn't be a good sign. At least, it wouldn't be if she still meant not to marry him. Somehow, she seemed to have fascinated him in some way. Either that, or Wayland had a silver tongue. However, as Pru colored up and glanced at Katherine, she seemed more tentative than usual. Was it Katherine's imagination, or might her charge have changed her mind about Lord Annandale?

With so direct an offer, the only answer was to accept, regardless of Pru's feelings for him. Katherine inclined her head. "Thank you, my lord. We would much appreciate your company."

As Katherine approached the carriage, it was not Lord Annandale, but Wayland who offered his assistance in helping her up the steps. She thanked him tightly as she tucked herself into the far corner, facing forward. Despite her hopes, Pru chose the seat opposite her, and Annandale installed himself at her side.

This left the seat next to Katherine free for Wayland to claim. The moment he did and the carriage lurched into motion, Katherine laid her hand on his knee to get his attention. He turned close enough for her to whisper, "Why are you and Annandale here?" After a moment, realizing where her hand was, she snatched it back.

With a frown, he glanced at the pair opposite them making polite conversation — though much to Katherine's chagrin, Pru appeared to be smirking at her. Softly, he answered, "Annandale has admitted to feeling lonesome up in Scotland, with only his sister for company, and hinted that he wouldn't be averse to finding a wife. So I'm doing what you asked me to do, promoting Miss Burwick to him."

"I never asked that!" Katherine bit her tongue before her sharp voice carried too far, for instance across the carriage to where the pair in question might hear. Thus far, the mood was cordial. Pru even smiled at something Lord Annandale murmured in her ear.

Wayland's frown deepened in contrast. "But you're trying to match her—"

"As a cover so I might investigate these thefts freely. There's a reason I left her mother in London. Miss Burwick doesn't want to be matched."

He pressed his lips together as he leaned back against the squabs. After a moment's pause, he muttered, "In that case, this may well prove to be an awkward evening."

Very awkward, indeed. How was Katherine to investigate when she had to play chaperone to Pru and Lord Annandale?

Fortunately, they reached the Theatre Royal before the atmosphere grew strained. Katherine disembarked last, aided by Wayland. She glanced up at the ornate façade of the massive theater, the carved swags beneath the eaves swathed in nighttime shadow.

Above, only the vaguest outline of the statue crowning the decade-old rectangular building could be discerned by the light of the lanterns flanking the broad door. With Lord Annandale escorting Pru, Katherine had no choice but to accept Wayland's arm. It seemed they were stuck in each other's company for the evening.

The antechamber opened to a wide arch leading into the bottom of the theater. Despite the ball held at the Assembly Rooms that evening, the ground-floor seats were packed shoulder to shoulder from the door to the stage at the far end. Although there were seats nestled in a ring directly on the stage, close to the performance, none of these was currently occupied. From candelabra twinkling in sconces between each of the three rows of private boxes, Katherine glimpsed several peers mingling. She couldn't estimate how many, given the distance and the movement of the people as they socialized.

See and be seen. That was the motto of polite society. It wouldn't surprise Katherine if several of those gathered here tonight later made an entrance at the Assembly Rooms. Hoping to avoid Wayland and the gossips placing them together in private, Katherine hadn't planned on moving locations tonight.

Lord Annandale paused just inside the entrance to

address Pru. "Ye've proved a right crack at loo. Do ye play as mean a hand of whist? They're apt to set tables on the second floor, if you're eager."

For a moment, Pru seemed speechless. She shot a pointed glance at Katherine, one that Katherine was able to read altogether too easily. *Wasn't playing loo supposed to discourage him?* With any other man, Katherine wagered it would have. He must be indebted to Wayland for some unknown reason, to encourage Pru at another unladylike activity. Granted, many ladies plied their minds to whist, but Katherine was willing to bet that in Pru's hands, the pastime would be rendered unladylike. Pru did nothing delicately.

Including accept the apologetic look Katherine sent. After all, the only reason Annandale had turned his eye toward her despite her attempts to rebuff him was because of Katherine. With the wry cock of her eyebrow, Pru turned to her escort and accepted.

"I take it you don't mean to follow," Wayland murmured for her ears alone.

"Hardly. She'll be in fine spirits at the card table alone. Let's greet the others here tonight."

He cast her a dubious look. Well he should, because she wasn't one for socializing with vapid men and women unless she needed to learn something. In this case, she was desperate to learn any clue that might point to someone other than the Juliens as having committed the crime. Who wore something silver that might have lost a sliver of embellishment?

To her surprise, as Katherine circulated the antechamber on Wayland's arm and then proceeded up the stairs to the corridor behind the first row of boxes, she spotted altogether too many people who she recognized. Had no one attended the dress ball tonight? As they strolled past the first box, Lady Dalhousie's voice carried.

"How dull it is in Bath of late."

"How can you say that?" Mrs. Oliver's voice was sharp. "I was robbed only yesterday. You'd think that would be enough *entertainment*."

Movement caught her eye ahead. Someone's wide cuffs as he greeted another in a private box two curtains down. The Marquess of Bath. Katherine's stomach lurched. She didn't see his grandmother at his side — thank Zeus for small favors — but panic seized her as she realized she had nowhere to run. At any moment, he would turn and find her in the company of Captain Wayland. If he sent word to her father...

The box next to the biddies had the curtain drawn. Was it occupied or empty? Katherine took a chance and dragged Wayland behind the curtain, pressing him against the divider with a hand to his mouth. Her heart thundered in her ears, and her knees weakened in relief, as she realized that the box was empty.

Next door, Lady Dalhousie's voice was unusually amplified by the roaring of blood in Katherine's ears as her pulse pounded. "*One* theft. They come so few and far between, it's not worth staying in Bath."

As the flood of panic weakened, Katherine became aware of how close she stood to Wayland. She dropped her hand from his mouth, the rough skin where he'd shaved scraping her palm. To alert him to remain silent, she raised a finger to her lips. She eased back, safely away from the heat of his body.

His eyes, wide and dark in the shadow of the private box, narrowed. "What are you doing? This time, I know better than to think you're stealing a kiss." His lips barely moved as he spoke in a whisper. His gaze dropped to her mouth.

"I spotted Lord Bath. He mustn't see us."

Wayland frowned. "Why not? Are you following him?"

"Far from it. You are the enemy of my father, and he is my father's friend..."

"He didn't seem to hold any rancor toward me. Besides, I wouldn't exactly say your father and I are *enemies*."

Not enemies? Hardly! Katherine knew her father did not approve of Wayland, but she didn't have time to think much about it as footsteps thudded along the corridor toward her. Her lungs seized. She bit her lip to stifle a gasp.

Wayland bracketed her shoulders with his warm hands. "You're being needlessly skittish."

She jumped at Lord Bath's voice. "Good evening, ladies. What's this about leaving Bath?"

"On account of the thefts," Lady Dalhousie said with a sniff.

"I assure you, we have the best investigators searching for the thief. You're in no danger should you choose to stay."

"No danger?" Mrs. Oliver parroted, her voice shrill.

Katherine pictured Lord Bath's cringe. She nearly mirrored it herself.

"Madam, my investigators are doing everything possible to find the thief and have your belongings returned. I promise, you won't be inconvenienced for long."

Lady Dalhousie scoffed. "It was only a string of pearls. So common, you can practically pick them out of the sludge. I thought the thief was more discerning..."

Wayland angled himself toward the curtain, reaching to pull back the drape. Katherine stopped him with a hand on his arm, shaking her head. She wanted to hear this while she still had a private moment. Perhaps the gossipmongers would have something new to say regarding the robberies.

Mrs. Oliver answered in a vicious tone. "The thief *is* discerning. Perhaps you need to check your jealousy!"

"Ladies, please, let's act civil. I can see all this talk of the robberies is doing us no good."

Katherine stifled a sigh as Lord Bath continued to placate the old women. She would learn nothing. Taking Wayland by the hand, she searched the corridor for occupants before slipping out with him and towing him to the nearest staircase. There, she dropped his hand to gather her skirts so she wouldn't trip.

"You're frightened over nothing. Lord Bath has nothing against me."

She stopped midway up the stairs to turn back toward him. "My father *does*."

"If you and your father would put aside your prejudices—"

"I know all I need to." Her father didn't make enemies lightly. The fact that Wayland had elevated himself to such a position spoke volumes. Papa didn't approve of his methods, and given that Katherine's methods closely mirrored her father's, neither did she. "Thank you for your escort, but I believe I can handle myself from here on. I would be at an acute disadvantage should word of my association with you reach my father."

"Why?"

"Because he would not approve." Her dowry was firmly hers, not belonging to the husband she never intended to take, or to her father. However, hers was an open, loving family. Her father trusted her.

"Of what, forming your own conclusions?"

She snapped her mouth shut, turned on her heel, and continued up the stairs. Katherine knew Wayland's character, much though he might protest. He wanted something, something he believed she would provide him. He must hold her abilities in high esteem if he thought she had the Burglar of Bath in her sights after only two days in town. Regardless, she didn't intend to share her information.

On the second floor, she set about her task: finding someone who wore shabby silver ornaments. Surely such a person couldn't be that difficult to find.

She approached the first box, where the curtain was

still drawn. Mrs. Quicke's voice wafted out of the box, laden with wistfulness. "Of course I asked Lord Bath to hold more events at Prior Park. I know how you love the plants they import, my dear. I tried hinting to him that Tuesdays are a perfect day to have a bit of a picnic and make a day of it, but he didn't seem very enthusiastic. We'll have to go on our own. But darling, do you think I should wear my ruby necklace or the citrines?"

"To the park?" That gruff, male voice must belong to her husband.

"Yes, of course. I have to look my best."

"You always look radiant, my dear. Wear which- ever tickles your fancy; the jewels are never as lovely as you. Perhaps I'll buy you another if you can't make up your mind."

"Oh, Mr. Quicke..." His wife giggled.

Katherine made a face. She referred to him by his surname? Granted, Katherine hadn't spent much time in their presence, but theirs seemed a superficial marriage. Katherine's stepmother was far younger than her father, so she knew firsthand that marriages involving an age difference could still be based on love and respect... not compliments and jewels.

If Mr. Quicke spent so much effort appeasing his wife with gifts, however... He might be desperate enough to steal someone else's gems and gift them to her.

As Katherine approached the half-open curtain, she stumbled. Her foot caught in the fabric, and what was meant to be a ruse turned into a genuine tumble as she fell into the box, landing squarely in Mr. Quicke's lap. The old man looked flabbergasted. No more so than she. She immediately kicked her legs to try to maneuver herself off of him, only to recollect that she was searching for silver.

None on his buttons. None on Mrs. Quicke's dress, or in the fan she was angrily snapping in front of her face.

Katherine turned to spill herself onto the floor once more, an apology pouring from her lips, when Wayland entered the room. He plucked her from the old man's lap by the waist and deposited her on her feet, brushing her down.

"Terribly sorry, sir" — he nodded to Mr. Quicke, his face impassive as he gave the same perfunctory nod to Mrs. Quicke as well — "madam. She tripped, and I wasn't quite able to catch her. Please, forgive her clumsiness."

Without waiting for a response, Wayland clasped her by the elbow. He steered her down the row of boxes, checking for occupants along the way. When he found no empty ones, he drew her into the shadows of the staircase leading to the boxes above instead. There, he rounded on her.

"Are you mad? What in tarnation were you doing?"

It seemed she wasn't the only detective to use foul language on occasion.

Katherine detangled herself from his hold. "Keep your voice down. I'm trying to investigate."

"By sitting in the laps of married men?"

She made a face. That hadn't been her intention, precisely. "I tripped on purpose to get close enough to see whether or not they were wearing anything with silver on it."

His eyes gleamed with interest, and his expression took on a keen edge as he leaned forward. "Silver?"

Tarnation! She hadn't meant to let that clue slip out. Thus far, she'd managed to keep it contained only to those who were helping with the investigation.

"Yes, I... saw a flash of it on the cloaked figure as they ran." She held her breath, hoping he would believe the hasty lie.

Unfortunately, it seemed as though she'd hesitated too long. Wayland leaned his hand on the wall opposite her, barring her exit and effectively trapping her.

She inhaled sharply, her nose filled with the cedar scent of his cologne.

"Is that the only reason, or have you found silver elsewhere?"

Katherine remained silent, thinking. *You could lie.*

"You can trust me."

He could not be trusted.

"I can help."

That might in fact be true. Reluctantly, Katherine admitted, "I found some silver among Mrs. Oliver's clothes. It could only have been transferred from the thief's person."

"And you think they will wear the same artifact the very next day?"

"Perhaps not," Katherine snapped, angry with herself for placing all her hopes on this one course of action. "But I need more suspects than the ones I have currently. If I can find someone with clothes worn enough to indicate they might own such an item, I'll have more to work on."

For several moments, Wayland studied her, his face impassive. He dropped his arm from next to her. "You must be desperate if you're resorting to falling into people to gain such knowledge."

"It seemed the most expedient means to do so. After Lord Northbrook's house party, it seems I've gained a reputation for clumsiness. I thought I'd use it to my advantage."

He released an audible breath. "Very well. I suppose I'll help."

Katherine bit back a laugh. "You suppose? You forget, I haven't asked."

"I just rescued you from a man's lap. At the very least, you should allow me the dubious pleasure of examining the men's clothing, and you, the women's. The silver could have come from a pocket watch, and that isn't immediately visible."

Why hadn't she thought of that? She smiled grimly, knowing that he had her cornered. She needed his help, and for that, he would surely exact a price.

"Very well. I concede."

"You don't sound happy about it," he commented as he steered her up the stairs to the third-floor boxes.

"I'm not. I'd prefer to do this on my own if I could."

"We'll work faster together."

She sighed as they reached the landing and turned to face him. "I know. That's why I've acceded to you joining me." She said nothing more, not a word of thanks or discouragement.

He caught her gaze and held it a moment, intense.

He broke the silence first. "Has anyone ever told you how exceedingly stubborn you are?"

"Several, but none manage it as eloquently as you." With a saucy smile, she turned to find their next target.

Wayland, as it turned out, was especially adept at turning a stumble from Katherine into an introduction with a couple or group. He flashed his dimple at the women, coaxed the men to brag about their pocket watches, and managed to extricate them from the group without consuming too much of their time. Even so, they only managed to make their way through half the theater before the production began and they sought out their seats. Thus far, the only person with shabby enough clothing to have been the thief was Sir Hugh.

By the time intermission arrived without Pru and Annandale having joined them, Katherine frowned. Fortunately, she felt comfortable enough in Wayland's presence not to worry for her safety. He might steal her investigation out from under her, but she felt secure in the knowledge that he would never harm her.

In fact, he was attuned enough to her distress that when she stood the moment the curtain closed, he did as well, frowning. "What ails you?"

"Have you seen Pru?"

He laid his hand on her back beneath her shoulder

blades, steering her toward the curtain of the box Lord Annandale had reserved. "I'm certain she's caught up at the card table. She was quite popular there on Saturday."

"Perhaps... If you'd like to continue searching, I'll check on her and meet you in the far boxes."

Without waiting for a response, Katherine turned to seek out the second-floor card tables. Instead, she found Mrs. Fairchild strolling with Mrs. Newcomb, the mother of her charge. Curiously, Miss Newcomb was not with them. Perhaps she was hanging on the prince's coattails — he wasn't nearby either, though Katherine had spotted him earlier.

She swallowed a groan and greeted the pair with a smile, hoping to slip around them and find the card tables without hassle. Instead, Mrs. Fairchild planted herself firmly in Katherine's path.

"Why, Lady Katherine, how nice to see you. I hear you're spending the evening with Captain Wayland again. Where has he run off to?"

Katherine clenched her teeth. "I wouldn't know," she bit off. "Contrary to popular opinion, we aren't joined at the hip."

"No?" Mrs. Fairchild raised her eyebrows with a smirk. "Only at the lip, then?"

"We have never kissed. Nor do we intend to."

Confound it, why did she have to rise to the bait? Mrs. Fairchild's smile grew. She looked sly.

"There's no need to deny it so effusively. All women get caught in the end." She tapped her wedding ring, a plain gold band.

Katherine considered stumbling into the pair, if only to break through them to the other side of the walk. Neither had been in Bath long enough to be the burglar. Instead, Katherine opened her mouth to counter. "My business, like yours, happens to be orchestrating such a happening for someone *else*, not for myself." She warmed to the subject as she realized it might be precisely the thing to quell this rumor once and for all, before it made its way back to London. She straightened. "In fact, that is the only reason I was speaking with Captain Wayland in private. I have a client who needs a marriage; he is a wealthy, unmarried man. I'm surprised you haven't considered him for your client. If you'll excuse me, I have to tend to my charge."

Her smile faded the moment she was past the two women and into the corridor once more. Hopefully, that would be the last she heard about the rumors regarding her and Wayland. Squaring her shoulders, she marched toward the private box repurposed as a card room.

And found it empty. Where was Pru? The cards and fish had been left on the table haphazardly, awaiting the return of the players. At least four, by the number of piles. Why had everyone suddenly left?

Uneasy, Katherine hurried through the theater to find Wayland. She kept on the lookout for Pru and her escort as she crossed the row of boxes and the antechamber. How difficult could it be to find a Scotsman, especially one with a brogue like thunder? Unfortunately, he wasn't to be found.

Wayland encountered her first, lingering by the staircase on the first floor of the boxes. "There you are! Did you find her?"

Katherine shook her head. "Have you seen her? Or Annandale?"

He frowned. "I haven't, but..."

"But?"

"I spotted Prince Karl loping for the exit. Miss Newcomb was following in his wake like a stray puppy. I assumed he meant to go to the dress ball."

Katherine frowned. Could something be happening outside? It was out of character for Pru to leave the building without telling Katherine, especially when Katherine had been so easy to find during the performance.

"Let's see if the doorman has seen them."

Wayland followed on her heels as she hastened to the exit. Outside, her eyes adjusted to the bright lamp-lights to either side, their luminescent halos fading fast after ten feet. They silhouetted Miss Newcomb's figure, a wadded handkerchief held to her chest as she peered down the street.

"Miss Newcomb!" Katherine raised her hand and trotted to the young woman's side. "What is amiss?"

With a sour expression, the mousy woman turned to glare at Katherine. "That hoyden of yours! She has the men eating out of her hand. Oh!" The young woman twisted the handkerchief violently.

What was going on? Katherine and Wayland exchanged a confused glance. As she did, a rumble started. She couldn't tell if she heard it first or felt it beneath her feet. She turned.

Horses raced around the corner, four of them. In the lead, Pru rode astride. Her hair tumbled from its pins down her back, waving in the wind. Her skirts were hiked to her knees, exposing her thick ankles and muscular calves. She whooped with glee as she galloped down the street, a nose ahead of Lord Annandale, who grinned just as broadly. As she caught sight of the finish line, Pru leaned closer to her steed's neck and urged it to a faster pace. She charged past, first by half a horse length. Annandale and Prince Karl came neck and neck, with Sir Hugh taking last place. He grimaced at his defeat.

Beaming with triumph, Pru turned her horse and trotted back to the entrance of the Theatre Royal. The other two men pulled alongside her, plying her with praises of her riding prowess.

Despite Pru's repeated proclamations that she didn't want male attention, Katherine had never seen her happier.

CHAPTER TEN

Katherine had never had cause to step into a pawnshop before. Her imagination hadn't quite conjured... this.

The quaint little storefront on the outskirts of Bath couldn't have fit her bedchamber back in London. It was a wonder she, Lyle, the proprietor, and a fourth man bent over what appeared to be a tray of spectacles could fit in such a confined space. Shelves lined the walls, each fitted with a removable tray to better examine the objects at hand. Larger, unwieldy items, including an ornate chest, a tattered valise, and a set of bagpipes, rested in the middle of the room. The proprietor, a thin man with an unshaven chin and an air of weariness, hovered over his customer as she and Lyle entered. The moment the door closed behind them, the man turned and crossed the small room in what seemed the blink of an eye.

His smile wide, he studied her for a mere second before he turned to Lyle. "What can I do for you today, good sir?"

Lyle glanced at Katherine. She shrugged and handed over the slip of paper on which she had listed a description of each of the stolen jewels to date. If the thief needed money quickly, this shop was perhaps the easiest place to sell the stolen jewels. Despite the unlikelihood that the Burglar of Bath would be careless enough to sell the jewels so close to where he had stolen them, Katherine had a better hope of identifying him had he done so here, rather than Bristol or London or... anywhere else, to be honest.

As Lyle engaged with the owner of the shop, Katherine used the man's irritating decision to under-estimate her to her advantage. She perused the trays of jewelry, most of it tarnished or in a slight state of disrepair. Some of it was utterly plain and likely wouldn't fetch much profit at all. A pair of diamond earrings, shaped a bit like a chandelier, caught her eye. Why were they familiar? The shop was so small that she had only to glance over her shoulder to read the paper that Lyle had now given to the shop owner. None of the items matched the earrings, so she continued to browse, cocking her ear to hear the conversation.

The proprietor harrumphed. "What is this? A list of items you mean to sell me?"

"No," Lyle answered. "We're looking to find those items."

"Your wife is looking at all my wares currently. Perhaps she'll find something there to suit her."

"My... what?"

Katherine bit her lip as she glanced toward Lyle. He turned crimson and stumbled over his tongue.

"No. Katherine... She isn't... Not to say that she's unappealing..."

She coughed into her fist to hide her laugh and took pity on him. He lost the ability to speak any time someone mentioned romance. And sometimes if he was in the mere presence of a woman he admired. Thankfully, he was comfortable enough with her not to count her among that number.

"We aren't married," she informed the shopkeeper.

"Forgive me. I assumed, given that you were in his company unchaperoned..."

What was modern society's fascination with chaperones? Katherine was perfectly capable of conducting herself with aplomb no matter with whom she chose to keep company.

"Chaperones aren't required," Lyle answered. "I would never harm Katherine. In fact, I barely even think of her as a woman. I mean..."

Katherine laughed, holding up a hand to stop him from another tongue-tied tirade. "We're here looking for those specific items. Have you bought anything that matches the description of one of those pieces of jewelry? Or perhaps someone has offered one to you and you declined. We'd be much obliged if you can point us in their direction."

With a frown, the proprietor peered at the list once more. "I don't believe I have, but let me consult my books. I record every item so I know the moment something is stolen."

Lyle stiffened. He raised one hand to his hip, where he carried his baton while on patrol. His hand closed on empty air. "I am a principal officer at Bow Street. I assure you, nothing will be stolen."

The shopkeeper hesitated a moment before turning and slipping through a narrow doorway into a secondary room of the shop. He left the door slightly ajar, though Katherine couldn't see inside. Lyle stepped closer to her to peer over her shoulder at the jewelry trays.

"Thieves," he scoffed. "Do we look like thieves?"

"Thieves don't always look like criminals," she

reminded him. "In fact, there must be one hiding in plain sight in polite society at the moment, for them to discover the best places to steal from their victims."

Lyle's nostrils flared as he released a short, disapproving breath. He didn't argue with her, however.

Katherine tapped him on the arm. "Before I forget again, were you in the Pump Room for the entire afternoon on Sunday?"

He straightened and turned away from the jewels. "Until you asked me to accompany Miss Burwick to the hotel, yes."

"Then you were there at the time of the robbery."

He stared at her, his lips pursed as he waited for her to say something more.

"Mr. Salmon told me that he and the Marquess of Bath were in the Pump Room when they heard Mrs. Oliver's scream, whereupon Lord Bath dispatched him to investigate. Is that true?"

Lyle frowned as he said, "I don't believe I saw them together. In fact I don't think I saw the Marquess of Bath at all while in the Pump Room. The pump drawing up spring water is located on the south side of the room, which isn't very large. I would have seen him. He's rather difficult to miss."

Mr. Salmon *had* been lying. Her pulse quickening

as her senses hummed with the thrill of the hunt, Katherine asked, "And Mr. Salmon? Was he there?"

Her hopes sank as Lyle nodded. "He was, at least initially. Making quite a nuisance of himself, if you ask me. I believe he'd left me in peace for half an hour or more by the time I heard Mrs. Oliver's scream. Good riddance. I'd prefer if he didn't prod at my inventions, thank you very much."

The other man in the room straightened and turned, identifying himself as Sir David. He greeted Lyle with a wry smile. "He's been hovering around me while I've been working, as well."

"David! I didn't expect to find you here." Lyle closed the distance between them to pump his friend's hand.

"Nor I you. Are you here on business?"

"Idle curiosity," Lyle answered. "Are you searching for parts for your device?"

"Always," the inventor answered.

"I forgot to mention yesterday, the Dowager Marchioness of Bath introduced me to a fellow who might be able to help you..." Lyle turned toward the door then paused. "Katherine, do you need me?"

She shook her head. "I know the way back to the hotel. Enjoy yourselves."

Sir David bowed over her hand. "It was lovely to

see you again, Lady Katherine."

"You as well," she answered with a smile.

As he and Lyle exited the shop, he didn't lower his voice enough for it not to carry. "It must be quite advantageous to have a noble patron."

"Katherine? She isn't my patron. Ours is an exchange of minds, not money."

"No? My friend, you're missing a great advantage. Think of all you could accomplish if she funded your inventions!"

Katherine frowned at the door as they strode out of earshot. Lyle never asked for money, but he lent her his expertise and inventions on occasion. Should she be funding him? He'd been reticent enough in accepting her insistence on paying for his lodgings while in Bath. However, if she offered him money directly, she feared it might interfere with their friendship. As he put it, they had an exchange of the minds, one that was beneficial to them both. Frankly, she enjoyed his company.

The door to the other room shut as the shopkeeper emerged. He offered the paper to her. "I'm afraid none of these descriptions match what I've sold. However, I cannot say whether they were offered to me without seeing a drawing of the items. An" — he frowned and peered closer at the page — "emerald ring with a spray of diamonds tells me nothing without seeing how the fixture is situated. It might be designed in one hundred different ways!"

Although Katherine might have been able to render a rudimentary drawing of Mrs. Oliver's pearl necklace from memory, she hadn't seen the jewels of the past victims. She smiled tightly. "Sorry to take up so much of your time."

He gestured to the tray of jewelry that she had already perused. "Might I interest you in something else? Maybe some antiquities that have been recently recovered from the area?"

"Antiquities?"

"As you know, the healing springs here have been popular since ancient times. Sometimes coins or artifacts are dug in the area and find their way to my shop. You look like a discriminating lady that appreciates history."

The man was clearly eager to sell her something. "Thank you, but I'm not in need of anything today."

She glanced toward the door, her mind awhirl. Sir David Brewster seemed particularly concerned with money. And although she hadn't inspected him closely for traces of silver, he wasn't particularly well off. He hadn't bought or sold anything while they were here but had distracted Lyle and removed him from the pawnshop instead.

Katherine asked, "The other man who was in here..."

"Oh, Sir David! He is making some kind of telescope... but not one to look at the stars. It is far beyond my comprehension."

"You know him by name?"

The shopkeeper shrugged. "Certainly. He's been a fixture in our little town for quite a few weeks now."

Weeks... or months?

Katherine asked, "And does he come in often?"

"Every few days. Always has something he wants to look at."

"Does he buy or sell?"

The shopkeeper sighed. "Neither, if I'm honest. He spends a great deal of time looking at all the new items I put on my trays, but he always leaves without purchasing anything."

How odd. Katherine thanked the man and exited the shop. She mulled over the information as she walked. Could Sir David be the thief? She'd hardly taken note of him, being that he was an inventor like Lyle and on the fringes of polite society. As a rule, she didn't care for status, but had it influenced her thoughts subconsciously? If so, he might have been lurking in the shadows of more than simply a pawn-shop and she had never taken notice. Considering that she prided herself on her observation skills, either she was lacking, or he had uncovered a role that allowed him to mingle with polite society without being noticed.

As she turned onto Sydney Place, she continued to consider her theory, examining it from all sides. However, a cluster of people caught her attention, including one abnormally tall man. What was Wayland doing chatting with the Juliens and their grandson?

Mr. Julien pushed Scott in his bath chair along the road while Mrs. Julien walked at his side. Wayland was having an animated discussion with Scott, though they were too far away for Katherine to make out the words. Unlike when she'd seen him at the King's Bath, in pain and miserable, Scott seemed lively and inter-ested in the debate. He wore a wide smile. It was mirrored by fond, relieved smiles from his grandpar-ents, though they didn't contribute to the conversation.

Wayland glanced up, noticing her. He raised his hands to bracket his mouth and called, "Lady Kather-ine! Come over here a moment and settle a dispute."

Why did he want her company? Covering her wariness with a polite smile, she joined them.

Wayland swept his hand to indicate his friends. "Lady Katherine, are you acquainted with Mr. and Mrs. Julien? This is their grandson—"

"We've met." Katherine smiled at each of them, ending with Scott. "Nice to see you again."

"And you, Kitty."

She fought back a grimace at that unfortunate youthful pet name.

Wayland smirked. "Kitty?" He cocked his eyebrow.

"The Juliens live near my father's country estate. Scottie and I spent several summers together when we were young." She emphasized the juvenile pet form of his name, raising an eyebrow.

"The years seem to have treated you kindly," Scott answered, unperturbed. He grimaced, his good humor falling away as he rubbed his thigh. "I wish I could say the same."

A curtain seemed to fall over the gathering, smothering their good humor. The corners of Mrs. Julien's eyes crinkled with empathy. Mr. Julien's expression fell.

Wayland coughed into his fist. In a light voice, he said, "Kitty..."

She glared at him. "That isn't my name."

His smile widened. "Katherine, then. I called you over here to settle an argument."

"What is the subject?" she asked, dubious.

"Dogs."

That didn't answer her question in the amount of detail she had hoped, but given that she kept a dog, she likely had an answer to their question. She nodded. "Very well, what is the argument?"

"Which dog breed do you think best suited to hunting? Scottie here says it's an English Water Spaniel, but I firmly believe that no dog can outhunt a Bloodhound. The Thrapston Association for the Prevention of Felons have been using them to hunt sheep-stealers for over ten years!"

"I don't know if owning a dog qualifies me to settle this dispute..."

Scott spoke over her. "Water spaniels flush birds out of the bush. I imagine you can appreciate how that might be useful to one such as I, who cannot walk. And if I trained him to bring me the fowl I shot from the sky..."

Mrs. Julien looked pained. "We'd love to get a dog, Scottie. Perhaps we'll be able to afford one this Christmas." She sounded as though she were promising a child a toy, but deep shadows of emotion crossed her face.

Scott frowned and looked at his leg. "If we hadn't come to Bath..."

"We're here for you, son," Mr. Julien answered, clapping his grandson on the shoulder. "Your grandmother didn't pawn off her jewels for nothing. These healing waters must help with the pain a bit, if so many people flock to them."

Oh dear. Katherine felt their pain acutely. Scott's, as well. Sullenness settled across him, displacing all hint of the joy from earlier.

If nothing else, she sought to distract him from that. "The best hunting dog is a pug."

Wayland barked out a laugh. "You must be joking."

She lifted her chin as they resumed walking down the street. "Not so. If you're hunting water fowl, perhaps the spaniel is best. If you want sheep-stealers, use a bloodhound. But Emma's had her uses as well. She has an uncanny knack for finding small items. Why, her knack for pilfering items gave me a vital clue at Northbrook's party... not that I realized it until later."

"What happened at Northbrook's party?" Scott asked, craning his neck. His withdrawn demeanor faded, replaced with open curiosity.

"Mr. Lyle Murphy of the Bow Street Runners—"

Katherine cleared her throat, earning herself a pointed look from Wayland.

He sighed. "Forgive me, of Sir John's Men."

Satisfied, she nodded, motioning for him to resume the tale.

"He apprehended the Pink-Ribbon Murderer, with help." Wayland nodded to Katherine. "Katherine discovered the fiend's identity, though in the process she nearly found herself killed."

Scott looked appalled. "Lawks, Kitty! You shouldn't dabble in that sort of dangerous business."

Even a man she hadn't met in over a decade thought he had a say in her life.

Wayland shot her an apologetic look. "I do wish she had been more careful, but if not for her, more women might have died. We should be proud of her."

Katherine opened her mouth, but she didn't know what to say. Was Wayland proud of her for solving the murders before he did? That made no sense. He was her father's rival — by extension, hers as well. Shaking her head, she fell back as he expounded on the tale of Northbrook's party, including the part where Emma stole the item that ended up giving her the final clue. He left out a few details, but she didn't correct him. Instead, her mind turned to her current case.

Mr. and Mrs. Julien were desperate for money to

help their grandson. She couldn't blame them, for she would have helped if she could. Even so, she couldn't stifle the voice asking if one of them was the Burglar of Bath, likely Mrs. Julien, given that her husband had such difficulty walking. As Katherine meandered around the back of the bath chair to reach Mrs. Julien's side, she paid particular attention to the state of their clothes. Worn — in fact, Mr. Julien had both elbows of his jacket darned — but neither of them wore any hint of silver. Not even on Mr. Julien's shoes, though those seemed to be caked in reddish clay on the heel.

When she reached Mrs. Julien's side, Katherine asked, "I was surprised not to see you and your husband at the King's Bath the other day. Scottie was there. Why not you?"

Wayland halted in his tale for a moment, giving her a peculiar disapproving look. Katherine ignored him.

Mrs. Julien glanced from her grandson to Katherine. She pasted on a smile, but it fluttered at the corners. "We would have liked to be there for him, but we weren't in Bath at all. You see, there's an apothecary down in Bradford-on-Avon that produces a special tonic that helps to reduce Scottie's pain. Where his injury is located, it's very difficult to find remedies that help. We need to see apothecaries that specialize in that sort of traumatic pain."

Mr. Julien added, "We were there all day, if that's what you're asking. The public coach didn't arrive until five o'clock to return us to Bath."

As much as Katherine would like to take them at their word, she would have to verify that what they claimed was the truth. She couldn't rule them out until then. Once she did, she would feel much lighter.

"I didn't mean to pry," she said as gracefully as she could manage. With the incline of her head, she said, "Don't let me keep you. I must return to the Sydney Hotel."

"As must I," Wayland added. "May I escort you there?"

With the Juliens as witnesses, Katherine couldn't protest. Instead, she laid her hand lightly on his sleeve and walked away with him. His arm felt as hard as stone. The click of their boots rang on the cobblestones, filling the silence between them.

When they were out of earshot, he hissed, "What business did you have asking them such questions?"

Katherine tried to retract her arm, but he laid his hand over hers, pinning her to him as he stopped and turned his head to examine her.

"I am investigating a string of thefts, as you well know."

The Sydney Hotel loomed not twenty feet away, the footman by the door too far away to be privy to their heated conversation. Given the tension between them — obvious at a distance, no doubt — the stranger seemed curious. He barely glanced at the women as he opened the door to guide them out of the establishment.

"Mr. and Mrs. Julien are kind, generous people. They've given everything to seeing that their grandson has the care he needs to survive. You don't know the scars the war leaves on a man, inside and out. Too many people aren't equipped to help, and so they abandon their loved ones to endure the aftermath alone."

The vehemence in his voice rendered Katherine speechless. He was a war veteran as well, so he knew precisely the pain Scott Julien endured. Perhaps not the physical pain, for he still seemed of whole body, but emotionally... His hazel eyes held shadows that she didn't dare ask to bring into the light. Who had abandoned him upon his return from the war with Napoleon?

"I know they are," she whispered. In truth, she wanted to give up thinking of them as suspects at all.

But she was a detective, and if she wanted to unmask the thief, she had to follow every avenue. She'd unearthed secrets before that people preferred to leave hidden. The truth would exonerate Mr. and Mrs. Julien.

Or it might implicate them further.

Firming her voice, she added, "They weren't at the baths on Sunday, Wayland. Don't you find that the least bit suspicious?"

He dropped his arm and moved a step away, gesturing at the distant pair and their grandson. "They were fetching medicine for their grandson. You want to suspect them for so altruistic a motive? I can't believe you, Katherine."

"Katherine!"

For a moment, she thought there was an echo. Belatedly, she realized someone else was calling her name. Harriet sprinted to them and slid to a stop, bracing her hands on her knees as she gasped for breath.

"Katherine, you must come at once. There's been another theft!"

CHAPTER ELEVEN

A nother theft.

"When? Where?"

Harriet caught Katherine's hand and dragged her down the street, past the Sydney Hotel. Wayland followed, keeping pace at an easy lope while Harriet babbled.

"It happened over an hour ago just down the street... or at least I think it did. You see, we don't know when it truly happened, for Mrs. Quicke wasn't home to find her jewels missing, and she's only just returned an hour ago. I've searched everywhere for you. I even ran down to the baths in case you were with Lyle in the Pump Room! I knew you'd want to be the first person to investigate the scene of the crime, lest something be disturbed. But it's taken so long to find you—"

Katherine dug in her heels and pulled her maid to a stop. "Harriet! Take a breath. You're turning purple."

As the other woman gasped for air, Katherine turned her. She bracketed Harriet's shoulders in her hands and schooled her to breathe evenly. When the maid seemed a bit less panicked, Katherine spoke calmly.

"Let's go through this slowly, now. Mrs. Quicke is the victim?"

Harriet nodded. "Her jewels were taken from the townhouse she rents on Sydney Place."

That was a good start. "Has she said which jewels?"

"The citrines. I don't know what, precisely, or from where in the house. You may have to learn that from her."

Katherine nodded. "And this occurred an hour ago?"

"So she thinks. The thief only took her citrines, so she's been saying that her return must have frightened him away from the other jewels."

"Where is Mrs. Quicke's townhouse?"

"This way." Harriet turned on her heel, this time not leading Katherine by the hand. She and Wayland hastened in the maid's wake, even though their destination became apparent before too long.

It seemed as though every gossip in Bath had amassed outside Number 10 Sydney Place. The growing crowd drew the attention of passersby, who invariably slowed or stopped to learn more about the disturbance. The Marquess of Bath waded into the thick of the crowd, reassuring everyone he passed that the authorities had the matter well in hand and they had nothing to worry about.

As Katherine drew closer to him, hoping to discover what he knew about the theft, Lady Dalhousie's loud laments drowned out any hope she had of gaining Lord Bath's attention.

"Why *her*? My necklace is worth far more than a few paltry citrines!"

Katherine groaned. Thankfully, the sound was devoured by more of Lady Dalhousie's mournful bragging. As if all of Bath didn't already know the origin and worth of her necklace!

Lady Dalhousie was rivalled in her enthusiasm by only one person — a hysterical Mrs. Quicke. The woman, no more than ten years older than Katherine, was far removed from her usual elegant, composed demeanor. Wisps of her hair had escaped her coiffure, thrown up in all directions as if the strands couldn't decide how best to free themselves. The woman's fingers dug into Katherine's arm as she stumbled into her path.

"Oh, Lady Katherine, the worst has happened!"

She, at the very least, did not seem the least bit pleased to have been robbed. Tears leaked from the corners of her eyes, tracking through the powder she'd carefully applied for her outing. She looked distraught.

Katherine tried in vain to detach herself. "All is not lost, Mrs. Quicke. I'm certain Lord Bath will see the culprit apprehended and your jewels returned safely."

"He violated my *bedchamber*."

Gritting her teeth, Katherine tried to wedge her hand beneath Mrs. Quicke's fingers. If the woman was going to go into vapors, Katherine would prefer she do so while holding her hand and not crushing her arm.

She amended that opinion a moment later when Mrs. Quicke proceeded to squeeze her hand in a grip like iron.

"I'm certain you're perfectly safe," Katherine muttered, trying not to show her pain. Nor her impatience to be rid of the victim — tarnation, she had a crime scene to investigate! "Lord Bath will increase the security on the street, and no one will bother you again."

"It won't help." Mrs. Quicke collapsed against Katherine's shoulder, sobbing.

Why now? It wasn't as though Katherine knew the woman personally. She simply happened to be the closest body who didn't seem to blame Mrs. Quicke for having been robbed instead of them. Even Mrs. Oliver seemed vexed that she was no longer the source of attention.

In between the woman's sobs, Katherine deciphered her words.

"Our butler... we hire... hired him when we rented the house... He was... stationed... by the *door*" — her voice heightened with distress on the last word — "the entire time! He... he never saw... nobody entered! They had to..." Her shoulders shook with sobs, and she buried her face in Katherine's sleeve, muffling her voice. Katherine gleaned only two distinct words after that: *climb* and *window*.

"You believe the thief climbed up to your bedchamber window and entered that way?"

Mrs. Quicke raised her teary, red-rimmed eyes and nodded. "He must have. I left my citrines on the vanity table when I went out in these." She touched the ruby pendant at her throat. "The window faces the alley. If he climbed in once, who is to say" — tears spilled down her cheeks — "he won't again! He left so much behind. We aren't safe!"

When she stumbled forward as if to cry into

Katherine's shoulder once more, Katherine deftly side-stepped. She guided Mrs. Quicke into Wayland's arms instead. At his irked expression, Katherine shrugged and gave him a look of apology. This was business. She had to investigate that alley before Mr. Salmon arrived on the scene — if she wasn't already too late.

The crowd, gathered around the front door to the townhouse, didn't seem to notice as Katherine slipped into the shadows of the nearby alley. Her slipper sank into moist earth instead of cobblestone. When she glanced down, she frowned. No, not earth. Clay, very like the clay affixed to Mr. Julien's shoe.

She hurried on, paying more attention to the ground, lest she disturb the evidence. As she found the first clear shoe impression, she grinned to herself. If only Lyle were near! He had a plaster that hardened in the print to leave a perfect impression of the boot size. Fortunately, she always kept string in her reticule. It would provide her with something.

As she kneeled next to the footprint and fumbled with the ties on her reticule, a man's boot wedged its way into her vision, squarely on top of the shoe print!

"Lady Katherine, what are you doing here? This is a restricted area."

Glaring, she craned her neck to face Mr. Salmon.

"You know very well what I'm doing here. I'm investigating."

"The Marquess of Bath hired *me* to catch the thief. Kindly remove yourself and stay out of my way."

"I can help you," Katherine said through gritted teeth. A blatant lie. She had no intention of sharing information with Mr. Salmon, especially when she suspected he might be the thief.

"I don't need your help," he said. "Now, will you leave, or shall I call for the marquess? He brought me over straight away when he heard the news."

Why was he so adamant to rub her nose in the fact that Lord Bath had hired him? Had he never been hired before? Katherine rubbed shoulders with marquesses and dukes all the time, so Lord Bath's title had little bearing on her esteem for him. Rather, that had been built on having interacted with him in the past as well as her father's good opinion of him. Although, given that he had fallen prey to a lazy, inept detective such as Mr. Salmon, perhaps she ought to amend her opinion of the marquess's intelligence and good sense.

Katherine straightened and shook out her skirts. *You ruined my evidence.* And judging by the trampled earth mere paces away beneath a second-story window, she was willing to wager that he had already destroyed any hope of finding untarnished evidence. She was wasting her time out here.

"Very well. I'll leave. Good day, Mr. Salmon."

She turned on her heel and strode back to the gathering, but she didn't go far. If Mr. Salmon had been preoccupied all this time in examining the alleyway, perhaps he hadn't yet had a chance to search through the townhouse. Katherine hastened toward the ajar door, hoping no one would stop her.

As she eased it open and stepped inside, she groaned. Footprints, outlined in clay, marred the floor, leading up the stairs. Mr. Salmon must already have been in here. She shut the door behind her.

"Salmon?" Footsteps sounded, and a moment later, the Marquess of Bath emerged from the staircase. He stopped short. "Lady Katherine, whatever are you doing here?"

"I thought I'd lend my eye," she told him succinctly. "Mr. Salmon seems quite at the limits of his capabilities with the alley."

Lord Bath hesitated. "I don't think your father would approve if I let you into a crime scene. It isn't good for your sensibilities."

Katherine balled her fists. Violence wouldn't be good for her feminine sensibilities either, but he tempted her sorely every time he sought to lay out her future and her choices. Tightly, she told him, "My father would encourage me to do so if it so pleased me. Mrs. Quicke has personally asked me to look into the matter, to make certain that she will be safe tonight."

When the marquess looked dubious, Katherine waved her hand toward the door.

"Ask her for yourself, if you'd like. She's currently with Captain Wayland, who is helping to calm her. She is in quite the agitated state."

As he released an audible breath, Lord Bath's shoulders bowed inward. He gestured to the stairs. "This way."

As Katherine followed him to the second floor, she noticed the clay clinging to his heels. With every step, he left a reddish imprint on the runner. Sard it all, had every person in Bath strolled through that alley today? Even Lyle, skilled though he was, would never be able to retrieve evidence from it now!

On the second floor, she found the bedchamber easily. The bed was neatly made, every ivory-backed comb and brush on the vanity was neatly in place, but if Mrs. Quicke was to be believed, the jewelry she had left there was absent.

"Do you know precisely what was taken?" Katherine asked.

Lord Bath frowned as he turned from his position by the window. "She didn't tell you?"

"She was sobbing over her citrines, but she didn't specify in what form they were taken. Was it a necklace? A ring? Earrings?"

"All of the above, I believe. If I recall correctly from the last time she wore the jewels, they came as a set."

"And they were all left on the vanity..." Katherine peered around the room, her hopes sinking. It didn't look as though there was much to be found here. Lord Bath had obviously been in the room, for there were footprints in places along the floor, including ones he had recently made when he'd entered. She would find no clues there. What else might the thief have disturbed? If, indeed, this theft was committed by the Burglar of Bath.

Katherine peered around the room. Atop the wardrobe was an ornately carved box. Her height granted her the leverage to see inside when she opened it. Myriad jewels winked back at her, some clearly more expensive than a set of citrines. Why then had the thief snatched the jewels they had, if not because they had been left in the open?

Opportunity. That seemed to be the thief's motive,

plain and simple. The quickest, easiest jewels to reach their fingers.

"Are we certain the hired butler didn't take the set? It was left on the vanity for anyone to see." The thief couldn't have known as much, however; it would have been a stroke of luck, if indeed the burglar had entered by the window to find the jewels right in front of their nose, ready to pluck.

"It is a possibility. Do you think I should have him detained and questioned?"

Katherine pursed her lips then shook her head. "If it were him, why didn't he abscond with all the jewels? The worth of that box must be enough to feed, clothe, and house a person for the rest of his days. Much more stability than a mere set of citrines will gain him."

"Then you think the theft committed by the Burglar of Bath after all."

At the mention of the name, the marquess looked a bit queasy. Katherine crossed to him, laying a hand on his sleeve. He had his cuffs rolled up for once, baring his forearms to the elbow. "Perhaps you're right. This is too much for my delicate sensibilities. Why don't you give me a moment more to search and make certain that Mrs. Quicke will be safe, and then we'll go down?"

Nodding, Lord Bath moved to the doorway, where he hovered as Katherine searched for traces of silver. If the theft had been committed by the notorious Burglar of Bath, perhaps they had left the same clue as they had at the last crime scene. She started at the window, where the shutters were open wide to let in the air. Mr. Salmon was still trampling the evidence below as he now ran his hand up and down the walls as if searching for a handhold.

Although Katherine was no acrobat, it was clear to her that the wall of the neighboring house was close enough that a person in good physical form, perhaps without skirts to hamper their progress, would be able to use the proximity to lever themselves between the two walls and climb that way. However, it would be conspicuous if they were caught. Therefore, the theft had occurred at a time when no one had been walking past, or else the thief was extraordinarily agile and quick at climbing. Which, given the speed at which Mrs. Oliver's necklace must have gone missing, Katherine couldn't rule out. The thief was quick enough not to be noticed.

"If this was the Burglar of Bath, I believe we should leave the matter for Mr. Salmon to handle." Lord Bath's voice began a bit tentatively but gained confidence as he spoke.

Katherine turned from the window. "The theft,

certainly. But poor Mrs. Quicke is worried over returning to her room tonight. I must make certain that it is safe."

"Mr. Salmon can handle that matter, as well. What would you know of matters of security?"

"Perhaps I can be of assistance."

Katherine heard Wayland's voice before he stepped up behind Lord Bath, lingering in the doorway. Wayland stood a head taller than the other man. His height, or perhaps his military posture, granted him an air of authority. His voice rang like steel.

"I am an expert in security. I'm certain you're aware of this, given my background. What seems to be of concern?"

For once, Katherine was pleased for his interruption. She beckoned him closer. "Mrs. Quicke is beside herself about returning to this room when it has been so violated by the thief. I'd like to reassure her of her safety."

Wayland shouldered past Lord Bath, who weakly repeated, "Shouldn't we leave this to Mr. Salmon? We don't want to disturb anything."

"I am a detective as well," Wayland answered, his voice commanding. "I assure you, we will disturb nothing. Come, Katherine, what do you know of the entry?"

"The thief entered by way of the window. It was unlatched and open when I arrived. I imagine it must have been so during the day as well, to provide air to the room, for the latch looks sturdy." Katherine demonstrated by pulling the shutter partway closed and showing him the latch.

As he leaned closer, their shoulders touched.

"What are you looking for?" he whispered.

"Silver," she shot back.

With a nod, he stepped back. "I concur, but we should check the room for any signs that the thief might have entered by another route."

"Is that necessary?" Lord Bath asked. "Like I said, Mr. Salmon needs..."

"It's necessary," Wayland answered, his voice flat.

"The thief might not have been an intruder," the marquess persisted. "Lady Katherine surmised that the butler might be at fault."

When Wayland glanced toward her, Katherine winced. She didn't like fingering suspects without proof, particularly those of the working class. Altogether too often, the nearest titled peer was happy to blame someone of a lower status without a shred of evidence, and the matter was closed. She hadn't thought Lord Bath to be such a sort, but it appeared she was wrong.

"It was one possibility," Katherine muttered under her breath. "I'm merely a matchmaker, so what would I know?"

It hurt her to speak the words aloud. She was much more than a matchmaker. She had the experience and intellect to rival Mr. Salmon. No, that wasn't much competition at all — to rival Wayland.

In this case, he didn't leap to her defense. He knew, as well as she, that confirming the suspicion that had slipped past her lips might lead to an arrest. They needed evidence to support such an eventuality. She wanted justice, not an easy answer. Though, given that Lord Bath had hired Mr. Salmon, he might have hoped for the latter.

Ushering Lord Bath backward a few steps, Wayland drew the door to the room shut behind him as he spoke. "I must examine the door in case this was the mode of entry. Do you think this looks sturdy? Katherine, perhaps you should lock it, so we might see if it poses much of an obstacle to intruders."

Lord Bath huffed. "If it were locked, the thief would not have been able to gain entry."

"We aren't looking for the thief," Wayland reminded him, his voice muffled by the closed door. "Our aim is to determine whether or not Mrs. Quicke will be safe in her room tonight. Katherine?"

Smirking, she turned away and started to search the room as thoroughly as she could under such circumstances. She couldn't take too long or else Lord Bath would certainly barge in again. As she looked, she called, "I don't see the key. Give me a moment, and I'll find it."

Upon finding nothing silver where it might easily be seen, Katherine dropped to her hands and knees on the clay-caked rug. She peered beneath the vanity, hoping that the daylight would catch on a sliver of silver and she would be able to say with certainty that this crime had been committed by the same person as the last. Not a glimmer of metal. She checked beneath the bed and along the windowsill for good measure, only to come up empty handed. Could this theft have been the fault of the butler, after all?

As she glanced out the window, she spotted the dark cloak of a figure lurking down the lane as they emerged from behind a bush on the corner of the house. The cloaked figure! This was the third time she'd seen them, the second time it had been a part of a theft. She burst out of the room, solidly colliding first with Lord Bath and then careening into Wayland, who caught her by the upper arms.

"Katherine? Are you all right?"

She detached herself and babbled as she hastened

toward the stairs. "I can't find the key. I'm afraid Mr. Salmon will have to do so after all. So sorry to disturb anything! I'd best get out of your way."

Her slippers clicked against the stairs as she took them at a jog. Dimly, she heard Wayland call her name again, but she didn't have time to stop. She exited the townhouse and turned down the alley.

The only person she saw was Mr. Salmon. *Sard it!*

No, she wouldn't admit defeat so easily. She hiked her skirts above her knees and bolted down the lane. Mr. Salmon shouted as she nearly ran him down, steering to the side at the last moment as he straightened. At the end of the house, near the bush, she peered down the adjacent street. Neat fences abutted the lane, without a single person to be seen. She was too late. Her frustration mounting, she examined the bush, but she didn't find a single trace that someone had been loitering there, not even a smear of clay aside from her own footprints.

Swearing under her breath, she used the lane to avoid the crowd at the front of the building as she meandered back to the Sydney Hotel. Once again, the cloaked figure had been lurking nearby. That must mean that Mrs. Quicke's and Mrs. Oliver's thefts were connected. This was, in fact, the Burglar of Bath.

Unfortunately, Katherine hadn't been quick enough to catch him.

Her route took her along a back entrance to the Sydney Garden Vauxhall. Just as well, for she wasn't in the mood to speak with anyone who might be loitering by the main door, as Harriet had been earlier. Dejected, she dragged her heels as she crossed through the Vauxhall toward the looming hotel at the front.

As she neared, she spotted a figure tiptoeing around the corner of the building and attempting to use the back entrance. Was that... Pru? Katherine quickened her step.

"Pru?"

Flinching, the other woman turned. She looked guilty.

"Where have you been?" Katherine had been out all morning and hadn't noticed Pru's absence, but the other woman didn't know that, judging by the expression she wore. She looked like a child caught stealing sweets from the pantry.

"I've been..."

Pru grappled for words, but a plausible excuse seemed to elude her. When she next spoke, Katherine hoped it was the truth.

Pru's breath gushed out on a sigh as her shoulders slumped forward. "Lord Annandale has just given me my first driving lesson. He let me take his coach around Bath!"

That was much more innocent an explanation than Katherine expected. What would she care if Pru learned how to drive? It was more unladylike behavior, but Pru ought to have realized by now that Katherine embraced such things in her own life and others.

"How did you enjoy it?"

A wide smile broke across Pru's face. "Why, it was exhilarating! It's so freeing to be able to act as I please without worrying whether a man will find me to his liking. I've been under Mama's thumb for far too long."

Given that she was older than Katherine, she had to agree.

"You must be doing well in driving away Annandale's romantic opinion of you, then." For all that he had given her a driving lesson, it wasn't precisely the sort of thing a man did when he was courting a woman... was it?

Pru's cheeks turned pink, and she gave a little shrug. "As well as can be expected. I've thoroughly demonstrated that I'm not at all like the insipid young girls who usually seek to catch his eye."

Did that mean she had successfully rebuffed Lord Annandale or not? Katherine frowned.

"Oh," Pru exclaimed. "I meant to ask how your

investigation was progressing. It slipped my mind earlier this morning, but I'd dearly love to help if you've a moment to apprise me on the situation."

Their agreement had been that she *wouldn't* interfere in Katherine's investigation. Then again, the Burglar of Bath was proving to be more elusive than Katherine had hoped. With so little clues, perhaps Katherine needed help.

She was spared the need to answer as Sir Hugh exited the stairwell, which led directly to the rooms above — near Lady Dalhousie's room if Katherine recalled correctly, far removed from the one Sir Hugh had been allotted. His face brightened as he beheld them.

"Miss Burwick, there you are! I hoped I might encounter you if I went into the garden."

Pru blinked rapidly. "You... sought me out? Why?"

Why indeed.

Sir Hugh held his hands up in surrender. "You play a wicked hand of loo, Miss Burwick. I wondered if perhaps you had a few moments to teach me how to better play. You never seem to lose."

Her cheeks flushed with pride. "I do sometimes lose. The key is in knowing when your cards aren't strong enough, and when you can outbluff your opponents. I have some time now, if you'd care to sit and play."

"Absolutely," Sir Hugh exclaimed. "I'll find us a table in the hotel straight away."

He hurried off, at which point Pru turned to Katherine, an apologetic look on her face. "Would you mind playing chaperone? I can't very well be seen alone with him."

And yet she didn't mind being seen alone with Lord Annandale during her driving lesson. How very curious.

Katherine accompanied her charge and resigned herself to playing chaperone for the rest of the afternoon. Pru barely sat at the table before they were joined by the other gentlemen who had chosen to take lunch in the hotel, including Prince Karl and, soon, Lord Annandale. As Katherine hovered in the background, trying to supervise the game without being noticed, a hot gaze pierced the back of her neck.

When she turned, she found Mrs. Fairchild seated at another table with Miss Newcomb and her mother. The rival matchmaker did not appear the least bit pleased. Her expression boded ill for Katherine's week ahead.

CHAPTER TWELVE

———————————

The Burglar of Bath had to have gained entry into Mrs. Quicke's townhouse somehow. Had it been through the window, as she had been adamant? When she had been in the room, looking down, Katherine had thought it possible. Now, the next morning, with the sun slanting down the tall side of the townhouse and into the alley where she lingered with Lyle, she started to second-guess her judgement.

"Mr. and Mrs. Quicke are taking breakfast at the hotel. Lyle, climb up to the window before they get back, would you? I want to see if it's possible."

He straightened with a sigh of disgust from the trampled footsteps he'd been examining. The clay had dried overnight, leaving myriad impressions, all of them likely belonging to Mr. Salmon. Her friend gave her a dubious look. "What makes you think I have the skill to scale the side of a building? I'm an inventor."

And a thin one at that, Katherine had to admit.

Still, she knew his physique to be deceiving. "And you're one of Sir John's Men. You chase down criminals all the time."

"Yes... through the streets, not up tall buildings!"

Katherine opened her mouth to argue further — after all, she couldn't possibly climb. Not only would her skirts hamper her progress, but she had never done so before. Seeing as the side of the building was made of stucco, with little handholds for purchase, she had no hope of being able to climb the wall. As a shadow fell across the back of her neck, abruptly cooling her, she shut her mouth and turned.

Wayland arched an eyebrow. "What are you arguing about?" His eyes gleamed. No doubt he hoped that they had found a clue as to the thief's identity. If only Katherine were so lucky...

"I want to see if it's possible for the thief to have climbed in through Mrs. Quicke's window. She isn't at home, so she won't raise the alarm at the moment, but that may change." She gestured at her reticent friend. "If Lyle would only try—"

Wayland reached for the buttons on his jacket. "I'll do it."

"You will?"

"Yes. I'm a captain, if you've forgotten. I keep myself in fighting shape."

As he peeled away his jacket then handed it to her and rolled up his sleeves, Katherine couldn't help but study his fighting form. She'd noticed in the pool that he had the defined muscles to indicate an athletic build. He proved it further with every inch of skin he revealed on his muscular forearms. The day was chilly, but he didn't appear affected.

In fact, Katherine no longer felt chilled. Perhaps it was the warmth of the jacket over her sleeve, but she suddenly felt rather hot. As Wayland caught her ogling his arms, he winked. Her cheeks warmed, but she tried stoically to ignore the reaction.

"Are you ready?" Wayland asked as he stretched his arms over his head, then from side to side. Was he doing that to warm up his muscles or to show off?

Katherine steeled her spine and nodded.

After taking a deep breath that expanded his chest and taxed the buttons on his waistcoat, Wayland backed to the mouth of the alley. He took a running leap and then, true to her prediction, used the close proximity of the wall opposite to clamber up to the second story. He hooked his fingers onto the sill, holding himself aloft a moment before he dropped back to the ground, bending his knees as he landed.

There was her answer. The Burglar of Bath could have climbed in through Mrs. Quicke's bedchamber window and left via the same means.

"Thief!"

Katherine stiffened at the call. Wayland straightened, whirling. The wooden rattle of a city watchman's alarm filled the air, calling his compatriots. It seemed Lord Bath had increased the number of men in the area, true to his word. The only problem was that the dark-clad group now converging on their position thought them to be criminals.

Wayland caught her by the hand. "Run!" he shouted. Lyle lurched into motion, Wayland on his heels as he dragged Katherine to follow. With her free hand, she gathered her skirts to keep from tripping.

"Shouldn't we stop and explain?" They weren't thieves — they were detectives!

Neither man seemed keen on the notion.

At the nearest street, near where Katherine had seen the cloaked figure, they split paths. Lyle turned right, whereas Wayland urged Katherine to the left. He didn't slow the punishing pace for even a moment. They raced past neatly fenced yards. At the next alley, Wayland turned right. He turned again shortly after, and again. Did he have a map in his head to follow, or was he choosing their retreat at random? Katherine didn't have the breath to ask. She was sorely pressed simply to keep running.

The sounds of pursuit grew dimmer, though perhaps that was in part due to the roar of blood rushing in her ears. Wayland turned them down another alley. Ahead, a long awning projected over a sunken door, the entranceway providing room and cover for the various crates stacked there. As they came abreast, Wayland stopped. Without preamble, he bracketed Katherine's waist and spun her to press into the door. It held beneath their combined weight as he pressed in after her, concealing her body with his.

The beat of his heart thrummed against her chest. His breath tickled the hair by her ear as she strained to hear whether or not their pursuers would find them. She heard the clatter of boots and held her breath, afraid to give away their position. Wayland pressed closer, stiffening as he waited for the danger to pass. His warm body surrounded her.

The noise faded away as the patrol continued down the street rather than entering the alley where she and Wayland hid. He held still a moment more, making certain no one else pursued them. She took shallow breaths, trying not to breathe too loudly.

When he pulled back slightly, she knew the danger had passed. He gazed down at her, his eyes dark as he hunched beneath the awning. Suddenly aware of her hands, she laid one on his chest, feeling the shift of his muscles beneath his clothes and the firm beat of his heart beneath the tips of her fingers. At that moment, she realized that she must have dropped his jacket in the scuffle, for she didn't have it.

"Tarnation," she muttered under her breath, snatching back her hand. "I lost your jacket on the way. I'll retrace our steps and search for it. It must be safe again by now."

When she tried to squeeze past him, he didn't move a muscle. "To the contrary, I think it's very dangerous, indeed."

Was he referring to the patrol? She frowned.

Wayland seemed to be holding his breath as he reached out to trace a lock of her hair that had fallen free. His thumb brushed her cheek, heralding a convalescence of tingling resonating from that spot. Her mouth started to tingle as well. She licked her lips to ease the sensation. Something akin to determination entered his expression as he lifted his gaze from her mouth to her eyes once more. He bowed his head, bringing them closer...

The door opened behind her, and she nearly

toppled into what smelled like a bakery. Wayland caught her and pulled her back beneath the awning before he slid his body between her and the person who had opened the door.

"Och! What are ye two canoodlers doing on my doorstep? Off wit'ye!"

Her cheeks burning hotter than her mouth, Katherine did just that. What had just happened? Had Wayland been about to kiss her?

No. Impossible. She was doing far too much matchmaking lately if she started seeing romance in her own life. Besides, he was not to be trusted, and yet she found herself trusting him more and more the longer he offered his support. He had an ulterior motive. She had to remember that.

Wayland caught up to her near the mouth of the alley. "Katherine, wait! It might not be safe."

She turned to face him but found that she couldn't look him in the eye. She didn't know what she hoped or dreaded to find in his gaze, but she wasn't ready to confirm her suspicions. Or realize that she'd let her imagination run wild with her. It was far too confusing.

Staring at the button of his waistcoat, she mumbled, "The patrol will be searching for a man and a woman. We'll be safer apart. I can see myself safely to the hotel."

Reluctantly, he nodded. They chose separate paths. Wayland turned right, retracing their steps. Katherine turned left, spotting the towering Bath Abbey ahead and using it as a landmark to find her way back to the hotel on her own.

ENSCONCED at a table near the wall of the common room at the Sydney Hotel, Katherine tried her best not to revisit the moment between her and Wayland in the alley. It helped that the object of her thoughts was not present at the table. Lyle, however, was — and he hadn't seemed particularly inclined to accept her explanation for how she and Wayland had parted ways, even if it was partially the truth. She'd left out a few details, and unfortunately Lyle knew her well enough to be able to tell when she wasn't divulging everything.

Fortunately, while at the table, sipping tea and enjoying a sweet bun with Pru and Harriet, Lyle chose to keep his suspicions to himself. For that, Katherine was grateful. Keeping her voice soft, she said to the others, "The only thing we've managed to uncover about the theft at Mrs. Quicke's townhouse is that the thief could have entered and exited through the window. However, as we proved earlier, it's especially difficult to do so without being seen. In truth, I don't know that we've narrowed down our list of suspects at all."

"What do we know?" Lyle asked. "We have the bit of silver, which might have been from someone's clothing."

"Such as Sir Hugh," Katherine suggested. He seemed reasonably fit, although she hadn't witnessed him perform any feats of athleticism aside from riding a horse. "He has had that recent influx of quid to fund his gambling, and I'm certain I've seen him wear silver before."

Pru added, "There's his mother's earring as well. Why would he bring an heirloom such as that to Bath?"

Katherine had forgotten about the earring, but she found it highly suspicious as well. She nodded.

Fiddling with her teacup, Harriet looked acutely uncomfortable. She glanced toward the staircase. "Perhaps Emma needs a walk."

Katherine pinned Harriet's hand to the table with her own. She took comfort from the presence of her closest friend, even if it was highly irregular for a maid to sit at the same table with her mistress and drink tea. "I need your thoughts on this. Please stay."

Harriet made a face. "I know you won't like what I have to say."

"Humor me."

After she heaved a long sigh, Harriet tore her bun to shreds as she suggested, "I know Mr. and Mrs. Julien seem like good people, but they have strong motive. I heard today that they had to turn out their maid because they could no longer afford her. They're a whisper away from landing in debtor's prison. They need the blunt."

Katherine shook her head. "It cannot be them." When Harriet looked ready to chide her, she added, "I'm not saying that because of personal sentiment. Neither could climb into Mrs. Quicke's window—"

"*If* the thief entered by that way," Lyle injected.

Katherine glared at him as she continued. "Not to mention they weren't even in Bath at the time of Mrs. Oliver's theft. They were in Bradford-on-Avon, south of here. Though I did notice clay on Mr. Julien's boot when Mrs. Quicke's jewels were taken..." How had he come by that? He'd been strolling with his wife and grandson, though the theft had occurred at least an hour before Katherine arrived on the scene.

Pru raised her voice a fraction and spoke over Katherine. "No, they weren't."

"I beg your pardon?"

"You must be mistaken. I saw Mr. and Mrs. Julien climb into a carriage while Lord Annandale was showing me his horses, shortly before Mrs. Oliver discovered her jewels missing."

"Yes." Katherine nodded slowly, but her stomach sank with every word she spoke. "The public coach stopping in Bradford-on-Avon."

"No, a private carriage with ornate metalwork along the sides. A landau, I think, though the hood was drawn. It looked expensive, but Annandale was arguing with me about how best to encourage speed from his horses, and I wasn't paying as close attention as I might have done. In fact, if not for the beautiful matched team of four pulling the carriage, I might not have noticed at all." Her cheeks turned a curious shade of plum. "Forgive me. Didn't I tell you this the other day?"

Katherine slowly shook her head. "You did not... but I didn't think to ask. I was more concerned with whether or not the pair were in the baths at the time of the theft." Which, obviously, they had not been.

Mr. and Mrs. Julien had looked her in the eye and lied to her! How could they have done so? Katherine didn't want to contemplate their motives, which she feared began and ended with Scott. They would do anything for their grandson — perhaps even steal.

Desperate to consider someone else, Katherine blurted, "The thief might be Mr. Salmon."

The other three at the table laughed. Even Harriet giggled behind her hand. "He's much too stupid, my lady."

Katherine gritted her teeth. "It might be an act. Although he acts inept, he might have been able to climb up to Mrs. Quicke's window."

Lyle raised his eyebrows. "Do you truly think he's pretending at being such an imbecile?"

"No." She blew out a breath. "We've known him through the Society for far too long."

Pru leaned forward with interest. "The Society?"

"The Royal Society for Investigative Techniques," Lyle answered.

She turned to Katherine. "They accept women as members?"

Katherine nodded. "I'm not the only woman who happens to be a member. The Duchess of Tenwick, for instance, is a personal friend and a key member."

Lyle turned a curious shade of magenta. He esteemed Philomena Graylocke greatly, even if he had yet to be able to speak in her presence without stuttering. "Her, I imagine they welcomed due to her sheer brilliance." She, like Lyle, was an inventor and supplied her inventions readily to detectives in need.

Pru rested her elbows on the table and tapped her chin. "What does one need to do in order to be accepted into the Society?"

"I'll explain the steps another time," Katherine answered. "For now, I need your attention on the thefts, if you please. Mr. Salmon may well be an imbecile, but he is also highly suspicious. Why would he have insisted that the cloaked figure is his primary suspect when it is obvious he hasn't so much as noticed the lurker?" She shook her head. "And his insistence upon being with the Marquess of Bath during the time of Mrs. Oliver's robbery, despite the fact that Lyle and Captain Wayland have both confirmed that the Marquess was not with him at the time, is highly irregular. If he is not the thief, I cannot guess his game."

"What of this lurker?" Pru added. "I spotted someone, cloaked as you described, during my drive yesterday morning. I wasn't close enough to espy too many details, and given the chill this September, I didn't think it particularly noteworthy to have seen a person so bundled against the cold, but the figure appeared to be lurking on Sydney Place when I embarked. Do you think they might be the thief?"

Biting her lower lip, Katherine nodded. "I spotted such a figure outside Mrs. Quicke's townhouse while I was searching for clues as well. Now that I have seen them for both thefts, I fear that the lurker might indeed be the Burglar of Bath. However, that brings me no closer to identifying them. They have proven wily thus far."

"The figure seemed tall to me," answered Pru. "Your height to be certain. Most men fit that description, but there are few women who do as well."

Softly, Harriet added, "Mrs. Julien is one of those women."

She was. But how could an old woman have outrun her? Katherine didn't participate in foot races, but she would like to think that she was more agile than a seventy-year-old woman.

Could the lurker have been Mr. Salmon all along? No... Katherine recalled seeing him at the Assembly Rooms, bungling his investigation, mere moments before she caught sight of the cloaked figure through the doorway. However, Mrs. Julien... or perhaps Sir Hugh... Katherine couldn't recall if she'd seen either in proximity to the lurker. As loath as she was to admit it, she had to consider Mrs. Julien again. Why had such a kind old woman lied to her?

Katherine chewed on her thumbnail. "I haven't

found traces of silver on Mrs. Julien to match the sliver I found."

Harriet raised her eyebrows. "Nor have you on anyone else."

If Katherine had, this mystery might be much more easily solved.

As she opened her mouth to answer, the group of matrons at the nearest table burst into raucous distain. "This is a disgrace." The speaker, Mrs. Oliver, sounded as though she'd stepped in animal droppings. She cast a news rag down upon the table. Katherine caught no more than the date — yesterday's issue of *The Daily Scandal*, a lewd pamphlet that did nothing more than tear down the reputations of the most esteemed men and women in polite society. Katherine never read it.

However, as Lady Dalhousie leaned over to read the article with glee, Katherine paid the conversation some mind. She held up a hand to stall Lyle from speaking as he started.

The biddy crowed, "Oh dear. Lady Carleton was spotted wearing that hideous emerald ring her husband gave her for their marriage anniversary. Wasn't she shaking the rafters last month with her shouts of being the thief's latest victim? I knew her ring wasn't comely enough to have warranted his attention."

At Lady Dalhousie's pointed glare, Mrs. Oliver gasped in affront. "*I* did not exaggerate my theft, I assure you! My necklace was missing. Everyone in the King's Bath saw as much."

"You might have hidden it," Lady Dalhousie accused her.

"Where? That heinous investigator, Mr. Salmon, shook out my clothing for all to see. Unless you think I stuffed my pearls down my shift and somehow didn't leave a bulge..."

A third woman chimed in, "We aren't accusing you, Mrs. Oliver. Nor Lady Carleton — she is getting to an age where she might be going senile. She likely forgot where she put her ring and found it again when she returned to London."

"Senile," Lady Dalhousie scoffed. "She was ready to turn out her maid, certain that the poor chit had taken it from her!"

"As I said, senile. It happens to a lot of women her age. Why, Mrs. Tatton thought her diamond-and-sapphire earrings were taken in July, but she wore them to the Duke of Tenwick's ball just before the Season closed. Women that age start to lose their memories, don't you know..." The third woman drew out her words as she raked Lady Dalhousie with a long look, implying that she would be next.

Katherine blew out a breath. She hated these sorts of backbiting machinations. She returned her attention to Lyle. "Forgive me, what were you about to say?"

"Have you looked for traces of silver on Mr. Salmon? You seem adamant that he might be at fault..."

Her mouth gaped as she realized that she hadn't thought to search Mr. Salmon for something that might connect him to her one clue. He had stomped about rather conspicuously, in a manner that, had she not retrieved the sliver of silver beforehand, might have damaged the evidence. Perhaps he had known it was there because he had left it!

Perhaps all Katherine had to do in order to prove that Mrs. Julien hadn't committed the thefts was find that bit of silver on Mr. Salmon! "No, I haven't. Lyle, that's brilliant. I could kiss you!"

He turned such a brilliant shade of ruby that his cheeks almost resembled jewels on their own.

CHAPTER THIRTEEN

F or a man bumbling his way through an investigation that ought to make him visible in Bath, Mr. Salmon was a difficult man to find. After a night and a day spent searching for a man she would have preferred to avoid under ordinary circumstances, Katherine accepted an invitation from the Marquess of Bath in the hopes that his hired detective would also be in attendance.

Lord Bath invited several vacationers, including the recently robbed Mrs. Oliver and Mrs. Quicke, to have dinner at his manor a short drive from the town. He even sent his ornate, silver-scrolled, black barouche for anyone who didn't have a carriage of their own. Since Grandma Bath had extended the invitation to the inventors in town, Katherine had the pleasure of escorting Lyle to the gathering.

He, on the other hand, was much less pleased with the arrangement. "I don't see why I have to be here," he grumbled from his position in the corner of Lord Bath's sitting room. The room was decorated in scarlet and gold, with flowers painted on the wallpaper, and tassels adorning every cushion.

Grandma Bath, thankfully, was seated in a red armchair near the mantel and hadn't yet noticed Katherine's arrival. The old woman had been deep in conversation with Wayland when she had arrived, and Katherine hoped to keep it that way for the duration of the gathering. The very last thing she needed was for Grandma Bath to try to push her and Lord Bath together. She was here to investigate!

"I'm trying to locate Mr. Salmon."

"Which you can do perfectly well without me," Lyle insisted. He shifted his position, shouldering closer to the wall and putting her body squarely between him and the gathering at large.

"Mr. Murphy!" Grandma Bath shouted, a wide smile on her face. "Come, sit by me and tell me how your invention is faring thus far."

Looking like a skittish dog, Lyle cautiously slinked forward. Katherine smirked — until Grandma Bath turned her attention to the corner of the sitting room.

"Lady Katherine, is that you? Come here, dear. There's plenty of room. I haven't seen you in days!"

Apparently, Grandma Bath hadn't realized that Katherine's avoidance had been by design. Reluctantly, she accompanied Lyle closer, searching the room for an excuse not to linger. That arrived in the form of Pru, scowling behind the chair as she stood on her own.

"Nice to see you again..." Katherine fought a grimace as she recalled the name Grandma Bath had asked to be called. After a moment's pause, she forced out, "Grandmama." Katherine *had* a living grandmother, one every bit as puckish as Grandma Bath seemed to be. She didn't need another, most certainly because this one would involve marrying Lord Bath. "If you'll excuse me, I believe Miss Burwick requires my attention."

"Coward," Lyle muttered as Katherine stepped between the chair and the divan in order to reach Pru.

As she did, Pru's scowl deepened. "I do not require your attention."

"Anything that takes me away from Grandma Bath's side before she can call over her grandson requires my attention." Katherine muttered the retort under her breath.

Pru snickered.

"Speaking of matchmaking..." Katherine darted a glance across the room, where Wayland now stood in conversation with Lord Annandale. "Have you adequately rebuffed a certain Scottish laird's attentions?"

Pru glanced down at the weak champagne in her hand. "He hasn't ventured over to greet me, so I would say I have."

She didn't sound nearly as triumphant over the notion as she had in the past. *I knew it!* Katherine buried her surge of satisfaction over the glum way Pru traced the rim of her glass before taking another sip. She *had* developed feelings of some kind for Lord Annandale, and if Katherine had to hazard a guess, she would venture that they were not feelings of loathing. Although Katherine didn't want to be cornered into life as a matchmaker, particularly because it would curtail her investigations, she had helped her sisters find matches and knew when a woman was falling in love.

Whether or not she wanted to admit it, Pru was falling in love with Lord Annandale. The question was, had her efforts succeeded in rebuffing him, or was there still a chance for Pru to find her happy ending? And would Pru even realize that was what she wanted?

"He doesn't seem like such a bad prospect," Katherine mused as she moved to stand next to her charge and face Annandale. The men remained oblivious that they had become the topic of conversation. "Respectful, wealthy, perhaps a bit unconventional, but that might be for the better seeing as you aren't the conventional lady, either. If you had to marry, he wouldn't be the worst choice."

Pru made a face and gulped down her champagne. "Don't tell me you agree with my mother."

"Your mother chose a name based on a title. You've seen the man. You tell me — is he more than his title?"

Pru blushed as she stared into her empty glass. "Of course. Aren't we all?"

Katherine nodded. The silence stretched between them as Pru glanced coyly toward Annandale. She averted her gaze the moment he turned to look in their direction. Wayland, noticing where the women's attention had strayed, raised his eyebrows as if he meant to communicate from across the room.

Are you talking about me?

Katherine gave him a bemused smirk and a subtle shake of the head. *In your wildest dreams.*

She turned to Pru, who looked a bit out of sorts. "You know, marriage isn't the worst fate a woman can have. My sisters have proven to be very happy in their wedded bliss."

With a dubious look, Pru mumbled, "Men are odd. They have strange likes and dislikes. It's impossible to gauge their moods sometimes."

Katherine laughed. "Men are simple. They aren't so complicated as you'd like to believe."

Pru hiked up her chin. "Very well. Tell me about Mr. Murphy. What drives him?"

"His intelligence, mostly. Even when he's talking to you, he's always thinking about his next invention or a puzzle he's in the midst of solving. He's also got an honorable streak, for he could have decided to become a thieftaker for hire and earn twice the pay he makes serving under Sir John. He solves more crime and keeps the streets safer as he is. And loath though he would be to admit it, he is as weak to a pretty face as they all are, especially if that face is paired with an intelligent mind."

Pru huffed, clearly unhappy with Katherine's analysis. "You only know that because of your long-time association with him."

Shaking her head, Katherine offered, "Very well. Choose someone else, then."

She half expected Pru to choose Lord Annandale.

Instead, she was surprised when the woman said, "Lord Bath."

Katherine mulled over her words for a moment before speaking. "The marquess is responsible and extremely attached to his tenants. He serves in Parliament willingly and eagerly, to give his people a voice. While here, he dotes on them as well. However, as you've seen with the way he dotes on his grandmother, he has a specific idea of how all women must be. He assumes that we are also simple creatures when the truth is the very opposite." Katherine offered Pru a smile, hoping to share it, but she got little response.

Instead, Pru's gaze strayed back to Lord Annandale. A smile curved her lips, but it appeared more devious than friendly. "And Captain Wayland?"

Tarnation! Why did she have to ask that? Katherine's gaze strayed to the man in question, who she found looking at her for a moment while he answered Lord Annandale. Her stomach suddenly aflutter, Katherine was forced to admit, "Him, I cannot begin to comprehend. He is an enigma."

She didn't care to be proven wrong, and Pru had chosen the one man in the room that Katherine couldn't read. She still couldn't fathom why he was in Bath. And that near-kiss in the alley yesterday... had that been her imagination?

She forcibly turned her back to Wayland, not wanting to face the questions he raised. Trying to regain control of the conversation, she informed Pru, "My point is that, Wayland aside, men are simple. You can point to any one of them, pauper or prince, and have a reasonable idea of what they want from you."

Pru smirked. "Oh, I think Captain Wayland is fairly easy to read as well. You simply don't care to admit it. And princes?" Pru snorted. "They're the easiest. It's obvious Prince Karl, for instance, is interested in a woman who *doesn't* hang off his every word. I batted my eyelashes at him yesterday and complimented him on his frankly abysmal card playing, and I haven't had to contend with him since."

Although Katherine opened her mouth, she couldn't quite find the words to express her mixed amusement and pride over Pru handling the matter on her own. Why, then, had she been so adamant to ask for Katherine's advice on the matter? She seemed perfectly capable of turning away unwanted attention as it was.

Upon noticing Katherine's expression, Pru wrinkled her nose. "I grew weary of having a passel of men hanging off my every word." She glanced at Lord Annandale then down into her glass once more. In an almost inaudible mutter, she added, "Perhaps I ought to have found another way."

At that moment, a herd of men and women, having been offered a tour of the manor by Lord Bath before Katherine arrived, re-entered the parlor in his cheery wake. How big was Lord Bath's table? There must be thirty people here! If this was what he referred to as a "small, private dinner party," Katherine would hate to discover how many he invited to a banquet.

Last in the line of guests, lingering two paces to the rear of the last couple to enter, was Mr. Salmon. Katherine's spirits buoyed. She darted toward the door, only to be stalled as Sir Hugh stepped into her path with a wide smile.

To her surprise, she wasn't the one he was eager to see. "Miss Burwick," he greeted her warmly. "A pleasure to find you here! Perhaps if Lord Bath is of a mind, we can set up a card game in the parlor after dinner."

Katherine turned, raising an eyebrow to Pru, who blushed. As she did, she noticed movement across the room. Wayland and Annandale were walking toward them as well. Annandale wore a peculiar expression, half wary and half... possessive. Perhaps he wasn't as deterred from courting Pru as she seemed to fear.

The last person Katherine had time to indulge was

Wayland. Excusing herself, she slipped away from the group as Annandale approached. In a room full of people, Pru was chaperoned well enough.

Mr. Salmon slinked along the perimeter of the room to one corner, where he accepted a tumbler of spirits from a livery-clad footman. Katherine wove between people as she attempted to cross the sitting room. Although it had seemed of modest size when she'd arrived, somehow the distance between her and her target grew ever larger.

Paying only half a mind to the people surrounding her, she nearly tripped over Mrs. Fairchild. *Tarnation!* Why had Lord Bath invited her? Katherine bit back a groan, glancing from her to Mr. Salmon, half-afraid that the slippery man would disappear into thin air the moment she turned away. She recalled, from multiple meetings at the Society, that he proudly sported a silver belt buckle. If that buckle had a sliver missing, then she would know for certain who the true Burglar of Bath was!

Unfortunately, Mrs. Fairchild seemed determined to prevent her from doing as she wished. The woman caught her sleeve as Katherine tried to slip past with no more than a polite greeting.

"I don't know what you're playing at, but I insist that you stop."

The only thing Katherine cared to be doing at the moment was searching for the Burglar of Bath. What-ever nonsense Mrs. Fairchild had cooked up, she didn't want to hear it. Unfortunately, she didn't seem to have a choice.

"To what are you referring?" she asked reluctantly.

Mrs. Fairchild pointed toward the mantel, where Pru now entertained a number of men, including Prince Karl. Miss Newcomb, hanging behind him, couldn't seem to get a word in edgewise as the group held an animated conversation. Given the way Pru's face was alight with enthusiasm, the topic must be either cards or horses, at both of which she had proven herself proficient.

"*That*," Mrs. Fairchild said, her voice dripping with condescension.

Katherine sighed. Either the sound or her dejected posture drew the attention of Captain Wayland. Frowning, he took a small step back from the group as he met her gaze. She shook her head. She did not need him to come to her rescue again. In fact, it might rekindle the rumor she'd recently put to rest.

She turned back to Mrs. Fairchild, hoping that her turned back spoke volumes. "A conversation?"

"They're speaking of things best left to the study! Hunting, gambling, horses. Surely you haven't snuck

Miss Burwick into their after-dinner conversations as well."

The woman's scorn was evident in her tone of voice and her look of distaste. Women had every bit as much right to enjoy hunting, gambling, and horses as did men. Unfortunately, Mrs. Fairchild was of the same mind as Lord Bath when it came to which activities it was acceptable for men and women to engage in. They both posed a problem to women like Katherine, who wanted to pursue a predominantly male profession. She held her tongue on the matter, however.

"They're having an innocent conversation. There isn't any reason for Miss Burwick or me to be ashamed."

With a grimace, Mrs. Fairchild stepped forward to more squarely block Katherine's path. Unless she cared to stumble back into Wayland's arms or topple into Grandma Bath's lap, she was cornered.

"There is every reason. You're deliberately monopolizing the attention of every eligible man in Bath. Was your victory with Lord Northbrook not enough for you?"

A throb started in Katherine's forehead. She pinched the bridge of her nose. "I am not seeking to bar your client from marrying the prince. She can have him if she wants. Though I've heard he isn't the type to come up to snuff."

The rival matchmaker sniffed and drew herself up. "I insist you stop these mad methods at once and play fairly. Make your client's match with Captain Wayland, if you will, but leave the rest of the men out of it!"

Katherine flinched at the sound of Wayland's name. At the very least, Mrs. Fairchild seemed to believe that that would be the only reason Katherine would seek out his company. Even so, if word of how she had rectified the rumor returned to him, she doubted he would be pleased with the lie. After all, he appeared to have worked hard to recommend Pru to his friend, Lord Annandale.

"If she's acting so deplorably, none of them will be enticed."

Mrs. Fairchild's expression darkened like a thundercloud. "And how well do you think they'll be enticed if they learn that the woman they so esteem might very well be the notorious thief? I saw her lingering outside the King's Bath on Sunday."

Katherine spoke through gritted teeth. "Lord Annandale confirmed that she was with him the entire time and wouldn't have had the opportunity."

"So he claims, but it's obvious he's as besotted as the rest of them!"

Leaning her head down closer to her rival so as to contain the conversation, Katherine hissed, "Miss Burwick was at Lord Northbrook's house party during the time of one of the thefts, and you well know it."

The woman harrumphed. "If you'd like for the whole of the gathering to continue to believe that, you'd best start playing fair. Make your match with Miss Burwick and take her *off* the marriage mart so someone else might have a go at one of the men."

Was she out of her sarding mind? As the adage went, love was lawless. *Playing fair* simply didn't apply. However, Katherine bit her tongue. If she prolonged the conversation much longer, the host would call that dinner was served and she would squander her chance to examine Mr. Salmon's clothing. That belt buckle loomed in her mind.

"Very well," Katherine muttered, as much acknowledgement to Mrs. Fairchild's lunacy as she was likely to get. Thankfully, it seemed to satisfy her rival, who removed her death grip from Katherine's sleeve.

Katherine wasted no time in navigating the room to install herself at Mr. Salmon's side. The moment she did, he rubbed his nose. "Lady Katherine." His voice held a note of superiority, despite the fact that she was many times the investigator he was.

As she opened her mouth to reply cordially, a footman by the door cleared his throat. "My lords and ladies, dinner is served."

With a wide smile, the Marquess of Bath lifted his arms and swung his wide cuffs. "Come! Escort your dinner partner down the corridor after me."

Mr. Salmon and Katherine exchanged a look of mixed horror and distaste. Anyone would be a better dinner companion than he. Unfortunately, with every other gentleman offering his arm to the nearest lady — Lyle escorting Grandma Bath, Lord Annandale with Pru on his arm, and Wayland taking charge of the mousy Miss Newcomb — she had no choice but to accept Mr. Salmon's escort. She gingerly placed her hand on his arm as they took up the rear. They maintained stony silence as he escorted her down to the formal dining room, where all the places at the long table were now occupied save for two on the near end. Katherine was forced to sit on the corner, with no one to converse with save for Mr. Salmon.

All is not lost, she reminded herself. After all, she had ample opportunity to match the piece of silver to his clothing! As she fished out the small vial from her reticule, she let her eyes fall to his belt buckle, searching for scratches.

Instead of the gaudy silver buckle, he wore a plain one tonight. It was dull bronze in color. Why the change? Katherine dropped her reticule on the floor, necessitating that she duck beneath the table to retrieve it. There, she discovered that he didn't wear any silver on his boots, either.

For some reason, he had divested himself of all silver. Had she waited too long or alerted him that she had found the silver?

As Katherine emerged from beneath the table-cloth, Mr. Salmon's eyes and his voice were dull. He offered only the barest of pleasantries before he chose from the dishes presented to him by a footman. Katherine stifled a sigh as chatter erupted around them.

This was going to be a very long dinner.

CHAPTER FOURTEEN

H arriet dove for the handheld mirror the moment Katherine reached for it. "No, my lady, don't!" She yanked it from the writing desk and stuffed it beneath the pillow on the bed. Emma, curious as to what needed to be so hidden, sank onto her front haunches and dug her nose into the bedclothes, her curly tail wagging.

Katherine bit back a sigh. "I want to check my reflection."

"You look beautiful, my lady. Stunning. Effervescent."

"Harriet." Her voice held a note of warning.

Pressing her lips together, the maid shook her head. "Forgive me, but it's for your own good. What if you break the mirror? Today *is* Friday the thirteenth."

"It's a silly superstition, and I'm not nearly as

clumsy as my reputation suggests. I can look into a mirror without dropping it."

Harriet sat on the bed. With her luck, she likely broke the mirror herself.

Exasperated, Katherine turned toward the door. "Very well, I won't use my mirror." She opened the door and stepped into the corridor before she added, "I'll use Pru's." She shut the door before Harriet crossed the distance to stop her.

In the corridor, she found no more common sense. One of the doors down the line was open to reveal a woman's sharp voice. "My rabbit's foot! The one I bought yesterday, where is it?"

A muffled response filled the air, followed by the woman's shrill reply.

"The thief must have stolen it! He's stealing animal limbs now, too? This day will be a disaster!"

Katherine gritted her teeth and marched into Pru's room. A moment before she shut the door behind her, leaning her full weight against it, she heard the woman exclaim, "Oh, thank heavens! I can go out now."

The lucky rabbit's foot must have been found, after all. What drivel.

Katherine sighed and turned her attention to the room, looking forward to interacting with someone who possessed some semblance of sanity despite the day of the week. Thank Zeus it didn't happen to be a full moon tonight as well, or the biddies in the hotel would never leave their rooms. Katherine refused to remain indoors. She had a thief to find, and today, with its unlucky omen, seemed like precisely the chaos a thief might capitalize upon in order to strike again.

Instead of a calm, reasonable atmosphere, she found Pru in nearly as irrational a state. The entire contents of her trunk were strewn about the room. Dressed in no more than her underclothes, Pru glanced toward Katherine.

"Please, I need help. I cannot decide what to wear."

"Why not the green?" Katherine suggested. After all, Pru had once suggested that a similar color on Katherine had washed out her complexion. If Pru wanted to dress unappealing, it seemed her best choice.

Wrinkling her nose, the brunette woman shook her head. "No, not the green." She dragged a jaunty yellow walking dress over her skin. "Does this make me look radiant or perhaps a bit too pink?" With her free hand, she pulled a puce dress closer, the dark pink a stark contrast against the yellow. "What of this one?"

Katherine considered them both then answered, "The pink compliments you better."

The tension drained from Pru's shoulders as she nodded. She tossed the yellow onto the bed and started to pull the puce dress over her head. Katherine narrowed her eyes. First, Pru insisted that she look unappealing, but now she wanted to look attractive. She must have grown fond of Lord Annandale, after all!

As Katherine stepped away from the door, Harriet burst into the room, Emma tucked beneath one arm. She pointed a finger at the writing desk. "I am confiscating your mirror, too!"

Pru's mouth dropped open. "Whatever for? I need it if I'm to apply my cosmetics."

Yes, she had definitely developed some sort of tendre for Lord Annandale if she was going through that much trouble to look appealing. She and Katherine usually didn't bother with cosmetics unless they intended to go out for the evening.

"I'll apply them for you," Harriet answered. "If I can make Lady Katherine look unappealing, I can make you shine, trust me."

Katherine snatched the dog from Harriet's arms. "I'm going to take Emma out into the garden."

"You can't go out alone! The day is unlucky!"

"I'll take my chances," she said between gritted teeth as she shut the door.

The day had dawned hours ago with frost on the ground, but in case the sun had yet to warm the air to a bearable level, Katherine donned her pelisse before she exited with Emma in tow on her leash. She took the back stairs, by Lady Dalhousie's room, hoping not to encounter anyone.

At the first landing, the Long Hall came into view, where a merry little quartet played a jaunty midday tune. The light, supplementing the thin daylight streaming in from the tall, wide windows, sparkled off of the ladies' jewels. Had they decided to wear every single piece of jewelry they owned?

Snatches of conversation met her ears.

"...a cat, I tell you. I know what I saw."

"Was it black?"

"It doesn't matter the color," answered a third woman. "It still might have been a witch in disguise. You know they abound today!"

I know you are all dolts. Katherine bit her tongue.

"...don't want the thief to help himself to anything I own today! I've instructed my maid to be vigilant. In the meantime, I'm wearing all I can..."

Yes, bacon-brained dolts, the lot of them.

Irritated, Katherine stomped down the remaining steps to the door leading into the garden. She stepped out into the bracing air, the chill permeating her even with the pelisse. Thankful that she'd taken the fore-thought, she pulled it closer around her shoulders and crunched over the path. Emma happily led the way. She seemed impervious to the cold. With so much rain throughout the summer, it hadn't proven to be much of a summer at all. If Katherine had to hazard a guess, she would suspect that they would have snow again this winter, despite usually receiving no more than a dusting or two throughout the winter months.

Following her eager pug, Katherine lost herself in thought as she mulled over the investigation thus far. She'd hoped to have found the Burglar of Bath by now and been ready to return to her regular life. Unfortu-nately, it seemed that she'd set her hopes a little too high. She had some investigating to do yet, but how? Barring searching people's rooms in the hopes of finding something silver that they'd worn, she didn't have any ideas.

Her one hope was that the thief would take the opportunity presented today by so many superstitious nincompoops and that they would make a mistake when they did so. Katherine intended to be vigilant. Given that the ladies of Bath seemed to be wearing all their jewelry in a gaudy, mismatched display, she should be able to keep them all under her eye.

If so, the thief would have to come to her.

"Haven't you heard you shouldn't walk alone on such an unlucky day?"

Katherine groaned as she pulled Emma to a stop and turned to face the speaker. "Don't tell me you believe in that drivel, too. We're detectives. We believe in evidence."

Captain Wayland, his hands stuffed into his greatcoat pockets for warmth, laughed. "I don't, but I thought you looked lonely nevertheless."

The statement hovered between them, begging an invitation on her part to walk with him. However, they hadn't been alone together since he'd nearly kissed her — no, since her imagination had run wild with her. Nothing between them had changed at all.

Stifling a sigh, she indicated the walkway in front of her. "Would you care to join me?"

"It would be my pleasure."

They walked on a ways, Emma pausing to sniff various plants with what seemed like a disproportionate amount of vigor given the subject matter. Certainly, she couldn't be doing so in order to give Katherine and Wayland some privacy. Emma was a conniving little thief, but she was still no more than a dog. She didn't understand complicated human emotions.

"How fares the investigation?" Wayland asked.

Katherine mulled over the question. She had confessed most of it to him already, as she saw fit to divulge details. Still he continued to ask... "Why do you care to know?" If he was, indeed, conducting his own investigation, he seemed to be using her as a vital font of information.

Pausing at a crossroads in the garden, he turned to face her. His collar was turned up against his neck, tickling the bottom of his clean-shaven jaw. The dimple in his chin winked in and out of sight as he confessed, "I'm hoping if I ask often enough, you'll request my assistance. My protection or my expertise."

"You want me to be in your debt?" That didn't make much sense. What could he hope to use that for in the future? She didn't trust... that was to say, she *shouldn't* trust him. She had been trusting him with far too much information as it was.

He corrected her, his voice firm, "I want to help."

Why? It made no sense. He had to have an ulterior motive. Unlike Katherine, he didn't solve crimes and bring criminals to justice because it was the right thing to do. He did it for payment, of which there was none in this instance.

He had no motive to want to help her that she could discern. He couldn't be trusted. He inevitably did what benefitted him in the end.

If so, why had he given credit for the capture of the Pink-Ribbon Murderer to Lyle?

She didn't know what to think of Wayland.

Seeming to sense her misgivings, Wayland sighed. "Give it some thought. I can be a useful ally. You know where to find me."

Without another word, he turned and strode toward the hotel. He didn't look behind him.

Katherine paused, leaning down to scratch Emma, who seemed dejected that their companion had left so suddenly. "We don't need him," Katherine whispered as she scratched Emma's favorite spot on her back, right above her tail.

Because her nose was starting to ache from the chill, she returned to the hotel and stashed Emma in the room with Harriet. Pru, she was informed, had already gone below to the festivities in the Long Hall. Katherine endured her maid's disapproving look as she handed over her pelisse and announced her intention to join. In order to catch the thief, she had to be near the goods he intended to rob.

———

By TEATIME, Katherine was blinded by the amount

of jewelry everyone insisted on wearing. The sky had clouded over again, chasing everyone indoors by the lit hearths. Some chose to dance to the music played by the quartet; most chose to mingle around the perimeter of the room. Plainer than the Assembly Rooms, the Long Hall held its own sort of charm. It felt more like a country ball than an elaborate affair. This atmosphere seemed to seep into the bones of those gathered. Once, Katherine even spotted Lady Dalhousie dancing, though the woman put a swift end to that when she stumbled over her hem and the proclamations of doom resumed.

Katherine strolled past a table nestled in the corner. Pru was at its center, though there wasn't a card to be seen. The men had proclaimed the day too risky to gamble. Katherine shook her head at the reminder that the men of Bath could be every bit as silly and superstitious as the women. Despite the lack of entertainment, the men seemed content to hold a rousing conversation, passing a flask between them. Sitting next to Prince Karl, Miss Newcomb accepted it from him and raised it to her lips. She coughed and spluttered, her eyes watering as she passed it along.

Poor girl. Katherine winced in sympathy. She must be trying to emulate Pru's success with the men and failing miserably. If Pru was correct, doing so wasn't even the way to earn the prince's affections. He seemed immune to the calf eyes cast his way by the debutante. She might have been his shadow, for all the reaction he gave her. Although Katherine didn't know her, she did feel sorry for the girl, as she seemed particularly dejected the longer Prince Karl interacted with people other than her.

Knowing that Mrs. Fairchild couldn't be far — even though Katherine doubted she would condone the consumption of spirits had she been watching closely — Katherine vacated the area quickly. Unfortunately, that left her at the mercy of another matchmaking-minded woman.

"Lady Katherine, over here!"

The length of the Long Hall likely could hear Grandma Bath's shout. Pasting on a smile, Katherine strode toward the table where the old lady rested. The crowd parted for her, whispering as she walked past. Katherine almost wished there *would* be a theft, so that she would no longer be the spectacle.

Grandma Bath sat at a table with her grandson, which came as no surprise to Katherine. She was, however, astonished by the third person seated among them. What business could Mr. Salmon have with Grandma Bath?

As Katherine approached the table, the old lady kicked out the fourth chair. "Come, sit and take tea with us. I've seen you bobbing around the hall since I arrived. You must be famished."

Katherine was a bit peckish but had decided that her duty to find the thief came first. However, she couldn't deny the old woman's request, especially when the marquess turned to her with a smile.

He stood, taking her hand. "Yes, Lady Katherine, please do join us. It would be our pleasure."

He settled her into the chair before resuming his own. Mr. Salmon had also stood at her approach and waited for his employer to sit before he did as well.

At Grandma Bath's behest, Katherine helped herself to the cold meats, cheese, and bread on the tray at the table. The old woman turned over a spare teacup and filled it from the teapot at the table. Katherine took a bite of her collation, suspicious. Had Grandma Bath prepared to snag her?

"Ernest has just been saying how he enjoyed your dance the other day."

Katherine highly doubted he had mentioned any such thing, but the marquess was nothing if not polite. He agreed with his grandmother and added his profuse hope to repeat the experience in the future.

"I'm not much of a dancer," Katherine answered,

hoping to quell the subject.

"Practice will help with that," Grandma Bath said with a wink as she nudged Katherine with her elbow.

Katherine didn't care to practice her dancing. All she wanted, at this point, was to find the Burglar of Bath and retreat from Grandma Bath's matchmaking efforts. She had been in town nearly a week! Shouldn't she have more to show for her efforts?

"Perhaps another time," Katherine mumbled.

"Have you seen Prior Park? Ernest loves the gardens. I'm certain he'd be willing to show you."

Unless the park also included a hidden cache of stolen gems, Katherine wasn't much interested. "Thank you," she said, looking from one to the other. "But that shouldn't be necessary. Bath has kept me well entertained thus far."

"I hear there are more thieves on the loose," Grandma Bath said in disgust. "And near here, too! Three of them, lurking up on Sydney Place, so says the old watch."

Oh dear. Katherine was fairly certain that those *thieves* were she, Lyle, and Wayland. How close a look had the patrol gotten to them?

Not close enough to identify her, that much seemed true, given the look of worry that spawned on Lord Bath's face. He leaned closer to her, lowering his voice. "My dear, are you certain you wouldn't consider accepting a room in my manor? Your father wouldn't forgive me if something should happen to you. Your friends are welcome as well, of course."

Given the smug look on Grandma Bath's face, that was precisely what she wanted to happen. She would trap Katherine and her grandson into marriage by the end of the week.

Katherine smiled tightly. "Thank you for the offer, but—"

Her words halted, halfway out her throat, as a scream split the air. The quartet stopped with a screech. For a moment, the room was dead silent. Then chaos erupted.

Katherine bolted between the panicking women, who clutched at the jewels adorning their throats and ears as if the Burglar of Bath would manifest from thin air and rob them blind in the middle of the crowded hall. The men turned in circles as if searching for a ghost. Katherine made it to the staircase, where the scream seemed to have emanated. As she searched for the source, she turned to find Lord Bath and Mr. Salmon on her heels.

"Thief! It's the thief! Somebody help!"

The woman's shrill voice emanated from the rooms above stairs. The Marquess of Bath looked horrified. "It can't be." He exchanged a worried look with Mr. Salmon, who looked grim. Katherine didn't have time to indulge her shock, not if she wanted to find the thief! She hiked her skirt to her knees and dashed up the steps as quickly as she could manage.

In the corridor, which ended at Lady Dalhousie's open door, she found the old woman on the floor by her bed, a bleeding gash on her forehead and a curious-looking statue on the floor next to her as she groaned. Her maid, with Harriet by her side, trying to comfort her, looked ready to swoon. Her eyes were huge, and her hands shook.

"He came in and hit milady over the head before he took her jewels! Then he ran out."

"Where?" Katherine asked, ready to run. She might still be able to catch the thief!

"D-Down the stairs next door."

Lord Bath looked grim. "He didn't enter the Long Hall. We arrived from there."

"He must have gone down to the gardens," Katherine snapped, turning away from the scene.

Harriet abandoned the shaken maid and gripped Katherine's arm in both hands. "Don't go, my lady! Not today."

Katherine shook her off. "I have to."

This might be the lucky break she needed in the

investigation.

As she brushed between the two men, into the corridor, Mr. Salmon drew himself up. He looked every bit as shocked as the maid to find Lady Dalhousie thus attacked. In fact, Lord Bath looked ready to lose his lunch as he rushed forward to help the old lady. The burglar had never harmed any of his victims before.

"Don't touch anything," Mr. Salmon ordered. "I must examine the scene precisely as the thief left it."

For once, he made a sensible choice.

Katherine barreled down the steps, nearly tripping over her hem before she pulled it higher. Her heart thundered as she pursued the thief into the cool afternoon air. Where was he? Katherine spotted no cloaked figure, but unless he had gone around the side of the hotel to the front — in which case she would never catch him — there was only one path he could have taken, into the gardens proper. She raced along the gravel walk, the hedges soaring high to enclose her. Where would the thief have gone?

At the bend in the path, she turned the corner and stopped abruptly as she nearly collided with Mr. and Mrs. Julien. Katherine lost her footing and fell, scraping her arms against the pebbles. Mrs. Julien straightened, her eyes wide.

"Lady Katherine! Goodness me, are you all right?"

Her hands and arms stung from her fall. The cold air raised gooseflesh on her exposed skin. She accepted Mrs. Julien's help to stand. "Did you see anyone run past?"

"No..."

Tarnation!

"Why do you ask?"

"There's been another robbery," Katherine answered absently. She turned, searching for any sign of the thief, then frowned. The couple was barely dressed for the weather, their outer clothes unbuttoned as they puttered around the garden on a day deemed too dismal by the guests to go out. "Why are you out here?"

"Oh, we wanted to see if the flowers had survived the early frost last night."

If Katherine would hazard a guess, she would say they had not.

"And you saw no one?"

Mr. Julien shook his head. "Sorry to say, we were much too engrossed by the plants. We didn't think to look for anyone out here with us."

The thief must have gone around the front of the building, after all. Tightly, Katherine thanked Mr. and Mrs. Julien and turned to head inside. Had she just been lied to again by the elderly couple? Could Mrs. Julien have run so fast as to vacate Lady Dalhousie's room and reach the gardens without being seen? No, wait — Lady Dalhousie's maid had referred to the thief as a *he*. Had the young woman seen his face and identified him?

Katherine's list of suspects was a small one. Mr. Salmon had been with her at the time of this theft. As much as she would have liked to prove he was the thief, it wasn't possible. Where had Sir Hugh been at the time of the theft?

Taking the stairs two at a time, Katherine hurried up the narrow staircase to Lady Dalhousie's room. She had gathered a crowd, Wayland among them. Katherine ignored him as she slipped past, into the room. Lady Dalhousie's maid was still being comforted by Harriet. Katherine stopped beside her.

"I know this is a difficult time, but I must ask you some questions. Do you think you would be able to answer them?"

The maid nodded stiffly. "Anything, if it will help."

"Did you see the man who hit your employer? Did you recognize him?"

"I'm sorry." The maid glanced down. "I was down the hall. I ran at milady's scream, but I only saw the back of him as he ducked down the stairs."

Across the room, where Lord Bath had now helped the old woman onto the edge of the bed, Mr. Salmon asked brusquely, "Did you see who attacked you? Was he wearing a cloak?"

"A cloak," the maid exclaimed. "Yes!"

Lady Dalhousie, pressing her hands to her pale cheeks, took over the tale. "I didn't catch a close enough glimpse of him to see his face, but I certainly saw that cloak. It was unmistakable. Black with thread-of-gold embroidery along the edges, wide enough to billow around him like wings when he swung the sculpture at me."

That was nothing at all like the cloaked figure Katherine had seen, but given Lady Dalhousie's penchant for embellishment, it still might have been the same person.

"You're certain?" Mr. Salmon asked, dubious. "Could you have misplaced your necklace? Perhaps you're feeling disoriented from your fall."

Katherine gaped, unable to believe her ears. Had Mr. Salmon just insinuated that a woman with a gash on her temple had merely misplaced her gems?

"He snatched them right from my neck, you imbecile! I did not forget them."

Considering that the woman wore her necklace even in the King's Bath, Katherine had every confidence that the woman slept with them at night. They were never away from her person.

Yet the Marquess of Bath didn't seem at all convinced, either. "This cloaked figure struck you with the sculpture and absconded with your jewels, you say?"

Lady Dalhousie drew herself up. "Exactly so."

"And you saw him approach enough to recall his cloak but no other detail."

"Yes." She paused, frowning. "He swooped in from behind me, and I was hit before I knew it. I am not lying! I was robbed!"

"I can see that, Lady Dalhousie," Lord Bath said. He held out his hands, cuffs flapping, to placate her. "But you must admit it is out of character for this thief. He has never before attacked someone."

"He must have wanted my jewels desperately! I never take them off, so he had no other opportunity. I cannot believe you are treating me thusly after I've been robbed in *your* town!"

As Lord Bath tried to placate her in a calm, cajoling voice, Grandma Bath elbowed her way into the room. "Quite right! I've had enough of this nonsense. Ernest, we must hire someone to find this thief at once! I can't have him harming people in my town."

"Grandmama, you should have waited below." Lord Bath abandoned the injured woman in order to help his grandmother to the chair by the writing desk. He tried to convince her to sit, to no avail.

"I am not here to rest my legs. I am here to seek answers!"

The air rang with the force of the old woman's conviction. Even the gossips outside the door quieted.

With a nod of determination, Grandma Bath continued, "Ernest, this must stop. Let's offer a reward—"

"No reward," he answered, his voice firm. "I have hired Mr. Salmon to find the thief, and he will do that very thing, won't you, sir?"

"Yes, my lord." Mr. Salmon squared his shoulders, looking inordinately proud for a man who had never successfully caught a thief in his life. "Posthaste, I assure you!"

Katherine stepped forward. "Lord Bath, I think it might be prudent if Mr. Murphy examined the sculpture with which Lady Dalhousie was struck. He is one of Sir John's Men, experienced in such matters, and will handle it with discretion. Not to mention, his invention—"

"Oh!" Grandma Bath exclaimed. "His invention!

Why didn't I think of that? Yes, Mr. Murphy must take a look at the sculpture at once."

Katherine removed a handkerchief from her reticule before she approached the artifact. Although she expected it to be a fixture of the hotel or perhaps something Lady Dalhousie had brought from home, the sturdy six-inch-tall statue of a woman appeared far older. Time had worn away the features of the woman. Earth, reddish clay like that found near Mrs. Quicke's townhouse, still resided in some of the cracks of the statue. Where had it come from? Had the thief brought it? Striking Lady Dalhousie seemed more a crime of opportunity than of forethought.

Unfortunately, the woman had dissolved into a fit of vapors, pouring out every sordid embellished detail of how she was attacked for everyone to hear. Mostly, lamenting loudly how *this* theft was far more devastating than Mrs. Oliver's because she had been harmed, whereas Mrs. Oliver had not. None of it was useful, and she didn't seem fit for questioning again that night. Katherine would have to speak with her again in the morning.

While Grandma Bath sent for Lyle, Katherine took advantage of everyone's preoccupation to sneak down to the gardens once more. Although she couldn't be certain which direction the thief had taken, he had certainly emerged from this stairwell. She examined the area immediately nearby for any clue she might use to identify the thief.

She found a large button in the shape of a flower. Frowning, she picked it up off the ground. Where had she seen it before?

Pru's hideous dress! But Pru had been at the table with the other men during the time of the theft... hadn't she? Confound it, Katherine's back had been turned while she was with Lord Bath and his grand-mother. Pru couldn't have committed the other thefts, not being in Bath at that time. But this one was different...

No, Katherine was being fanciful. Pru didn't have time to become a thief. She was too preoccupied with her courtship — or lack thereof — with Lord Annan-dale. However, if she'd come outside for some air, she might have seen the thief as he ran away. Katherine slipped the button into her reticule until such a time as she could show it to Pru.

She found no other clues. By the time she returned above stairs, Lyle had arrived to take charge of the handkerchief-wrapped statue. He informed everyone that he needed access to the Pump Room in order to test his invention. Grandma Bath was only too happy to oblige.

"Thank you, my lady," Lyle answered as he followed her painstaking progress out of the room and past Katherine. "I am much obliged. With the waters from the spring, I believe I'll be able to show a shadow of the imprint of the thief's hand on the statue. If nothing else, we should know how big his hand is, and we might be able to identify him from that information."

"Anything to stop this thief from terrorizing my town sounds grand," the old woman proclaimed.

"This should be interesting," Mr. Salmon muttered under his breath.

Katherine jumped. Until he spoke, she hadn't realized that he'd been standing beside her. He paid her no mind as he followed after Lyle, seemingly eager to discover what the inventor was able to glean from the makeshift weapon.

Katherine started to follow then hesitated. Did she have time to wait for Lyle's experiment to come to fruition? She had to catch the Burglar of Bath — before his newfound violent streak turned deadly.

To herself, Katherine muttered, "Perhaps this day is unlucky, after all."

CHAPTER FIFTEEN

Katherine tugged her pelisse closer to her neck to ward away the early-evening chill as she strode along the cobblestone street toward the Pump Room. It had taken her longer than expected to calm Lady Dalhousie and try to extract more information from her. With everyone agog over the excitement, Lady Dalhousie had thrived in recounting the tale, adding more dramatics to every retelling.

By the time Katherine had sat her down to try to uncover some useful clues, the old woman had twisted the tale to such an extent that she couldn't believe a word of it. Perhaps Lady Dalhousie had noticed something important, but with all her penchant for embellishment, she had blurred the details to the point that Katherine doubted the woman knew what pieces of her tale were false and which were true. The latest

308 LEIGHANN DOBBS & HARMONY WILLIAMS

rendition had involved some sort of pirate. Perhaps the old woman had been struck on the head a bit too hard.

A cursory examination of the room once Mr. Salmon vacated it earned Katherine no further clues. Too many people had come and gone, trampling the rug, moving small artifacts, and preventing Katherine from searching outright for the clues she needed to solve the case. In front of so many witnesses, she needed to keep up her ruse of playing the matchmaker. Under the guise of gossiping as much as the other women who congregated in Lady Dalhousie's room, she'd managed to search very little and had found nothing, not even a small sliver of silver.

Nothing save for the flowery button in her reticule. That must be coincidence, mustn't it?

Footsteps sounded from behind her. Katherine glanced over her shoulder, quickly averting her gaze when Wayland's tall figure stepped beneath one of the freshly lit streetlamps. Why was he following her?

"Lady Katherine," he called.

She didn't slow her steps, but her skirts prevented her from matching his long-legged stride. He reached her easily and caught her arm, pulling her to a stop.

"What do you think you're doing?"

She hiked up her chin, mulish. "I'm walking to the

Pump Room to join Lyle, though I don't see how that's any of your concern."

"Don't be daft. There's a thief on the loose — one who has now escalated to violence. You should have taken your carriage rather than risked walking alone."

Katherine frowned at the vehemence in his voice. Why was he suddenly so protective of her? They were... not precisely rivals, but not friends, either. Yet he'd stated he wanted to help her investigation. Help... or glean insights he could use to identify the thief himself? She didn't know whether to trust him.

However, this newfound concern over her safety seemed genuine. He didn't want to see her hurt. Was that the honorable part of him, the same part that had driven him to serve in the war against Napoleon? Or was it something more...

"Why are you here?" she asked, her voice quiet. His hand on her arm anchored her even though he only bracketed her bicep, rather than gripping her tight.

"Harriet told me you'd left without sending for the coach—"

"No, why are you in Bath?" Her voice gained strength. She examined his expression for any shadow of dishonesty.

"Perhaps I'm here on holiday, like so many others."

For all that he had taken a bath in the healing waters, she couldn't picture him relaxing on holiday. He was as driven as she and no doubt needed to keep himself as busy. Otherwise, why would he have turned to the life of an investigator upon his return from the war? As the heir to a viscount, he needn't work.

"You don't lie very convincingly."

He dropped his hand with a shrug. "Perhaps I don't care to make the effort to lie to you. I'm not here in Bath to disrupt your efforts."

As long as he didn't get in the way of her investigation, perhaps she shouldn't waste so much time wondering. The Marquess of Bath was adamant that he was employing Mr. Salmon and no other on the case; his refusal to provide a reward even when his dear grandmother asked proved that much. With no monetary incentive, the only reason Wayland would have for solving the case before her would be to spite her. Perhaps she was softening toward him too much, but she didn't think she was in danger of that. He wasn't that good a liar.

"I don't have time to dawdle. Lyle might have already found something of use."

"Then let's not waste time." Not taking her hint to leave her to the investigation alone, Wayland fell into step alongside her and escorted her the remainder of the way to the Pump Room.

When they came within view of the dormant King's Bath, Katherine spotted her father's seal on a carriage door hitched outside. She speared Wayland with an ornery look. He didn't seem bothered by her displeasure.

Calmly, he informed her, "I sent Harriet on ahead, in case I was unable to find you."

She ignored him and entered the Pump Room.

The building next to the King's Bath was designed to impress. In the darkness, she couldn't make out the carvings on the exterior, but the interior of the room was no less opulent. A short corridor led to a vaulting room on the right. The clean white walls led up to a domed roof two stories above. Corinthian pillars supported a balcony at the far end of the room, where a grand piano resided, now devoid of a player.

The rest of the room was a wide-open space, with little to furnish it save for the counter in the middle of the south wall where the fountain allowed easy access to the healing water. For the moment, the only person manning the counter was Grandma Bath as she fussed over Lyle. If the look on his face was any indication, the old woman was hindering more than she was helping. Hopefully, Sir David, on Lyle's other side, was proving to be of greater use.

The only light in the room wafted from the candles set atop the counter near the pump. However, the meager light must have been enough to identify her, for the moment she walked into the room, two other people gathered caught her by either arm and pulled her into the space between the nearest door and the one by which she had entered. Pru and Harriet.

"Captain Wayland is right," Harriet hissed as she released Katherine. Her voice didn't carry far, though it seemed to echo in the wide, mostly empty space. "You shouldn't be taking chances with your safety! One woman has already been harmed today."

When Harriet sank into a curtsey, Katherine glanced over her shoulder to see that Wayland had followed them to their private location. The only other person she saw in the room, Lord Bath, hovered near his grandmother, trying to convince her to sit. Movement stirred in the shadows of the far wall, near the piano. Katherine's heart skipped a beat before she recognized Mr. Salmon. Although he might be loath to admit it, Lyle's invention provided *his* best chance of catching the thief, as well.

Harriet babbled, "Thank you, Captain, for looking out for her. We are in your debt."

Katherine returned her attention to her friends. "He walked with me to the Pump Room. We were in no danger. I'm certain I spotted at least one watch patrol along the way." After the incident today, Lord Bath didn't appear to be gambling with the safety of the visitors to his town.

What if the patrol scared off the thief?

Although it nettled her to admit such a thing, Katherine had to acknowledge that it might be for the best. If the thief had escalated to violence, more people might be harmed. Perhaps even killed... Katherine touched her throat. She'd had more than enough of murderers for the time being, hence why she had chosen a thief this time. Thieves resided in the shadows, trying not to be seen. They didn't hit ladies with old statues simply so they could abscond with a very distinctive necklace.

"We cannot be too careful," Wayland admonished her. "I'm worried that the thief is growing bolder."

Truthfully, so was she.

"I will solve this as soon as may be. We'll have to wait for Lyle's invention to tell us what he can about the attack tonight."

Pru frowned. "What have you learned since we last spoke of this? Can we point more definitively to any of the suspects?"

"It isn't Mr. Salmon," Katherine answered, inwardly sighing. "I was at the table with him and Lord Bath when Lady Dalhousie screamed."

"Who, then?" Harriet asked. She opened her mouth, but Katherine cut her off.

"It isn't Mrs. Julien, either. Lady Dalhousie and her maid described a man, and Mrs. Julien would have had to move exceedingly quickly to reach her husband in the garden before I arrived. She wasn't wearing a dark cloak, which Lady Dalhousie described."

"I don't know how much stock I would put in Lady Dalhousie's recount of the event," Wayland added, "but I concur. The thief is not Mrs. Julien, nor her husband."

"We've seen a cloaked figure around town at both the robberies that have occurred. I believe that she saw a cloaked figure, but whether that figure looked precisely how she described or acted as heinously, I cannot say."

"She was struck over the head rather hard, from the look of it," Pru interjected. Whether that was a point in Lady Dalhousie's defense or one against her, Katherine didn't know.

"The only clue I found in the garden, by the door leading to the back stair..." Katherine trailed off. She dropped her gaze to her reticule, frowning.

"What is it?" Pru asked.

After a moment's hesitation, Katherine dug her fingers into her reticule and groped until she found the button. She offered it wordlessly to the other woman.

Pru recoiled the moment she recognized it. "It isn't mine! Or at the very least, if it is, I must have dropped it the other day. I was with Lord Annandale, searching for a deck of cards from the hotel staff when I heard the scream. If you don't believe me, Miss Newcomb can attest to that fact. She's been following me about like a lost kitten."

Katherine took a moment to absorb that information. She *had* encountered Pru by that very door the other day, shortly after Mrs. Quicke's theft. Perhaps it had fallen off her clothes then.

Pru added, "I'm not even wearing that dress today."

No. She was wearing her prettier dress, no longer attempting to appear dowdy. Her nicer dresses certainly weren't adorned with these atrocious buttons. Katherine slipped the button into her reticule again, chiding herself over suspecting Pru. They had been at Lord Northbrook's house party together! Not to mention, the woman had become a friend.

Unless... what if Pru had an accomplice? She had been so insistent that Katherine accept her mother's job, which ultimately led to them traveling to Bath together, without Mrs. Burwick. Katherine had been so caught up in the investigation that she hadn't had time to consider Pru's whereabouts. What if during the times she allegedly was with Lord Annandale, instead she was off stealing jewels?

Don't be ludicrous. Katherine was grasping at mist. Pru wasn't a thief, and she certainly wasn't a violent person... the incident with the Pink-Ribbon Murderer notwithstanding. The Burglar of Bath had to be someone else.

"The only person left is Sir Hugh. He claimed that earring I found in the hotel."

Pru nodded. "And he has an influx of quid for the card tables. He must be selling the jewels as fast as he receives them. He isn't a skilled enough player to have earned all that blunt."

"I went to see a pawnbroker the other morning. He hadn't seen any of the jewels we described."

Wayland nodded. "I think I know the shop to which you're referring. It might not be the only place to sell jewels within driving distance of Bath."

"I'll ask Lyle. He has contacts he might be able to put to use to point us in a better direction. The stolen jewels must have turned up for sale somewhere by now unless the thief is taking out the stones and selling them by themselves." As she spoke, she turned away from the group to cross the distance toward Lyle. They desperately needed another clue if they had any hope of unmasking the true thief.

Wiping away the sweat on his brow, Lyle straightened. He looked pleased with himself. Above the sound of his invention as it boiled the pump water into steam, he loudly said, "It'll take a few minutes before the steam does its trick."

Katherine sidestepped the humongous contraption. How did Lyle mean to bring this back to London? Shaking off the question, she beckoned him closer.

He begged a moment from Grandma Bath, who waved him off, and joined Katherine in a quieter corner. "I don't yet have an answer for you."

"I know. I have a favor to ask."

Although she studied his face for signs of trepidation, all she found was his exuberance over testing his invention. He truly was the happiest when inventing; he ought to make more time for it, rather than accepting a back-breaking workload of patrols.

"What do you need?" he asked.

"You have contacts near Bath to track stolen items, don't you?"

He frowned but nodded. "It's how I knew of the pawnshop. But they aren't all in Bath, and there might be others evading the law that I haven't been able to locate."

"Could you reach out to your contacts to see if anyone has sold them the jewels or the gems from them? I have a hunch, but without catching him in the act or someone confirming that he sold the jewels to them, I cannot prove it."

Lyle narrowed his eyes. "I'll ask and let you know should any of them confirm the sale. Who is your suspect?"

"Sir Hugh. I'm certain I've seen him with tarnished and scratched silver on his clothing, and he'd had a recent influx of funds." Everyone else, either she'd ruled out, or was... unthinkable.

As the air filled with more steam, escaping Lyle's contraption with a hiss and intermittent whistle, the stench of rotten eggs assaulted her. She wrinkled her nose and stepped away, even as Lyle stepped closer to look. At the front of his invention was a foot-wide glass-encased space. The statue rested within. With the steam, the glass had fogged to the point that she had to squint in order to discern the silhouette of the sculpture.

"Drat, I can't see anything." Lyle opened a hinge on the top of the glass box, revealing a small door wide enough for him to stick his arm inside. Sir David adhered himself to Lyle's elbow as he peered within. Steam billowed out of the hole, intensifying the horrid smell.

Pinching her nose to ward away the smell, Grandma Bath leaned closer. As she did, she jostled her spectacles, and they slipped off the tip of her nose and tumbled into the box. "Oh dear!"

"Don't touch that," Lyle warned her. "The steam will be scalding."

"I'll retrieve that for you, my lady," Sir David volunteered. He rolled his sleeves to his elbows and donned a leather glove before he carefully slid his hand into the hot box. As he removed the spectacles, he muttered under his breath and peered closer at them.

Katherine stepped closer, able to see a fractal pattern on the lenses of Grandma Bath's spectacles. Sir David's hand trembled as he stared at it, mesmerized.

"Eureka, that's it!" He handed the spectacles to Grandma Bath and turned to Lyle. "Murphy, I have to run. Best of luck with your invention." He doffed the glove, clapped Lyle on the shoulder, and bolted out of the Pump Room.

Where was he going? Had he seen the imprint on the sculpture and ran before it implicated him?

Lyle peered into the contraption and swore.

Katherine wasn't sure whether to run after Sir David or help Lyle.

"I'm sorry, Katherine. Something's gone wrong. It didn't work."

His shoulders slumped as he slipped on the discarded glove and reached into the box to remove the statue. Moisture beaded on the surface as the cooler air struck it. At the base, a shimmer of metallic flecks wrapped around the sculpture. Excitement stole Katherine's breath for a moment before she registered the size of the imprint. She glanced down at her hand. It was smaller — much smaller.

Sir Hugh couldn't have hands *that* small, could he? Katherine hadn't noticed the size of his hands when they'd spoken. If she didn't know better, she'd think the burglar must be a woman. But Lady Dalhousie had been adamant that her attacker was a man...

Looking lost, Lyle turned to her. "I don't know what happened. The steam must have shrunk the residue left by the attacker's hand. I'll try again, but I'm not certain if there's anything left to find on the sculpture."

Katherine patted his shoulder. "I don't blame you, Lyle. Even this is more than we would have been able to determine from looking at the statue ourselves. Thank you for trying."

He sighed but nodded. "I only wish I'd been of more use. It looks as though discovering where the jewels are being sold is our last hope of finding a clue."

Katherine prayed that, this time, a stroke of luck would befall them. She was running out of suspects.

CHAPTER SIXTEEN

L ady Dalhousie could very well have died from the last attack. That knowledge swam in Katherine's mind. She was unable to sleep, tossing and turning in the bed she shared with Harriet until her maid glared at her, gathered some blankets and a pillow, and moved to the floor.

Even Emma didn't like the tossing and turning and soon joined Harriet. Katherine couldn't help it. Every time she shut her eyes, she recalled the Pink-Ribbon Murderer.

Mere weeks ago, she had stumbled across the prone and strangled body of a young woman on the brink of death. Only her fortuitous arrival had stopped the killer from completing the task he'd set out to do. *Sard it!* Katherine had chosen the Burglar of Bath as her next investigation *because* the thief had yet to harm anyone. They slipped in and out of homes, public places, private rooms. Like a ghost. That was the way it was supposed to stay.

Now? If she didn't catch the thief soon, Katherine feared that she would face another frightening moment when she stumbled over a nearly dead body. Perhaps this time, she wouldn't be able to save the victim.

I have to do something. Unable to sleep, Katherine resolved to catch Sir Hugh in a suspicious act. In order to do that, she had to follow him.

There were no places at all to hide in the guest wing, with only a narrow corridor dividing the two rows of rooms. The narrow stair exited near Lady Dalhousie's room, whereas the wider main staircase surfaced in the middle of the hallway. If Katherine lingered in the common room on the ground floor, she might not catch Sir Hugh in the act of leaving the hotel.

However, the first floor, where the Long Hall was located, provided a better vantage point of both staircases. If she hid near the servants' stair, she had a splendid view of the main staircase in case Sir Hugh used that one instead. Because she expected a long wait, she busied herself jotting down her every suspicion in a slim leather volume, chewed in the corners from Emma's pilfering. At first, it was difficult to read the words she added, but the light grew as she slanted her page toward the nearest window.

When she heard footsteps on the main staircase, she scrambled to her feet and prepared to follow the culprit. She was in luck! With his collar curled up around his chin and his shoulders hunched, Sir Hugh snuck down the staircase. If only he'd been wearing a dark cloak, she might have apprehended him on the spot! He looked up to no good.

After a count of five, she hurried down the stairs after him, stepping lightly in the hopes that she wouldn't be noticed. When she reached the common room, she expected it to be deserted. To her surprise, she found a sleepy-eyed maid cleaning the tables and settling the chairs around them for visitors.

As the woman spotted her, she straightened, but Katherine waved her off. Since Sir Hugh was leaving the hotel, she didn't intend to stay either. The door swung shut behind him, and she quickened her pace so she could peek out and discover which direction he had taken. He strode toward the center of town, where Bath Abbey loomed.

The early-morning chill was bracing. Fortunately, the air was dry; Katherine feared that, had it been humid, her breath might have formed ice crystals in her eyelashes. As it was, she wished she had thought to bring mittens despite it only being mid-September. She tucked her cold hands beneath her pelisse instead to warm them from the biting air.

When she judged Sir Hugh to be sufficiently ahead of her, she strode away from the hotel in pursuit. Unfortunately, she didn't get far.

"Lady Katherine!"

Tarnation! Katherine inwardly swore as she heard the caller's Scottish brogue. She couldn't be rude to Lord Annandale, of all people, not when she suspected that Pru might be developing a preference for him.

As she turned, he jogged to reach her. "I cannae say I'm disappointed to find you're an early riser. Can we speak a minute?"

Every second she spent with him, Sir Hugh strode farther away. However, Katherine was wise enough to know that she had little hope of following her best suspect this morning. She might as well capitulate to Lord Annandale's request.

With a wave of her hand, she indicated the hotel. "Why don't we speak indoors?"

He nodded and opened the door for her to enter.

Inside, the serving girl quickly settled them at a clean table with a cup of steaming chocolate and a Sally Lunn still warm from the oven. In all, a far preferable way to spend the morning. They sat next to a lit hearth, the crackle of the flames soothing her as much as the warmth shed by them.

When Lord Annandale said nothing to further their conversation but stared into his cup, Katherine prodded him. "I must admit to some surprise seeing you out of bed so early. Don't most peers prefer to lie abed until noon?"

He frowned, the corners of his mouth disappearing into his auburn beard as he studied her. "What slug-gard has time fer that? There's work to be done in a day, at least there is back home." He passed a hand over his beard. "Miss Burwick doesn't lie abed all day, does she?"

When he spoke Pru's name, he rolled the *r* almost as if he were purring. Katherine started to understand how Pru might have been pulled under his spell. Lord Annandale was an attractive man, not to mention one of the few lords who took his duties seriously.

"She does not," Katherine answered.

The set of his shoulders relaxed a bit. He took a sip from his cup, cleared his throat, and glanced around the nearly empty room. Aside from the maid, they were the only two people occupying it, since the sun had scarcely risen. He met Katherine's gaze then studied the contents of his cup.

"Ye're Miss Burwick's matchmaker, are ye not?"

"I am," Katherine answered, wary.

He coughed into his fist as a flush climbed up his neck to disappear into his beard. "I've nae done this before." He cleared his throat again and fiddled with his collar. "I knew you've got yer eye on Wayland for her—"

Katherine winced. How far had that rumor spread? Pru would not be pleased.

"—but I ken he has nary the least bit o' interest in her. Not to say that she isn't lovely." Annandale raised his hands, as if trying to ward away an attack. "She is. But Wayland..." He scrubbed the back of his neck with one hand. "Wayland has his eye on a diff'rent bit o' muslin, if ye ken my meaning."

Katherine didn't know how he could have made himself plainer. Wayland didn't want to marry Pru; that she knew already, and it was a fortunate thing at that, for Pru would be more likely to slap him than kiss him.

"I know Wayland has no intention of making an offer for Miss Burwick," Katherine answered. What a bizarre statement to say aloud. For some reason, she couldn't picture Wayland making an offer for anyone. Perhaps that was due to the fact that she thought of him as more of a detective, perhaps a thorn in her side, but a professional worthy of respect and perhaps envy rather than a man with... desires. Again, that moment in the alley when her imagination had run wild with her flashed across her mind. Wayland's body close to hers. For a moment, she'd considered kissing him. But he...

She shook the thought from her mind.

Fortunately, Lord Annandale didn't seem to notice her sudden preoccupation. His blush climbed into his cheeks now as he admitted, "I'd like ye to match me with Miss Burwick."

Had she just gotten her first proposal? In the past, the men who found themselves attached to her clients — whether said client was an official one or merely a sister she hoped to help — had always asked the object of their affections directly. She had never had anything to do with arranging the marriages themselves. What was she to say?

If Mrs. Burwick ever learned that Lord Annandale had come begging to Katherine for Pru's hand, Katherine would have far more notoriety and clients than she wanted. Even if she must pretend at playing the matchmaker in order to hide her true objectives, she had hoped not to earn a reputation for being good at it. A good reputation put pressure on her to try to arrange the matches she agreed to.

Though in this case, she believed Pru craved the match more than she let on. However, she couldn't accept a proposal without speaking first to her friend. In fact, it was likely for the best if she wasn't put in the middle of this.

Choosing her words carefully, Katherine answered, "I'm hired more as an advisor than someone meant to handle all the particulars of marriage. You'll have to ask Miss Burwick directly, and if she's so inclined, she will accept. I'll remember you to her and encourage her, but the decision is ultimately hers."

"Aye, of course." He bit his lip and glanced at Katherine out of the corner of his eye before he asked, "Do ye ken if she has any preference for me at all? If she has her heart set on Wayland..."

That rumor might be preferable to the one of Katherine matched with Wayland, but it still aggrieved her to hear it flaunted. Why must people gossip at all? Perhaps she shouldn't disparage the habit, as she sometimes learned pivotal information pertaining to her investigations in such a manner.

"I don't believe Miss Burwick will be heartbroken to learn that Captain Wayland is disinclined to make the match."

Lord Annandale straightened. His blush faded, and

his smile grew. Zeus, the poor man was smitten with Pru. Katherine had to do something to facilitate the match, since it seemed obvious to her that Pru returned his affections. If she only spent a bit more time alone in Lord Annandale's presence, perhaps Pru would realize it herself. But how? Now that Miss Newcomb had taken to stumbling after Pru no matter where she went, it was impossible. Unless... perhaps Katherine could arrange for Miss Newcomb to be too busy to serve as an impediment to Pru's match! Although Mrs. Fairchild was an early riser, Katherine expected that she still had an hour before the rival matchmaker awakened.

Annandale said, "There's hope, then?"

Katherine smiled. "I don't see why not. Spend a bit more time with her, and we'll see."

"What do ye think might tip the scales in my favor?"

How was she supposed to answer that? After a moment's thought and another sip of the rich, bitter chocolate, she said, "Miss Burwick enjoys the freedom to act as she pleases. She doesn't care for the trappings of polite society."

His lips tipped up at the corners, the look in his eyes softening. "I've noticed. 'Tis refreshing. Some say I'm a bit wild, too."

"If you don't mind my asking, you're friends with Sir Hugh, are you not?"

"Aye..." He frowned, focusing his full attention upon her. "Has Miss Burwick asked after that scoundrel?"

"She hasn't." At least, not as anything other than a suspect in the robberies. Katherine leaned forward, her senses humming. "Why do you refer to your friend as a scoundrel?"

Annandale scowled. "The blighter's been spending far too much time in Miss Burwick's company after he knows she caught my eye."

Jealousy. Katherine bit her tongue before she laughed.

"I hear he came into some money of late. I must admit, I found it odd that he carried around his mother's earrings as a keepsake. Do you know anything about that?"

The Scottish lord looked at her as if she'd grown a third eye. "He does carry his ma's earrings about. E'er since her passing, he's been selling 'em steady to pay off his debts."

If Sir Hugh had sold his mother's jewelry here in Bath, could he have slipped in an item or two that hadn't belonged to her?

Katherine asked, "Would those be debts incurred by gambling?"

"His da's debts." Lord Annandale gathered an air of disapproval, deflating a moment later with a defeated sigh. "He's nae done well to turn to cards as a means to cover them. 'Tis why I followed him to Bath. He's a good lad, but he thinks he can win and square away his life. It does not work like that."

"No," Katherine murmured, "it doesn't."

Had Sir Hugh grown tired of losing at cards and decided to supplement his income by stealing jewels instead? Why, then, had he chosen to lose his newfound money in a card match? Katherine couldn't fathom it, but then she didn't see the appeal of risking money at the table to begin with.

"Have you and Sir Hugh been in town long?"

"Months," Annandale confessed.

The timeline fit.

She smiled, though it felt a bit forced. "Perhaps it's fortunate that Miss Burwick and I decided to venture here after the close of the Season, then. You might have missed us, otherwise."

"That'd be a sore pity."

After draining his cup, Lord Annandale set it in the saucer with a click. He scraped back his chair and stood. "Many thanks for takin' the time to hash this out with me, Lady Katherine."

"My pleasure." She hastily stood as well. "If you'll forgive one more question, I'm curious."

The marquess cocked his head to the side then nodded.

"When did Captain Wayland contact you requesting to stay at the townhouse you were letting?"

"Ah, that." Annandale laughed. "The mad blighter showed up on my doorstep one eve and begged me a favor. Said he'd followed a bit o' muslin to town and he feared she'd be up to no good. He ne'er did tell me her name, but I think his affections are obvious enough, don't you?"

The one thing obvious to Katherine was that Lord Annandale was exceedingly gullible. Katherine knew that Wayland had to have ventured to Bath in order to solve the mystery of the stolen jewels. However, the fact that he'd arrived spur of the moment without asking Annandale in advance informed Katherine that he'd only arranged the trip after learning that Katherine intended to solve this mystery. He pretended to play fair, but he'd had an ulterior motive all along. He must have taken offense in some way that she had solved the Pink-Ribbon Murders before him.

Well, I intend to solve these thefts first, as well.

Katherine parted ways with Lord Annandale, venturing above stairs as she searched for Mrs. Fairchild. Pressing her ear to the woman's door along the way alerted Katherine to the fact that the woman had risen, even if she hadn't yet left her room. Unfortunately, Katherine wasn't quiet enough to fool Emma. Her pug whined from behind the closed door to her room.

With a sigh, Katherine detoured to fetch Emma's leash and escort her out of doors to void her bladder. Harriet was still asleep on the floor. Katherine must have tired her out more than she'd thought, with all the restless tossing and turning throughout the night.

The air was no less brisk for Katherine's foray next to the fire. If anything, it felt even colder. She rushed Emma through their jaunt in the gardens. Unfortunately, once she did her business, the pug was not at all interested in returning inside. Instead, she yipped and pulled with her full inconsiderable weight on the leash, leading Katherine deeper into the gardens. To keep the poor dog from strangling herself, Katherine followed.

Emma led her all the way to the Marquess of Bath. What was he doing out here, on such a bitter cold morning?

"Lady Katherine," he greeted her with a smile, not

seeming to notice the way Emma begged for his attention.

"Lord Bath. What an unexpected delight. Why are you out in the garden and not inside the hotel?" She twisted, looking over her shoulder toward the looming building. She didn't espy any movement, indicating that the bulk of the residents were still abed.

A furrow forming on his brow, the marquess followed her gaze toward the hotel. "I'm worried over this latest theft," he admitted. "It isn't like this thief to harm someone in the process of his robbery."

"That means we have yet another danger to look out for," Katherine completed.

Lord Bath nodded once, tersely. "Precisely." His jaw was clenched, his usual jovial air replaced by one of seriousness. "I thought I'd take a walk in the gardens to clear my head. These afford a good view of the hotel, in case the thief returns. I can head him off."

The marquess was attempting to catch the robber himself? "That is... an admirable yet surprisingly direct approach. Haven't you hired Mr. Salmon to handle matters such as this? Granted, you know my opinion of his professional acumen..."

"I'm beginning to worry it might be too much for him to handle," Lord Bath admitted. "I've had reports from a patrol who, only the other day, encountered a group of robbers and chased them off from a town-house near here. I'm afraid every would-be thief will now come out of the shadows and try to take advantage of the situation. We could have several thieves in town. They'll drive away visitors, for certain." His face fell. "Until now, most have seen the thefts as a sort of entertainment, but if people continue to get hurt..."

She laid her hand on his sleeve, wincing. "The group the patrol encountered, they weren't thieves."

"They must have been. They were climbing into a window near the scene of a previous crime."

She examined the sky as she admitted, "Or investigating the crime." As she met his baffled gaze, she cringed. "I was one of the group. Mr. Murphy and Captain Wayland were with me. They can attest that we were only searching for clues so we could end this."

The expression on the marquess's face turned to stone. "Katherine," he admonished her. "What would your father think?"

"He would applaud my initiative." Though perhaps not her choice of company.

"I highly doubt he would approve of you putting yourself in such danger. You ought to leave the matter to professionals."

I am one such professional. Since she couldn't

point that out, she settled for "Such as Lyle Murphy, you mean?"

Lord Bath exhaled, exasperation and irritation clear in the flare of his nostrils and set of his eyebrows. Whatever disparaging thing he meant to say regarding her friend, a whimper from the dog at his feet caught his attention. His forbidding expression faded, replaced with a softer one.

Wagging her tail, Emma jumped on her hind legs to plant her paws somewhere in the vicinity of his kneecaps. Her mouth open, her tongue lolled as she whined again, canting her head to the side and offering him the saddest eyes Katherine had ever seen. Emma was quite the actress when she wanted to be. If Katherine didn't know better, she would think Emma one of the most neglected, flea-bitten strays.

The dog fooled Lord Bath, for he bent to rub Emma's ears. With a yip of glee, the dog thrust her head into his wide sleeve. He yelped with a laugh. "That tickles!"

"Emma." Katherine tried to herd her pet away, but the pug refused to move. Her tail wagged a mile a minute as she buried her face even farther up his sleeve. "Emma, what is the matter with you?" Katherine grasped her dog around the middle and pulled.

The dog squealed, grasping something in her teeth and drawing it out of Lord Bath's sleeve as Katherine tugged on her. Why, it was his cuff! As the wide cuff straightened, some crumbs that had fallen into it fell to the ground. Emma attacked them with exuberance.

Wry, Katherine commented, "She must be hungrier than I expected, if she's so adamant to get at what has fallen into your cuffs."

"Oh dear." He laughed. He straightened out his other cuff beneath his greatcoat sleeve. As he shook it out, more crumbs fell. "I usually try to ensure my sleeves don't catch on anything, but I didn't notice while I was eating breakfast this morning. How embarrassing."

"Think nothing of it," Katherine said with a smile and a wave of her hand. "I'm only sorry that Emma was so bothersome to get at your food. Is that a crumble of bacon?"

"It well might be." Lord Bath grinned, inviting her to share the joke.

At least he was no longer chiding her for trying to follow her passion and solve this case when he did not. She collected her dog from the ground. "I should feed her before she finishes and searches you for more. Good day, my lord."

"Good day, Lady Katherine." He rubbed his hands together for warmth.

Hurrying back into the hotel, Katherine lingered by the fire to warm up as Emma shamelessly begged for breakfast. The serving girl promised to deliver a bowl of chopped meat for the dog straight away.

The moment Emma finished her meal and Katherine felt warm enough to return above stairs, approaching footsteps warned her of someone coming down to meet her. Katherine crossed to the foot of the staircase just in time to block Mrs. Fairchild's path.

The woman sniffed, pulling her shawl closer around her shoulders. Given the lack of outerwear, Mrs. Fairchild must have come down to break her fast and had no intention of leaving the hotel at this early hour. Katherine had time yet to plant the seed that would keep Miss Newcomb far too busy to pester Pru.

"Good morning," she said cordially.

Mrs. Fairchild returned the greeting between gritted teeth.

"How is Miss Newcomb faring in her attempt to emulate Miss Burwick?"

Mrs. Fairchild scowled, her expression filled with malice. "This has been your aim all along. You've... you've paid the men to pay attention to your... hoyden of a client! And in so doing, you've managed to wrap me around your little scheme and ruin Miss Newcomb's chance of happiness!"

Happiness... or wealth and prestige? Katherine wasn't certain what Mrs. Fairchild's aim was for her clients, other than the fact that she was highly competitive and wanted to outmatch Katherine. Ordinarily, Katherine might be happy to let her do so, but not if it would mean Pru's unhappiness. She genuinely wanted the best for Pru, and if that happened to be a marriage to Lord Annandale, then she wanted to do her part to facilitate that.

Even if it meant tricking Mrs. Fairchild in order to ensure that Miss Newcomb was well occupied and give Pru and Annandale some privacy. And she knew exactly how to make Miss Newcomb more attractive to the prince. Pru had said the prince wanted a woman that didn't hang off his every word. Her rival would never trust her, but if she couched her advice to help Miss Newcomb catch the prince's eye in disparaging words or even discouragement... that seemed more the sort of language Mrs. Fairchild preferred to speak.

She tried for a laugh and hoped it didn't sound too forced. "Miss Newcomb will never be able to prove to the prince now that she values him over his title and money. She might as well throw herself at his feet and beg him to have her, for all the good it will do. She's but one more fawning female in his circle, unlike Miss Burwick, who will have nothing to do with him. Yet who does he seek out?" Katherine tapped her lips. "In fact, it might be better if you and Miss Newcomb packed up and left town, what with the escalation of these thefts."

To her surprise, Mrs. Fairchild looked genuinely frightened. "I don't like that a woman has now been harmed in the pursuit of these jewels."

Katherine softened toward her. She kneeled to gather her dog. Emma was only too happy to sit in Katherine's arms and have her belly scratched. In a soft voice, Katherine confessed, "I don't like it any better than you. I had hoped to escape more violence."

Mrs. Fairchild had nearly lost a client to the Pink-Ribbon Murderer. Although Miss Young had lived, she had departed the house party as soon as possible, a testament to her good sense. *Would* Mrs. Fairchild choose to leave with her client instead of pursue the match? Katherine had expected her to do the very opposite, but it would solve Katherine's problem either way. And it would be one less person in town who might be hurt if she didn't solve these thefts soon enough.

"I'd half hoped it was you following Miss Newcomb around in a cloak, hoping to scare us off."

Katherine frowned. "I beg your pardon?"

Mrs. Fairchild's shoulders slumped. "Miss Newcomb has told me that, several times when she's out following your client and her would-be paramours, she has seen a tall figure in a dark cloak. They're never close enough for her to see their face. After what Lady Dalhousie described..."

"It might be the thief."

The woman nodded. "It might be."

The silence stretched between them as Katherine contemplated that information. Miss Newcomb had seen the thief. How often, and where?

Mrs. Fairchild broke the silence first. "I don't understand it. It makes no sense, to be honest. I would understand if the thief was following the prince, for he sparkles more than most of the ladies! But Miss Newcomb? She doesn't even own a pair of earrings. She has nothing to steal."

Neither did Pru, nor Annandale. What was the thief's motive?

"Perhaps it might be better to leave Bath," Katherine muttered under her breath. "Before it's too late."

Mrs. Fairchild drew herself up and stormed down the rest of the stairs, past Katherine. "Not on your life," she hissed as she marched past. "Miss Newcomb is getting her match, and nothing you can do will possibly interfere. That, I vow."

The thief seemed to be escalating, but as Katherine watched her rival walk away, one thing was for certain: Mrs. Fairchild was frightened, but not enough to call off this unspoken competition. Which meant that she would undoubtedly use the words of advice Katherine had dripped into her ear. Pru and Annandale would find the privacy they needed in order for Pru to realize that she had developed feelings for him.

That, at least, was going according to plan — even if nothing else was.

CHAPTER SEVENTEEN

W hen Katherine next saw Lyle later that afternoon, her stomach sank. He didn't look like a man who'd come bearing good news. In fact, he barely bent to scratch Emma's head as she wagged her tail and ran to greet him in the threshold of Katherine's room. With a sigh, she held the door wide and ushered him in.

"No luck?" she asked as she shut the door.

He shook his head. "I've heard word from or personally visited all my contacts in the area. A few have heard from Sir Hugh — in fact, the pawnbroker we visited the other day was sold a pair of diamond earrings. Sir Hugh wanted the blunt, not to retrieve the jewels at a later date. However, no one has been approached with any of the jewels we are searching for."

"The earrings—"

Lyle shook his head. "Not on our list."

Probably the earrings of his mother he'd had in his pocket. Was that where he was going earlier in the morning — to pawn them?

On the bed, Harriet paused in darning a hole in the hem of one of Katherine's dresses. "Do you suppose he might be holding onto the stolen jewels to sell them last? It would be very conspicuous to sell them now."

Katherine started to nod then frowned. She sat on the hard stool in front of the writing desk. "You're right, but... Oh, sard it! How are we supposed to know which of the past thefts was true?"

"Language," Harriet chided her.

Lyle didn't seem bothered by it. Just as well, for he had taught her most of the foul language she knew. "What do you mean?" He crossed to the bed and perched on the end.

Emma made a wild leap to land next to him, only to slip off the edge and fall to the floor once more. Absently, his gaze fixed on Katherine, Lyle bent to retrieve the pug and set her on the coverlet. She climbed into his lap instead.

"Careful," Katherine warned him. "She'll have your pocket watch out in a moment."

That watch was Lyle's pride and joy, having been awarded to him on the basis of merit for consistently solving the cases presented to him by Bow Street. He hooked Emma around the middle and perched her on his knees as he scratched her beneath the ribbon tied around her neck. She seemed pleased with the compromise.

Katherine added, "There have been accounts in the scandal rags of ladies who reported their jewels stolen wearing them to recent events. Lady Carleton, for instance. They can't all have been mistaken thefts, but that leaves us with a list of jewels that may or may not have been stolen."

"And a man who may or may not have stolen them," Lyle answered solemnly.

Katherine frowned, thinking of Lord Hugh again. Why would a man who had been adamant that he retrieve his mother's precious earrings turn around and sell them a moment later? Because he needed the money, as Lord Annandale had attested. Those earrings had meant nothing to him beyond the value they represented.

"I'm certain Lord Hugh was selling the earrings that belonged to his mother," Katherine muttered.

Harriet lowered the dress and needle onto her lap. "He still might have hidden away the other jewels. I've made friends with a young woman in the hotel who happens to have caught the eye of Sir Hugh's valet. If you'd like, I can ask her to have him search the room for us, to see what he finds."

"That would be helpful," Katherine agreed with a nod. At the very least, they weren't sitting and twirling their thumbs while they waited for the thief to make a mistake.

"What of the Juliens?" Harriet asked.

Katherine pressed her lips together and stared at her lap, refusing to answer.

"You said they were in the garden at the time of Lady Dalhousie's theft. Mrs. Julien might be the cloaked figure you have been following, the one you think is the thief. It wouldn't have been terribly hard for her to sneak down that passage unnoticed."

"I ran for the stairs the moment I heard the scream."

Harriet pointed her finger. "But you've admitted that you were across the room. There were multiple people between you and the door. Mrs. Julien might have hidden the cloak somewhere in the garden and pretended to have been there all along."

Tarnation! Katherine hated when her maid formed such a coherent argument. She didn't want to consider the Juliens — in fact, she had been adamant to rule them out. Unfortunately, the evidence wasn't allowing her to do so.

Lyle mentioned, "They have a grandson, don't they? Perhaps he might know whether or not his grandparents have been acting suspiciously during their foray in Bath."

Katherine sighed. She leaned forward, propping her elbows on her knees and laying her head in her hands. The room was so small that Emma was able to stretch across the narrow distance to lick Katherine's forehead. She patted her pet.

"I am no longer close with Scott. We haven't spoken in years."

"I've seen Captain Wayland speaking with him," Harriet put in. "Perhaps they've become friends."

If he had been angry with her for considering the Juliens earlier, he wouldn't be any happier with this new line in the investigation. It was time to discover precisely how much he meant his offer of help.

Reluctantly, Katherine said, "I'll ask Wayland and see if he'll help."

———————

"Tell me this is a joke."

Katherine jumped at Wayland's biting tone. Even bracing herself for it, she wasn't ready for the vehemence in his expression. She cast a quick look over her shoulder, into the hotel common room teeming with people, before she turned back to him. The moment he had arrived at the hotel, she had beckoned him into a nook at the end of the room. A door led into the kitchen, and from time to time, a footman or maid passed with vittles for the patrons. Otherwise, they were undisturbed.

The heat from the kitchen climbed up Katherine's back as she faced Wayland. "You said you wanted to help. I'm asking for your help."

He swore under his breath and turned away from her. For a moment, she feared he would storm out of the hotel. At the corner of the nook, he turned back to face her. "This is asking too much."

She lifted her chin. "Then refuse."

He swore again, so vehemently that it made the serving girl jump as she emerged from the kitchen. The teapot nearly toppled off her tray. Katherine helped her to right it, and after a moment, she scurried past Wayland without looking at him.

Katherine said, "I'd rather not suspect them either, but I've found nothing to rule them out. If they have been collecting the jewels, they must have stashed them in or near their place of residence. Scott has access."

"Then why don't you ask him yourself, *Kitty*?"

She scowled, crossing her arms beneath her breasts. "That isn't my name. And Scott and I haven't spoken in years. You're on better terms with him than I am. You understand him better. He'll be more likely to listen to you."

"This investigation has addled your mind if you think for a moment that I will make those poor people feel worse for being suspected of being thieves!"

He approached her, cornering her against the wall as he spoke. Another person exited the kitchen, paying them no mind. Katherine swallowed. She breathed shallowly, staring up into Wayland's forbidding expression.

Softly, so others wouldn't hear and come to investigate, she whispered, "You claimed to be waiting for me to ask for your help. Well, I'm asking, Wayland. If you want to help, this is what I need in order to solve the case."

He held her gaze and didn't say a word. His nostrils flared with every breath.

Her stomach shrank as she realized that she had asked too much of him after all. For all that he'd professed to want to help, he was in Bath for a different reason. She might have given away her hand, but he didn't seem keen on pursuing that line of questioning.

Would she have to approach Scott herself and hope that he didn't shut her out? Or worse, expose her for a detective. Polite society wouldn't give her entry into the places she needed to be in order to investigate some of the most puzzling cases if they thought her no better than a Bow Street Runner.

Which, in her opinion, was a valiant profession, not that society at large agreed.

Katherine shoved past Wayland's body, breaking the strained silence between them. "Forget I asked."

As she walked away, she hoped that Sir Hugh's valet was persuaded to search his room and find something, because frankly, she was running out of options.

CHAPTER EIGHTEEN

The frigid predawn air didn't do much to wake Katherine the next morning as she urged Emma to make water so they could both return to the soft, warm bed. Harriet had been snoring like thunder, and Katherine had been reluctantly awake when Emma had scratched on the door. The light of the moon inched toward full, shedding enough light for Katherine to see. The round orb seemed as bright as the sun, close to the western horizon. Once Emma trotted back to her, she had to grope her way up the stairs to the guest floor.

There, she was surprised to find a light along the corridor. She scooped Emma off the floor and held her to her chest while she hid in the narrow stairwell, slowly peeking around the side. A man exited a room on the far end of the corridor, holding a lantern. The light glinted off his golden hair. Was that... Sir Hugh? Where could he mean to go at such an early hour? Surely not to sell more jewels, as was his suspected destination when she'd tried to follow him yesterday. It was too early for any shops to be open.

To keep herself from freezing while she took Emma outdoors, Katherine had pulled yesterday's dress over her head and donned her pelisse. She was far from presentable, but with her bare feet stuffed into her slippers, she was dressed enough to follow. Her senses hummed as she wondered if this was perhaps the moment he made his mistake and she caught him in the act.

She couldn't bring Emma. That little thief would give away her position! Quickly, she stuffed the dog into her room and hurried in pursuit of Sir Hugh. With luck, this time Lord Annandale wouldn't waylay her.

At this hour, no one else lingered in the streets. They were as still as death as Katherine tiptoed after Sir Hugh. Although he was easy to pinpoint with his lantern, walking toward the setting moon, the rising sun at her back afforded her some additional light so she didn't trip over her feet, albeit a thin sort of pinkish light. After five minutes, Katherine was certain they were moving toward the center of town.

Church wouldn't begin for several hours, yet Sir Hugh led her unerringly toward the tall cathedral. Was he plagued by guilt over what he'd done? Perhaps he was seeking guidance. As they reached the shadow of Bath Abbey, she slowed, waiting to see if he would sneak inside. Most chapels weren't locked. However, he did not; instead he walked past.

Could he be going to the King's Bath? It was closed at this time of day, and likely locked. Though as he slipped around the side of the building, Katherine had to wonder if he intended to sneak through one of those wide windows described to her near the alley.

He did not. He stopped so suddenly that, for a moment, her shoe rang on the ground and she was afraid he might be alerted to her following him. She quickly hid in the doorway to the nearest building, pressed against the wood. She breathed shallowly through her mouth, straining her ears to hear whether or not Sir Hugh stepped nearer.

Nothing. No sound. She chanced a glance around the wall to the King's Bath, half expecting him to have disappeared. Instead, she found his body hunched over something on the ground. What was he doing? It almost looked as though he were digging. That couldn't be right.

Unless... Could he have buried the jewels he stole? She had to get closer.

Katherine inched forward. The open square separated her from Sir Hugh. If he turned around, she would have nowhere to hide and a very poor excuse for having left the hotel. She concentrated on stepping swiftly and softly as she approached.

Her toe dug into a raised cobblestone, and she tripped. The soles of her slippers clattered against the ground as she pumped her arms for balance. Sir Hugh snatched for his lantern. She dove for the nearest object, a wooden bench near one side of the square. She landed on her stomach behind it on the cool stone. Her heart raced, drowning out her hearing. Had he seen her? She craned her neck.

He must not have. Instead of searching for her, he snatched up his lantern and bolted in the opposite direction. He was getting away! Katherine pushed herself to her feet and followed. Whenever he paused to look back — far too often for her comfort — she paused in the shadow of a doorway or alley. After ten minutes, she realized that he was leading her back to the Sydney Hotel. She stopped following but remained watching until he disappeared inside.

Her hands were like icicles. She warmed them with her breath. What had he been doing at the King's

Bath? Curiosity overwhelmed her. With Sir Hugh likely too frightened to lead her to anything worthwhile, she returned to the spot where he had been digging. The sun had risen, providing her with some light as she bent over the hole.

It didn't look like anything special — an ordinary hole. Judging by the chipped piece of cobblestone lying inside, she thought he had been using the stone to dig. But why? Had he hidden something inside the hovel? Katherine knelt, using the cobblestone to work at the dirt. It was compact but easier to budge that she anticipated. The warm spring waters must have prevented the ground from freezing during these past few nights of frost.

Nothing. Just as she was ready to give up, Katherine spotted something bronze. Bronze? That didn't match any of the missing jewels. Katherine unearthed a small coin. Upon dusting it off, she found the worn stamp of a bust. It looked vaguely Roman. The coin itself felt old, far older than anything she'd ever seen...

Save, perhaps, for the statue the thief had used to bash Lady Dalhousie over the head! Perhaps Sir Hugh had made his mistake, after all.

Katherine palmed the coin for proof and returned to the hotel. As she reached the top of the stairs, she was met with an exuberant face and wagging tail. *Tarnation!* In her haste to leave, she hadn't shut her door properly.

Emma spat out a lady's glove, one made for a hand much smaller than Katherine's. She sighed, bending down to pick it up. Excited to play, Emma sank her teeth into the thumb, refusing to relinquish her prize so easily. As Katherine gritted her teeth and tried to wrestle the glove from the pug in order to find its owner and return it, she couldn't help but think that she should perhaps have remained asleep this morning instead.

CHAPTER NINETEEN

I n spite of Lord Bath's fears, the recent, more violent theft didn't appear to have dampened any of the bacon-brained ladies' enthusiasm for the subject. If anything, they were sensationalized. Mrs. Oliver and Mrs. Quicke couldn't compare to the thrilling tale of being attacked by the Burglar of Bath himself! Lady Dalhousie capitalized on everyone's attention by recounting her tale for anyone willing to listen. Katherine noticed that it seemed to change slightly with each retelling.

After church, the ladies eagerly congregated at the King's Bath. In fact, they seemed to take pride in arranging their jewelry just so atop their clothes. *The ninnies.* Katherine lingered near the dressing room in case the thief struck once more, but she wasn't optimistic that he would revisit the scene of the crime. He never had before.

Therefore, she was likely the only woman unsurprised by the fact that the jewels remained untouched. As the women dressed, she slipped out of the building and breathed in the cool, fresh air. It granted clarity of mind. The other ladies in Bath ought to try it.

This morning, Lyle had gone next door to examine his contraption still taking up a good portion of the floor space in the Pump Room. Katherine joined him, eager to see if he had worked out the trouble that had resulted in bungling the imprint on the sculpture used to strike Lady Dalhousie. As she reached him, he straightened from fiddling with the underside of the pipe that led from the furnace part of the invention to the place where he had set down the object.

Sighing, he shook his head and rubbed his hands clean on a handkerchief. "I don't understand it. Unless one of the additives I put into the water to make the minerals re-form from their soluble state somehow affected the sculpture as well, I don't know why it didn't work as expected. I can find nothing out of place."

Katherine patted him on the shoulder. "It was worth a try, if nothing else. I appreciate your willingness to test your device on the evidence." Usually, he took an invention through an extensive number of tests before allowing her to use it while solving a crime.

"I only wish I could have been of more use."

She caught movement from the corner of her eye as ladies and their escorts spilled into the room in order to partake in the refreshments served. Due to the odor of coal and rotten eggs clinging to Lyle's invention, a table had been moved near the piano and laden with food and drink for the arrivals. Nevertheless, the ladies cast scathing, distasteful glances at Lyle and Katherine as they walked past.

To Katherine's delight, she witnessed Miss Newcomb laugh at something Sir Hugh said and brush her hand lightly over Prince Karl's sleeve in the process. When she turned away a moment later without acknowledging him at all, his gaze followed her. She was halfway to the refreshment table — alone — when he hurried after her. He offered his arm as he reached her.

Brilliant. Katherine smiled. It seemed her trick with Mrs. Fairchild had gone according to plan. Now that Miss Newcomb seemed to have caught the eye of the object of her affections, she would no longer be trailing after Pru and Lord Annandale. They would be free to spend time together and fall in love.

If Katherine could manage to catch the Burglar of Bath, her work here would be complete.

A tall, familiar figure entered the room, his wide shoulders seeming to devour the space as he paused to search for someone. When his gaze reached her, Wayland lingered. Their eyes met, the air charging between them despite the size of the room. Had he done as she had asked and asked Scott for insight into his grandparents' actions? Katherine couldn't approach Wayland and ask while in public, so she turned away, trying to banish the lingering thought in her head just as firmly.

Lyle tapped her on the shoulder. "Katherine? I think Harriet is trying to get your attention."

He pointed to the other side of the room, where a narrow corridor near the piano likely led to a servant entrance. Harriet stood on the threshold, beckoning.

"Thank you. I'll see what it is she needs."

Fortunately, everyone in the room seemed much too preoccupied in speculation or recollection about the Burglar of Bath to notice Katherine as she skirted the perimeter of the room. When she neared Harriet, her maid turned and disappeared down the servants' corridor. Katherine followed.

The noise and temperature dropped significantly down this narrow, plain hallway. Harriet halted halfway down and waited for Katherine. The moment she stepped within earshot, the maid hissed, "I have news from my friend."

Katherine had spotted Sir Hugh among those gathered. This must have given his valet the time needed to search his room! Eagerly, she leaned forward. "What news?"

"Sir Hugh's valet found none of the stolen jewels in his room."

Her hopes sank. "None at all?"

Harriet shook her head. "The only jewels he has are the ones he brought with him to Bath."

That didn't mean that he wasn't the Burglar of Bath. All it meant was that he didn't keep the stolen items in his room. Katherine had stumbled upon him digging a hole. She'd heard that antiquities were sometimes dug up here in Bath. What if Sir Hugh had dug up more than coins? What if he had dug up the statue and then used it to clobber Lady Dalhousie, knowing it could not be traced to him...

"Furthermore, none of his silver items are obviously scratched in a way that could match the sliver of silver you found. Most of the items are too small to have been the cause."

Katherine swore. Although finding nothing didn't mean that Sir Hugh was exonerated, without any evidence, she couldn't arrest him. In fact, unless Scott had found a similar situation in his grandparents' abode, the evidence seemed to be piling against the Juliens instead.

Katherine didn't want to discover that such pleasant, caring people were in fact criminals. However... She pursed her lips. What if Lyle's invention hadn't malfunctioned? What if the person who had attacked Lady Dalhousie was not a man but a woman? Mrs. Julien might have small hands. Katherine had never paid close enough mind to her hands to measure them. Could Mrs. Julien be the cloaked figure who Lady Dalhousie claimed had rendered her unconscious?

Katherine bit the inside of her cheek as she struggled with that question. She needed advice. As much as she didn't want to consider it, she had no choice. She had all but ruled out everyone else in the investigation.

"You've suspected Mrs. Julien of the thefts from the start. Do you still?"

Harriet lifted one shoulder in a cautious shrug. "Nothing has happened to change my mind."

"You think that we'll find the jewels in her house."

Harriet raised her eyebrows. "They let go of their maid. Perhaps the reason wasn't only lack of funds, but also because they have something to hide."

Would Scott search the house for her? Katherine had hoped he might listen to Wayland instead, but if she had no other choice but to ask...

Hesitantly, she said, "Mrs. Julien is near the right height to be the cloaked figure I've been seeing around town."

"Indeed, she is. Have you ever seen her and the figure at the same time?"

Katherine couldn't recall if she had. Thinking on the cloaked figure made her wonder what the thief might be up to.

After a moment, she pursed her lips together, thinking. "Mrs. Fairchild confessed to me that Miss Newcomb has been seeing the cloaked figure shadowing her. It makes no sense, seeing as she doesn't have any jewels to steal."

"Makes perfect sense to me. That silly young woman has adhered herself to Prince Karl's shadow the whole time she has been here. Prince Karl wears more jewels than any of the women here."

Blast, Harriet was right. The prince could be in danger!

"I have to go."

Katherine turned on her heel, hurrying back to the Pump Room. She couldn't sit idly by and allow someone to be robbed, even an idle, self-centered man like the prince. Pausing on the threshold, she searched the room for the glimmer of jewels. Unfortunately, there were far too many of those to be found, not one of them attached to a man. Where were the prince and Miss Newcomb?

When she couldn't spot them, she approached Mrs. Fairchild. If nothing else, the woman was known for keeping a strict eye over her charge. She might not part with the information willingly, but if Katherine expressed the direness of the situation... The thief was escalating. If they managed to catch the prince alone, perhaps they might even be desperate enough to resort to murder! Katherine had to stop them first.

"Mrs. Fairchild."

The woman scowled. "Here to gloat, are you?"

Katherine frowned. "About what? I thought I spotted your charge with the prince earlier." Had they since parted ways?

"Oh, Miss Newcomb has Prince Karl playing to her tune, as I knew she would. No thanks to you. Your Miss Burwick seems to have done her damage on the Marquess of Annandale. If he was your hope all along, why did you need her to draw the attention of every other man in Bath?"

Katherine didn't have time for this nonsense.

"Where are Miss Newcomb and the prince now? I don't see them."

Mrs. Fairchild sniffed. "They've got out."

Katherine's heart skipped a beat. The pair, alone, where the thief might happen across them? "You let your charge into his presence unchaperoned?"

Mrs. Fairchild drew herself up. "Hardly. They left to walk back to the hotel with Miss Burwick and Lord Annandale. It's frigid out there, but I will give her a few moments before I follow in the carriage."

Would Pru and Lord Annandale be enough protection from the thief? If Miss Newcomb had managed to lose her chaperone, she might be clever enough to find herself in the prince's company alone. No, Katherine had to find them.

Without another word, she bolted from the Pump Room into the square. The brisk afternoon air had warmed from the sun. It wasn't suitable for short sleeves, but with her long sleeves and pelisse, Katherine barely felt the autumn air. She grabbed handfuls of her skirt, lifting it above her ankles as she bolted through the streets in search of the prince. Her heart hammered in her ears. Would she make it to him in time?

Halfway to the hotel, she spotted the foursome strolling ahead. Relief swept through her as she leaned against the corner of a building to catch her breath. They were unharmed and in so formidable a group, surely the thief wouldn't strike. She had time to warn him so he might take the proper precautions.

As she straightened, Katherine spotted movement from the corner of her eye. A figure skirted the shadows of the nearest alley ahead, slinking into the one just beyond. A *cloaked* figure. The thief!

Katherine didn't have the breath to shout, so she lurched into motion instead. The figure heard the slap of Katherine's heels on the cobblestones and yelped. Their black hat fluttered to the ground as they bolted down the alley. Katherine smashed it beneath her slipper on the way past.

As she did, the noise drew Pru and Lord Annandale's attention ahead. Pru turned, calling Katherine's name. She didn't have time to answer. The thief was getting away!

The black cloak ahead fluttered around the woman's shoulders, lifting enough for Katherine to discern her skirts beneath.

So it *was* a woman! Although the thief hiked them to her calves, she was too far ahead for Katherine to make out any identifying detail.

Could an old woman like Mrs. Julien run so fast? Katherine ran full tilt after the figure, determined to catch her. When the woman darted down another passage, Katherine barely slowed to change her course. Footsteps pounding against the ground behind her drew her attention for but a moment; she didn't have time to wait for Pru or Lord Annandale to reach her to explain. She dashed down the alley instead.

By the end, she was nearly on the woman's heels as she darted into the street. A carriage rumbled past, nearly clipping the thief as the driver cursed the air blue. Katherine stopped so suddenly, she nearly pitched forward into the black conveyance as it sped past.

"Katherine!"

She didn't wait. The moment the road was clear, she grabbed her skirts and raced after the figure just as the cloak disappeared around another bend. This was the best chance she would find to capture and arrest the Burglar of Bath. If the culprit slipped away again, the prince — or someone else — might be in danger. Katherine stumbled as if she'd staggered across Miss Young's nearly dead body again. She couldn't let that happen. Not while she remained on the case.

She turned the corner and gained ground on the thief as they galloped down the narrow alleyway encased by tall buildings. Did the woman ahead seem to be flagging? Triumph surged through Katherine's veins as she followed. A strand of gray hair escaped from the side of her hood as she paused to glance behind her. The contours of her profile seemed familiar. Who...

The thief turned the corner. Katherine rounded it only to find that the woman had been cornered by the back of another building. She had nowhere to run.

Katherine demanded, "Take off your hood and turn around slowly."

The woman did, revealing her white-threaded steel-gray hair. As she turned, she looked Katherine in the eye, fearless.

"Mrs. Burwick?"

———————————

CHAPTER TWENTY

K atherine couldn't believe her eyes. Pru's mother was the burglar? What was Pru's mother doing in Bath? They had left her in London.

But she couldn't be the Burglar of Bath since she had been at Lord Northbrook's party during the time of one of the thefts. Or could that have been when Lady Carleton had been robbed? Katherine couldn't recall the order of the victims. The blood roared in her ears as she stared, unable to fathom why she'd found Mrs. Burwick here, of all places.

"Why are you following the prince?"

"What prince?" Mrs. Burwick pulled a face, her nose wrinkling with befuddlement.

"Prince Karl of Prussia." When the older woman's face remained without any trace of recognition of the name, Katherine realized that, despite what Mrs.

Fairchild had mentioned, the cloaked figure had never been following Miss Newcomb. "If not him, then who are you shadowing?" she asked, afraid she already knew the answer.

Her suspicions were confirmed as Mrs. Burwick answered, "I was following Prudence."

Miss Newcomb had been dogging Pru's heels the past few days. The cloaked figure wasn't the thief at all, but merely Mrs. Burwick keeping a close eye on her daughter.

Footsteps echoed down the alley, growing closer.

The older woman's gaze gleamed as she leaned toward Katherine to whisper, "I've seen the way Lord Annandale has been drinking in her every word and making every excuse to insinuate himself at her side! You've done very well, beyond my greatest imaginings. And in so short a time!"

All this, because Pru had been determined to draw attention to herself that first night by acting in every way she shouldn't. Who was to know that it would result in catching the eye of a wild-at-heart marquess?

The footsteps paused abruptly. Katherine turned to meet the astonished gazes of Pru and Lord Annandale. Annandale rolled up his sleeves, balling his fists and stepping between Pru and the cloaked figure. His protective stance dropped the moment Pru spoke.

"Mama? What are you doing here?"

Katherine sighed and rubbed her temples. "Yes. I believe that will take some explaining, but not here. Let's return to the hotel."

"Aye," Lord Annandale agreed. "Why don't we start by swallowing a wee dram, lest we start seein' evils 'round every corner?"

LORD ANNANDALE HAD TAKEN his leave with more aplomb and grace than Katherine would have been able to muster had she learned that the mother of her romantic interest had been spying upon her. Now settled next to the warmth of the hearth in the Sydney Hotel common room, Katherine faced Mrs. Burwick over a cup of tea and readied herself to hear the tale. Pru, glaring with her arms crossed, seemed much less willing to accept a rational explanation.

Mrs. Burwick tapped her daughter's arm. "Don't scowl like that, dear. If Lord Annandale comes back, you'll frighten him back to the highlands."

Katherine smirked. She didn't think Annandale would be so easily frightened off given his adamancy over making the match, but she held her tongue on the subject.

Pru's scowl only deepened. "Why are you here? You promised to stay in London and allow Katherine the freedom to work her magic."

Mrs. Burwick turned to Katherine with a sheepish look. "It wasn't that I don't trust you—"

Katherine suspected it was precisely that.

"But this is my only daughter's happiness we're talking about. I wanted to see how she was getting on with Lord Annandale. Is that so terrible?"

"*Yes*," Pru said with feeling. "You promised you would let me decide my future this once. For heaven's sake, you tried to marry me off to an old man with one foot in the grave!"

"He is a duke," Mrs. Burwick answered with a sniff. She fiddled with her teacup but didn't drink.

Pru rubbed her eyes, seeming weary of this same argument. "Did you ever think that maybe I don't care to marry a duke?"

"Don't be ridiculous, dear. Everyone wants to marry a duke."

"Not Katherine."

Sard it, she was dragging Katherine into this argument now, too. She took a sip of her tea and tried not to be noticed.

"Lady Katherine already has a title, of sorts. You do not."

"I don't care about titles…"

Mrs. Burwick wagged her finger. "You say that now, but when you're my age with a willful daughter of your own, you might feel differently!"

Pru clenched her jaw but didn't respond.

Smug at having won a moment of silence, Mrs. Burwick sipped from her tea before she added, "Of course, you refused the last duke, and there aren't many to be found. A marquess will have to do. You *do* see the sense in marrying Lord Annandale, don't you?"

Pru colored, her cheeks turning the same shade as her teacup. "Perhaps I don't care to marry at all. Like Katherine."

Tarnation! Pru's mother was ruining all the careful work Katherine had laid down. Why did she have to come to Bath?

Before the conversation devolved further and Pru became even more stubborn over the fact that she would not capitulate to her mother's wishes, Katherine intervened. "How long have you been in Bath?"

Mrs. Burwick tapped her fingers on the table. "I followed you straight away, of course. I've been here since the first night. I found lodgings near the outskirts of town."

"You were in the corridor of the Assembly Rooms."

"For all the good it did me," Mrs. Burwick mumbled. "I didn't so much as see Prudence's shadow, and you nearly caught me then! If not for your companion..." She paused. "Were you trying to convince him to make an offer for Pru? I heard a rumor."

"I beg your pardon!" Pru bolted upright, dropping her arms to clutch the side of her chair. She turned her wide, fearful eyes on Katherine. "Tell me that isn't true. I heard you were matching me with Captain Wayland, but I knew such an audacious rumor couldn't possibly be true..."

"It isn't," I informed her.

She relaxed at once.

"If you were at the Assembly Rooms, then you were at the King's Bath when the thief struck."

"In a manner of speaking," Mrs. Burwick answered, turning away. She looked guilty. "I was far too busy trying to elude you to have seen anything."

"And outside Mrs. Quicke's townhouse? I saw you in the bushes."

"That was wretched timing," lamented the older woman. She glanced from Katherine to Pru and back again, seeming a bit out of sorts. "I was trapped there for a time. I was following Prudence, but she left with

Lord Annandale driving a carriage, of all things. Someone called out, and I feared I was caught! I hid just in time to avoid the Marquess of Bath as he strode down the alley to speak with someone else. He didn't see me, but for a time I was too frightened to move, and then the scene swarmed with people soon after. I only learned later that there was a robbery there."

Katherine narrowed her eyes. "That places you at two robberies. Don't you think that's a tad suspicious?"

"Three," Mrs. Burwick admitted, seeming reluctant. She fiddled with her cup. "But I was only looking for Pru, honest! I was about to enter this hotel by the back door in the garden when I heard a frightful scream. I ran as soon as I did and later learned that Lady Dalhousie had been attacked and robbed!" She nibbled on her lower lip. "I do hope you're able to convince Lord Annandale to come up to snuff soon, for I don't think it's at all safe here."

Unfortunately, Katherine was inclined to agree.

"Mother," Pru spat, her tone cautioning.

The wheels in Katherine's mind spun as she processed Mrs. Burwick's confession. She opened the reticule on her wrist and removed one large floral button. "This wouldn't happen to be yours, would it?"

Mrs. Burwick's eyes lit with enthusiasm. "You found it! I lost it off my favorite dress. See?" She pushed aside the cloak to show a gap on the bodice where one of the ornamental buttons was missing.

Pru made a thin noise of despair. Katherine ignored her, the muscles in her body tensing with anticipation as she leaned forward.

"If you were there, in the garden, when Lady Dalhousie screamed, then you must have seen the thief as he ran from the hotel. He escaped through that stairwell."

Mrs. Burwick's eyebrows pulled together. "Are you certain? I didn't see anyone emerge, though I admit I dashed away the moment I heard the scream." Her frown deepened. "Although..."

"Yes?" Katherine's fingernails dug into her palms as she fought against a tide of impatience.

"I saw Mr. and Mrs. Julien, the old couple who bring their grandson 'round in a bath chair, come around the corner of the hotel soon after. I had to duck behind the hedges to keep from being seen! I found it unspeakably odd that they moved *away* from the scream rather than toward it."

Mrs. Julien again. *Tarnation!* Katherine had been so close to omitting her as a suspect. Her heart ached knowing that the evidence pointed more and more toward the only woman left standing.

Although if the cloaked figure wasn't the thief,

did Katherine need to search for someone so tall? Her head throbbed with the onset of this new evidence.

And Mrs. Burwick continued to speak, pouring out more information that Katherine wished she hadn't heard.

"Come to think of it, I also saw them while I was hiding from Lord Bath. They spent a good deal of time in the alley."

Mr. Julien couldn't possibly scale those walls, nor could Mrs. Julien… though perhaps he could have lifted her high enough for her to pull herself over the windowsill…

Katherine shook her head. What was she thinking? Mrs. Julien was an old woman! She wasn't in her prime, like Wayland.

"What were they doing?" Katherine asked.

"I… I cannot say. I was trying not to be seen, but I'm certain I noticed them."

"How soon did you see them before Lord Bath arrived?"

"Lord Bath?" Mrs. Burwick frowned. "No, I'm certain I saw him first. I was already hiding when I glimpsed the Juliens. Wasn't I…?" She pursed her lips as she thought but seemed conflicted.

"What does it matter?" Pru answered bitingly.

"You were spying on me! You shouldn't have been there. I'm old enough to mind my own future."

"Ah, but will you? I swear, dragging you to the altar is more difficult than wading against a current!"

"I don't *need* to marry anyone. Katherine, tell her."

Rather than get in the middle of such a bullheaded argument, Katherine excused herself and left mother and daughter to work out their differences in private.

CHAPTER TWENTY-ONE

W hen a knock sounded on the door to Katherine's room, Harriet opened it to reveal Pru. The young woman looked ready to tear out her hair. She stormed into the room.

"My mother has revealed her presence here for *one day*, and I'm already hoping she will be the thief's next target. Perhaps if he strikes her over the head hard enough, he will knock some sense into her."

She turned her gaze to the ceiling, blinking hard to shed the glimmer of tears now clinging to her lower lashes. When she lowered her gaze to find Lyle seated at the writing desk, she wiped her cheeks hurriedly and composed herself. She turned away from him, meeting Katherine's gaze where she was seated on the edge of the bed.

"Forgive my tardiness. You wanted to speak?"

Katherine held tighter to Emma, who wiggled as she lunged toward the new arrival, hoping to beg for attention. At least Katherine could be reasonably certain that Pru wasn't hiding crumbs in her sleeves, but the pug would undoubtedly find something else on her person and decide to relocate it. She had been busy over the past couple of weeks.

"I wanted to discuss the investigation thus far and hope you or someone else might have some insight I've missed. I've gone through it a thousand times, and the only person I can point toward as the thief is Mrs. Julien."

Despite the fact that she couldn't perform the same feats of athleticism as Wayland.

Katherine added, "But if you're preoccupied with other matters, don't let me keep you." She held herself straight, her shoulders thrust back as she hoped for Pru to opt to join the party.

She was in luck. Pru blew a strand of hair away from her eyes before she strode forward and dropped heavily onto the mattress next to Katherine. Happy, Emma bounded onto Pru's lap and begged for attention. Pru vigorously rubbed the dog's stomach, which caused no end of joy. It was infectious and seemed to seep into Pru and lighten her mood.

Softly, she said, "I'm free for the moment. My

mother's gone to ready herself for the dress ball tonight. She'll be back by four o'clock to help me dress, but that should give us an hour to speak."

"Hopefully it won't take that long. We've had three thefts occur since we've been in town. There must be something about them that I've overlooked."

Lyle leaned his elbow on the desk. "What are your clues?"

Katherine held up a finger. "The sliver of silver, which I've been unable to match to anyone's clothing. The stolen jewels — which we've now learned are not in Sir Hugh's chambers, nor have they been sold to anyone in the area. But I did follow him the other day and find him digging along the perimeter of the King's Bath, outside the building. I looked in the hole, but I didn't find the stolen jewels, or much of anything, to be honest. An old coin that means little in regards to the investigation. I assumed he'd reclaimed the jewels he'd hidden there, but if he had, wouldn't he have them in his room?" Shaking her head, Katherine pinched the bridge of her nose to stave off a headache. She was desperate to find a way to connect Sir Hugh to the thefts, but the evidence refused to cooperate.

Lyle said, "Brewster and I are putting together his invention this afternoon in the square outside Bath Abbey. While I'm nearby, I'll take a tour of the

perimeter of the baths and check for more such distur-
bances. Perhaps he simply moved the jewels."

Katherine clung to that thread of hope. "Thank
you. I appreciate your help."

Her friend gave a one-shouldered shrug. He
mumbled, "I only wish I could have been of more help
the last time."

"We don't know for certain that the results were
wrong. Perhaps the wielder of the sculpture had small
hands." Katherine turned to Pru, on her other side.
"Have you noticed the size of Sir Hugh's hands?
You've seen him play cards."

"I recall them being rather large."

Her spirits sank once more. If Lyle's invention had
worked as designed, then Sir Hugh could not be the
thief. However, Mrs. Julien still could.

"That leaves Mrs. Julien." Katherine sighed. She
dropped her head into her hands. "I still don't know
whether she is keeping any jewels in her lodgings."

From the door, Harriet murmured, "They have no
servants, or else I'd try to have them search the Juliens'
rooms."

"I know." Katherine straightened. "If Wayland
hasn't done so, I'll have to ask Scott."

She paused, thinking. Could there be another
way to discover whether or not the Juliens were at

fault? Mrs. Julien had told Katherine that she had
been in a public coach bound for Bradford-on-Avon
when the theft of Mrs. Oliver's pearls had occurred.
However, Pru had spotted her entering a carriage
with fancy scrollwork along the sides, far too expensive to be a public coach. Not to mention, the cost of
hiring such a vehicle would have been tremendous.
Mrs. Julien purportedly didn't have that money
to spend.

Had Pru recalled incorrectly? Had Mrs. Julien lied
to her? Katherine couldn't be certain. Tracking down
the driver of the public coach might prove impossible,
and Pru hadn't seen enough of the carriage to identify
it, preoccupied as she had been with Lord Annandale
at the time. If Katherine confronted Mrs. Julien with
her lie, would she tell the truth instead?

The last time she had spoken to Wayland about
confronting the Juliens, he had been furious. Even if
they were... perhaps not enemies, but certainly not
friends... Katherine wouldn't feel right if she marched
up to the Juliens' doorstep and demanded to know the
truth. If she had to pursue this avenue — and it
appeared as though she had no other choice — then
she first had to speak to Wayland. If he felt strongly
enough about it, perhaps he could concoct an argument to sway her mind.

386 LEIGHANN DOBBS & HARMONY WILLIAMS

With a sigh, Katherine stood. "Thank you for your help. I know what I must do next."

Pru scrambled to her feet alongside her. "Wait. I'll come with you."

When Katherine hesitated, Pru's eyes filled with tears. "You must let me help," she begged. "I feel so..." She hesitated, searching for a word. "Decorative. There's nothing to recommend me. I've done nothing this entire time but act in every way I should not, and although it's distracted me for a time, I..."

Katherine frowned. "Distracted you? From Annandale's suit?"

"No." Pru looked down. "From Mary's absence. She was my dearest friend in the world. I thought finding her killer as we did at Lord Northbrook's and bringing justice might bring me some measure of peace, but it hasn't. She's only been dead a few weeks, but it's as though everyone's forgotten her. Mama wants me to marry, but it feels as though I'm leaving Mary behind." Her voice caught on a sob, and she wiped her cheeks.

Katherine looked around the room. Harriet muttered an excuse about taking Emma for a walk and absconded with the dog. Lyle made his excuse as well, vacating the room so Katherine could speak with the grieving woman in private. The moment the door shut behind them, Katherine urged Pru to sit next to her on the bed once more.

"I didn't know you felt this way."

Without looking her in the eye, Pru shrugged and wiped her cheeks. "I thought you understood. Mary was your relative."

"Miss Rosehill was a distant cousin, yes." Katherine squeezed Pru's hand. "I didn't know her like you did."

"I miss her."

Katherine said nothing, not certain how to mend the hole in Pru's heart. Although she had lost her mother at a young age, nothing had truly happened to heal that wound and help her move on. She'd spent more time with Papa, who had helped her to understand when he remarried that his new wife was not meant to be a replacement for her mother. Merely another addition to their family, with more to come. Mama was still there, still a part of Katherine and her older sisters.

"Falling in love and getting married was Mary's dream, not mine." Pru looked down. "She was always prettier than I was. The only reason I'm earning any male attention now at all is because she isn't here to stand beside me."

"That isn't true."

Pru scoffed.

Katherine squeezed her hand tighter. "Lord Annandale is quite smitten with you. He asked me for your hand."

A fleeting smile curved Pru's lips as she glanced up from beneath her eyelashes. "He did not."

"He did. He wants to marry you."

Pru's smile faded. Her chin wobbled. "I don't know if I can. I don't know if I'm ready. If Mary were here..."

"Have you spoken with him about how you feel? Have you told him about Mary at all?"

Pru swallowed audibly and shook her head. "I've been trying not to think of what a betrayal this is to her memory."

"Is it a betrayal? Or would she want you to be happy?"

Pru didn't answer.

Katherine stood, using her hold on Pru's hand to tug her friend to her feet. "I think, before you make any decisions or lack thereof about your future, that you ought to speak to Lord Annandale regarding the matter. See what he has to say about it. Perhaps he might be willing to wait."

Pru took a deep breath, squared her shoulders, and

nodded. "Very well. Do you know where his town-house is?"

"I was hoping you would be able to point me in the right direction."

Pru nodded and led the way from the room. With luck, Wayland would be inside as well, and Katherine would be able to complete her reason for visiting, too.

KATHERINE ADJUSTED her pelisse as she stared at the blue-painted door where Pru had informed her Lord Annandale resided. Their knock seemed to echo in her ears as she awaited an answer. Were the men at home?

After what seemed an eternity, Pru seemingly unusually withdrawn next to her, the door opened to reveal a tall man with a full mane of ginger hair. He grinned. "Well, lass! Ye're a sight fer sore eyes. M'laird will be some pleased to see you. Come right in!"

"Thanks, McTavish."

Katherine raised her eyebrow at Pru, who shrugged. "He's Lord Annandale's valet."

The brawny man ushered them into the front parlor, where he bid them wait while he fetched the lord of the house. With a smile, Katherine asked, "Is Captain Wayland in as well?"

She didn't care for the twinkle in the man's eye as he said, "Och, ye must be that lass he came to town fer. Wait yer wee pretty head right here."

Katherine frowned as the valet disappeared.

Pru guffawed. "You should see your face!"

"I've never been told to 'wait my wee pretty head' before."

"You get used to it," Pru said, wiping her eyes as she grinned.

Fortunately, the men didn't take long to enter the parlor. Katherine turned to Pru. "Are you comfortable with me leaving for a moment?"

Although she held her lower lip between her teeth, a sure sign of nervousness, she nodded.

Katherine caught Wayland's eye. "Can I speak to you in private?"

He nodded, leading her into the corridor. There, he placed a hand on the small of her back and drew her toward the door. The door had a crack in it, unnoticeable from outside due to the vivid blue paint. A tendril of chill air drifted in through the crack, raising shivers along the exposed back of her neck.

Wayland didn't seem bothered by the hint of cold. He stood near to her, so she had to tilt her head up to meet his gaze. Before he said a word, she held up her hand. "I know you aren't going to like what I have to say, but I felt I should inform you that I must look at Mrs. Julien again as a suspect. I've tried every other avenue, Wayland, believe you me. The story she told of visiting Bradford-on-Avon is a bald-faced lie. She or her husband were seen near the sites of all three thefts. I have to ask her for the truth or else have Scott search their residence. I—"

Cutting her off, Wayland laid his hand over her mouth to silence her. When she pressed her lips together, piqued, he dropped his hand to his side and cocked an eyebrow. "If you'll listen to me a moment, I'll tell you what Scottie found in his grandparents' home."

Her mouth dropped open. "You... you asked?"

He nodded once curtly. "I did."

"But I thought..."

"I didn't *enjoy* it. Scott was none too happy to have been asked such a thing, either."

The muscles in her back tightened with anticipation as she awaited the verdict. "He searched the townhouse?"

"He did. He found nothing. No stolen jewels."

Had he lied? Katherine nibbled on her lower lip. Could she trust Wayland's results, or should she verify them herself? Mrs. Julien had lied about her where-abouts during the theft of Mrs. Oliver's necklace. However, if she didn't have the necklace...

Damn! She still might have hidden it. If Katherine suspected Sir Hugh of the theft on that account, then she had to suspect the same of Mrs. Julien.

"Thank you," she said, even though his help had brought her no closer to solving the string of crimes. After taking a deep breath, she reached for the latch on the door, intending to leave Pru with Annandale to sort out her feelings.

"Wait." Wayland leaned his palm against the door, preventing her from leaving. The movement brought him close enough to her for her to smell the cedar scent of his cologne. "There's something else."

She tipped her head back to read his expression. He seemed to be hiding something. "Regarding the investigation?"

"Yes... but I think you might like to hear it from Mr. and Mrs. Julien yourself. Wait a moment for me to fetch my greatcoat, and I'll take you to them."

KATHERINE SIPPED THE WEAK, lukewarm tea in her

cup as she stared across the low table to the elderly couple seated side by side on the couch. The house they had let was small, their flat on the ground floor to make it easier to move Scott in his chair in and out of the house. He wasn't in the room with them, for which Katherine was glad. She didn't want to have to confront the Juliens in front of him. Her spirits sank by the minute. The ominous tone of Wayland's voice and the fact he'd brought her here to hear them in person indicated that the Juliens had something to confess.

Since the couple didn't seem forthcoming, and Wayland appeared to be waiting for her to speak first, Katherine lowered her cup and saucer to the table and dusted off her hands. "You lied to me, Mrs. Julien. You told me you and your husband were in Bradford-on-Avon at the same time a witness saw you enter a private carriage — not a public coach."

Mrs. Julien pressed her lips together and exchanged a glance with her husband. Neither spoke.

Katherine drew herself up straight in the armchair. "You've been here since the thefts first began."

"Shortly after," Mrs. Julien interrupted. "The first theft had already occurred and been publicized through the news rag, which was how we knew of the thief."

Katherine narrowed her eyes. "You've been spotted by witnesses at all three crime scenes since I've been in Bath. How do you care to explain that?"

The air in the room grew stiff. When Wayland changed position, the rustle of his clothing sounded loud and ominous.

"Tell her what you told me. You can trust Katherine."

She didn't know whether to be relieved or baffled by his apparent support. But what would she do once they confessed? Keep it a secret? Is that what Wayland wanted? Had he brought her here knowing she would feel empathy for the old couple and not tell a soul that they were actually the Burglar of Bath? She could hardly do that. Could she?

Mrs. Julien nibbled on her lower lip, glancing down. She groped for her husband's hand. He held it tight as he answered, "The reason we're in Bath is not only for Scottie's sake. It's to solve the mystery of the thefts."

"Solve the mystery?" Katherine frowned. "You mean you weren't stealing jewels? But why keep solving it a secret?"

His wife added, "We're desperate for money, you see, and we met the Dowager Marchioness of Bath years ago. She's always cared zealously for her tenants, and we hoped she might be willing to offer a reward. The private carriage we entered on the day of Mrs. Oliver's theft belonged to the dowager. You can seek her out and ask her to verify the truth."

"She hired you to search out the thief?"

The couple exchanged a worried glance. "Not precisely," Mrs. Julien ventured.

Her husband added, "She wanted to, but her grandson has control of the money. He hasn't been willing to part with it for anyone other than that crock detective, Mr. Salmon."

"We're still hoping…"

"We didn't want to tell anyone in case they tried to hone in on our reward."

Katherine wasn't able to provide them with a reward. However, they might be able to help her with the investigation, seeing as they had been in Bath longer than she. She glanced at Wayland, wondering. How long had he known of this? His impassive expression offered no answers.

Mr. Julien harrumphed. "Mr. Salmon certainly won't solve the crime with the way he's sniffing around women's skirts. If he hadn't been so enamored with Lady Dalhousie's maid, he might have caught the thief in the act a week ago at Mrs. Quicke's house!"

"What do you mean?" Katherine asked.

"Well, you see, I was first on the scene of the crime that day," Mr. Julien explained. "Not long before we spoke to you, in fact. I left the house to fetch Scottie's wheelchair so we might take a stroll with him around Sydney Place. Lo and behold, Mr. Salmon!" He said the word scathingly. "I found it odd that he would be strolling alongside Lady Dalhousie's maid. I didn't know they knew each other at all, and if she's hoping to find a husband, frankly, she can find better."

"Mrs. Quicke's carriage, my dear. Don't forget the carriage."

Mr. Julien nodded. "Yes, the carriage. I had to wait at the side of the road for it to pass on my way back with the bath chair, mere moments before I spotted Mr. Salmon. I passed the chair along so Scottie could ready himself, and hurried out to follow Mr. Salmon and see what he was about." The old man shook his head. "Never trusted that fellow. He had a look to him."

Katherine pressed her lips together but shook her head. "He cannot be the thief. He was with me at the time of the attack on Lady Dalhousie."

"Yes, well, be that as it may, I followed him. He wasn't far from Mrs. Quicke's townhouse when she came out, shrieking to all and sundry over her missing jewels. Well, I was closer than he, and I zipped down that alley while he bid his ladylove adieu. See what I might see, as may be."

That must have been how he'd gotten clay on his shoe! But if so, he might have seen some clue that Mr. Salmon, in his ineptitude, had eradicated. "Did you find anything?" Katherine asked, the question pouring from her in a rush. "A footprint?"

Mr. Julien nodded. "Looked like a boot print, yes."

"Small, perhaps? Belonging to a woman?" The imprint Lyle had managed to show on the sculpture jumped into the forefront of her mind, insistent.

Her hoped dwindled as Mr. Julien shook his head. Perhaps it had been a mistake, after all.

"It was a large boot, definitely belonging to a man."

Katherine sighed. "Just as well... Did you happen to find anything else?"

He shook his head, but he added, "It took a confounded while for Mr. Salmon to arrive! I had ample time to go over the alley, but if someone entered the bedchamber by the window, I found no sign other than the boot print."

Tarnation. She needed some other clue, anything to point her in the direction of the thief. When she glanced at Wayland, he seemed remarkably calm considering that, with Mr. and Mrs. Julien omitted, they had no viable suspects. Nothing she could prove, at the very least.

"Have you discovered anything else at any of the other thefts?"

Mrs. Julien shook her head, seeming wan. "We've found nothing, save that Mr. Salmon isn't to be trusted. Did you know this cloaked figure, the one he claims to be his most promising suspect, was not even in Bath until recently? No one appears to have seen the figure until Mrs. Oliver's theft."

Katherine cleared her throat and nodded. She didn't want to embarrass Mrs. Burwick by letting on that she was really the cloaked figure.

Mr. Julien added, "And he seems far more interested in sniffing around the maids than in investigating. At least, so it has seemed for two of the thefts."

"But," Mrs. Julien said, drawing out the word and raising Katherine's hopes.

"But?" she echoed.

The old woman exchanged a glance with her husband. "Lady Dalhousie's theft is different from the others, isn't it? No one else was attacked. This... well, I have to wonder if someone else committed it."

Katherine had discounted Mr. Salmon as a suspect because he had been sitting next to her during the time of Lady Dalhousie's theft. However, what if he had made an arrangement with Lady Dalhousie's maid to rob her? His skirt sniffing, as Mr. Julien put it, might have been him arranging for the next theft on his roster. If he'd spent time with other maids, he might even have arranged to be let into Mrs. Quicke's home while she was away — and speaking with Lady Dalhousie's maid straight away after would provide him with the alibi he needed should anyone ever look in his direction. Could he be clever enough to have conducted these robberies?

He knew Katherine was an esteemed detective. He would have needed to be present in front of her in order for her to discount him for the thefts, and he knew it. It was all the proof Katherine needed. Now, all she had to do was find Lady Dalhousie's jewels in Mr. Salmon's possession — or perhaps in the possession of his accomplice, her maid.

Finally, Katherine had the clues she needed to proceed with this investigation!

CHAPTER TWENTY-TWO

Katherine's heels clicked on the cobblestones as she hurried from the Juliens' townhouse to the Sydney Hotel. The night was still young. With luck, she would find Lady Dalhousie with her maid at this very moment, preparing for the dress ball at the Assembly Rooms. She might be able to end this investigation this very evening!

Stretching his legs to accommodate her quick pace, Wayland turned to her. "Now, will you admit that I was right all along, and there was no need to suspect these people?"

"Perhaps. I'll have to ask Grandma Bath, but I'd like to discount them. You know I would."

"Is that where you're off to all of a sudden? Your excuse in the drawing room was thin."

The hotel loomed ahead. "No. I have a different idea to pursue."

"Would you care to share that idea?"

Katherine pressed her lips together. Considering that Wayland seemed bent on dogging her steps anyway, he would find out soon enough. "I discounted Salmon as the thief because of the assault on Lady Dalhousie. He was present at the table with me during the time it occurred."

"Yes..." Wayland drew out the word, clearly waiting for more.

They reached the door to the hotel. A footman opened it in order to allow them to enter. Katherine stepped through first then waited a heartbeat for Wayland to follow before she resumed the conversation. "What if he convinced Lady Dalhousie's maid to commit the thefts for him? The same could be true of Mrs. Quicke and Mrs. Oliver, different maids each time. Every household has them."

A few older women clustered in the corner of the common room, near the hearth. The drone of their conversation sounded like the ebb and flow of water on the shore. Katherine glanced at them briefly on her way to the stairwell; Lady Dalhousie was not among them. The afternoon was late, but evening had not yet blossomed, so Katherine had every hope of catching the old woman in her chamber before she left for the dress ball beginning at six of the evening.

As they reached the first-floor landing, Wayland asked, "Are you certain confronting the maid is the best course of action?"

She paused. "I'm not only confronting her. I'm searching her room for the necklace. If she stole from her employer..."

"And kept the necklace where? It would be madness to stash it in the very room where Lady Dalhousie sleeps, and unless there's a wing of this hotel I don't know of, there isn't enough room here for the maid to have been given a room of her own. She likely sleeps on the floor."

Katherine threw her hands into the air in frustration. "It isn't as though a lady of Dalhousie's stature would deign to rummage under the bed."

He shook his head, his mouth thin. "There is too much risk. I wouldn't do it, and I'd like to think I'm at least half as clever as this thief. He did somehow manage to slip in and out of the hotel without being remarked upon."

"What would you have me do? Mr. Salmon might have absconded with the necklace, but I don't have any servants I can ask to search his room. Lord Bath would never believe that his beloved investigator was pulling the wool over his eyes. I have no other course of action for the moment."

Wayland hesitated for a moment. In a soft voice, he said, "This might be a mistake. You could be endangering this woman's livelihood."

He was right, of course. Katherine gnawed on her lower lip as she thought.

"I'll bring Emma."

He cocked an eyebrow. "I don't see what your dog has to do with any of this."

"She's a thief, as well."

"Perhaps, but she doesn't know the item you hope to find. If she filches something, it might be anything."

Katherine resumed mounting the steps. From the vibrations in the stairs, she could tell Wayland followed her. She continued the conversation. "What she steals doesn't signify, so long as she finds something. I can use it as an excuse to chase her about the room and search for myself."

He chuckled. "That will be quite a sight."

At the top of the stairs, she turned to glare at him. He smirked.

After pausing at her room to let out the pug, who was altogether too happy to be freed, Katherine herded the animal down the corridor to Lady Dalhousie's chambers. She rapped sharply on the door. Wayland stood to one side, waiting.

"It's about time! I ordered hot water half an hour ago. Come in."

Despite the fact that Lady Dalhousie was clearly not speaking to her, Katherine lifted the latch and let herself in. Wagging her tail, Emma bounded in and buried herself beneath the bed. Katherine tucked away a smile. The first portion of her plan was unfolding in precisely the right manner!

As Lady Dalhousie twisted her head to look in Katherine's direction, she yelped. She jerked away from her maid, causing the woman to fumble with the laces to the stays over the old woman's underclothes. She caught the laces at the last moment, pulling them so tight that Lady Dalhousie released a loud gasp.

"You!"

Lady Dalhousie pointed a bony finger at Katherine as she uttered the breathless word. She gasped for breath and touched her side as if in pain. Her maid scrambled to loosen the laces to provide the woman with some air before she fainted.

The moment she could draw a full breath again, she added, "I am dressing! You shouldn't be here!"

Katherine glanced to the side in time to catch Wayland hiding behind the wall once more. If Lady

Dalhousie spotted him in her undressed state, she might have an apoplexy.

"Get out!"

It seemed the old woman didn't care at all for what reason Katherine had chosen to intrude on her abode. Katherine nodded. "Of course. I must fetch my dog."

"That *animal!* Fetch my dressing gown, quick. Don't leave the door open," Lady Dalhousie snapped.

Katherine didn't know whether the woman was speaking to her, the maid, or both. She opted to ignore both commands and drop to her hands and knees to retrieve her dog. "Emma, come here, girl."

The pug crouched at the farthest end of the bed, the light glinting off her eyes. Did she have something in her mouth? The shadows were too deep for Katherine to properly tell.

"Oh! Here you are, milady. Terribly sorry."

A woman gasped.

"No! Get out of there at once."

The maid grabbed hold of Katherine's arm and hauled her to her feet. Her cheeks were high with color, making her eyes seem unusually bright.

"Why don't you want me to look beneath the bed?"

The maid dropped Katherine's arm at once. Averting her gaze, she took a step back and mumbled,

"I haven't had time to clean beneath the bed. There is terrible dust there, I'm certain."

"I must retrieve my dog."

"I'll do it," the maid volunteered. She climbed over the bed to the other side to peer beneath for Emma. Katherine knew her pug wouldn't be so easily caught.

The maid, on the other hand, was shortly to be exposed as a thief. She had nowhere to turn, and the way she squirmed informed Katherine that she was, in fact, guilty. All she had to do was corner the woman and force her to confess.

"Where did you say you were the evening that your mistress was attacked?"

"D-Down the corridor. Why?"

"Yes, *why*?" Lady Dalhousie added, her voice sharp. "What gives you the right to barge into my room and accost my maid?"

As the maid thrust her hand beneath the bed in search of Emma, the pug burst through the other side, carrying a white silk purse in her mouth. The moment Lady Dalhousie spotted her, she shouted, "You are the thief!" and dove to catch the dog. She caught the ribbon around the pug's neck instead, tugging on the end until it unraveled. Thus freed, Emma bolted for the open door with her prize.

Wayland appeared to block the dog's path. Despite

her fondness for him, Emma refused to relinquish the pouch. When Wayland surveyed the interior and paused with his attention on the pug, she dropped onto her haunches and wiggled her back end, taunting him. He took the bait and reached for the pouch. Emma bolted to the other side of the bed.

Her eyes wild, the maid lunged to catch Emma. She succeeded in gripping the bag. Although the dog's strength was no match for a human's, she was tenacious and held tight to the bottom edge of the pouch. The maid yanked on it, her fingers tightening on the drawstrings. As she pulled, the mouth of the pouch opened, and out spilled Lady Dalhousie's prized diamond-and-aquamarine necklace. Both maid and mistress ceased their squabbles, horrified.

Katherine drew herself up. She pointed to the maid, confident. "Emma is a hero, not a thief. She's found the Burglar of Bath! Madam, your maid helped Mr. Salmon to steal your necklace!"

CHAPTER TWENTY-THREE

T o Katherine's surprise, instead of demanding that the woman be arrested at once, Lady Dalhousie burst into tears. Shaking like a leaf in the wind, she lowered herself onto her bed. Wayland, who had squeezed into the room next to Katherine, paused.

"No, that isn't true at all," Lady Dalhousie exclaimed, sobbing into her hands.

Katherine frowned. That wasn't the typical reaction of the elite upon discovering that they had been robbed by their servants.

Her voice muffled, Lady Dalhousie confessed, "She only became familiar with Mr. Salmon because I asked it of her, so she might steer his investigation appropriately. Agatha isn't the thief. I am!"

Wayland exchanged a glance with Katherine, his

eyebrows raised. He bent to retrieve the hidden necklace from Emma before she chewed off one of the strings of jewels or swallowed it by accident. As he held the necklace aloft, the pug raised her forelegs, begging for her new toy.

Katherine scooped her off the ground to keep her out of further mischief.

His voice dry, Wayland echoed, "*You* are the Burglar of Bath?"

Lady Dalhousie looked up from her hands, her eyes red. "Of course not. Don't be absurd." She glanced at her maid, who stood as still as a statue as she watched the scene unfold, as if she feared to so much as breathe.

The old lady confessed, "I stole my own necklace. At least, I made it seem that way. I hid it in the pouch beneath the bed and instructed Agatha to strike me over the head with that hideous sculpture she'd won in a card game from Sir Hugh one night."

"I rather liked that statue," the maid mumbled, almost too low to be understood.

Lady Dalhousie begged, "Please, don't have her arrested. She was only doing as she was told!"

In the ringing silence, Emma stretched out her neck, nipping at the necklace Wayland still held. He offered it to Lady Dalhousie, who stuffed it out of sight beneath her pillow.

"Why don't you tell us everything?"

Lady Dalhousie scrunched her nose as she beheld him. "It's simple. My necklace is worth ten times the value of some of the stolen jewels. It is unique and beautiful, and yet I have to stomach the likes of Mrs. Oliver rubbing my face in her misfortune. I couldn't take it any longer. The thief should have stolen *my* necklace!"

Perhaps he would have if she had not been constantly wearing it. Katherine pinched the bridge of her nose to stave off a mounting headache. How feather-headed did a person have to be in order to turn so green with envy that she robbed and injured herself?

Judging by the look on Wayland's face, he thought the same.

Lady Dalhousie trembled as she looked from one person to another. She seemed to shrivel and draw in on herself. "Please, don't tell anyone. My reputation would never survive!"

Baffled, Katherine carried her dog through the open door into the corridor. Where had she gone wrong? If the maid and Mr. Salmon *weren't* the burglars... who was?

As if from a distance, she heard Wayland say firmly, "I won't speak a word, provided you do not as well. Cease crowing over this false theft immediately, and no one need know the truth."

What was the truth?

As Wayland stepped into the corridor and shut the door behind him, Katherine muttered to herself. "At least Lyle will be happy to learn of this news."

"I beg your pardon?"

She tilted her face up to meet his. "Lyle's invention worked, after all. The maid has small hands, and it was her print that was rendered on the sculpture. He can rest easy." Shaking her head, she petted Emma. "Unfortunately, it brings me no closer to discovering the true thief. What have I missed?"

At the door to her room, Katherine paused. Wayland stopped her from entering with a touch to her shoulder. Sapped of energy, she'd forgotten he still kept her company. She turned to him, to find him wearing a serious expression.

"What makes you think you've missed anything? You're brilliant, Katherine. I'm certain you already know this answer. The moment you stop latching onto the first idea that seizes you, it will all become clear."

He held her gaze for a moment, his words

spreading like warm honey through her extremities. *Does he truly think I'm brilliant?* She said it often of men like Lyle, who had a quiet sort of genius that emerged in his inventions and his insights. But her? She had a passion for investigation and a stubborn drive to succeed. At the moment, with so little suspects left, she didn't think herself brilliant at all.

"I'll see you shortly at the dress ball. Good evening."

"Good evening," she echoed, still confused as he walked away.

As she entered the room with Emma, Harriet straightened from where she had been examining her choice of Katherine's dresses for the evening. "There you are! What's happened to Emma's ribbon?"

Absently, Katherine muttered something about her having lost it. She couldn't be certain if she spoke the words in the right order, for her mind was still on the thefts. Mr. Salmon *must* be the thief. She had discounted him because he had been with her during the robbery of Lady Dalhousie's necklace, but that hadn't been the act of the Burglar of Bath at all!

He had claimed to be with the Marquess of Bath during the theft of Mrs. Oliver's necklace, but that was impossible. Wayland had spotted Lord Bath in his carriage, leaving the bathhouses. Not to mention, he had lied about considering the cloaked figure as the thief, for Katherine had already determined that she was none other than Mrs. Burwick, and she hadn't even been there prior to this week.

Despite his ineptitude, Mr. Salmon had managed to gain Lord Bath's confidence, something that made him all the more likely to be the thief. He could direct the investigation anywhere he pleased. The longer Katherine mulled over the problem, the more certain she was that Mr. Salmon was the culprit.

However, Wayland was right. She couldn't go haring off in search of Mr. Salmon to accuse him. Lord Bath would never believe her if she did. She had to think this through properly. Before she pursued another lead, she had to eliminate all her current suspects so that she could prove to Lord Bath that Salmon was the only one who could be the burglar.

"I'll be back in a moment."

"But the ball—"

Harriet heaved a sigh as Katherine slipped into the corridor and shut the door behind her.

Sir Hugh's door was at the other end of the corridor, not terribly far. How could she possibly eliminate him as a suspect? Although she didn't yet have a full plan in her mind, she rapped on the door. As she awaited an answer, she dug out the old coin she'd unearthed from the hole where Sir Hugh had been digging. The old sculpture had originated with him as well. Had he been searching for this all along?

The door opened to reveal Sir Hugh in a half-dressed state. His shirt was open at the throat, his cuffs flapped as wide as Lord Bath's, and he hadn't yet donned his waistcoat or jacket. His eyebrows soared as he beheld her waiting for him. "Lady Katherine, how may I help you?" He didn't sound the least bit in a helpful mood.

She offered him the coin nevertheless. "I believe this belongs to you."

His hand shook as he took the coin, though his expression remained impassive. "Why would you think that?"

"I followed you to the King's Bath the other day. I found this in the hole where you were digging."

He swore under his breath. "I knew someone was following me."

She held up her hands in surrender. "All I want to know is how you found that cache to begin with."

Although his nose wrinkled with reluctance, he admitted, "It was a stroke of luck, to be honest. I've never been fond of Bath's healing waters. I came here for the gambling, not for the baths. What else is there to do while Annandale goes for a swim but walk the perimeter of the baths?" He shook his head. "One day, I tripped. I dug up the offending article, which turned out to be that sculpture used to smash Lady Dalhousie over the head." He recoiled, taking a step back. "I didn't strike her with it, I swear on my mother's grave. And I'll have you know the only jewels I've sold while in Bath belonged to my mother. My father left the estate in such a sorry state... It doesn't signify. Suffice it to say, I've robbed no one."

Katherine opened her mouth to inform him that she already knew who had robbed Lady Dalhousie, but he didn't appear to be listening. Muttering under his breath, he stepped back into his room.

"In fact..." He snatched something out of the drawer of his writing desk and returned to thrust it beneath Katherine's nose. "There we are. All I got for those worthless bits of pottery at the pawnshop. And I doubt the statue would have gotten even as much as I wagered for it in the card game where I lost it to Dalhousie's maid. What is her name... Aggie?"

Curious, Katherine accepted the slip of paper. It was dated the afternoon of Tuesday, September 10 — the same date and time that Mrs. Quicke had been robbed. It stated that he had sold a few old shards of pottery to the pawnshop for eleven shillings. For pottery that old, even broken, Katherine would have expected a much greater profit. But the receipt proved that Sir Hugh could not have stolen Mrs. Quicke's jewels because he was in town at the time of the theft.

Shaking his head, Sir Hugh brushed a lock of blond hair from his eyes and confessed, "I returned to the site where I'd found those things, hoping for greater luck."

"You might have it with that coin," Katherine predicted. "Don't sell it to a pawnshop. I suspect it's far older than it appears. Find an antiquities dealer in London. It might just give you the fresh start you're trying to achieve." She raised her eyebrows pointedly as she added, "A good player knows when it's time to fold."

He held up the coin and asked, "If you think it so valuable, why are you giving it to me?"

Why indeed? Choosing her words carefully, she confessed, "Lord Annandale must see something in you to consider you such a stalwart friend. Don't prove him wrong."

As he shut the door, Katherine's thoughts returned to the Juliens. With Sir Hugh acquitted of the crime in her mind, she still had one more thing to do in order to eliminate the Juliens from her list once and for all. She had to speak with Grandma Bath.

If she had to face that clever old woman, Katherine was going to need a buffer. She returned to her room to fetch Emma one last time.

CHAPTER TWENTY-FOUR

A s Katherine strolled into the square in front of Bath Abbey, the lit street lamp cast a halo in the twilight that glinted off the silver scrollwork on a carriage, which gleamed as if freshly painted. The barouche was empty, abandoned but for the driver stroking the matched team of horses at the fore. The seal of the Marquess of Bath caught her eye on the door and buoyed her spirits. Pru had reported seeing Mr. and Mrs. Julien climbing into a carriage with scrollwork such as this! Their tale might be true, after all.

Emma seemed just as eager to find the truth — or, perhaps, simply search out the marquess in the hopes that more crumbs had fallen into his cuffs. She pulled on her leash, attempting to approach the barouche. Katherine knew she wouldn't find him there, so she reined Emma in to heel as they approached the cluster of people in the center of the square.

Despite the waning sunlight, Sir David Brewster worked diligently in the center of the square as he built an enormous apparatus. Although Katherine couldn't tell precisely what it was at this stage, it looked rather reminiscent of a fat telescope to her. A young boy stood holding a lamp, his arms shaking as he hefted it over his head for the inventor to see. Lyle helped, conversing with Sir David in the absent way he did when his mind was more fully on a different problem. Should Katherine stop him to tell him that his invention had worked, after all? In this state, he might not even register her words.

More important at the moment was that she speak with Grandma Bath. The old woman leaned heavily on a cane as she oversaw the work being done on the apparatus in the center of the square. Although she smiled and exchanged a few words with anyone who passed, her attention was devoted to the invention being mounted on the cobblestones. For the most part, she stood alone, her grandson nowhere to be seen.

Perfect. With luck, Katherine would be able to confirm the Juliens' story and leave without being thrown into Lord Bath's path as a potential bride. Once she had eliminated the Juliens, Lady Dalhousie's maid, and now Sir Hugh as well, she would have reasonable cause to confront Mr. Salmon.

As she strode forward, her step faltered. Hadn't Mr. Julien claimed to have seen Mr. Salmon strolling with Lady Dalhousie's maid during the time of Mrs. Quicke's robbery? *Tarnation!* If she managed to confirm the Juliens' alibi, then she would at the same time eliminate Mr. Salmon as a suspect. Who was left?

"Oh, Lady Katherine, what a delight!"

Grandma Bath had seen her now, so she had no chance to reconsider this course of action. She smiled and approached the old woman. "How are they getting on?" she asked, gesturing to the inventors.

The old woman beamed. "Quite well, I think. Sir David says he should be ready to unveil his invention tomorrow at noon! Ernest is out spreading the word so everyone knows to gather here. If you wait a moment, I'm certain he will return soon."

As tempting as that was...

"Actually, I have a question for you, if you have a moment."

"Yes, yes, of course!" She reached out to clasp Katherine's hands with a smile. Her skin was delicate and cool to the touch. "How can I help?"

"It's about Mr. and Mrs. Julien. They mentioned that they visited you on Sunday, and perhaps you had sent a carriage to this very square to drive them to your estate?"

Grandma Bath retracted her hand and turned away stiffly. "I met with them, yes. But I'm afraid I cannot reveal the nature of our visit. That is confidential."

Katherine smiled. She dropped Emma's leash for a moment so she could take the old woman's hand in both of hers. "That's perfectly all right. I meant only to verify their presence with you."

She scarcely spoke the words before Emma yipped and bolted for Lord Bath's carriage, trailing her rope.

"Emma, no!"

Katherine hiked up her skirts and dashed after her pet, hoping to lunge and grab the rope. Despite her legs, Emma was quick. She evaded the driver and the whinnying horses' hooves and dove into the boot of the carriage. Katherine slowed to fetch the dangling leash, wrapping it around her fist. As she straightened, her knuckles brushed against the scrollwork. Sharp. A little piece of the metal embellishment had broken off! She stared at her marred skin, lamenting the fact, but her gaze caught on the ornate decoration. The shape...

Emma wiggled her rump as she chewed on something in the boot. "No, Emma!" She clasped her dog around the middle and pulled her out of the carriage boot, only to draw out the pug's newest toy as well. A string of gray pearls dangled from Emma's chops. Katherine was so startled, she nearly dropped the dog. After a moment that seemed to stretch into forever, she gathered enough of her faculties to wrestle the necklace free.

When she turned, Grandma Bath had crossed half the square and now stood within hearing distance. Katherine held up the string of pearls, flabbergasted. "*You're* the Burglar of Bath?"

Grandma Bath stumbled to a halt, mouth agape. The color drained from her face, and in the light of the street lamp, she looked as though she might fade away.

"How in the world did you happen to have Mrs. Oliver's necklace in the boot of your carriage?" Katherine could see no other explanation than to believe that Grandma Bath was the thief. But she'd been with the Juliens at the time of this particular robbery, hadn't she?

No, Pru had only mentioned seeing the carriage, not that Grandma Bath had been inside it.

"No, you have it all wrong!"

While Grandma stood speechless, Lord Bath dashed from one of the nearby shops and planted himself squarely between Katherine and his grandmother.

"Grandmama isn't the thief. I am."

"You are?" The old woman found her tongue long enough to force out those two words, but they seemed to sap the energy from her. "Ernest, tell me it isn't so!"

As she swayed on her feet, Lord Bath hurried to steady her. With a grimace, he glanced at Katherine. "Can we move this someplace where she might sit down?"

TEN MINUTES LATER, Katherine and Lyle stood in the antechamber of the King's Bath. The lonely room was lit with a single branch of candles, throwing the shadows into the far corners and making it seem even lonelier. Grandma Bath sat on the red divan, clutching her grandson's hand as he prepared to confess the true tale. Emma squirmed in the old woman's lap as she begged for attention.

"Please, Ernest, tell me this was a bad joke. I know you're a good man, not a... not a thief."

He bowed his head, color blooming in his cheeks. "I'm afraid I cannot answer that. I am the Burglar of Bath."

"You robbed the people who came to your town for the healing waters?"

"Yes. No." He grimaced.

Katherine crossed her arms. "Which is it? Yes or no?"

The marquess's stubbornness seemed to flag along with his strength. When he squeezed onto the divan next to his grandmother, Emma happily climbed into his lap. He patted her absently with his free hand.

Grandma Bath squeezed his hand so hard, her knuckles turned as white as her face. "We were so afraid of driving off our patrons. How could you do this, Ernest? I raised you better than this."

"The first two robberies were not committed by me. Nor was Lady Dalhousie's." He glanced from his grandmother to Lyle and Katherine, as if trying to stress with his gaze that he spoke the truth. "The first two were actual robberies. I don't know who committed them. But when tourists started flocking, I thought it might be wise to continue. However, I would never *harm* anyone. If I'm honest, I was never able to discover the true culprits in the first two cases, but I certainly will do everything in my power to find the culprit who harmed Lady Dalhousie."

Katherine raised her hand, stalling him. "There is no thief. Lady Dalhousie took offense to being overlooked and arranged for her maid to strike her." She turned to Lyle. "The results of your invention were genuine, after all."

A small smile fluttered across Lyle's lips. "I must admit to some relief there. I was doubting my abilities. But what's this about a *true* thief?"

Lord Bath sighed. "Yes, Grandmama and I were frightened upon the initial thefts. So much cold rain this summer affected the harvest, and our tenants are barely surviving. I've kept the price of bread to a manageable number by the skin of my teeth, but I cannot do more for them. The only thing keeping the town flush enough in pockets to provide for everyone is the healing waters. Especially with this brutally cool summer, the baths seem to be the only thing that is able to provide relief for many people. But with the thefts..."

He exchanged a long look with his grandmother then paused to shake Emma out of his sleeve.

"None of that, you sneaky telltale." He patted her rump and raised his gaze to Katherine once more. "With the initial thefts, we thought they would do harm to the number of patrons who visited. Instead, by the second, it had done the very opposite. More people flocked to Bath than ever, but when the thefts didn't continue, it looked as though that interest would wane again. So I... took the initiative that they might continue."

"You stole from the visitors."

"I borrowed, more than anything." He grimaced. "I know you probably don't see much distinction, but I arranged for the stolen gems to find their way back into their owners' possession shortly before they left Bath. The ladies liked the attention too well to admit that they hadn't been robbed and... until now, it worked brilliantly. The reason you found Mrs. Oliver's necklace in the boot of my carriage is because I had planned to return her jewels to her room tonight while she was at the dress ball."

That explained why the society rags had described some of the previous victims as wearing the same jewels that had been previously stolen. It wasn't senility. The gems really had been secretly returned. The victims most likely thought they had merely misplaced them and were too embarrassed to admit they found them amongst their belongings.

Suddenly, his faith in Mr. Salmon made sense. "You knew of Mr. Salmon's reputation as a shoddy detective from the very beginning. You didn't want him to discover you had committed the thefts."

"I beg your pardon?" Lord Bath shook his head. "No, that isn't it at all. Mr. Salmon has proven invaluable to me. Granted, I never hired him to uncover the thief. You see..." He pressed his lips together as if wondering how much to divulge.

Everything. Katherine raised her eyebrows.

His shoulders falling forward with defeat, the marquess admitted, "If anyone was going to take the danger of robbing someone, I couldn't fathom it be anyone but me. I have access to anywhere in Bath, you see, and I circulate enough that my presence will go unremarked. However, just in case certain people ventured to town to attempt to solve the crimes on their own" — he nodded to Lyle — "I needed to have an alibi. *That* was Mr. Salmon's job. He was to keep a lookout in some cases, but mainly ensure that if anyone asked where I was at the time of the thefts, he would say that I was with him."

That accounted for the inconsistencies in Mr. Salmon's tale to Katherine. It even followed the reports she'd gotten from Mrs. Burwick and Wayland that they had seen Lord Bath near the robberies he had committed. Here, she had been certain the inconsistencies had been because Mr. Salmon had committed the crimes. She hadn't even thought of considering the man who had been such a stalwart friend of her father's. Her judgement and her focus on Mr. and Mrs. Julien even when she hadn't wanted them to be the culprits had clouded her investigative instincts. This entire time, Katherine had been battling herself and trying to lead the investigation to a desirable answer rather than letting it take its course.

Sard it, even Emma is a better investigator than I am! She bit the inside of her cheek rather than admitting as much aloud.

Lyle asked, "What of the piece of silver you found at the King's Bath?"

"Oh." Katherine fetched the vial out of her reticule and showed it to Lord Bath. "Is this yours?"

He frowned. "How am I to know? It's a small piece of silver. Although..." He paused, a crinkle forming in his forehead as he thought. "Oh, it matches the scrollwork on the carriage. I do remember my cuff catching on the scrollwork. A piece must have come loose and dropped in my cuff. It happens more often than you might think. My cuffs are forever getting caught or collecting crumbs, as Emma has discovered." He patted the dog as he shrugged. "It is the price I must pay. If my cuffs are too tight, I feel as though I cannot breathe. I've always been that way."

In the silence that followed, Lord Bath turned to his grandmother and patted her hand. "I'm terribly sorry to have caused you so much grief, Grandmama. I only did it for you. As the crops failed, you too seemed to wither away. You care so much for the tenants here, as do I, and I only wanted to see everyone remain happy and prosperous through these difficult times. Can you bring yourself to forgive me?"

After a long, drawn-out silence, Grandma Bath harrumphed. "I can forgive you, you rascal."

He brightened.

She held up her index finger. "On *one* condition. The jewels must be returned. And there will be no more thefts."

"Of course, Grandmama. I'll return everything tomorrow, while everyone is gathered in the square."

"And I want a reward to be given to Mr. and Mrs. Julien. They've been doing some work to gather clues as to the Burglar of Bath. We'll tell them their clues led to the man's capture and we have remanded him into our custody to be dealt with according to the law. This will account for the end of the thefts, as well."

Lord Bath sighed. "Very well, Grandmama. I'll scrounge together the money for a reward."

Satisfied, the old woman pointed her finger at Lyle. "You have no jurisdiction outside London. Bath has its own watch, and I won't see you arresting my grandson."

Lyle rubbed the back of his neck. "He's a

marquess. Even if I tried, I imagine you'd be able to bribe him free within the hour."

"So don't try," Grandma Bath said, her voice waspish.

Lyle sighed. "I suppose if the jewels were all returned—"

"They were," Lord Bath exclaimed. "Or they will be."

"Then so long as the thefts cease, I'll consider the matter closed."

"Of course." Lord Bath frowned then turned to his grandmother, looking sheepish. "But without the entertainment of the thefts, what if no one elects to visit Bath?"

The old woman smiled. "Oh, I doubt that will be the case. We have Sir David's new invention, after all! He's calling it a kaleidoscope, and I must admit, it sounds thrilling. Well worth coming to Bath to see." She patted her grandson's hand. "We'll do just fine, Ernest. We always have."

CHAPTER TWENTY-FIVE

T he sun winked from between fat gray clouds, cheerily looking down at the line of people assembled to see Sir David's kaleidoscope. He stood to the left of the telescope-like contraption, explaining how to turn the crank on the side as they peered through the lens. Katherine had yet to step up and peer through it herself, but judging by the exclamations of those who had attempted it, she knew the kaleidoscope produced a sight to behold.

While Sir David preened beneath the attention of the gathering, freely acknowledging Lyle's help in constructing the apparatus and working out some of the math, Lyle seemed oblivious that he was once again the source of someone's praise. He stood off to the side, where he examined one of Agatha's hands. As he did so, Lady Dalhousie's maid turned pink.

The color deepened when Lyle murmured something too soft for Katherine to catch. If she knew her friend, he was likely only holding the maid's hand in order to verify that his invention had worked properly. As she said something in response, Lyle turned a shade of red to rival hers and dropped her hand, seeming to stutter over his answer.

"And one for Lady Katherine!"

"Oh." Katherine turned just in time to juggle a steaming mug between her palms.

Grandma Bath stood like a general, directing two trailing servants in the Bath livery to hand out more such mugs. As they did so to the people near Katherine, the old woman gave her an exaggerated wink.

Loudly, she said, "My grandson is out fetching more. Never fear! Everyone will get a mug. And a Sally Lunn."

Mutely, Katherine accepted the bun. She offered a wan smile to the old woman, who wasn't as subtle as she likely thought. With luck, the group was far too distracted to wonder what the marquess was truly doing at that moment. Katherine spotted Mrs. Oliver and Mrs. Quicke in the crowd; he shouldn't have any trouble finding a place to return their stolen jewels.

But wait, where was Mr. Salmon? Perhaps he was aiding Lord Bath with this one last task.

A man cleared his throat on the opposite end of the gallery. Katherine turned to find Lord Annandale raising his mug to capture everyone's attention. Sir Hugh, Pru, and her mother were by his side. Katherine could only imagine how the poor man felt about Mrs. Burwick's sudden insistence on remaining close.

"I'd a moment, if 'twill not bother ye. I've an announcement."

The gathering quieted, the attention shifting from the kaleidoscope to Lord Annandale. He puffed out his chest and took Pru's hand in his. "It gives me no end o' pleasure to announce that Miss Burwick has agreed to make me the happiest of men. We're to be married!"

Cheers sprang up around the square, along with some awkward applause as everyone attempted to juggle their mugs. As the noise abated, another man cleared his throat.

"I have an announcement as well," said Prince Karl. He turned to Miss Newcomb, at his side, and took her hand. "Miss Newcomb, I have met no other woman like you, and I doubt I'll find anyone who might compare." He sank to one knee, his attention on her face. "Will you consent to make me the happiest of men and become my wife?"

"Yes! Oh, yes!"

Gasps and cheers rang around the square. Cringing, Katherine glanced at Pru to find her scowling. Lord Annandale leaned down, but his Scottish burr was rather distinctive as he placated her.

"I'll be happier, lass. That, I vow."

Pru turned a delighted shade of pink.

When Katherine turned back, she found Mrs. Fairchild standing near the prince and Miss Newcomb, both of whom were receiving the congratulations of those alongside. The matchmaker drew herself up, smug.

Katherine raised her mug. Those nearby quieted. It spread like a ripple until there was a lull in the chatter. "To the match of the Season!"

"Hear, hear!"

Although Mrs. Fairchild's expression remained stern, she acknowledged the praise with a slight nod. Katherine swore she noticed a slight curve to the woman's lips. Could the woman actually smile? Katherine had not thought it possible.

As Mrs. Fairchild tended to Miss Newcomb, Katherine lifted her glass toward Pru and Lord Annandale, catching their gazes before she took a sip in order to let them know that she thought their love the true crowning moment.

As she did, Lord Bath slipped into the gathering

from the back. He caught Katherine's gaze and nodded, hopefully an acknowledgement that he had accomplished the mission he'd set out to do. When he paused to ask Mrs. Burwick about the commotion, she must have informed him of the new developments at once, for he offered his hearty congratulations to both Pru and Annandale.

Katherine suspected that Mrs. Burwick neglected to mention the second pending marriage on purpose.

Although Lord Bath had returned, Mr. Salmon did not accompany him. Had he returned home in disgrace?

As a pair of women strolled behind Katherine, snatches of their conversation met her ears.

"I thought Mr. and Mrs. Julien had solved the thefts. I'm certain that's what Lady Bath told me..."

"Then the old lady has gone senile! There was an article in the Bath Chronicle this morning directly stating that Mr. Salmon had caught the thief. I suppose he also transported him to London, for I've heard not a whisper of the thief's identity. A shame. I would have liked to know who it was..."

Mr. Salmon must have ridden through the night to reach London so quickly! And for what, to claim the solved thefts for his own benefit? That blackguard! The next time Katherine crossed paths with him at the

Royal Society for Investigative Techniques, he would rue the day he ever stole the credit from another investigator.

"Now, does that bun deserve such treatment?"

Katherine glanced down at her fist, which had crumpled the Sally Lunn in her hand. She met Wayland's dancing gaze as he stepped alongside her.

"Did you hear Mr. Salmon took credit for the capture of the Burglar of Bath?"

Not that the man in question had been captured, certainly not by Mr. and Mrs. Julien, but Katherine abhorred seeing them so ignored when it should have been they who received the credit and the thanks as opposed to that inept weasel.

"I had not. Lyle shared what happened, however. Allow me to offer my congratulations for tying up all loose ends. It appears as though everyone is happy with the outcome."

When he glanced toward Pru and Lord Annandale, Katherine wasn't certain whether he referred to the end of the thefts or the forthcoming marriage. Katherine could take credit for neither.

"I never doubted your investigative abilities," he murmured as he turned his gaze upon her once more. "Your skills are impressive."

Katherine drew herself up. Just as she opened her

mouth to accept the compliment with grace, Wayland gave her a wicked grin.

"Emma's skills are equally impressive," he added, his smile widening.

The man was clever enough to know when he should walk away. As he turned his back on Katherine, she gritted her teeth. Had he come to Bath simply to poke fun at her?

Now that her time in this town was over, she might never know.

****

More books in the Lady Katherine Regency Mystery series:

An Invitation to Murder (Book 1)

Sign up to join my email list to get all my latest release at the lowest possible price, plus as a benefit for signing up today, I will send you a copy of a Leighann Dobbs book that hasn't been published anywhere...yet!

http://www.leighanndobbs.com/newsletter

IF YOU ARE ON FACEBOOK, please join my VIP readers group and get exclusive content plus updates on all my books. It's a fun group where you can feel at home, ask questions and talk about your favorite reads:

https://www.facebook.com/groups/ldobbsreaders /

IF YOU WANT to receive a text message on your cell phone when I have a new release, text COZYMYS-TERY to 88202 (sorry, this only works for US cell phones!)

IF YOU LIKED THIS BOOK, you might also like my Hazel Martin Mystery series set in 1920s England:

Murder at Lowry House (*book 1*)
Murder by Misunderstanding (*book 2*)

Cozy Mysteries

Hazel Martin Historical Mystery Series

***

Murder at Lowry House (book 1)

Murder by Misunderstanding (book 2)

Lexy Baker Cozy Mystery Series

* * *

Lexy Baker Cozy Mystery Series Boxed Set Vol 1 (Books 1-4)

Or buy the books separately:

Killer Cupcakes

Dying For Danish

Murder, Money and Marzipan

3 Bodies and a Biscotti

Brownies, Bodies & Bad Guys

Bake, Battle & Roll

Wedded Blintz

Scones, Skulls & Scams

Ice Cream Murder

Mummified Meringues

Brutal Brulee (Novella)

No Scone Unturned

Cream Puff Killer

Kate Diamond Mystery Adventures

***

Hidden Agemda (Book 1)

Ancient Hiss Story (Book 2)

Heist Society (Book 3)

Silver Hollow

Paranormal Cozy Mystery Series

***

A Spell of Trouble (Book 1)

Spell Disaster (Book 2)

Nothing to Croak About (Book 3)

Cry Wolf (Book 4)

Mooseamuck Island Cozy Mystery Series

* * *

A Zen For Murder

A Crabby Killer

A Treacherous Treasure

Mystic Notch
Cat Cozy Mystery Series

* * *

Ghostly Paws

A Spirited Tail

A Mew To A Kill

Paws and Effect

Probable Paws

Blackmoore Sisters

Cozy Mystery Series

* * *

Dead Wrong

Dead & Buried

Dead Tide

Buried Secrets

Deadly Intentions

A Grave Mistake

Spell Found

Fatal Fortune

Lady Katherine Regency Mysteries

***

Sam Mason Mysteries

(As L. A. Dobbs)

***

Telling Lies (Book 1)

Keeping Secrets (Book 2)

Exposing Truths (Book 3)

Betraying Trust (Book 4)

Romantic Comedy

***

Corporate Chaos Series

In Over Her Head (book 1)

Can't Stand the Heat (book 2)

What Goes Around Comes Around (book 3)

Contemporary Romance

***

Reluctant Romance

Sweet Romance (Written As Annie Dobbs)

Firefly Inn Series

***

Another Chance (Book 1)

Another Wish (Book 2)

Hometown Hearts Series

***

No Getting Over You (Book 1)

A Change of Heart (Book 2)

***

Sweetrock Sweet and Spicy Cowboy Romance

Some Like It Hot

Too Close For Comfort

Regency Romance

* * *

Scandals and Spies Series:

Kissing The Enemy

Deceiving the Duke

Tempting the Rival

Charming the Spy

Pursuing the Traitor

Captivating the Captain

The Unexpected Series:

An Unexpected Proposal

An Unexpected Passion

Dobbs Fancytales:

Dobbs Fancytales Boxed Set Collection

———

Western Historical Romance

***

Goldwater Creek Mail Order Brides:

Faith

American Mail Order Brides Series:

Chevonne: Bride of Oklahoma

——————————

Magical Romance with a Touch of Mystery

***

Something Magical

Curiously Enchanted

ROMANTIC SUSPENSE

WRITING AS LEE ANNE JONES:

***

The Rockford Security Series:

ABOUT LEIGHANN DOBBS

USA Today bestselling author, Leighann Dobbs, discovered her passion for writing after a twenty year career as a software engineer. She lives in New Hampshire with her husband Bruce, their trusty Chihuahua mix Mojo and beautiful rescue cat, Kitty. When she's not reading, gardening, making jewelry or selling antiques, she likes to write cozy mystery and historical romance books.

Her book "Dead Wrong" won the "Best Mystery Romance" award at the 2014 Indie Romance Convention.

Her book "Ghostly Paws" was the 2015 Chanticleer Mystery & Mayhem First Place category winner in the Animal Mystery category.

Find out about her latest books by signing up at:

http://www.leighanndobbs.com/newsletter

Connect with Leighann on Facebook
http://facebook.com/leighanndobbsbooks

Join her VIP readers group on Facebook:
https://www.facebook.com/groups/ldobbsreaders/

About Harmony Williams

If Harmony Williams had a time machine, she would live in the Regency era. The only thing she loves more than writing strong, funny women in polite society is immersing herself in the nuances of the past. When not writing or researching, she likes to binge-watch mystery shows and spend time with her one-hundred-pound lapdog in their rural Canadian home. For glimpses into the secrets and settings of future *Regency Matchmaker Mystery* books, sign up for her newsletter at http://www.harmonywilliams.com/newsletter.

CPSIA information can be obtained
at www.ICGtesting.com
Printed in the USA
BVHW040221040121
596922BV00020B/951